The Road ~~Not~~ Taken

What Readers say….

The book was a delight to read. The characters were real and the situations were plausible. **Amazon Customer**

Specifically, the book delves into the emotions, tensions, and experiences families and loved ones go through when a loved one is deployed. Once the book was delivered, I couldn't put it down!. – **Natalie Finley**

It was both heartwarming and refreshing to read such a charming and uplifting story of young love with characters you find yourself wanting to meet in person. I will definitely be reading more from this author. – **K. Turner**

"The Road Not Taken" offers a marvelous opportunity to pause and reflect on all that we can be thankful for in this life. – **Richard Follett**

I was engaged from the beginning of this book! A contemporary story with strong, vibrant characters. Interesting backstories and "histories." Themes resonate with today's times! Most enjoyable!! Most!! – **Mary G.**

Not the simple love story it started out but more suspense and atmosphere. It kept my interest and I wanted to read quickly to find out what happened next. I recommend it to anyone wanting a good read. – **Margaret Nelson**

We all love a good love story with a happy ending, and E.A. Coe, has shown (in this book and his last) that he can deliver both very well. **Elizabeth Cottrell**

This is an uplifting book and great read. Pick it up and you won't want to put it down. Two enthusiastic thumbs up! – **AK**

Order this book today! A charming story by Mr. Coe. – **Jmac42**

Something soothing about this story just kept me going and not wanting to stop. I loved this simple yet brilliant romance." – **Reviewed By Rabia Tanveer for Readers' Favorite**

The Road ~~Not~~ Taken

E. A. Coe

This book is a work of fiction. References to historical events, real people, or real places are used fictitiously. While some places, businesses, and events named in the book exist, the activity that occurs in these, involving the fictitious characters of the book, is entirely imagined. Other names, characters, places, or events are also products of the author's imagination and resemblance to actual people, places, or things is coincidental.

First Printing: 2020

ISBN 9798617749719

F. Coe Sherrard Jr.

818 Forest View Rd

Edinburg, Virginia 22824

coe@eacoe.online

DEDICATION

I dedicate this book to the strong women in our world. I'm the grandson of one, the son of one, the brother to one, the brother-in-law to two, the father of one, the father-in-law to two, and the husband to the greatest one of all. In my long professional career, I have been fortunate to work with many, and even luckier that many have worked for me.

E. A. Coe

Table of Contents

1 The Reunion 1

2 Siena Tyson 19

3 Tyrell Harrell 31

4 Woodstock, Virginia 35

5 Tartan Springs 51

6 Todd Foster 61

7 USMC Birthday 65

8 Pastor Tom Burns 73

9 The Review 79

10 Holidays 89

11 Spring 107

12 Deployed 115

13 Fox Uni 123

14 Water Problems 127

15 Trouble Brews 139

16 Chopper Down 147

17 Disconnected 161

18 The Operation 189

19 Recovery 213

20 Gina McCaskey 217

21 Meeting of Minds 229

22 Business To Finish 245

23 Life Planning 255

24 Uninvited Guest 261

25 McCaskey Energy 267

26 Big Event 279

ACKNOWLEDGMENTS

Thank you to the many people who provided support and encouragement during the preparation of this book, starting with my wife, Jean, and my sister, Holly. I also thank my artist sister for her assistance in creating a cover design. To Dave Adams who provided early assistance in the technical details of piloting helicopters, and to my dear friend and former Marine, Perry Miles, for his early attempts to help me edit, thank you. Jim Fitzsimmons, I am so appreciative for your complete review of an early edition of the story and for the flaws you noted. The final draft is better for your comments. Thank you, Sondra Johnson for making me back the story up a few years, so that the coronavirus emergency of 2020 would not have to be considered. Thank you to all the friends who took the time to read early drafts and provide input. Your criticism and feedback improved the book. To all the friends and family who provided inspiration for the characters of the book, thank you. While this story was fiction, the characters were real … because they were you. Thank you, 99Designs and Ferdi Ka for your amazing book cover design services.

To all who read this novel, I hope it may bring a smile during a time in our world's history when we need one.

Prologue

Is there a difference between the Road Taken and the Road *Not* Taken in life, or is there only one road?

Most agree a well-lived life ensues from intelligent reactions to things we can change, within the unyielding framework of those we can't. At the end of the path, our legacy depends only on the life we lived. We can leave a bit of dust commemorating the small waste of the planet's limited resources during a lifetime; or, we can leave something that will live on after we don't: a song, a painting, a well-written sentence, an inspiration, a lesson, a memory, or love. We thank our Creator for the gifts bestowed on us at birth when, at our departure, we leave something more than a handful of ashes.

The Road ~~Not~~ Taken

What is it we'd have found
On the road that wasn't taken?
That's something that we'll never get to know
Life's path goes forward, only,
Leaving past crossroads forsaken
Going back is just a place which dreamers go

So, pick your pathways well
And with wind or gas or water
Choose one you can maintain by yourself
You'll never get ahead
If you always follow others
Winners find the right way by themselves

In the end, all paths conclude
In the very same location
And, too often, travelers find on their last day
That the journey's more important
Than the final destination
So, enjoy the sights and sounds along the way

1 The Reunion

Memories, even good ones, are often lost among mounting layers of life's history, but not this one. The aroma, a fresh essence of soap and shampoo perfumed with a hint of lilacs, was distinctively hers, and Ty knew who stood behind him before turning around.

"Hi, Ty," greeted Siena Tyson.

"Hey, Seeney. Nice to see you." Ty Harrell, attending his ten-year reunion, had not returned to his old hometown since graduating from Tartan Springs High School.

"I didn't expect you at this event. Have you been to any of our other reunions?" asked Siena.

"No. This is the first. Until this year, the Marines kept me in places that made traveling to West Virginia difficult."

"So I heard. You're stationed at Andrews Air Force Base in DC now, right?"

"Right. The base is located across the Anacostia River from DC, in Maryland, and the Marines keep a detachment stationed there. Do you still live in town?

"Afraid so. Can't find a way to break out as you did. I own a bookkeeping business here."

"That doesn't sound so bad," said Ty, surreptitiously glancing toward her hands. "Is Jack with you tonight?"

Holding up her ringless left hand, Seeney acknowledged she had seen Ty's furtive glance. "Nope. Jack Stiles is old news—but someone will undoubtedly fill you in on that gossip later tonight. How about you? Are you here by yourself?"

Embarrassed to have been so obviously caught, Ty said, "Oh—sorry. I don't keep up with much that happens here. But, yes, I'm by myself."

"Then save me a dance. Right now, my busybody friends need interrupting. We'll talk more later."

And—she was gone, immediately immersed within a group of former classmates. If he was candid with himself, Ty knew he had a teenage crush on this girl ten years earlier—no different from nearly every other boy in Tartan Springs.

Siena, or Seeney, the nickname used by her friends, had been the most popular girl in school and the most attractive. Ty's challenge back then lay in the fact she dated only older guys, ran with a faster crowd than Ty's, and was just generally out of his league. Despite that, the two had become friends when they worked on the yearbook staff together as seniors.

"Ty Harrell! Look at you!" It was Sheila Morgan, the coordinator for the event, still short and about thirty pounds heavier. "Except for the mustache, you haven't changed since the day you graduated. I don't think you need a name tag, but here's one in case."

"Thanks, Sheila. You look great as well."

"Ha! Did they teach you to lie like that with a straight face in the Marines?"

"Not at all." Ty's face colored but then recovered. "I'd recognize that smile anywhere."

"Right! Only now it occupies a bigger package. I bet you could still wrestle in the one-forty-five-pound weight class."

"Only with a twenty-pound allowance," Ty said, laughing.

"Well, at least two of your old wrestling buddies are already here. Jude Stevens is over at the bar, and Bill Busby and his wife were heading toward the buffet line."

"Thanks, Sheila. I'll find them."

The drive from Andrews to Tartan Springs, West Virginia, had been pleasant on this beautiful fall day, and Ty's earlier walk across the old high school campus brought back many memories. His enjoyment of the day surprised him.

After he graduated and went to West Virginia University, Ty's parents sold their home and moved to Florida. With no reason to return to Tartan Springs during summer breaks, Ty stayed at his Morgantown apartment. He joined the United States Marine Corps during college and earned aviation wings as a helicopter pilot. After that, the Marines took him to places like Pensacola, Florida, the Kashir River Valley in Bektistan, and now, Andrews.

Most people who graduated from Tartan Springs stayed in the area. The town benefited from its location at a busy railroad junction, which facilitated the transportation of things like coal and broiler chickens. Folks not engaged in the mining industry or agriculture found jobs in various distribution facilities and trucking.

Unlike many West Virginia coal-mining-oriented communities that had lost relevance and fallen into disrepair, Tartan Springs had aged well. While the town was old, it remained quaint. It was close enough to well-heeled Maryland and Northern Virginia metropolitan centers to attract affluent retirees seeking the beauty and solitude of rural living. Main Street boasted several boutiques and craft stores, as well as a variety of dining options. In addition, the town's proximity to a larger town, Compton, to the north, gave constituents choices for goods and services from a selection of bigger stores located there.

When Ty came through the gymnasium doors moments before, the familiar smell carried him back a decade in time. The odor wasn't offensive—just the unique by-product of a well-used athletic facility. Non-specific and complicated, the scent, created over time by years of competition, musty locker rooms, polyurethane floors, and dust beneath the wall of bleachers not easily reached, permeated the space.

No amount of vivid description or even video could duplicate this olfactory phenomenon—which then helped to uncover other memories of long-ago events: the student parking lot where he had put his first dent in the car borrowed from his parents; the sidewalk where he and Jillian Sherman had walked hand-in-hand to the junior prom; the hum of the giant turbines of the nearby power plant that permeated the town. Finally, punctuating the memory before the gym doors had closed behind him, Ty viewed a relic from the town's industrial past, a large tanker truck rumbling over Main Street on its way to the McCaskey Coal Company's mines fifteen miles west.

As Ty now turned back to the crush of once-familiar people who surrounded him, the next fifteen minutes encompassed a blur of smiling faces, shaking hands, and covert glances at name tags. Surprised he recognized as many as he did, Ty was more surprised by those he didn't—but should have.

A decade had treated some folks well—and others not. As he headed for the makeshift bar set up in the gymnasium, he observed Todd Foster, loudly holding court with a group of former classmates and constituents. Ty knew Foster casually a decade ago but held no desire to reacquaint himself. Foster graduated a year ahead of Ty and had been Seeney's primary boyfriend for much of her junior year in high school. After starting Colgan County Junior College, he abruptly dumped her.

Shocked and hurt, Seeney dated nobody else regularly for the remainder of her senior year. Foster, always a loudmouth, was usually at the perimeter of any trouble occurring at the school, and Ty wondered what Seeney had ever seen in him. Now he questioned the collective intelligence of residents who elected Foster their mayor.

Trying to skirt the edge of the bar area, furthest away from the mayor, Ty heard, "Hey, Flyboy! Welcome back to our humble town."

"Hi, Todd." Ty continued toward the other side of the bar. "Thanks."

"If you ever want to bring the president out this way, let me know." The mayor laughed, and several others in his group chuckled. "We'll sponsor a parade or something."

"Yeah, right," Ty responded, trying to disengage politely. "I'll keep that in mind." Ty flew in the elite Marine Corps helicopter unit specifically assigned to service the President of the United States.

The mayor, enjoying the attention of his entourage, held a beer in his hand, likely not the day's first. Ty kept walking, mentally noting to find a seat in the dining area as far away from Todd Foster as possible. As he reached his destination, Ty recognized another familiar face coming in his direction.

Tom Burns approached from the mayor's end of the bar, and Ty blinked twice to believe his eyes. Tom's appearance had changed little in ten years, but Ty's old friend appeared to be wearing a clerical collar. Tom had been Ty's next-door neighbor from elementary school through high school. They rode the same school bus, played on the same Little League team, and attended almost every class together throughout their youth. While Ty did his best to avoid trouble, Tom embraced it. He had not been an evil child but an always mischievous one who embarrassed his parents often.

Tom had graduated with the rest of his class, but only after spending every summer since the eighth grade in summer school. Tom's highest grade in a high school course was a C+—in tenth grade Industrial Arts. Yet, he shocked all in the school's administration when he recorded a near-perfect score on the SATs. Despite the potential for certain scholarships because of the high SAT and ACT scores, Tom drifted toward juvenile delinquency when Ty left for West Virginia University.

"Hey, neighbor," said Burns, as he reached to shake Ty's hand. "Long time, no see. How are you?"

Ty, dumbfounded by Burns' attire, wondered if it was one of his old friend's jokes. "I'm doin' fine, Tom, or is it, Pastor Tom?"

"Around here, I'm Pastor Tom, but just Tom is fine for you. I've managed to track your accomplishments since we left here ten years ago. Way to go, man!"

"Thanks, but I'm embarrassed to say my record for keeping up with folks isn't as good. So, when did this happen?" Ty asked, pointing to the collar.

"Oh, about four years ago. I knocked around after high school and finally found something interesting to me. The Lutheran Church up in Compton organized a missionary trip to South America, and I thought it would be an easy and cheap opportunity to experience someplace new. I think the pastor up there had an idea of what I might find, and he was right."

"What was that?"

"Not enough time for all that tonight, Ty, but the trip reoriented my world, changing my life dramatically. I finished seminary in 2012 and now hold the position of assistant pastor at the Lutheran Church in Compton."

"I'm impressed and would like to know more about your journey sometime. How are you so familiar with mine? I haven't spoken with anyone from around here in years."

"Hey, man," Tom said, looking skyward. "I have connections now."

Ty was uncertain how to respond to the religious insinuation until Tom laughed, punching Ty lightly on the shoulder. "Joking, Ty. You can find just about anything these days on Google. Have you seen Siena Tyson yet this evening?"

"Yes, almost as soon as I came in the door. She hasn't changed much, has she?"

"No, but she suffered a tough year. Didn't know if you were aware of all that, and I remember you two were friends in our senior year."

"She mentioned Jack Stiles is no longer in her picture and joked that someone would most likely give me the details of the break-up tonight."

"Yeah." The pastor fidgeted in quiet contemplation before continuing. "You might, but don't believe everything people tell you. Stiles is a piece of shit!"

"Are pastors allowed to say that?"

"Only in private to friends," said Tom. "Let's meet sometime in DC and grab a beer. I'm there quite a bit for work."

"Sure thing, Tom."

They shook hands, and Ty refocused on getting to a location at the bar where he could find a drink.

After Seeney left Ty to visit a group of her old classmates, her mind remained preoccupied with her short conversation with him. "He's looking damn fine, isn't he?" Susie Thompson interrupted Seeney's reverie. Susie had been a cheerleader with Seeney and, like her friend, had already been married and divorced since graduation.

"Who? Ty Harrell? Yes. The Marine Corps suits him well."

"How come he didn't show up on our radar back in school?" asked Sally Howell, another former member of the Tartan Springs cheerleading squad, circa 2006. Sally was also Tartan Springs' long-standing police chief, Tim Howell's daughter.

"Because we were too cool to date boys our age back in the day," said Seeney, laughing.

"Right," chimed in Susie. "That worked out for some of us, and others—not so much."

"I did sort of notice him in high school," mused Seeney. "We worked on the yearbook together in our senior year and became friends. He's not as skinny as he was in high school, but he hasn't changed much."

"I think you're right, Seeney," said Sally. "He hasn't changed, and most the other guys we graduated with have—for the worse. That makes Ty look good by comparison. I remember you used to talk about him toward the end of our senior year—which made the rest of us wonder a little. We thought you might be looking for an easy rebound after breaking up with Todd."

Seeney laughed. "I didn't break up with Todd. I got dumped! I didn't need a rebound, but Ty was a friendly boy to talk to, wrestling kept him in shape, and he didn't obsess about getting into my pants. That made him different—and attractive to me."

"I don't remember you two dating any. Did I miss something?" asked Susie.

"Nope. I couldn't lure him into asking me for a date. Time ran out when the school year ended."

"Ha!" giggled Susie. "Maybe only the first period ran out. The second period just started a few minutes ago. I didn't see a wedding ring on his hand."

"Don't be a silly romantic," said Seeney, chuckling. "But, for the record, I did check his hand when he came in. He's not wearing a ring. Even better, I caught him checking out my hand!"

"Bingo!" said Sally. "This could be the start of a love story. Stranger things happen, Seeney. You're single, and he's single. So why are you still standing here talking to us?" As her friends stood smiling at her, Seeney glanced around the room to see where Ty had wandered.

With a beer in his hand, Ty surveyed the dining area created in the gymnasium. His old friends, Jude Stevens and Bill Busby were with several others at a table that seated ten, so he headed in that direction.

"Ty Harrell!" said the smaller man in the group. "What a surprise, friend!"

"Hey, Jude," said Ty. "They told me there would be an alumni wrestling match tonight, so I thought I better come. I don't see it on the schedule, though."

"Ha!" said the larger man with the attractive wife. "There better not be one of those. I doubt anyone around here stores tights large enough for me anymore."

"No, Bill, I think you're right." Reaching his hand to Bill's wife, Ty introduced himself. "You must be Judy? I'm Ty Harrell."

"Nice to meet you in person, Ty," said Judy. "These two have told me about you. I guess I'm the one responsible for taking Bill from a heavyweight to an extra heavyweight."

Bill Busby was the high school's heavyweight wrestler from 2004 to 2006 and placed third in their senior year in the Northern West Virginia AA wrestling tournament. In those days, he weighed in at about two hundred fifty pounds. Today, Bill was in the three-hundred-pound range. He carried the extra weight reasonably well at six-foot, four inches, but he seemed embarrassed by his physique.

"It isn't Judy's fault," said Bill. "Totally mine, but my doctor and I have a plan. Tell me what your secret is, Ty. You're not any heavier than when we graduated."

"I wish, but the military requires annual physicals for pilots, and we still need to pass a physical fitness test every six months. So, my job sort of demands I stay in shape."

"Well, you're an inspiration!" said Busby. "When you come to the reunion next year, you'll see a smaller man sitting next to Judy."

"Darn, I'm sorry to hear that, Bill." Then, looking at Judy, Ty asked innocently, "Judy, is the new guy anyone we know?" The group laughed, and Judy hugged her burly husband. Seeney Tyson then appeared at the table with a drink and a plate of food.

"Is this seat available?" Seeney pointed to the chair next to Ty's.

"Absolutely, Seeney," said Jude, "but you sure you want to sit with a bunch of ex-wrestling jocks? The basketball guys are all over there."

"Tonight, I'm looking for a little protection, so wrestlers may be a better choice," she said.

"Got it," said Jude. "Those round-ball pussies would be worthless for that, but who do you need protection from?"

"Oh, I'm fine," said Seeney. "The mayor is a little drunk and has been pestering me, but I can handle him."

"Trying to re-strike the old flame?" asked Bill.

"That train departed ten years ago. His wife might also have something to say about that."

"What wife?" asked Judy. "Shirley shoved Todd to the street about six weeks ago."

"I didn't know," said Seeney. "That explains some things."

"Sit down, Seeney," said Ty with a wink. "We'll take care of you. Hold this seat for me while I visit the buffet."

After going through the line for food, Ty returned to the table, finding the mayor standing next to the chair occupied by Seeney. Foster was preparing to sit despite Seeney's objection. "Sorry, Todd, I'm sitting in that seat, I'm afraid," said Ty, as he placed his plate on the table.

"Whoa there, Flyboy! I didn't see any reserved signs on seats for this function."

"There aren't. I was talking to my old wrestling teammates before going to the buffet line and left my drink here to hold the place to sit with them."

"I see." Foster still gazed luridly at Seeney. "But she doesn't look like one of your old wrestling teammates. She looks like one of mine." Seeney blushed and dropped her fork. Before anyone could say anything, Foster added, "Yep, makes me hanker for the old Mercury convertible I used to own with the big back seat."

Bill Busby and Jude Stevens rose to their feet, but Ty held up a hand to them. "Mayor, with due respect, I don't think Seeney wants to talk about old times with you. Why don't you find another table?"

"OK, OK," he said, looking at the three standing men. "Perhaps another time, Seeney."

"Not likely, Todd," she said.

When the mayor gave a mock toast to the table and left, Ty said, "Wow, Seeney! Sorry about that."

"No problem. Todd's harmless—just a nuisance."

"What kind of a mayor is he?" asked Ty to the rest of the table?

"A drunk one, for the most part," said Judy Busby. "He got elected a couple of years ago, running against a former convicted felon. Not so sure the town wouldn't have been better off with the felon."

"So, tell me what else has happened in town since I left," said Ty. Accompanied by choruses of laughter, the group gladly covered the juicy gossip of the past decade.

After dinner, Bill, Ty, and Jude began to regale Judy and Seeney with wrestling stories. "Remember the best match you ever lost?" Bill asked Ty.

"I think I know the one. Was it against Keystone our senior year?"

"Exactly! Keystone was the defending AA state champion, and it was our last match before the state tournament."

"Wait a minute," said Seeney. "I went to that! I remember it. Didn't we upset Keystone? It came down to the heavyweight match, and you pinned your guy, right, Bill?"

"I did, and we won by a point. I got to be the hero, and the boys tried to carry me to the locker room, but they couldn't lift me. The real hero was Ty, though."

"But—he lost, didn't he?" Seeney asked hesitantly.

"I did," said Ty. "But why were you at that match? I don't remember you being a wrestling fan."

"I wasn't," admitted Seeney. "It was the only high school wrestling match I ever attended. You and I worked on the yearbook together, and I remember your apprehension about the match. You told me you were wrestling some famous guy and that you might not fare too well. You were my friend, and I worried about you, so I came to the match to cheer."

"Wow, I didn't know that," said Ty. "You never mentioned it."

"Well," said Seeney, "since you lost, I didn't think you wanted anyone to bring it up."

"Right," said Jude. "He might have lost, but he's the reason the team won the match—other than wonder boy's miraculous pin. Ty wrestled Gabe Sullivan, who was a three-time AA state champion. Gabe had an eleven and zero record that year, including nine pins. High school matches were scheduled for six minutes, but Sullivan rarely wrestled more than three or four minutes in a match. He pinned his opponent in the first or second period most of the time."

"OK," said Seeney. "I'm listening, but what made Ty's loss so important?"

Ty tried to interject, but Bill stopped him with a raised hand and a stern expression. "Because, Ms. Tyson, Sullivan was supposed to pin Ty. Keystone would earn five team points for a win by pin. Ty didn't get pinned, so Keystone only earned three team points for a win by decision. Tartan Springs won by one point. If Sullivan had pinned Ty as Keystone planned, we'd have lost by a point."

"Wish somebody had told me the significance of that then, Ty," said Seeney. "As I remember it, the match was close, and you even had a chance to win near the end."

"Your memory is correct, Seeney," said Jude. "After spending most of the second period on his back avoiding a pin, Ty almost pulled off a miraculous victory in the third period. Behind seven to four, Ty kept pressing Sullivan, who was out of steam. Finally, as time expired, Ty managed to take him down and get Sullivan's shoulders to the mat—but just out of bounds. Sullivan knew he got lucky."

"Yeah. If the match had gone thirty seconds longer, Ty'd have won," interjected Jude.

"Thank you for sharing the story with me," said Seeney, looking at Ty. "A heroic performance, Ty."

"Jude and Bill make it sound that way, don't they?" said Ty. "The thing I remember most about the match was the second period I spent mostly on my back, face to face with a referee ready to slap his hand to the mat. My neck was sore for weeks!" The conversation continued a few minutes more until most of the group left the table to view the photo display of old class pictures at the front of the gym. Seeney stayed behind, so Ty did as well. "I wish I had known you were in the gym that night," started Ty, "... or maybe I'm glad I didn't know until now."

"You were my friend, and I liked you," said Seeney. "I didn't want to bring the match up while we were working on the yearbook, just in case..."

"I understand," Ty interrupted, "but that wouldn't have bothered me. To know you had come to the match to watch me would have been a big deal—because you were like the queen of the school."

"Ha! Being the queen had its issues—but if you thought I was a queen, why didn't you ever ask me out?"

Ty stared into Seeney's face for a few seconds, trying to judge whether her question was a joke or not. "Seeney, you were at a different level from me in high school. I was a relative nobody, and you were the most popular girl in school. In my best dreams, I had no chance of a date with you."

Seeney smiled. "Yet we worked on the yearbook together, and for some reason, I thought it important to come to that last wrestling match. Not sure, Ty, but the old saying, 'faint heart never won fair lady ' comes to mind. Do you remember I didn't go to the senior prom?"

"Yeah, I do. I didn't go either. I assumed you didn't because you were still upset about the break-up with Foster."

"Nope. My parents were more worried about that than me. Lots of boys asked me, but I was holding out for one who never did. When that boy didn't even go to the prom himself, I never quite understood why he wouldn't have asked me."

Ty stared at the woman sitting across from him. "What an idiot I was! Why didn't you give me a bigger hint—been a little more forward? I was the naïve one in high school, not you."

"Since then, I learned the value of being more direct. I may not always get what I want, but if I don't, it isn't because I don't ask."

"I guess I blew it," said Ty. "I'm not sure I wanted to come to a reunion ten years later to find that out."

"I wouldn't say that. I'm a divorced bookkeeper living in the same town we grew up in, and your life has been rather exciting. I think you've done alright. Let's go watch the video Sheila put together of our class."

Ty had more to say, but Seeney put a period on the conversation for now, so he replied, "Good idea."

They walked to the school's small concert auditorium with several friends, and Ty picked a row with empty seats. He allowed Seeney to lead the way, and she chose a place with one vacant seat on each side of it. Ty sat in the one to the right of her.

As the hall started to fill, Ty noticed Mayor Foster heading down the aisle toward their row. He quickly nudged Seeney to move over one seat so that the empty place would be to Ty's right and not on Seeney's left. When Seeney saw Foster approaching, she understood Ty's request and quickly complied. When Foster realized the new seating arrangement, he went to a different row. Ty winked at Seeney and softly rested his hand on her knee. "This guy never gives up."

"Apparently not." Seeney gazed toward her knee. "Thank you."

The entertaining video managed to incorporate clips including virtually every graduating senior from the class of 2006. Seeney appeared in many of the videos, and Ty appeared in more than he expected. One video showed Ty discussing something with the yearbook's copy editor, and just inside the frame, a pretty girl gazed at him intently. It was the same woman who now sat next to him ten years later.

Did he miss something in high school that he was too naïve to understand? What sort of crazy fate caused him to come back to Tartan Springs for this reunion? His mind was still spinning with these thoughts when Seeney nudged his arm. "Since the video is over, do you think we should leave?"

Coming out of his trance, Ty said, "Oh gosh, yes. Sorry. It brought back a lot of memories, and I lost track of where I was!" As the couple walked to the gym, a band began tuning up, and most people were crowding around the bar for a drink.

Someone had concocted a container of West Virginia moonshine punch, and since nobody stood in the line for this drink, Ty used the spigot to pour a sample into a plastic cup. Seeney corralled a glass of white wine, and she led them to a quiet corner of the gym where several two-top tables sat against the wall.

"How romantic," Ty joked.

"Yes, I thought so. This will give us a chance to finish our conversation from earlier."

"Looking forward to it." Ty tasted the punch, and his face contorted as he looked desperately for a place to spit. Finding none, he swallowed. "This is awful! ... my God... I'm not sure what's in it, but it tastes like something you should apply, not drink. Would you happen to have some gum or a mint?"

With her eyes locked on Ty's, she took the gum she was chewing from her mouth and handed it to him. "Just this one."

"Perfect."

"It's been an interesting evening, hasn't it?" asked Seeney.

"Yes," said Ty, trying to determine to what Seeney might be referring. "I'm glad I came to the reunion this year."

Seeney stared at Ty for a few moments. "I'm glad you came too, Ty, but can I tell you a bit of a problem I'm having? Can I be direct?"

"Sure," Ty said with some concern.

"When I allow a man to touch the inside of my knee without slapping his face—that man better have a bigger plan than my knee!"

Ty smiled, concealing his shock at Seeney's seductive insinuation. "I understand and apologize if I was too forward earlier. Would a big house with a picket fence and a dog be enough of a plan? Of course, the dog is optional."

"Is the dog big or little? I don't like little dogs."

"It's a big dog," said Ty, playing along with Seeney's flirtation.

"OK, but that seems like a comprehensive and somewhat presumptive plan. Doesn't something of such scale need a dress rehearsal?"

"Wow! You must be a mind reader? That's almost exactly what I was thinking, but I was afraid you might think my idea was inappropriate. Since we're being so direct, though, I'll tell you—I was considering more of an undress rehearsal."

Seeney could no longer keep a straight face. "We're on the same page then. I think I can make that kind of a rehearsal happen." She didn't continue, waiting for Ty's response.

Ty stalled and finally said, "OK. You beat me at this, and I'm not sure what I'm supposed to say now."

"Well, most men at this point would ask the lady if she'd care to dance."

"Right. Would you like to dance, Seeney?"

"Yes, I would."

Seeney, always an exceptional dancer in high school, was still an attraction. Not intentionally showy, her moves were smooth and elegant, occasionally spiced with an unusual twist or spin, which appeared choreographed for a specific part of a song. Ty was comfortable as the accompanying act, not flashy, but always in step. He danced with relaxed confidence, demonstrating experience in a dance environment.

They stayed on the floor for three consecutive songs, the last one an original by the band written by the lead singer. *The Road Not Taken* was the name of the song, and as Seeney glanced at the man across from her, the lyrics seemed eerily prophetic. When they sat, Seeney complimented Ty. "You're an excellent dancer. I don't remember that from high school days."

"Except for the junior prom, you never saw me dance. I didn't go to many of the high school dances, but I was a regular at the Rave up in Compton."

"I didn't know that about you. My parents allowed me to date older guys and host parties at my house and all kinds of wild stuff but, can you believe they wouldn't let me go to Compton? They weren't racists, but they thought the Rave a little too ethnic and too dangerous."

"Well, it was ethnic but no more dangerous than a high school dance. Of course, troublemakers show up wherever young people gather, but the adult chaperones who stayed quietly visible in the background kept things under control at the Rave."

"Didn't you bring a girl from there to the junior prom?"

"Yes. Jillian Sherman came from Compton."

Seeney smiled. "You created quite a community stir with that. Interracial dating occurred when we were in high school, but people in our town still considered it rebellious. You were a new friend for me in our junior year, but I remember admiring your courage that evening."

"Funny. I never thought about the date as being controversial. I brought a girl I had done a lot of dancing with to a dance function at our high school. We had a great time."

"Whatever happened to her? I don't remember you dating anyone in particular during our senior year."

Ty laughed. "No, Jillian and I experienced sort of a falling-out in the summer—when she got pregnant."

"Oh, my God, Ty! I'm sorry! What did you do?"

"Nothing much I really could do. But, since I was still a virgin at the time, I had no responsibility for the baby—so I suggested she marry the prospective father."

Uncertain how to react to this news until she realized Ty was smiling, Seeney laughed. "Wow! I had no idea. Did they get married?"

"Yep, but they didn't have a ceremony. If they had, I most likely wouldn't have made the invite list." Seeney and Ty still chuckled over this history when Todd Foster lurched toward their table.

"Well, you two put on quite a shhow," slurred Foster. "Ty, this is one a' the townz bess danzers, and I think you need a' share her with a' ress a' us."

"Not tonight, Todd. I'm danced out," said Seeney.

"The band's playin' a sslow song. 'At won't take mush energy." Then, Foster grabbed one of Seeney's hands, attempting to pull her toward the floor.

Alarmed, Seeney retracted her hand. "Sorry, Todd. No."

When the mayor reached for Seeney's hand again, Ty stood to face him. Several in Foster's group of sycophants now gathered around the table. "Sorry, Todd, but she doesn't want to dance anymore tonight."

"Siddown', Flyboy!" ordered Foster, having difficulty maintaining a steady focus on Todd.

Ty didn't move, glancing around at the gathering crowd. "Look, Todd, I don't want any trouble tonight. This has been a terrific event, so let's leave it that way. Seeney isn't going to dance with you."

Foster swayed closer to Ty. "Maybe you dint hear me. I said, siddown!"

"My hearing is fine, but you aren't in my chain of command. And, if you're seriously considering some kind of juvenile physical altercation, my advice to you is to think again. You're drunk, at least thirty pounds overweight, and out of shape. I'm none of those. Before you decide, though, let me do this."

Ty retrieved his cell phone, took a quick picture of Todd and the small group with him, then dialed a three-digit number. Foster's face turned beet red, but he watched Ty curiously.

"Hi 911," spoke Ty into his phone. "This is Ty Harrell, and I'm down at the high school reunion. I think you should send a squad car down here. Mayor Foster is a little drunk, and he's about to get himself killed in a fight." Ty paused, holding his hand up to the mayor and the little group. "Sure, I'll hold." After a short pause, he said, "Oh, hi Chief. Yes, I'll tell him."

Ty lowered his hand. "That was your police chief, Tim Howell. He said he'd be here in about five minutes to give you a ride home, Todd. If you decide to go with your original plan, remember I took a picture of you and these witnesses."

Foster, livid and swaying precariously, stared at Ty, who didn't move. One of the mayor's friends said, "Come on, Todd. This isn't worth it. Let's get out of here."

"I'm goin'." The mayor turned to see which friend had made the last suggestion and almost fell in the process. Catching himself, he addressed Ty and Seeney. "You don' know who yer dealin' with, Harrell, and if yer smard you won' set foot in thiss town agin. And you, Shiena Tyshon—you live 'ere, but you made bad choizes ta' nighd!"

"To me, Mayor Foster," said Ty, "that sounds like a drunken threat, which isn't such a bright idea since my cell phone now contains a picture of at least six people who witnessed it. If anything happens to either Ms. Tyson or me in this town, you, sir, will be suspect number one. I wish I could say that it was a pleasure seeing you again after all these years."

"Get fugged!" replied Foster.

"Thanks, whatever that is, I'll think about it," said Ty.

Foster slapped a full drink from the table, splashing everyone in the process, and departed the gym. Seeney stood and said to Ty, "We've had enough fun tonight. Let's leave."

"I'm right behind you." On the way to the parking lot, Ty asked, "Is Foster going to be a nuisance to you or your business?"

"I doubt it. What can he do? With your warning in front of a bunch of folks, he'd be crazy to try anything. Thanks—by the way. Evidently, my judgment in picking boyfriends back in the day left something to be desired."

"Maybe it's improving?" smiled Ty.

"Could be. Where are you staying tonight?"

"Oh, I'm at the Hampton Inn at the edge of town."

"Wrong answer," said Seeney.

"That's what I hoped you'd say. Do you own a spare toothbrush?"

"No, but you can use mine."

"Done!" said Ty.

"What time do you need to be on the road tomorrow?"

"Early enough to check-in at the unit in the afternoon. Ideally, I should leave here by nine or ten."

"Then, we need to leave now so you can get some sleep at some point," she said, winking at him.

On the following morning, Seeney lay awake in Ty's arms but facing away from him. She enjoyed the gentle comfort of a warm body next to hers, and she committed to not making a move to disturb that any sooner than necessary.

Nevertheless, her mind kept replaying the song the band played the night before, *The Road Not Taken*. When she first heard the words, she imagined an unkind fate delivered the tune as a sad message to her. The lyrics recounted how life moves only forward and that people can't revisit past crossroads except in dreams. Was her dance with Ty a part of a metaphoric vision meant to tease her about a chance she missed years earlier? The notion depressed her.

This morning, after a dreamlike evening, she conjured a more promising alternative that perhaps the songwriter didn't contemplate. When two people take different paths in life, no opportunity exists to rewind for a revised decision. As the song rather fatalistically pointed out, all roads lead to the same place in the end. But, she thought, don't different paths sometimes cross again? And don't these occasional intersections provide a chance to change directions? The logic made her smile, and she resolved to make the best of her reconnection with Ty Harrell.

"Are you sleeping?" asked the voice behind her.

"No, and I guess you aren't either. How long have you been awake?"

"Maybe a half an hour. I didn't want to move because I didn't want the evening to end," Ty said.

"I've been thinking the same thing for about an hour."

"This sort of first date is unusual for me, Seeney. These last twenty-four hours were incredible, and I'm glad I decided to come to the reunion. I guess what I'm stuttering about here is—I hope this was more than a date."

Seeney rolled over so that her face almost touched Ty's. "For the record, you're the first man to share this bed since I kicked my former husband out. I haven't enjoyed evenings like this for a long time either. Truthfully, I never had a date like this in my life. But you aren't a man I met last night, Ty. We've known each other for over ten years, and this is a date I believe we should have had a long time ago. I'm glad it was special for you—and I hope to hell you have more plans for me than just last night!"

Ty held Seeney's stare without speaking right away. "As I told you, I'm struggling a little to express myself well, but the most important part of my evening didn't occur after we arrived at your house. It happened after I entered the gymnasium when you told me to 'save a dance.' I didn't know I had missed you for the past ten years until you hinted to me that I should have. I can make plenty of plans for you but understand that my life and career now aren't always predictable."

"Good speech, Captain. I like it. So, what happens next?"

"I'm not sure. Neither of us had a plan for this, so I guess we see how it plays out. I'll be at Andrews for at least another eighteen months and don't know where the government may send me after that. Andrews is only three hours away, so I can make trips back here easy enough."

"Right, and my friends in DC would allow me to stay with them for visits your way."

"You won't need a place to stay," said Ty.

"Mmm. You have room for me?"

"Plenty. I have a tiny, one-bedroom condo."

"Perfect!"

"Then, that takes care of the next few months," said Ty. "I'll warn you. My flight schedule can be erratic and hard to work around sometimes."

"I understand. My schedule, on the other hand, is controlled entirely by me. I can be completely flexible. My only firm commitments are the junior college night classes on Tuesdays and Thursdays. I'm trying to earn enough credits to be able to apply to Shepherd University eventually. Someday, I want to take the state CPA exam."

"That sounds great."

"Good," she agreed. "One last question—is that your knee on my thigh?"

"No."

"That's what I hoped you would say."

Later, while Ty showered and shaved in Seeney's spacious bathroom, he performed a quick inventory of her toiletries. He noted she used a relatively common soap, Dove, and everyday shampoo, Pantene. In addition, she had several bottles of perfumes in front of her vanity mirror. One bottle carried the brand, Caswell-Massey, and when Ty opened it, he recognized the distinctive scent of lilacs.

2 Siena Tyson

Siena Tyson, born on February 29 in a leap year, 1988, only celebrated the actual anniversary of her birth every four years. Her parents never quite solved the dilemma of which day to observe their daughter's birthday. Some years it was the last day of February, and other years, the first day of March.

She had been an unexpected baby, occurring late in her parents' life. According to them, her conception resulted from a massive flood that paralyzed the town in the spring of 1987. Jim and Emily Tyson had been confined to their home with their twelve-year-old daughter, Mildred, for three days, waiting for the floodwaters of the Siler River to retreat. Without electricity for almost a week, the community experienced a spike in births the following January and February.

Siena's sister, called Millie, was almost thirteen years older than Siena. More like a mother than a sister, Millie picked Siena up from school as much as her parents did. As a result, Siena's friends often thought her parents were her grandparents. Jim and Emily were only in their mid-forties when Siena started school, but they were older than most other parents of children in her classes.

Millie married a local trucker, Adam Whorton, after high school. Not long after the wedding, Adam discovered hauling fruit and vegetables was less taxing than coal, and he moved to Salinas, California with Millie. The west coast was a long way from West Virginia, and family visits from the couple were infrequent.

Siena began dating Todd Foster as a junior at Tartan Springs High School. Todd, a senior and president of the student council, also owned a car. A somewhat rebellious student leader, Todd was popular among classmates, but not so much with school administrators. Candidates for status boyfriends were scarce at Tartan Springs, and Todd filled the role as the default choice for the high school's most popular girl. The match was far from perfect, but the relationship sustained for nearly a year. The pair broke up unceremoniously after Foster went to junior college in Siena’s senior year.

Siena's excellent academic credentials and high ACT/SAT ensured acceptance to many colleges or universities. She was undecided about what she wanted to accomplish in life, however, and tying herself to massive student-loan debt didn’t seem an intelligent first step. The two junior colleges in the area were relatively inexpensive, so she decided to enroll at the one her former boyfriend didn't attend. She started dating Jack Stiles, the son of the owner of the local Chevrolet dealership, in the summer before fall classes began.

Four years older than Siena, Jack was different from the boys she had dated in high school. More mature, he also had things the boys in high school didn't—starting with a high-paying job at his dad's business. As a result, he could afford to take her to upscale restaurants, always in a new "program car" from the dealership.

When Jack succeeded in taking their relationship to a sexual level, Siena became even more impressed. Sex for Siena had been an obligatory, if infrequent, part of the high school dating ritual, but it had never been particularly satisfying. Boys typically possessed a raging, white-hot passion—that dissipated as quickly as it began. Just as her own body started to warm to the stimulation of sex, boys were done and ready to move on to something else, leaving her physically aroused, sexually unfulfilled, and mentally frustrated.

The experience with Jack was different. Somebody had taught him how to intensify his own pleasure by increasing his partner's. What an epiphany Siena's first intimate encounter with Jack had been! And, like many girls who didn't know better, Siena equated this tremendous difference in lovemaking to love itself.

Jack proposed in September, Siena accepted, and the couple married three months later. Her parents couldn't afford a large wedding, but Jack's could. Jack Junior was an only child, and his parents insisted on paying for the luxurious and well-attended event.

Siena completed her first semester of courses at the junior college but didn't return for the second semester. Within months of the wedding, Jack Senior retired and named Jack Junior President of the dealership. Neither Jack nor Siena wanted children right away, so Siena threw herself into learning all she could about the bookkeeping for the dealership. Her husband didn't give her a paycheck, but for Siena, the free labor was a way to contribute to the partnership.

Jim and Emily Tyson were tragically killed in a traffic accident on I-68 in 2008, and Millie came back home to help Siena with funeral arrangements. She also assisted Siena in settling their parents' modest estate, but she didn't bring Adam. Because of their age difference, Siena and Millie had not been close as sisters, but they completed the estate negotiations unemotionally and amicably. They split the proceeds from the sale of the family home and the funds in their parents' savings accounts evenly.

Rural Valley Electric (RVE) owned the tanker truck responsible for the accident, and their driver also perished in the crash. Lester Miles' family sued RVE for liability in the driver's death, and the attorney representing Lester's family contacted the Tysons' insurance company. After consulting with Siena and Millie, the insurance company joined in the Miles family's lawsuit.

The sisters wouldn't have considered suing anyone and had little interest in the insurance company's negotiations with RVE. Claiming collective damages of five million dollars, the attorneys settled out of court with RVE for ten percent of that. After the attorney's recovered a forty percent contingency, Siena and Millie split a bit over one hundred thousand dollars from the settlement; Siena filed the legal package, which came with the check, in a file cabinet without ever opening it.

The court found RVE's only negligence to be allowing the tanker truck to travel with a slightly overweight load. This caused control problems for the vehicle as it came downhill on the icy expressway. Millie returned to California, and the sisters exchanged Christmas cards but had no other opportunities to see each other. Jack invested Siena's portion of the insurance settlement in one of the many funds he owned.

The car dealership earned exceptional income, the couple lived in a spacious house, and both drove late-model cars. For eight years, except for her parents' unfortunate accident, life seemed good, if unremarkable, for Siena.

Until February of the past year.

Jack had been irritable for several days and avoided intimacy for almost a week. The interlude didn't bother Siena, but the abstinence was unusual for Jack. Siena presumed something at work was bothering her husband, but he had been abrupt with her when she questioned him.

Alternatively, he had asked her several times for no reason about whether she, herself, was feeling okay. She was fine until, on a Saturday, she became annoyed by an itch in the vaginal region. The sensation was worse on Sunday, and she suspected a yeast infection. These occasional occurrences were ordinary for women, but Siena found them embarrassing, and she committed to seeing her doctor the following day.

Doctor Chavez fit Siena into her busy schedule that Monday and Siena visited Chavez's clinic while Jack was at work. Marie Chavez, a striking Cuban woman, forty-five years old, had practiced medicine in the town for almost fifteen years. Doctor Chavez was Siena's friend, besides being her physician. They worked out together at the local gym and found time for lunch several times per month. After Chavez's examination, the physician told Siena she didn't see anything alarming and no sign of yeast.

"I see a slight irritation on one side of the vaginal wall, but nothing else. The results of the blood test will be here by tomorrow, which may provide additional detail. Your sexual activity hasn't changed in any way, has it?"

The question from her physician seemed strange. "No, Marie, of course not. What exactly do you mean? Jack and I haven't been intimate this week, but nothing else has changed."

"No reason to ask, other than an irritation we can't currently explain," said Doctor Chavez, laughing. "I was just making sure you hadn't found a younger man or something."

"No, nothing like that." Seeney smiled but wondered about her doctor's unusual question.

"Okay," said Chavez. "I'm sure it's nothing, but I'll give you a call when we get the blood test back."

Seeney didn't mention her visit with Doctor Chavez to Jack when he came home. She felt guilty about that, but he didn't seem to be in a talking mood anyway. She was glad, and both went to bed early after a light dinner.

Doctor Chavez called at three the next day and suggested Seeney come to the clinic. Before she left the house, Seeney received a call from Tom Burns. Surprised to hear from the pastor, she took his call but told him she was on her way out. They made plans to speak the following day.

At Doctor Chavez's clinic, the receptionist led Seeney back to the doctor's private office. Chavez looked somber, and Seeney intuitively knew whatever the doctor would tell her would probably not be good.

Seeney sat down in front of her, and Doctor Chavez pulled no punches. "Seeney, you contracted gonorrhea."

The blood drained from her face, and Seeney gasped, "What? It can't be! How could that happen?"

Chavez remained quiet until she was certain Seeney had nothing more to say. "I'm sorry, but only one possible way exists to contract this disease. You should not be frightened for your health. We can treat gonorrhea easily, and you will recover completely."

"Then, I got this from Jack?" asked Seeney, tears now forming beneath her eyelids.

"If what you told me yesterday is accurate, Seeney, then yes, only Jack could infect you."

"That son of a bitch! He infected me with a venereal disease? I'm going to kill him!"

"Relax, Seeney. Don't overreact yet. You're my friend, and I feel your pain, but we must consider other things now. He may be the only one possible to infect you, but he may not be aware he, himself, is infected. The gestation period for this disease varies among people. If he does know it, then so does his doctor, who I believe is Doctor Carruthers. Is he still your husband's personal physician?"

Trying to think through the furious stir in her mind, Seeney said, "Yes. He still sees Doctor Carruthers."

"Then, I'll check whether Carruthers filed a report yet with the county's Public Health Department. Public Health requires notification of any cases of discovered STDs. Also, the medical protocol directs infected people to contact known sexual partners of the past sixty days. Since nobody has contacted you, your husband may be unaware of his own infection."

"That may well be," said Seeney, "but it doesn't make him any less guilty."

"No, it doesn't," agreed Doctor Chavez, "but it could affect his legal liability. If Jack infected you after knowing he was carrying the disease, he might have other problems besides you."

"Oh my God, Marie! What do I do?"

"I'm not in a position to advise on those matters, Seeney, but let's start by getting you a shot in the butt to kill this thing. Then, I'll call you tomorrow when I find out if someone filed a report with Public Health."

Barely able to contain her rage with Jack that evening, Seeney decided she wanted the element of surprise on her side. She said nothing about visiting Doctor Chavez, going to bed early feigning a migraine headache. She received another call from Tom Burns the following morning.

"Sorry, I'm so persistent," said Burns, "but I have something important to tell you."

"It's okay. I was going to call you later. I had a tough day yesterday and was slow to get myself together today."

"Well, I'm afraid I'm not going to make your day any better."

"Don't worry. You can't possibly make me feel any worse today."

"One of my parishioners approached me on Sunday after services with something terrible on her mind. I invited her to my office, and she told me an awful tale. She discovered she had contracted a venereal disease the previous week, and her doctor told her to contact all recent sexual partners. There were only two. One was a trucker who passed through Compton several weeks ago, and the other was someone who lives in Tartan Springs."

"And," interrupted Seeney, "his name is Jack Stiles."

"Yes. Did you know already? I'm sorry."

"Don't be sorry, Tom. You're trying to protect me, and I appreciate that. But, unfortunately, you're a little too late. I found out I had gonorrhea yesterday. That was the appointment I had when you called. Who is this woman?"

"I can't tell you the name," said Tom. "It would break an ecclesiastical trust. I think you'll be able to figure it out easy enough on your own if that becomes necessary. But the woman was upset, and she said the man in Tartan Springs had threatened her when she told him her condition. That's why she came to me. She was frightened for her safety and didn't know where to turn. So, I helped her file a restraining order to prevent further contact from the gentleman in Tartan Springs."

"Thanks. I understand."

"Can I make a suggestion?" asked the pastor.

"Sure, Tom. I don't know what to do. Murder is probably out of the question. Divorce is fairly certain, but I don't know where to start with that."

"A friend in my poker group is the meanest divorce lawyer in the state. His name is Buster Aldrich, and he's done more to reduce infidelity among males in our county than all the ministers combined. Nobody wants to go up against him in a divorce case, and he's personally responsible for a lot of rich ladies up this way. Could you drive up here today to meet him?"

"Sure. Can I schedule an appointment on such short notice?"

"I can handle that. Just bring a copy of the medical report and any financial records you can conveniently access. You do the books for the dealership, right?"

"Yes, as well as our personal banking and taxes."

"Great. Bring everything. I'll give you a call back with a time and an address."

Seeney arrived at the law offices of Aldrich, King, & Delaney with a folder of paper files, several USB drives, and the medical report of her current condition. The distinguished-looking Buster Aldrich reviewed her records and asked a list of questions. When he finished, he asked her what her goal was.

"I think I want a divorce, Mr. Aldrich. I'm embarrassed by my medical condition, and wider publication of it would be humiliating to me. I'm not sure how to get a divorce without that being a matter of public record, though."

"Okay," said Aldrich, "but leave that to me. What about money?

How much do you want?"

"Mr. Aldrich, I'm not doing this for monetary gain. That isn't why I'm here or even something I thought about."

"Well, you need to," said Aldrich. "What this man did to you is worth a lot. You've earned a share of the profit you created together over the past eight years. That business won't support you anymore once you leave it, but the dealership will continue to support your husband. Let me review these documents tonight, and I'll call you tomorrow morning with some ideas."

"Okay. What do I owe you now, and what is this going to cost me to pursue?"

Aldrich studied Seeney in thought, then relaxed back into his chair. "My rate is four hundred dollars per hour, ma'am, and a divorce trial like this one could cost in the range of fifteen to twenty thousand dollars. My initial thought is to avoid a public trial with a mutually acceptable negotiation. My guess—not my promise—my *guess* is my services may cost you nothing. I think, in the end, your husband will gladly pay my fee for you." By the following day, Buster Aldrich had a comprehensive plan which he discussed with Seeney by telephone. To strike swiftly, Mr. Aldrich proposed he drive to Tartan Springs to meet with Jack Stiles that afternoon at the Stiles' residence.

Jack arrived home and saw Aldrich's Lexus in the driveway. He proceeded inside, where Seeney met him at the door. He asked, "Do we have company?"

"Yes, we do. Let's go to the living room."

When the couple came through the arched entrance, Aldrich stood in front of the coffee table. He extended his hand to Jack. "Good afternoon, Mr. Stiles. My name is Buster Aldrich. I'm an attorney, and I represent your wife. She would like a divorce, and I would like to make this as easy for the two of you as possible. Take a seat."

Jack looked at the attorney, then to Seeney with a confused expression. "Seeney, do you want to tell me what this is about?"

"Mr. Stiles," said Aldrich, "this will go much easier—and quicker if you allow me to do the talking. Sit here at the table, and you'll see several documents which I'll explain." Jack still looked confused but sat down in a daze. "This first document is the medical diagnosis your wife received on Tuesday from her physician, Doctor Chavez. She contracted gonorrhea from you. The second document is your agreement to an amicable, no-fault divorce based on irreconcilable differences. This type of divorce is allowed in West Virginia without a public trial or hearing. The third document details the financial part of your agreement with Mrs. Stiles for her to accept the terms of the no-fault divorce."

Jack's face was white, and he didn't speak for a long time. Then, finally, he faced his wife. "I'm devastated, Seeney— and so sorry. I would have never done this to you—I just—just—didn't know—and..."

"Stop it, Jack! Of course, you didn't know you caught the clap from one of your employees. I'm sure you're sorry about that and about passing it to me. But I don't want to be married to you anymore—and it isn't because you gave me a disease. It's because I can't trust you. You made your choices. Now I'm making mine!"

"Please review the second document," continued Aldrich, unfazed, "and you'll see the language is straightforward. This sort of divorce involves no trials, subpoenas, or embarrassing public testimony. It also preserves your privacy relative to the infidelity, as well as the medical consequences of it. In short, it allows your reputation not to be impugned, thereby protecting your business enterprise. Finally, the third document provides your wife's conditions for this nonpublic solution."

Jack began reading the third document and became angry. "Are you crazy? You're suggesting I give her this house, her car, and most of the money in our banking and savings accounts in return for her agreement to the no-fault divorce?"

"Yes, that is correct," answered Aldrich. "If I were representing her in a divorce court, I would ask for much more, including a portion of your business investments, a monthly stipend for her support, and some percentage of the business you own. Your wife, in my opinion, is being extremely benevolent under the circumstances."

"The bank still owns a mortgage on this house, and the car she drives belongs to the dealership. So, I can't just give her the titles to those," complained Jack.

"On the contrary, Mr. Stiles, you can—and you will if you don't want a very public divorce trial. I have a complete record of your financial holdings right here." Aldrich held a folder up for Stiles to see. "Your wife is a meticulous bookkeeper, and your records are both well maintained and well organized. You control more than adequate resources to eliminate the mortgage on this house and pay for her car. Whether you liquidate existing assets to do this or obtain a new personal loan from your bank is of no consequence to me. Still, these transactions must be completed by six o'clock, Monday."

Jack then turned to Seeney. "You filthy bitch! You gold-seeking whore!"

Aldrich broke in before Jack could say more. "Excuse me, Mr. Stiles, but that third document on the table has just become outdated and is no longer accurate." He took the document and replaced it with another one from his briefcase. "This new document now stipulates you will also turn over the funds in Fidelity Investments account number 1732402 to your wife as part of the settlement."

"What the hell?" exclaimed Stiles.

"Mr. Stiles," said Aldrich. "I don't like your attitude, and you're wasting my time. If you continue to verbally assault the wife you so carelessly infected with a venereal disease, I have several other documents I can show you in my briefcase. I told you what I would demand in an open divorce court, so your wife is letting you off cheap. For your information and your additional consideration, I also offered to represent Mrs. Tyson in a personal injury lawsuit against you. Such a suit is outside the parameters of the divorce settlement. I would take her case at no cost to her on a contingency basis, and I'm quite sure I'd win. Mrs. Stiles has, to this point, declined my generous offer, but you may give her reason to reconsider. Now, shall we proceed here or not?"

A shaken Jack said, "Alright. We can proceed. I understand, but can we go back to the other document on the table, not your new one? I only said seven words, and by my calculation, it cost me ten thousand dollars per word. That seems a little high."

"No," said Aldrich. "Time only goes forward, never backward. So, let's try not to do anything more which would delay or further change our negotiations."

Jack, speechless, seemed afraid to move. Then, at last, he asked, "Can my attorney look at these documents before I sign them?"

"Yes. You may, but that would require, yet again, a different third document. Your best deal is on the table. If you want your attorney involved, I will add your 401(k) holdings to our request. Additional lawyers cause delays and more paperwork, and neither your wife nor I have time for either. Our stipulations for document number three will change if you choose that option." Then, he pulled another paper from his briefcase.

Stiles knew Aldrich had defeated him. "Never mind. Keep your document. I'll sign these."

"That is smart on your part, Mr. Stiles. However, I hope you noted in the stipulations that you're not to discuss this agreement with anyone at any time. You're further warned not to disparage your wife either publicly or privately. In my professional opinion, you're getting off exceedingly easy."

As Jack rose from the table, Seeney told him, "Jack, please leave your keys to the house on the table, and I would like the spare key on your key ring for my car. I packed your things into four suitcases and a trunk which are in the garage. You can take them when you go. Keep the suitcases and trunk."

The sudden breakup of one of its "power couples" shocked the community, and the inevitable rumors surfaced. Most presumed Jack Stiles did something terrible to leave Seeney as peacefully as he did and as generously. A few knew about Jack's infidelity, and others guessed it. Cheating husbands, however, were common in Colgan County. If citizens didn't condone cheaters, they at least accepted them as part of the county's fabric. Lucrative divorce settlements created jealousy among some women— and enemies among men.

Seeney endured the social judgments stoically and abided by the conditions of her legal agreement with Stiles. Jack also maintained the terms of the deal, allowing his business to continue to thrive.

3 Tyrell Harrell

Born on St. Patrick's Day in 1988, Tyrell was the only child of Orville and Mavis Harrell. The couple moved to Tartan Springs from Chantilly, Virginia, when Ty was a baby. A lifelong United States postal worker, Orville became the postmaster in Tartan Springs when the position opened in 1991.

The family lived in a modest but well-kept neighborhood near the school. Orville and Mavis made sure their son participated in Boy Scouts, Little League, Sunday School, and other local organizations available to youths growing up in rural communities. The family also made frequent trips to Washington, DC, where Ty explored the art, history, and science inside the walls of the many Smithsonian Museum buildings.

In elementary, middle, and high school, Ty distinguished himself as a good student, a good musician, a good athlete, and an excellent young citizen. But, doing nothing poorly, he also did nothing extraordinarily. As a Little Leaguer, he made the All-Star team, but he wasn't the star. He was selected to the All-County band as a trumpet player but never made first chair. Ty placed twice in his weight class in the County AA Wrestling Tournament but never as a champion. Academically, he finished in the upper ten percent of his class but was neither the valedictorian nor the salutatorian. That Ty never achieved the top in his endeavors didn't bother either Ty or his parents. Orville and Mavis were proud of their son, and any team he chose to join always welcomed him.

Ty enrolled at West Virginia University after high school. Tuition for in-state students represented an education bargain at West Virginia's largest university. In addition, Ty obtained a student loan for the costs not covered by a partial scholarship he earned.

He tried out for the university wrestling team, making the practice squad as a freshman. This squad consisted of neither varsity nor junior varsity athletes but rather wrestlers who practiced with the team and provided reserves to fill holes created by injuries in varsity lineups. In his first season, the coach noted that Ty out-performed nobody—but out-hustled everybody.

The coach, impressed with Ty's work ethic and tenacity, promoted him to junior varsity as a sophomore. By the time he was a senior, Ty wrestled on the varsity squad. In his last year at WVU, fate awarded Ty a re-match with his old high school wrestling foe, Gabe Sullivan. This time, Ty beat Sullivan, who wrestled for Slippery Rock University, by a score of eight to five, the same score he had lost to the wrestler four years earlier in high school.

During Ty's freshman year, he met with a United States Marine Corps recruiting officer who visited the school. Ty discovered he could earn income for college through the USMC Platoon Leader Program, and he drove to Quantico, Virginia, one weekend for a battery of qualifications tests.

He did well, and the USMC invited him to join the Platoon Leaders Officer Candidate School program. Ty attended a six-week summer training course at the Quantico Marine base after his sophomore year. After that, he took the Marine Corps Aptitude Battery test to qualify for flight training.

As a result of the aptitude tests, the Marines accepted Ty into the flight program and awarded him funding for twenty-five hours of flight school, which he completed during his final years at college. Commissioned as a second lieutenant in the Marines when he graduated from college, Ty reported to Quantico for Officer Candidate School. From there, he went to Pensacola, Florida, for military flight training.

After achieving Navy wings, his first active-duty orders were to the Kashir Province of Bektistan, where he flew logistical support missions in the H-53, Sea Stallion helicopter. In the year he deployed to this volatile area of the world, he was fortunate to encounter no direct hostilities toward his aircraft. His squadron received a Naval Commendation for the number of successful missions flown during the tour, and the marines promoted Ty to Captain after the tour.

From Bektistan, Ty received what many USMC aviators considered "dream orders" to prestigious HMX-1 based at Quantico, Virginia. The squadron maintained an elite permanent detachment at Andrews Air Force Base to support the transportation needs of the President, Heads of State, Department of Defense officials, and various VIPs/dignitaries.

Ty flew both the venerable H-3 and the newer H-60 helicopters in his aviation duties and acted as the squadron's legal officer on the ground. Within six months of the tour, scheduled to be three years, Ty thought he had fallen in love.

Her name was Jennifer Hayes, the Disbursements Officer for the base exchange. Ty met her at a function held at the officer's club, and the two became dating partners soon after. A graduate from George Washington University with a degree in finance, Jenny had quickly climbed to one of the top administrative positions in the Air Force Exchange system.

At only twenty-seven, she was intelligent, aggressive, and attractive. However, Jenny also had a wild side. She loved the nightclub scene at nearby National Harbor, and she was a frequent visitor to the casinos in Charlestown, West Virginia, and Atlantic City, New Jersey.

Ty's critical flying duties often required him to maintain a "ready-alert" status for aviation missions that might materialize on short notice, precluding his participation in some of the things Jenny planned. As a result, Ty's duty commitments sometimes challenged Jenny, but they never stopped her.

When Ty had the chance to take a week of vacation leave, he proposed they go to Lake Tahoe. The resort location represented a place that could meet Ty's expectations for outdoor activity, like skiing, and Jenny's desire for nightlife. Unfortunately, the trip turned into a disaster.

Jennifer skied two hours on the first morning and complained about the cold. When Ty came back after a day of challenging skiing, his body struggled to keep up with Jenny for a night of casinos and dancing. After the vacation, the couple realized they lived in socially different hemispheres. Shortly after returning to DC, they amicably and metaphorically kissed each other goodbye.

Ty's recent visit to his old hometown for a high school reunion created a pleasant but unanticipated distraction in his now well-ordered life. His fortuitous re-connection with a woman he had coveted a decade earlier provided a girlfriend who lived an inconvenient distance away, who he wanted to work into a career that often found personal relationships inconvenient. Of course, such obstacles can be overcome in fiction, but only time would tell if the challenges might be handled in real life.

4 Woodstock, Virginia

Two weeks after the reunion, Ty was anxious to return to Tartan Springs to visit Seeney. The couple talked several times on the phone and exchanged a series of emails. Their relationship was progressing as both hoped it would, and their prospects exhibited signs of becoming exciting. On one phone call, Seeney said, "I was thinking, Ty. The weather is still nice out here and will probably stay that way for another month or so. The leaves are starting to change, and I want to explore a trail near here. Would you want to meet me and hike it together some weekend?"

"I'll meet you to do anything together," said Ty. "I can't make it there this week, but I'm not scheduled at work next weekend. Should I plan to come to Tartan Springs?"

"Next weekend would be perfect. The leaves won't be at peak at the lower elevations but close to full color on the mountaintops. The trail I want to try is about two and a half hours from here, which is about the same distance for you. The name of the trail is Big Schloss—you can

Google it—and it's near a little town in Virginia called Woodstock."

"Sounds exciting. I'll look it up. Is that spelled S-C-H-L-O-S-S?"

"Yes, and the trailhead starts in the Wolf Gap Recreation Area."

"Got it," said Ty. "I might not be able to leave until after work on Friday. Will we stay somewhere around Woodstock on Friday and Saturday night?"

"Yes. I can make those arrangements. But, unfortunately, at this time of the year, rooms can be hard to find in the Valley so, if you're game for the plan, I should start working on that right away."

"Sounds fine to me, but remember, sometimes in my business, things come up that can change my plans without much notice."

"I understand. Most motels have an easy cancellation policy, though. If your schedule changes, let me know, and we'll make a new plan."

After they hung up, Seeney smiled and entered a Google search for Woodstock, Virginia. Within a half-hour, she secured a reservation at the Comfort Inn and had all the information she needed about the historic little town.

Two weeks later, she was waiting in the lobby of the motel for Ty. The trip from Tartan Springs had taken her under three hours, and she had already checked in. Ty texted her when he left Andrews Air Force Base at four o'clock. She suspected his trip would be a little longer than hers since he would be in the middle of the DC rush-hour traffic, leaving the Northern Virginia area.

Seeney saw his Cherokee pull into the parking lot at seven o'clock. He entered the motel with one small suitcase, and she greeted him near the counter with a hug. He was still in his military uniform, and he apologized, "Sorry, Seeney, but I left straight from the base, and I didn't have a chance to change clothes."

"I'm glad you didn't." Seeney openly admired the man in front of her. "I like you in that uniform."

"Well, thanks, but I'll change quickly, and we can leave for dinner. Sorry I was late. Traffic around the city was bad this afternoon."

"No problem. I checked in for us, and if you don't mind, I think you should throw your suitcase in the room, and we'll head to town right away. The desk clerk says Woodstock rolls up the sidewalks early and that dining options are limited."

"OK, if you say so," said Ty, sounding not so sure this was really OK, "but won't I seem a little out of place in a uniform around here?"

"Listen, Captain. You should only concern yourself with how one person thinks you look this weekend. Any problem with that?"

"We should leave, then," said Ty.

Seeney laughed. "The clerk said a cute café on Main Street has terrific food, but sometimes it gets busy on weekends. I didn't make reservations, but let's give it a try."

Fifteen minutes later, they found a parking space not too far from the Woodstock Café. Situated almost in the center of town, the cafe sat directly across from a courthouse. Fall flowers in planters lined the streets, and attractive iron benches appeared in front of many businesses. Noticing no meters, Ty parked, and the couple proceeded to the café. The relaxing solitude of the quaint town contrasted with the bustling activity inside the restaurant. The cheerful sounds of a packed room of diners created a pleasant cacophony, and a young hostess greeted them near the door with a smile.

"Do you have a reservation?"

"No, we don't," admitted Seeney, "but our motel clerk recommended we eat here. Is there a possibility you can accommodate us? We don't mind waiting."

At that moment, a cute blonde woman appeared behind the hostess and greeted Seeney and Ty. The hostess relayed to the woman that Seeney and Ty had no reservations. The blonde looked around the room and then back at the couple. "Certainly, we can accommodate you, but maybe not right away."

Ty thanked her. "That would be fine. We aren't in a hurry. Can we wait someplace, perhaps with a cocktail?"

"Sure," said the blonde, "but you'll have to settle for wine or beer. These seats by the window are available—but can I make a suggestion?"

"Sure," said Ty.

"My name is Natalie, and I'm one of the owners. We'd love to host you for dinner, but it might be an hour before we can seat you. Our town has an outstanding local brewery located less than a block away. Go have a beer or wine over there and, if you give me a telephone number, I'll text you when a table opens."

"Thank you," said Seeney. "That sounds perfect. How do we find the brewhouse?"

As Natalie gave Seeney the walking directions to the brewery, Ty wrote his cell phone number on the café's reservation log. An attractive couple leaving the Café said goodbye to Natalie as they departed, and Natalie told Ty and Seeney, "That's our mayor and his wife."

Seeney looked at Ty, then asked Natalie, "Do you think your town would consider making a trade for a mayor located in West Virginia?"

Chuckling, Natalie said, "I don't think so. Jason and Donna are popular here in Woodstock. You're all set. I'll send you a text when we're ready, but don't worry if you're in the middle of a beer when the message comes. We'll hold your table if we need to. We try to stop taking orders at nine o'clock, but that still gives us plenty of time."

"Thank you so much," said Ty.

"No. Thank you, sir—and thank you for your service."

Ty and Seeney walked to the Woodstock Brewhouse, a spacious establishment bustling with activity. Like a German festhaus, the crowded business was loud and friendly. Ty located a table and ordered an IPA for himself and a cider for Seeney. When the young waiter returned with the drinks, Ty reached for his wallet, but the employee stopped him.

"You don't owe anything," said the waiter. "The man with the beard up at the bar paid for these. He told me to tell you 'thank you for your service.'"

Ty thanked the young man, whose name tag read Jerome, and gave him a five-dollar tip. "Please thank my generous friend at the bar as well, Jerome."

"Yes, sir."

Ty held his glass to Seeney's in a toast. "I guess wearing this uniform was a good idea after all. It seems to be doing something for us."

"It's definitely doing something for me," Seeney said with a flirtatious wink.

"Don't tease me with that kind of talk. I won't be able to think about drinks or dinner."

"Wouldn't want that to happen. You're going to need your energy this weekend." Seeney touched Ty's foot with hers softly under the table.

The couple finished their beers, and when Natalie's text arrived, they proceeded back to the café. The hostess was no longer at the front, but Natalie was, and she appeared happy to see them. She seated them at a two-top in the front windows, provided menus, and said their server, Misty, would be over shortly. The menu surprised them. While it listed limited entrees, the descriptions reminded the couple of something they'd find at a fine dining restaurant in DC. "I don't think short-order cooks work back in the kitchen," said Ty. "A real chef is back there somewhere. How'd you find this place?"

"Just lucky, I think. The hotel clerk recommended it."

"We need to thank that clerk, then."

When Misty arrived at the table, Seeney asked the server for a local white wine recommendation. "I'm not a connoisseur myself," said the humble Misty, "but people who come here enjoy the Viognier from Cave Ridge or the Thalia from Muse Vineyards."

"Thalia is a new variety for me, so let's try that," said Seeney.

"Make it two," said Ty, "and I think we're also ready to order."

The braised short rib was one of the best Ty thought he ever had, and Seeney was equally enthusiastic about her maple miso-glazed salmon. Before they left, the chef, Joaquin, visited their table with Natalie. It was apparent the two were a pair. Seeney and Ty thanked the couple for accommodating them and praised the outstanding dining experience. On their way to the car, Ty complimented his partner's travel planning. "Seeney, this little town is kinda' magical, or is that just a glow I'm feeling from the company?"

"Well, I'm glad for the glow, but I agree. The café would shine without any help from personal glows. That may be a tough benchmark for the rest of the weekend."

"Tell me about the hike tomorrow."

"Well, we have a choice. Big Schloss is the more famous trail, but I'm inclined to pick the sister trail called the Tibbets Knob Trail after talking to some other people. That one, according to my friends, is more difficult but offers better views than Big Schloss. The total hiking time is also less at about two hours versus four for Big Schloss. So, I thought if we hiked the shorter trail tomorrow morning, we might still have time for some other things in the afternoon—like maybe visit the winery in town."

"Either one sounds fine to me, but I like your plan. I wouldn't mind exploring the town a little more. What time do you want to start?"

"I get up early, Ty, but we don't have to tomorrow. We can go anytime."

"I'm up by five-thirty in the morning to exercise, so you better not give me a choice if you don't want to wake up that early on the weekend."

"How about seven? The motel offers a complimentary continental breakfast."

"Sounds like a plan." Pulling up to the motel, Ty said, "I'm ready to get out of his uniform finally."

"I'm ready for that, too," said Seeney.

The couple started early the following day and arrived at the Wolf Gap Campground by eight o'clock. Ty had a small backpack with some trail mix, bottled water, and a first aid kit. Both wore appropriate boots, seeming experienced hikers. They had no problem finding the trailhead, and just before beginning the climb, Ty said, "We're the only ones out this early. Should we be concerned about meeting the wrong kind of wildlife on the trail—like, for instance, bears?"

Seeney smiled and retrieved a small container from her fanny pack. The spray bottle pictured a bear with four red Xs placed over it.

"You always carry bear spray with you?" asked Ty. "I didn't know Tartan Springs had a bear problem."

"This stuff works as well on a two-hundred-pound man as it does on a three-hundred-pound bear. In addition, this is stronger than normal pepper spray, cheaper, and readily available at most sporting goods stores."

"I'm glad you're always prepared, but, for the record, I only weigh about one hundred sixty-five pounds."

"I brought this along for the bears on this trip, not the men."

The ascent was strenuous but not dangerous, and the couple didn't encounter another hiker on the entire trail. At the lower levels, the path was wide enough for the pair to hike next to each other; as they got higher, this became impossible. Ty assumed the lead sometimes, and other times Seeney would.

As they neared the summit, the trail provided the hikers two alternatives for reaching the top. One path continued along a mild traverse lined with trees; another appeared to go straight up a craggy rock cliff. While the route up the ridge required no special rock-climbing equipment, it was unquestionably the more demanding route to the summit and, most likely, the more scenic. Ty deferred the selection to Seeney.

"You kidding me? We didn't come out here for a walk in the woods." She started up the rocky trail with Ty behind her, admiring her stamina, her sense of adventure—and her muscular legs.

Despite their several stops to admire striking scenery, they accomplished the summit in under two hours. The views from the top were even better than advertised, and they sat silently at the crest, taking it all in. As Seeney predicted, the foliage at lower elevations was still mostly green, but autumn colors began to show at the peak. The air was crisp but not yet cold, and the spectacular panoramas from this part of Virginia looking into West Virginia were breathtaking. Ty finally broke the silence. "Seeney, this is one of the most beautiful places I've ever been. Thank you."

"Thanks for coming with me. I'm glad we discovered it together."

"Can you imagine what it must look like at sunset? Or, at night with a full moon? You'd feel like you could almost touch the sky from this rock, I bet." Seeney glanced at her watch, then back at Ty. She thought for a moment, then looked again toward her wrist. Ty noticed and asked, "You in a hurry? Got someplace else to go?"

"No, Ty. You just gave me a crazy idea, but it may not be practical."

"OK. I'm curious. What was it?"

"Well, this may be nuts, but the time is only nine-thirty, and going down the trail wouldn't take as long as coming up. Let's say we're back to the car by eleven. If we head to the Walmart in Woodstock and buy some cheap camping gear and a few provisions, it would be possible to be back at the trailhead by two. Even if we don't climb the trail as fast as we just did, we could be back here before four. Sunset isn't until about five, and guess what? The moon is full tonight."

"That's my kind of adventure, but what about the other things you wanted to see in Woodstock?"

"That winery isn't going anywhere. Neither is Woodstock—but when in our lifetime will we ever have a chance to spend a night on this mountain, in October, with a full moon in the sky?" asked Seeney.

"We better start moving," said Ty.

The couple stood at the Walmart checkout counter at noon, with a small list of items, including a pop-up tent, a double sleeping bag, a lightweight solar blanket, two thin roll-up foam cushions, and a mountaineering-style backpack. While Ty gathered the camping supplies, Seeney visited the grocery area and picked up bottled drinks, ready-to-eat food, fruit, and bread. Seeney put the grocery items in Ty's smaller backpack in the parking lot, and Ty filled the bigger one with the camp supplies. They bought lunch at Burger King's drive-through window and arrived back at the Wolf Gap trailhead by one-thirty.

Ty was smiling as he strapped on the heavier backpack. "Seeney, I can't tell you how much I'm enjoying this."

"Thanks. I hope my legs can handle two mountains in one day."

"We can take our time. Even with some extra weight, we'll easily make the top before sunset. Do you know the elevation of Tibbets Knob?"

"I think around three thousand feet. Why?"

"Just thinking," said Ty with a mischievous smile. "Do you know what the Mile High Club is?"

"You may be surprised to learn I *do* know about that club ...and what the membership requirements are. Jack's dad owned an airplane, and Jack had a pilot's license. He was always bugging me about joining the Mile High Club. I never did."

"Well, I'm a pilot and still not a member either. So, I thought maybe I could fix that today, but this mountain might not be tall enough."

"Hmmm. I think you better reorient your mind back to hiking, or you won't even earn membership to the half-mile club." Then, she started up the trail.

The couple reached the summit in a little over two hours this time. A combination of tired legs and heavier loads created an extra hour for the trip over the same one completed in the morning. Still, they got to the top well before sunset and set up a campsite, including a small fire.

As a massive, red sun was setting over the state of West Virginia, Ty and Seeney enjoyed a front porch view with no obstructions. They sat on a boulder, facing west, sipping a lukewarm canned beer, and munching on Route 11 sour cream potato chips as the sun descended over the autumn-inspired geography. "Unbelievable!" said Ty.

"It was worth the effort," agreed Seeney.

"I doubt anyone on the planet has a better view than this with any better cocktails or hors d'oeuvres. Where did you say these chips are from?"

Seeney leaned into Ty's shoulder, holding the bag to the fading light. "They're Route 11 chips and made in this county. The founder is the daughter of someone who had a famous restaurant in DC. Several cuisine magazines have reviewed the chips favorably, and folks around here are proud of them."

"They should be. The chips are outstanding."

Before the light faded entirely, Ty placed his cell phone on a convenient rock, set the timer on his camera, and took a picture of themselves. "Might not be enough light," he said, "but we'll see."

The sun had almost disappeared, and Seeney said, "The beanie weenies are getting warm over the fire you made. We've also got fruit and bread for dinner—oh, and I almost forgot—one more lukewarm beer apiece."

"My God, Seeney! You're beautiful, *and* you can cook? Where was my head ten years ago?"

"Apparently in the yearbook and not on me."

The air on the mountaintop cooled after sunset, and the couples' light jackets began to lose the battle against temperature. Ty held Seeney's shoulders a bit tighter. "My mind was on you back then, Seeney. I just didn't know you were in my reach. I was a naïve kid with not much confidence, and you were already a grown woman even though we were the same age. Since the reunion, I thought about that a lot, and, as I look back, I'm not sure I'd change anything, even if I could. Both of us have seen some life now. We know things we want in a partner and things we don't—that we wouldn't have known back then. So, I think we have a better chance of a meaningful, strong relationship today than we might have had ten years ago."

Seeney cuddled and sighed. "Maybe you're right, Captain. But I keep thinking—it would have been nice to enjoy this for the last ten years."

"We're making up fast enough," said Ty.

"I like that part. Speaking of which, if you want your membership in the half-mile club, we should move to inside the tent."

Smiling, Ty warned, "Tonight is going to be a little chilly in that tent, Seeney."

"I doubt it," she said confidently.

Before leaving the dying campfire, the couple watched the full moon rise over the mountains to join a starlit sky. As romantic as the setting was, the dropping temperature made a sleeping bag inside a tent more tempting. Ty announced he needed to step up the path to 'water the flowers' before retiring, and Seeney did the same on the opposite side of the trail.

They met back at the entrance to the tent a few minutes later and crawled inside. Light physical activity kept them warm initially, but Seeney was the first to realize that sleeping naked in a sleeping bag covered only by a lightweight solar blanket was a lousy idea this evening. Survival trumped romance, and she said, "Sorry, Cowboy," as she put her hiking clothes back on.

"No apology necessary. I didn't know how much longer I could hold out. Do you want me to restart the campfire?"

"Unless you plan to move it inside the tent, the fire won't help us much. But I think we'll be fine with the extra clothing. Just stay close and keep your arm around me."

"No problem." Fully clothed in the sleeping bag under the solar blanket within the small space of the tent provided enough heat for the couple to sleep relatively comfortably for the rest of the evening. They woke to the first rays of the sun at around six-thirty.

A little stiff from sleeping on the thin foam cushion, Ty crawled from the tent and gazed at where their small campfire had been. The fire was long gone, and Ty would need to gather more dry wood to start it again. He didn't think restarting it was worth the effort, so he called to Seeney inside the tent. "What would you think about gathering everything this morning and heading down the mountain? To start a fire would take about half an hour, or we could enjoy fresh coffee and hot showers in about two hours at the motel."

"I'm not sure which sounds better. Hot showers or hot coffee, but I'm with you. The sooner for either or both, the better—but I wouldn't have traded this adventure for anything. This was awesome!"

"Agree. Let's do it again sometime. We'll know to bring warmer clothes next time."

"Or next time might be in warmer weather. I bet we're the only ones who slept in a tent on a mountain anywhere around here last night."

"Probably right."

"If you put the tent and solar blanket back in the big backpack, I can fit everything else in your smaller one. I'm going to leave the bread and fruit for the critters," said Seeney.

They were hiking down the trail by seven and reached Ty's

Cherokee by eight-thirty. At nine, back at the Comfort Inn, they helped themselves to giant mugs of hot coffee from the breakfast bar. As they ascended in the elevator to their floor, Ty welcomed Seeney to use the shower first.

As he enjoyed his coffee and rested on the bed, waiting for Seeney to finish in the bathroom, he reflected on the past two days. This weekend, he'd done precisely the things he liked to do, and he wondered if the same were true for Seeney. She had undoubtedly been willing company, but had she, perhaps, only been trying to accommodate him? He had an idea for a different kind of future weekend he thought he would test on her later in the morning.

Seeney, her hair still dripping when she stepped from the bathroom, held a bath towel around herself. At five feet, two inches, she was compact, but she obviously cared about her physique. Her naturally curly hair was dark brown with hints of red, and a single dimple attractively dented her left cheek. Legs made shapely by well-defined muscle seemed long for her otherwise petite frame. Hazel eyes and an effervescent smile complimented a face that needed no makeup for most occasions.

Seeney caught Ty staring at her. "I like the way you're looking at me, Mister. Can I help you with something?"

Ty laughed. "I'm not sure how you expect me to react when you walk in here wearing nothing but a towel."

"Oh, I'm sorry. Does the towel bother you?" She let it drop to the floor.

"Geez, Seeney. Why don't you climb under the covers and wait for me? I'll be right back."

"OK. Check-out isn't until noon, so we could take a quick nap."

"Or something ...," Ty replied.

Sensual morning exercises ended with a nap in the comfortable motel bed, and when Ty opened his eyes, the clock on the nightstand displayed eleven-fifteen. He squeezed Seeney gently. "We should think about getting up."

Sleepily, she acknowledged. "OK, but that was so relaxing. I was looking forward to getting something to eat downstairs, but I think the breakfast bar closed at eleven."

"You're right. Why don't we go back to that café where we ate

Friday? The owner told us they served brunch on Sundays."

"Sounds good to me. We'll still have time to visit the vineyard in town. Or do you need to start back to DC?"

"The vineyard would be fine. If I'm back to Andrews by evening, I'm OK."

The couple dressed and stood at the Woodstock Café's hostess podium by twelve-thirty. Customers occupied every visible table, but the owner, Natalie, greeted them as she removed dishes from a nearby table. "Hey, you came back. How was the hike?"

"Terrific," said Ty. "Looks like we always get here at your busiest times."

"Sunday brunch is popular," said Natalie as she handed the dishes in her hand to a server, "but tables turn over quickly. You can sit here at this booth I'm cleaning after I wipe it down."

Ty and Seeney sat, and a bubbly server named Renée brought menus. "Hi," she said. "Natty told me you two were here on Friday night. Welcome back."

Ty ordered eggs benedict on Renée's suggestion, and Seeney ordered French toast. When their entrées arrived, Seeney's eyes widened at the presentation, and she said to Renée, "I don't think I ever saw French toast that looks like that. I'll never eat it all."

"Joaquin makes the brioche bread for the toast here, and the fresh blueberries come from a local farmer. If you can't finish it, this guy next to you looks like he could help."

Seeney soaked up the last bite of toast with syrup on her plate as Renée returned to their table. Ty's dish was also clean, and he asked Renée, "Would you tell the chef those were the best eggs benedict I ever ate? The béarnaise sauce was amazing."

"Sure thing. Joaquin—we call him Joe—makes the sauce himself. Are you two from around here?"

Seeney said, "No. Ty lives around DC, and I'm from Tartan Springs, West Virginia. This is our first visit to Woodstock."

Renée eyed the two of them curiously, an unasked question lurking on her lips. At that moment, Natalie appeared and asked the couple how their meal was. Before Ty or Seeney answered, Renée said, "Duh—Natty—look at their plates. I don't think we need to put them through the dishwasher."

Natty laughed and gave Renée a light hug. The two ladies enjoyed more than just a professional relationship it seemed. Natalie said, "Sorry folks, sometimes Renée doesn't let customers get a word in edgewise."

"No problem," said Ty. "She's right. The food was outstanding—just like Friday night, and we're already making plans to come back."

As Renée cleared the table, Natalie asked the couple what they had seen in the area the previous day. When Seeney told her about hiking to Tibbets Knob twice and spending the night at the top, Natalie said, "Shut up! Tibbets Knob twice in one day? Are you two triathlon athletes or something? I had no idea camping facilities even existed up there. Joe and I haven't hiked that trail yet."

"Well," said Ty, "the only camping accommodations are what you bring on your back, and I would warn you to take some warm clothes if you plan to do what we did in October. The view at sunset is amazing, though."

"Going on my list," said Natalie. "Thanks. What's on the schedule for today?"

Seeney glanced at Ty, then told Natalie, "We thought we might visit the Muse Vineyard before we headed back, but what would you recommend?"

"Muse is one of my favorites, but if you can hold that off for a little while, you should stay here a bit longer. Benny V is performing today, and he starts in about fifteen minutes. We feature entertainment every Sunday from two to four, and Benny's whole band is with him today. The group has another gig later this evening in town, so all of them plan to join Benny for his performance at our place. The band is outstanding."

"Thank you," said Seeney. "You sold me. Can you bring me another glass of that Thalia I had on Friday night?"

"I'm with her," said Ty. "And, I'll have an IPA."

"I'll let Renée know."

Natalie's suggestion proved sound, as Benny V's band was exceptional. To find this level of talent in a small agricultural mountain community ninety miles west of DC, performing at a small cafe surprised Seeney and Ty. When the entertainers finished their first set, Ty suggested ordering another drink. "I think we're going to be coming back here again, and we can always visit the vineyard another time. I'm enjoying sitting here listening to the music and talking to you, so let's stay until the band finishes at four."

"Fine with me," said Seeney. "I love this place."

"Find Renée and order us another round if you can. I need to visit the restroom facilities."

As he waited for the restroom to become available, Ty read newspaper articles clipped on the walls in this area. The numerous positive reviews proved the café had been a "discovery" for many others besides him and Seeney. He suspected it wouldn't take long before the business needed more wall space, and he recorded a note on his cell to remind himself to post a review on Yelp and TripAdvisor.

Ty saw the server, Renée, sitting across from Seeney on his way back to the booth. When Renée noticed Ty approaching, she smiled at Seeney, and the two exchanged a quick fist bump. Then, as she left the booth to allow Ty back in, she turned her back toward Seeney and whispered, "Good pick here, Mister. Don't blow it!"

Renee left before Ty had time to respond. When he sat down, he asked Seeney, "What was that about?"

"Oh, nothing. Just girl talk. Renée has worked at this café for almost fifteen years, and I don't think she misses much. She's a sweet lady with a beautiful heart, and my impression is she considers nobody in here a stranger."

Ty thought about that—and about what the server had quietly said to him as he sat down. "I think you're right. Whatever your conversation was, Renée felt compelled to tell me not to 'blow it' with you."

Seeney laughed so loud it drew people's attention in the next booth, and she covered her mouth. "That doesn't surprise me at all. Renée thought we were a cute couple and wanted to know more about us."

"Well, she's at least two-thirds right about that. You're cute—and we're a couple."

"She doesn't work on many Sundays," said Seeney. "She's devout, and Natalie allows her to take Sundays off. They needed her today, though."

"A lot of things worked in our favor this weekend."

"I was thinking that, too," said Seeney, contemplating. "When we leave today, you should give Renée a substantial tip in exchange for the good one she gave you."

"I plan on it," said Ty, with a wink. "While we've got a few minutes before the band starts, can I run an idea by you relating to our next visit?"

"I'm all ears. When is it, and where is it?'

"Well, it would be up my way and much different from this weekend. I think the event might be fun for you, and I would like you to come."

"I'm listening—and I'm inclined to accept without knowing what it involves, but you're acting a little hesitant," said Seeney.

"I'm not—really. Just—well, it's the United States Marine Corps birthday party. The date is November tenth, and, for Marines, the celebration is a big deal. This year the party is on a Tuesday. So, if you came up for a long weekend, we could go to the dinner on base together."

"Thank you, Ty. I don't think that would be a problem, but what am I missing? What are you holding back?"

"The commitment is bigger than it sounds," he said. "It's formal, which means all the Marines will be in their dinner dress uniforms. Also, a lot of traditional military BS goes on that you might have to tolerate. Lastly, you're going to end up with a pretty bad hangover on Wednesday. Sort of goes with the territory on this event."

"Well, that hangover sounds appealing, so I'm not sure how I can decline. I'll need to go to Compton next week for a dress."

"That won't be necessary. I'm sure you have something in your closet that would work fine. I don't want this to cause extra expense."

Seeney stared at Ty's face a few moments before answering him—calmly and deliberately. "Ty Harrell, you may still be a bit naïve, but you need to learn to never stand in the way of a woman with a good excuse to buy a new dress."

"OK, OK. I'm sorry. I know how you react to men in uniform, though, and my hands will be full as it is. I'm up for the challenge, but don't do anything to make my job more difficult."

"That *does* sound like a challenge—for you," answered Seeney coyly. "I can't promise I'm going to be able to help you with that part, though. If I come, I'm going to be looking damn good, and you'll have to deal with the consequences. Tell me more about this hangover. Is there no way we can avoid that?"

"We can try. Once the main dinner is over, most of the younger officers uber to National Harbor with their wives and girlfriends, where there are many clubs. DC is a patriotic town, and on the Marine Corps' birthday, a Marine in uniform has a difficult time buying his own drink anywhere. Not wanting to disappoint our generous fans, we tend to finish any drinks purchased for us. We attempt to dance off as much of the excess alcohol as possible, but we generally lose the battle by two in the morning. It doesn't hurt much—until the next day."

"And past experiences—remembered pain, wouldn't help to create a better course the next time?"

"Marines can be pretty dumb, I guess," said Ty.

"OK, I'm warned, and I accept."

"That's what I was hoping you'd say."

After Benny V and his band concluded their final set, Ty paid the bill. Surprising him, Renée gave he and Seeney a warm hug, saying she hoped she'd see them again soon. Natalie also caught the couple as they were leaving to say goodbye. Ty dropped twenty dollars in the band's gratuity basket, and the couple proceeded to their two cars parked in front of the café.

Seeney said, "With the twenty dollars you left for the band and the twenty you gave Renée, this turned into an expensive brunch."

"It was a bargain. The whole weekend was. Thanks for the planning."

"Ha! The only thing I planned was the location. This trip had a mind of its own."

"Every once in a while, things work out like that," said Ty. "Sometimes, *we* make the path, and sometimes the *path* makes us."

"Well, I enjoyed this one," said Seeney.

"I did, too."

The server, Renée, watched the couple leave the café, and she went to the front windows as they walked to their cars. They engaged in a conversation, and if Renée hoped to witness a last, long, romantic kiss between the two, their tender G-rated embrace disappointed her. Even in this, though, she sensed a latent intimacy that made her smile. She lightly touched the small cross on her necklace as she returned to wiping tables.

5 Tartan Springs

Seeney watched Ty's car, ahead of hers, turn right to go east on I-66. She sounded her horn as she continued up I-81 to her exit to go west and saw Ty's hand wave out of his side window as she passed.

In her mind, the past weekend couldn't have gone better. The trip she planned turned out to be only partially the trip the couple experienced. The one they shared, however, was better than the one she intended. Her thoughts wandered again to that song from the reunion about the "road not taken"—then to the unusual conversation between the server, Renée, and herself.

"Can I ask you a personal question?" asked Renée.

"Renée, I only met you an hour ago," said Seeney, "but something tells me you're going to ask me that question no matter what I say."

"Yeah. You're right. Sorry. It's just—I see a lot of people come in here, and sometimes I get this overwhelming curiosity I can't control.

You two are an attractive couple—and that man you're with looks like a good catch to me. Why is he in DC, and you're in West Virginia?"

Seeney couldn't hold back a laugh about this intimate inquiry from a woman she didn't even know. "Renée, you're amazingly bold—but, for some reason, I like it. Of course, it's possible we have similar tastes in men."

"Well, that could be—but yours is a little young for me. I'm almost thirty-five. Still, I don't understand the separation. Sorry."

Seeney then provided the inquisitive Renée with a short history of her relationship with Ty. As she ended, she chuckled. "Men can be clueless sometimes, and they all seem to be born with an inexplicable macho drive to be in charge. Males don't react well when they believe someone is pushing them, yet I find they're often easily led. Ten years ago, as classmates at the same school, my attempts to lead Ty might have been too subtle. I've improved my technique since then."

Renée laughed with Seeney and said, "You go, Girl! You learned that in less time than me, but you're dead on. Do you have faith?"

The question blindsided Seeney for a moment, but she realized Renée posed it without an ounce of judgment. "I'm not as well-equipped in that area as I should be," admitted Seeney. "I attend church and have a dear friend who is a pastor, but I haven't yet found all the answers I'm looking for."

"No problem," said Renée. "You're still a seeker—good. My faith is strong, though, so I'm going to pray for you."

Renée had delivered this message with no recrimination, and Seeney was respectfully appreciative. "Renée, you're a wonderful person. Thank you. I can use all the help I can get from wherever I can get it."

As Renée noticed Ty returning to the booth, she said, "You're more than welcome. I do lots of praying for a bunch of people I like—and I know it works." She then gave Seeney a friendly fist bump and got up from the table.

When Ty told Seeney what Renée quietly said to him as he exchanged places in the booth, it made her laugh.

Now, as she continued her drive back to Tartan Springs, she didn't laugh—just thought deeply. Three miles before her exit from the interstate, she passed the spot near the end of a long decline where her parents perished eight years earlier. A few minutes later, she caught sight of the McCaskey mansion overlooking the town, and she took the exit for Tartan Springs. Seeney met a tanker truck going the opposite way on Main Street, but other than that vehicle, the streets were empty.

When she came to the sign identifying the Tartan Springs Bottled Water Company, she stopped the car for a moment. The natural spring and town's namesake sprang from among boulders just behind the sign. A series of pipes connected the spring to the water business's building, where the spring water-filled plastic bottles that the company distributed throughout the Mid-Atlantic region. The small business, located at the bottom of the hill from the McCaskey mansion, represented ground zero for where the community started over two hundred years ago.

Natural springs are geological phenomena that occur due to an aquifer filled to the point water overflows to the land surface. Springs can range in size from intermittent seeps, which flow only after much rain, to pools producing hundreds of millions of gallons daily. Sometimes spring water emanating from water traveling from great depths in the earth that passes over layers of hot rocks creates thermal springs.

The water flowing from a natural spring is often clear, cold, and fit for immediate human consumption. Subsurface rocks crudely filter this water, and during its travel, underground debris falls out of suspension. Additionally, the lack of sunlight precludes many microbes, viruses, and bacteria from living. However, not all these living things die automatically, nor are agricultural or industrial pollutants that may seep into the aquifer permanently removed.

Once home to the native Iroquois People, the area around the Siler River saw its first European settlers in the early 1700s. After the French and Indian wars, more people arrived, pushing west from the cities of the Mid Atlantic. Around 1830, a Scottish immigrant named Samuel McCaskey built a modest cabin near the outcropping of rocks from which the spring in the area surfaced. He called the water feature Tartan Springs. Thus, his home behind the spring and the community that evolved around it became known by the same name.

Samuel's experience with coal came from two generations of Scottish coal mining ancestors. His discovery of open seams of the energy-laden sedimentary rock near the tops of the nearby mountains encouraged his recruitment of a company of neighbors to help him extract it. The small operation grew to a larger one as the demand for the resource expanded proportionally to the rapid increase in the populations of the country's eastern cities.

When railroad tracks connected the area to Baltimore and Philadelphia, McCaskey couldn't keep up with the demand. So, he expanded the enterprise. His primary customer, the Pennsylvania Electric Company, provided financing for the significant capital project, and using the same funding, Samuel constructed a mansion beside his cabin. Then he knocked the cabin down.

The Civil War was unkind to a divided nation, but not to McCaskey Coal. During the war, battles raged to the north, the east, and the south of Tartan Springs, but never close to the remote mountain town. Because of the importance of McCaskey coal to the union effort, a small militia remained near Tartan Springs for the duration of the conflict. Samuel Jr. volunteered to fight for the Union Army, but his only action was as a supply clerk stationed in Washington, DC.

After the war, he became president of his father's company, and when Samuel Senior died, Junior tripled the mineral rights holdings on surrounding mountaintops. McCaskey coal was, by far, the largest employer in the county by this time and a rather significant energy company for the country. Federal oversight of the coal industry was sporadic at best and nonexistent in some administrations. State regulation of the booming sector was no better.

Mining accidents occurred frequently, and one of those killed Samuel Junior's oldest son, Samuel McCaskey III. An engineer educated at Virginia Polytechnic Institute, young Samuel was repairing a leak near the bottom of a massive slurry pond when the earthwork on the downhill side gave way, drowning Samuel III. As a result, Samuel Jr.'s second son, George Milton McCaskey, became heir apparent to the family business and the family's significant fortune.

George Milton and his son, George Milton McCaskey Jr., were relentless businesspeople and astute politicians. Between 1898 when George assumed leadership for McCaskey coal from his father, and 1980 when George Jr. died, company revenues grew from four million dollars annually to over fifty million dollars per year. The company employed over five hundred, and the McCaskeys controlled much of the area's political initiatives.

George Milton McCaskey III, called Milton, didn't fare as well as his father and grandfather in either the business or political categories. That wasn't entirely his fault, as the importance of coal to the country diminished considerably after World War II. Coal had also become the favored target of environmentalists, causing the regulatory environment to be more demanding for the industry.

Even if this were not the case, Milton didn't have the energy or instincts of the McCaskey's before him. Born into wealth, he had no economic incentive to work hard. So, while the declining revenues from the business depressed him, he knew the inherited family fortune was enough to allow him a luxurious lifestyle until he died.

Milton's son, George Milton McCaskey IV, who all in the county called "Four," didn't think the family fortune would last his lifetime. As president of a coal company long past its prime, Four shouldered the responsibility for balancing rising expenses against progressively declining revenues. Managing a positive net profit at the end of this yearly exercise became ever more difficult.

Penalties and fines resulting from safety and environmental violations now represented a significant and continually increasing annual line-item expense. In addition, state and federal regulatory agencies legislated demanding and more stringent operating conditions faster than the company could address them.

McCaskey coal remained one of the larger employers in the area, but the workforce was nearly half of what it had been in its peak operating years. Employees also no longer represented a friendly or extremely loyal group. The world had let coal miners know their work was both challenging and dangerous, and the few willing to perform the task wanted higher pay with fewer hours.

The McCaskey mansion overlooking the town still appeared majestic, but close observers noted signs of deterioration. Four and his wife, Lisbeth, with their only child, Georgina, moved into the house in 2005, after Milton's wife, Jules, passed away.

Milton's declining health necessitated a full-time nurse, and he lived in the western wing of the home; Four and Lisbeth occupied the eastern side; Georgina stayed in the apartment over what was once a carriage house.

In 1954, Milton's younger brother, Earl, brought an idea for a new business to the family. Earl didn't gravitate to the coal business like most of the McCaskeys. He graduated with a liberal arts degree from James

Madison College and could contribute no engineering expertise to the operations side of the McCaskey Coal company.

Milton showed little patience with his younger brother and often made fun of him for attending a school that, until recently, had only accepted women. Earl's concept, however, required almost no investment, kept Earl out of Milton's hair, and diversified the family's business with a product besides coal. Using water from the natural springs on the McCaskey property, Earl began selling Tartan Springs Springwater in 1955.

Earl designed a sign for the front of the business depicting a local hillbilly catching water in a jug from a small mountain waterfall. The water for the display was natural, coming from a pipe connected to the spring's outlet. It fell into a three-dimensional jug attached to the sign with a drainage line behind it. The billboard was popular with visitors and became a tourist attraction in the area.

Next, Earl started self-distributing the product to local grocery stores and restaurants using his pickup truck. With the product's primary ingredient free to the McCaskey's, the new company's only costs resulted from marketing, packaging, and distribution. Earl proved to be a savvy businessperson and kept overhead down while personally expanding the territory for the bottled water.

The company took a giant leap forward when a major regional corporation selected the product for distribution in West Virginia, Virginia, Pennsylvania, Maryland, and Washington, DC. By 1964, Tartan Springs Water shipped five thousand cases weekly, grossing over six million dollars per year. Even with the hefty percentage paid to the distribution company, the Earl's business netted over two million dollars per year in profit.

Unbeknownst to anyone but the immediate McCaskey family, Tartan Springs Water quit using water from the town's natural spring in 2008. Earl's son, Jacob, installed a hidden check valve in the piping between the spring and the production facility, drawing water instead from the town's water supply. An out-of-town company completed the necessary plumbing in the dead of night, and even the business's few employees seemed unaware of the change.

The morning after her return from Woodstock, Seeney placed a call to Pastor Tom. He lived in Compton, and Seeney hoped she might have lunch with him when she went there later in the week for a dress for the Marine Corps Birthday Bash. Like Ty, Tom Burns was a classmate at Tartan Springs High School. However, Seeney and Tom didn't become good friends until the past year, when the pastor helped her through the difficult situation with her former husband.

Not sure which day she would be able to go to Compton, Seeney decided the day might depend on Pastor Tom's schedule. As she glanced at her business calendar, she noted it was busy, but nothing on the calendar was day-specific. She had five payrolls due by Wednesday, weekly bookkeeping required for four other small businesses, and some coordination of several reports for her most significant account, Tartan Springs Ford.

She picked up the Ford account after her divorce earlier in the year. John Beckham, the local Ford dealership's owner, was Jack Stiles' primary competition in the community. Operating similar businesses in the same small town didn't make Jack and John enemies—but neither were they friends.

After the divorce, Seeney no longer did the books for her husband's business, and Beckham wondered if she would provide the services for his business. He used the largest CPA firm in town for his bookkeeping but thought he could save some money by having the everyday QuickBooks entries done by Seeney and then having the more complex tax filings prepared by the CPA firm. He was correct, and the result was a five hundred dollar per week check for Seeney and a ten thousand dollar per year savings to the dealership.

Payroll was an easy bookkeeping function within the robust QuickBooks accounting platform, and it was lucrative for Seeney on a payment-for-time basis. Each of the accounts other than the Ford dealership was small, with few employees, and the QuickBooks payroll module, once set up, was simple to use. Seeney charged about half the price the country's largest provider for these services, ADP, did, and her total time per account was about a half-hour every two weeks.

Her payroll services income was now over fifteen thousand dollars per year, and this part of her business was growing without any effort from herself. Word-of-mouth was the source for almost all her business in this specialty bookkeeping area.

She earned about two thousand dollars per month from the Ford dealership and another three thousand dollars per month, collectively, from the other five businesses for which she provided weekly bookkeeping services. By learning QuickBooks thoroughly to help her former husband manage his company, she was now earning over seventy-five thousand dollars per year with her own small business.

Seeney attended night classes at the junior college to eventually earn enough credits to apply for admission to Shepherd University. Shepherd offered an online studies program that could provide her with a Bachelor of Science degree in Accounting. With that, she could one day sit for the state's CPA examination. Seeney calculated she might be a Certified Public Accountant in about four years.

As a result of her divorce, she lived in a large house with no mortgage and owned a good car. She also had almost two hundred thousand dollars of savings in her bank account. This didn't make her rich, but with her frugal lifestyle, Seeney knew she would never again need to depend on someone else for support. By not attending college out of high school, she had put herself a bit behind, but she was catching up— on many levels.

After the trip to Woodstock, Seeney received another voicemail on her home telephone from Todd Foster. She used her landline as her business telephone because it gave her the option of screening calls through the voicemail system. Since the reunion in September, Foster had left two messages for her, which Seeney ignored. However, she knew if Foster continued to annoy her, she would have to take one of his calls. That opportunity presented itself two days later.

"This is Siena Tyson."

"Hi, Seeney, this is Todd. I'm glad to hear you using the name Tyson again."

"Hello, Todd. I know you've called a couple of times since the reunion. How can I help you?"

"I wanted to apologize for my behavior. Seeing you there reminded me of our high school days, and I guess I got a little jealous."

"Yeah, well, ok. Not your best performance, but it's over. I accept the apology, so thanks for calling."

"Hold on, hold on there, Seeney," reacted Foster. "I didn't call just for that. I was hoping you might have dinner with me sometime. You may have heard Shirley and I are getting divorced."

"Thanks, Todd, but no. That isn't something I'd be interested in now."

"Well," said Foster, "you're sort of blunt. We had quite a romance in our high school days. Doesn't that count for something?"

"Are you serious, Todd? We dated over a decade ago, and you unceremoniously dumped me in my senior year for a pole dancer from Beckley. Not that it matters, but no, what happened ten years ago doesn't count for anything. Thank you, but I don't want to have dinner with you, so don't call me anymore." Then, she hung up.

Since she received no additional calls from the mayor, she assumed he got the message. He did, but his significant ego, now bruised by Seeney's rejection, turned his mind to revenge. A day after his call to her, the mayor contacted local businessman Jack Stiles.

6 Todd Foster

Todd Foster and his parents, Peggy and Bill, arrived in Tartan Springs when Todd was five years old. The couple and their young son moved from Philadelphia, where Bill had been a pharmaceutical salesman. When Mr. Foster lost his job in Pennsylvania, he brought the family to the more rural West Virginia environment. He found another sales job with a Midwest company that manufactured textbooks.

Bill's territory included most of the Northeast portion of the United States, easily accessible by automobile from his new West Virginia location. However, the position required weekly travel, and on one trip to New York City, Bill decided not to return to Tartan Springs.

Peggy was neither surprised nor particularly unhappy about her husband's decision, and young Todd didn't even notice his father's absence for several months. Bill spent little time with his son during Todd's first five years, so Todd didn't have much to miss when the man left permanently. Peggy worked as a secretary for the local poultry plant, a job that provided enough income for her and her son to live comfortably but modestly, in Tartan Springs.

An average student in school, Todd passed each grade successfully, if not remarkably. He became involved with the student council when he reached high school and enjoyed the social aspects of politics. Elected as student council treasurer as a sophomore and vice president as a junior, Todd became the president as a senior.

Peggy found it challenging to sync her work schedule to pick up her son from his many after-school meetings, so she purchased an old used car for him from one of the poultry plant managers. As an upperclassman and a rebel-leader with a vehicle, Todd's status made him attractive to junior cheerleader Siena Tyson. A born politician, Foster projected a gentlemanly facade for Seeney's parents, which caused them to trust him.

Seeney was, however, far more trustworthy than Todd, and she put limits on Todd's wilder plans. On many nights after dates, she drove his car back to her home with Todd in the passenger seat. Her boyfriend often drank too much, and Seeney didn't much care how he got home if she got herself home safely. She fulfilled the role of attractive accompaniment for Todd, but she wasn't a party girl herself.

The couple dated through Todd's senior year and into the summer. Todd started Colgan County Junior College in the fall, and Seeney presumed they were still a pair. Dates became more sporadic, though, and Todd blamed this on his junior college schedule. Seeney was surprised a community college curriculum would be so intense, but she maintained her own busy agenda as a high school senior. So, she didn't mind having more free time. In addition, having a boyfriend gave her the excuse she needed to turn down the many date requests from boys at Tartan Springs for whom she had no interest.

It turned out that Todd's crowded calendar resulted from his activities with another woman, not school. The See All Sho Bar, located about a half-mile from the junior college, became Todd's favorite after-school break for a costly beer. Besides beverages, the bar advertised exotic dancers, a somewhat misleading claim. To promote the performances of the all-female cast as "dancing" represented a stretch, and the costuming reflected anything but exotic. Costumes were, in fact, nonexistent. Nevertheless, Faith Lord, an attractive girl about Todd's age, became his favorite employee, and Faith thrilled Todd when she appeared to like him.

Faith's sexual experience far exceeded Todd's, and she, unlike Seeney, exhibited no inhibitions. Todd finally called Seeney before the

Thanksgiving vacation to officially break up with her. Unfortunately for Todd, however, just before Christmas, Faith broke off her relationship with him. She utilized a gun to do it and demanded a significant cash transaction from Todd in the process, citing a need to depart the area on short notice. Soon after the episode, Foster began dating Shirley McCaskey.

Todd finished two years at Colgan County Junior College with uninspiring academic results and no ambition for continued education. However, his high school friend, Jacob McCaskey, gave Todd a part-time job as a sales representative for Tartan Springs Water. Todd then married Jacob's younger sister, Shirley, during his final semester at the junior college.

Todd believed he managed to marry into the McCaskey fortune, but the McCaskey family wealth no longer amounted to close what local folks thought. Todd, in reality, had only achieved a part-time job in the deal.

Four McCaskey's brother, Winston, resigned as the town's mayor in 2005, and Four hoped he could find another mayor who would be *considerate* of delicate McCaskey Coal matters. So, he convinced his former accountant, Cyrus Clinton, who had recently completed four years of prison for tax fraud, to run for the position, offering to fund the campaign.

He presumed Cyrus would lose, so privately, Four also asked Todd Foster to seek the job. Four secretly funded Todd's campaign with money diverted through Tartan Springs Water. His simple goal was to maintain influence over the next mayor of the town, whoever that might be. He correctly guessed that others would be discouraged from announcing candidacy, with two diverse candidates already declaring intentions to campaign for the relatively modest paying position.

McCaskey believed Todd Foster to be a weak and unqualified candidate but thought he could win for two reasons: 1. Foster represented the opposite choice to the candidate seemingly backed by McCaskey Coal. 2. Cyrus Clinton was a convicted felon who had served prison time. No other candidates declared for the position to Four's relief, and Foster won by a large margin. The result, McCaskey thought, allowed him to keep control over vital town issues critical to McCaskey Coal's business and reputation. Shortly after the election, Four invited Foster to the McCaskey mansion for a confidential meeting.

7 USMC Birthday

The night before the Marine Corps birthday celebration, Seeney and Ty had dinner and drinks in the upscale area around the Washington Nationals baseball stadium. On Tuesday, Ty took off early from the base, and the couple spent part of the day kayaking a scenic stretch of the Potomac River that passed in front of the Jefferson Memorial.

They returned to Ty's condo to dress for the evening, and Ty waited in his evening dress uniform as Seeney stepped from the bedroom. "Oh, Lord! You aren't going to make it easy on me tonight, are you?" he said, whistling softly.

"Does that mean you like the dress, Captain?" She did a modest pirouette in front of him.

"Yes, and so will every other Marine at the party. You look beautiful."

The dress Seeney had purchased in Compton was bright red with a broad blue sash at the waist—not by accident, the Marine Corps colors. The design was simple and elegant, with the length ending just below

Seeney's knees. A large slit in the front of the dress revealed one leg almost to her thigh when Seeney walked. Thin straps held the top part to her bare shoulders, but the V-neckline didn't show cleavage. Still, the lightweight material above the belt was tight enough to present her petite dimensions positively.

"I'm glad you like it," said Seeney. "You don't look too bad yourself. I'm looking forward to the evening."

Ty had prepped Seeney so much for the event that the dinner part seemed tamer than what she expected. Everyone in attendance looked splendid, and Seeney found Ty's Marine Corps friends to be gentlemen. She also enjoyed learning the traditions of the celebration and participating in the rituals. At one point, as she waited for Ty to retrieve cocktails from the well-attended bar, an attractive woman of about her age sat down next to her.

"My name is Jenny Hayes," the woman said, "and I noticed you came with Captain Harrell. He's a friend of mine, and I wanted to introduce myself."

"Hi, Jenny. Ty mentioned you. I'm Seeney Tyson."

"I thought so. Ty has told me about you, too. You probably know Ty and I dated for a while, and I'm glad we're still friends. We couldn't get our lives synced, but I still respect him a lot. You've got a good man there."

"Thank you, Jenny," said Seeney. "Ty and I couldn't quite get on the same path ten years ago in high school, but we reconnected recently, and things seem to be working better this time."

"Well, I'm glad for him—and, for you. It was nice to meet you." Jenny left the table and, as Ty approached the table with fresh drinks, she passed him. "Hey, Ty. She's beautiful!"

The formal part of the birthday dinner may not have been as wild as Seeney expected, but the next phase of the evening was. After the formal dinner, the younger Marines departed with their wives and girlfriends to National Harbor, and the night escalated to a different level of activity. The Marines in their dress uniforms presented a colorful and impressive sight at the private clubs, and guests welcomed them enthusiastically.

Seeney found herself not only succumbing to the atmosphere but enjoying it. She was with other young people, having fun among an adoring and patriotic audience. If the Marine Corps' fans didn't always bring Seeney the same kind of drink she last enjoyed, she drank the next one they offered. The Marines and their dates gave their best effort to dance off both the effects and the excess content of the alcohol, but they started losing the battle in the early morning hours.

Seeney walked out of the last club with her shoes in one hand to the waiting Uber. The cold November pavement under her bare feet felt refreshing, and she remembered little about the ride back to Ty's apartment. She also didn't remember getting into the condo and thought it quite likely Ty had carried her; she supposed it equally possible she had carried him.

The fancy red dress doubled on this evening as pajamas. Ty's dinner dress blue uniform served the same purpose, and Seeney remembered waking up several times wishing Ty had removed his shoes before getting in bed. That was only a passing thought amidst a deep, alcohol-inspired sleep.

When her eyes first fluttered open in the morning, Seeney found it incomprehensible that the fun from the previous evening was worth the pain she felt now. The couple lay next to each other, and Seeney asked, "Did Jenny Hayes allow you to come to bed with your shoes on? My rules might be different."

Ty moaned, "No, and I took them off at least a dozen times— in my dreams. Sorry. I saw you talking to Jenny last evening. Were you comparing notes?"

"Obviously not, or she might have warned me about the shoe habit. But she's personable and still thinks highly of you. I liked her."

"Jenny's smart, attractive, and a wonderful person. Unfortunately, we didn't share enough things to be compatible long-term partners."

Seeney thought for a few moments, then said, "But the things you did share—those must've been pretty good, right?"

Ty hugged Seeney a little tighter. "Those things are nothing you need to worry about."

"I'm not. Believe me, Ty. I'm here with you this morning. She isn't, and I'm not the least bit jealous. Instead, I was curious because I experienced the same sort of confusion about things like that relating to important relationships in the past. My naivete caused me to make decisions far worse than picking an incompatible girlfriend." Then Seeney rolled over to face Ty.

Ty thought before answering. Finally, he said, "Seeney, I don't believe we're much different than most young people. Our early experiences with romance tend to be propelled by instinctual and intense sexual urges. Knowing no better, we equate these feelings to the elusive concept of *love*—which nobody ever explained to us well. It takes some time and experience, sometimes some mistakes, to figure out what the term is all about. I'm reasonably sure a lot of people never do."

"Go on," Seeney encouraged.

"Here's what I know. I enjoy times like this morning, Seeney, but I also like a lot of other times with you as well ... such as sitting in a car next to you, following you up a mountain, watching a sunset from a high rock, and just talking on the phone about nothing. I like you whether your clothes are on or off, and my favorite part of life without you is planning the next time I can be with you. I didn't feel the same about Jenny—or anyone else yet in my life—so I think I'm starting to understand what the term *love* may mean."

Seeney listened intently to Ty's explanation and couldn't keep a tear from escaping to her cheek. "I'm sorry," said Ty. "Did I upset you?"

Sniffling, Seeney punched Ty playfully in the ribs. "No, Ty. You need to learn that women don't only cry when something's wrong. We also cry when something's right. If I read what you just said in a novel or had seen it in a movie, I would have cried. Shoot! I'd have cried if you'd written it to me in a letter. But you said it, unrehearsed, out of the blue, and from your heart. I'm the only woman in the room and the only one who heard it. So, you meant those words for only me—which makes them that much more meaningful. I'm certain I'll remember this moment as one of the most romantic ones in my entire life." Then she hugged Ty tightly as she continued to sniffle.

Ty wasn't sure how to respond or whether he should, so he didn't. In a few seconds, Seeney loosened her grip. "So, Captain, if you like me so much, why did you inflict this horrendous hangover on me? Why am I lying here in an expensive dress I've been in all night—and why are you still in a full-dress uniform with your shoes on?"

"Because I wanted some company. Want to try coffee?"

"Hot, black, and lots of it!"

The couple spent a long morning moving slowly, and they took an extended walk in the crisp air of November before lunch. By the afternoon, both Ty and Seeney had recovered enough from the previous night's activities to be able to keep food down and to mentally function.

When it was time for Seeney to leave for West Virginia, Ty brought her suitcase from the bedroom.

"Thank you, Ty. Except for the hangover, this trip was wonderful."

"Sorry about the headache but thank you for coming. You made it a memorable event for me."

"What you told me this morning made it special for me," answered Seeney. "I wish I were as eloquent as you."

"Oh, that. It just sort of came out. I may be getting a little ahead of myself, and I don't want you to feel uncomfortable if you aren't in the same place I am." He gently reached for her two hands.

"Ty, don't misinterpret my silence. I'm certain I *am* in the same place you are. I think I got here before you did! But, after *presuming* I was in love with men like Todd Foster and Jack Stiles, I'm not sure I'm qualified to use the word anymore. And, if *love* was the right term for them, then I need a whole new term for you—which I haven't identified yet."

"I understand. I think we're both seekers, trying to figure this out together."

"Seekers?" said Seeney thoughtfully. "That's the second time the word has come up in the last couple of months. I like it. I'm also glad we're on the same path again. Do I need to tell you I'm not sharing that path with anyone else now?"

"No, I didn't need to ask. I'm not either."

"Good. Call or text me when you get home."

"Will do, Captain." she said, adding with a smile, "I love you—or something."

"Me too—whatever that is."

Several days after the USMC Birthday Party, Ty arranged to see his friend, Pastor Tom Burns, who was in town on church business. Entering the neighborhood tavern, Ty saw Tom at the far end of the bar and sat down on the stool next to him. Tom's trip to the city related to his work with the Lutheran Children's Ministry. They settled on the Eastside Tavern, off Anacostia Boulevard, as a convenient location to meet for a beer the following afternoon. Ty questioned his friend about the clerical collar. "Are you required to remain in uniform when you're off work?"

"No. Not at all. The collar keeps me from being mugged, sometimes results in a free beer in bars, and always reduces the level of vulgarity and profanity occurring around me. How 'bout you? Does your uniform do the same?"

"I think it does now that you mention it. Except when I wear the uniform into the Officer's Club on base. Then, it causes an *increase* in the level of vulgarity and profanity." Both laughed, and Tom ordered Ty an IPA from the bartender.

"Uniforms are useful in their time and place," continued Pastor Tom. "Sometimes they symbolize what the people who wear them stand for, and other times they mask that."

"Very philosophical, but why not? You're in a sort of philosophical profession that suits you."

"Ya' know," said Tom, "it does, doesn't it? Who'd have ever thought? My job includes many things people don't think about, though."

"In what way?"

Tom glanced at Ty and abruptly changed the course of the conversation. "I'm delighted to see that you and Seeney reconnected after the reunion. She's become a real friend of mine."

"I understand," said Ty. "She says you helped her quite a bit around the time of her divorce."

"Yeah, a little, and two weeks ago, I assisted her in picking a dress for the Marine Corps Birthday Bash. How did she look—did you like the dress?"

Ty laughed. "I hated it, Tom! She was the prettiest lady at the ball, and I spent the entire night fighting off a battalion of horny Marines. That sexy dress didn't help any. She told me she had lunch with you in Compton, but she didn't tell me you helped her with the dress."

"Well, I didn't do much," admitted the pastor. "My only role was to approve it when she modeled it."

"It worked. Seeney says you're also joining us for Thanksgiving in a couple of weeks."

"She asked if I would come down to Tartan Springs for the day after she came home from DC last week. Is that OK with you?"

"Absolutely! The only meal Seeney ever prepared for me was hot dogs and beans when we hiked together in Woodstock. Do you know if she can cook?"

"Seeney can do anything she puts her mind to," said Tom. "And she doesn't put her mind to anything she can't do well. So, I'm sure it will be a culinary tour de force."

"Well, I'm looking forward to it. So, what brings you to DC this week?"

Pastor Tom then told Ty about his work with the Lutheran Children's Ministry. Soon after his missionary trip to South America, he became involved with the organization and stayed engaged while attending Gettysburg College. After graduating and being ordained, Tom became the assistant pastor for the Lutheran Church in Compton. His mentor there, Pastor Sinn, allowed Tom considerable latitude in participating in the Children's Ministry, collateral to his duties in Compton. His work with the organization took Tom to a wide variety of unusual countries, and he coordinated charitable efforts in high levels of several foreign ministries.

"This is fascinating," said Ty. "I think everyone in our high school knew you had the intelligence and energy to do great things. You only needed the right platform."

Pastor Tom reflected on Ty's observation for a moment, taking a sip of his beer. "I guess you're right, Ty. Our world is a troubled place now, and none of us can afford to withdraw, as I did in high school. We all share a responsibility to do our part to make things better." Tom took another sip of beer, staring at Ty. "You're doing that in one uniform, and I'm doing it in another."

"It appears," mused Ty curiously. "Does all the work you do for the Children's Ministry involve children and the church?"

"I'm not sure exactly what you're asking, Ty, so I don't know if I can answer."

"Can't answer? Or won't answer?"

"You want another beer, Ty?" asked Tom, changing the subject.

Tom never returned to talking about Children's Ministry as the two friends finished their second beer. Ty also didn't press him for additional information. Instead, after shaking hands at the door, they went in separate directions, with Ty wondering about his mysterious friend.

8 Pastor Tom Burns

Born to Lily and Jonah Burns on April 1, 1988, Tom was the youngest of two children. Adele, his sister, was eight years older than Tom. Jonah worked as the financial manager for Colgan County Trucking, and his wife taught kindergarten in Tartan Springs. Their house was next door to the home of Ty's parents, and the adults were friends. The two families were similar in many ways, including the fact that each had boys of the same age.

From her birth, Adele was a "princess"—not metaphorically, but literally. She won her first beauty pageant in the Compton Beautiful Babies parade at age two. As a six-year-old, Adele won the Colgan County Fair's "Little Miss" contest; she was the Fair's " Junior Miss" as a twelve-year-old and the "Queen" as a sixteen-year-old. Adele also took part in various other regional and state pageants, and the year she graduated made it to the quarterfinals of the Miss West Virginia beauty pageant.

Typical pageant parents and proud of their daughter, Lily and Jonah spared no expense in helping her compete well in the pageant endeavors.

Some of Tom's earliest memories were of being carted all over the state for his sister's competitions.

Not only pretty, Adele was also smart. Always near the top of her class academically, she made the honor roll consistently. Her perfection in school became so important to herself and her parents that even an occasional grade of "B" caused concern in the Burns household. Despite the potential for academic scholarships for college after high school, Adele, with her parents' approval, delayed higher education to pursue her pageant activities.

At eight years old, Tom remembered hearing his sister vomiting in the bathroom between their bedrooms. Concerned for her, he called to her through the door, but she said she was okay. After that, the vomiting became a frequent occurrence, and Tom confronted his sister one night. "Adele," he said, "you're sick all the time. You need to tell mom and dad."

"Oh, Tom, I'll be fine but thank you for worrying. Come here for a minute." She hugged him for a long time, and Tom sensed that she might have been crying. Then, finally, she said, "Tom, never let anyone try to make you into someone you don't want to be. Do you hear me?"

Five years later, his sister died. Only twenty-two years old, Adele succumbed to an overdose of a prescription drug. An empty pill bottle lay on the bed next to her, but no record existed confirming a physician's prescription for the pills. She left no note and no mess. She had cleaned her dishes, made her bed, and paid her rent through the end of the month. The week before her death, she had failed to qualify as a final eight contestant in the Miss West Virginia beauty pageant.

When Adele died, the town went into shock, and the tragedy devastated her parents. Lily Burns required hospitalization for a mental breakdown, and Jonah didn't speak for weeks. Tom cried for two nights before the funeral but appeared to be the most emotionally stable family member at Adele's services. During the minister's eulogy, Pastor Ewell ended his sermon, saying, "We all grieve the untimely passing of this beautiful woman, so young, and with a full and exciting life ahead of her. The hopes and dreams held for her by her parents and her community end here as her all-too-short life has. We now commit her soul to your loving hands, Dear Lord. Amen."

The congregation responded, "Amen," and lined up to pass the closed casket at the front of the church. When Tom's turn came, he placed a small white rose on the casket and whispered, "Thank you, Adele."

The family handled their grief differently, with Tom's performance in school and athletics declining after the funeral. His parents and all in the community believed this to be a reaction to his sister's death. That wasn't the case. Instead, he responded to something his sister told him years earlier that he didn't fully understand until she died.

Tom realized now that his sister had warned him not to make the same mistakes she had. From the day of his sister's death, he vowed to himself that he wouldn't try to live up to the expectations of others but only to those he created for himself. He understood that the consequences of this attitude might often disappoint his parents, his teachers, and his friends; he also knew his sister paid a high price for her relentless attempts to please others.

Sometimes people learn the wrong things from life's lessons, which was perhaps the case for Tom. During his high school years, he purposely chose a different path than everyone else. His extreme efforts in this at times illustrated, strangely, Tom's intellectual brilliance.

As hard as it is for even the brightest students to keep a straight-A average, it may be even more challenging to maintain a consistent straight-D average. Tom did this, however, constantly failing at least one class, so he would have to take summer school. For Tom, an academic requirement to attend summer school reduced the parental and peer pressure to participate in competitive summer sports.

As a sophomore, Tom became sorely disappointed when the industrial arts teacher awarded him a grade of C+ in the elective course. He requested a private conference with the teacher, Mr. Hovatter, to review the grade. Surprised by Tom's disappointment, Hovatter showed his student how he calculated the grade. While Tom's academic average in the semester was a D, the final exam score comprised forty percent of the semester's grade. Tom had received a B+ on the test.

"Wait a minute," said Tom. "The exam included fifty questions, and I'm certain I only got thirty-one of them right. So that should be sixty-two percent, right?"

Hovatter seemed stunned for a moment. "How do you know you got exactly thirty-one answers correct? I haven't shared those test results with students yet."

Tom gulped. "Well—just guessing. I checked my answers after I finished the exam and was pretty sure of the ones I got right."

Hovatter stared at the young student, then shook his head in amazement. "Yes, Mr. Burns. You got thirty-one test questions right, and the nineteen you answered wrong happened to be among the easiest on the exam. The anomaly completely baffled me. The examination proved difficult, and because so many students did poorly on it, I graded on a curve. A sixty-two percent score equated to a B+."

"But," complained Tom, "are you telling me that if you grade on a curve, and everyone does bad on the test, the best of the bad scores can still equal a good grade?"

"Yes," said Hovatter. "That's one way to look at it."

"What if everyone does great on an exam?" asked Tom. "If you grade on a curve, that means the worst of the good scores can still equal a bad grade, then. That doesn't seem fair."

"No, it doesn't," said Hovatter, "but sometimes life works that way." Tom had learned a valuable lesson from the industrial arts teacher about both grades and life that he never forgot.

When high school ended, Burns stayed in Tartan Springs, unsure of what might be next for him. His exceptional SAT and ACT scores afforded Tom the possibility of college, despite his poor academic school record, but Tom didn't feel ready for that. So, when he heard about a mission trip to South America organized by one of his friend's churches, he applied to go. He had never been outside the country, and, for Tom, this trip offered the opportunity for an all-expenses-paid lark.

What he found in Guyana was far from what he expected. The eight missionaries, including himself, lived in the same squalid conditions as their hosts, ate the same minimal quantities of food and took part in the same activities of the village. Initially horrified by where he had ended up, Tom realized he wouldn't survive the four-week visit with a D+ performance.

The mission's organizer, Pastor Sinn, helped to kick Tom into action. His youthful energy and natural intelligence were a welcomed resource for both the other missionaries and the impoverished residents of the village, and he found many ways to employ these assets. His ideas for re-engineering a failed drinking water facility proved successful, and before he left, the villagers honored Tom by naming their facility "Tommy's Idea."

When Tom returned to West Virginia, Pastor Sinn invited him to a series of conferences in Compton, and Burns' new path began. He graduated from the Lutheran-based Gettysburg College with a divinity degree in 2011 and completed the college's seminary courses the following year. Sinn offered Tom a position at the Compton Lutheran Church after he became ordained.

Before assuming his role with the church in West Virginia, Tom accepted an invitation by the Lutheran Children's Ministry (LCM) to participate in a unique training course funded by that organization. An international non-profit dedicated to children's issues worldwide, the LCM had sponsored Tom's early trip to Guyana. The leadership of the LCM remained in contact with Tom throughout his education at Gettysburg College. Tom never spoke about either the location or the nature of the three months of training they sponsored for him.

9 The Review

When Seeney noticed the Facebook post from the local Chamber of Commerce about the Small Business Alliance Initiative, she tapped the screen for details. The post indicated the proposed alliance would offer networking opportunities, free classes, and media promotions to help area small businesses expand their clientele. Existing Chamber members would be able to access the services at no charge. The only requirement for paid members was to complete some online information.

Seeney joined the Tartan Springs Chamber of Commerce the previous spring, shortly after her divorce from Jack. The number of employees determined annual dues for a business, and with only one, herself, Seeney's dues amounted to eighty-five dollars per year. She enrolled under the name ST Bookkeeping and attended several after-hours networking functions.

Results from being a member of the chamber so far remained mixed, but she had only joined recently. Her Chamber of Commerce filing caught the attention of the town's licensing department, which contacted her about obtaining a town business license, which cost her one hundred-forty-five dollars. She did, however, pick up one new bookkeeping client from the networking events.

Eastern Hydroponics was a new company in town, founded by a group of young agricultural science engineers. With locations in Pennsylvania and Virginia already, the entrepreneurial business was growing fast. The founder's strategy included purchasing tracts of inexpensive open land convenient to interstates and well-located within easy distance of several metropolitan areas.

Utilizing solar energy and supplied by well water, massive climate-controlled greenhouses produced high-demand organic vegetables year-round for urban restaurant businesses. Teresa Miller, one of the founders and the manager for the Tartan Springs location, made it clear to Seeney in their first meeting, Eastern Hydroponics would focus on operations, not administration.

With minimal payroll and not many moving parts, the company needed nothing more than an efficient bookkeeping service in their other locations. Teresa hoped the same would be true in Tartan Springs.

The town didn't regulate single entity small business operating out of a residence. However, if Seeney's business ever grew big enough to need additional employees, zoning would force her to rent commercial space.

While she set up her business with a town license, she also filed with the State Corporation Commission to create an LLC. As a result, West Virginia now officially recognized ST Bookkeeping, LLC as a single entity, woman-owned, limited liability company. Seeney smiled when her first business cards, ordered from Vistaprint, arrived, identifying herself as the sole owner of the LLC.

The online form for the Small Business Alliance Initiative (SBAI) requested her contact information, including an email address. The document also asked applicants to "like" the SBAI's new Facebook page.

Seeney needed to create a distinct "user" account with personal login identification and a password to complete the form. She entered the same login and password she used for all her accounts: styson@satsun.com, with the password ST26537?, her initials with her ZIP Code, and a "?" symbol. The password satisfied most online requirements and was easy for her to remember.

When she logged into the new SBAI site, she found it mostly empty, which didn't surprise her. As a brand-new program, all the site's tabs indicated *under construction*— new content coming soon.

Within a few hours of the time Seeney first logged onto the SBAI site, Mayor Foster noticed it. The chamber's initiative for this alliance was his idea, and Foster retained special administrative privileges to monitor the website. Dick Stockton, the current chamber president, questioned Foster about the need for a site, noting the new sub-organization had no relevant web-based material yet. The mayor assured Stockton that content would be coming, reminding him of the importance of a reliable website for businesses to access.

After reviewing the information, Seeney provided, Foster was happy to see she had clicked on the box to like the SBAI Facebook page. Since the SBAI was now one of her official Facebook friends, Foster knew he would be able to monitor her random posts to other friends on Facebook. He tapped on her profile, disappointed to find she included almost no personal information there.

Her timeline contained few posts making it clear Seeney spent little time on social media. Foster scrolled to her "friends" page, finding over three hundred contacts, many of whom he also knew. When he didn't see himself listed, he suspected she had blocked him many years prior.

Ty Harrell's name appeared in Seeney's list of friends and several of Seeney's bookkeeping customers in town. One of those business Facebook friends, someone at Tartan Springs Ford, had sent Seeney a copy of a ServiceRate review. The customer had submitted the review recently, awarding Seeney's bookkeeping service five stars. ServiceRate was a relatively new social media review organization, like TripAdvisor and Yelp, specializing in service industry businesses.

The review gave Foster an idea, and he opened a new tab on his computer for the ServiceRate website. After filtering his search to services in Tartan Springs, he found three reviews on Seeney's small business site. All the reviews displayed five stars which didn't surprise him. Foster decided he should add one.

When Pastor Tom called, Seeney assumed Tom would be confirming his plans to join Ty and her for Thanksgiving. That, however, was only part of the reason for his call. "Hi, Tom. You're still coming on Thursday, aren't you?"

"Absolutely. I wouldn't miss it. What can I bring?"

"Well, a date if you want. Other than that, nothing."

"Well, I'm between partners now," laughed Tom, "but I could scare up someone if we need a fourth for bridge."

"No. You're crazy. I doubt we'll be playing bridge, and I know darn sure we won't be playing poker. Someone warned me of your reputation in that arena. Bring yourself, and that will be fine. We're going to eat around four—or whenever I have it ready."

"Sounds great, Seeney! Thank you. Tell Ty I'll bring a couple of growlers of a good IPA our brewery up here makes." Then, in a more serious tone, the pastor asked, "Do you track the reviews your business gets on sites like Yelp and TripAdvisor?"

Seeney replied cautiously, "I pull those up occasionally, but I'm such a small business I don't receive many. Why do you ask?"

Tom hesitated. "Well, you have a new one on ServiceRate. Five stars. I read it yesterday."

"OK. What's wrong with that? Who wrote it, and why would you be looking for reviews on bookkeeping businesses?"

"I'm not, Seeney. I overheard someone talk about the review, so I looked it up. You should read it. Mayor Todd Foster posted it, and I don't think you're going to like it."

"What? Hold on. I'm going over to my computer." From her desktop, she pulled up the ServiceRate site and scrolled down to the new reviews. There it was, posted several days earlier by Foster:

ST Bookkeeping is, without a doubt, one of the best full-service businesses in town. Siena Tyson's work is fast, efficient, and reliable. Her attention to detail is remarkable, always leaving her customers completely satisfied. Five Stars.

Todd Foster

Mayor, Tartan Springs, West Virginia.

When Seeney finished, she shouted into the phone, "That bastard! That sorry excuse for a man! Who told you about this, Tom?"

"Nobody told me about it. I overheard a group of men laughing about the review at the Renegade up here in Compton. Todd was in the group. So was Jack Stiles."

The Renegade, a popular bar and restaurant located just south of Compton, was about fifteen miles north of Tartan Springs. Ironically, despite the business's name, the bar catered to an upscale clientele, including ministers, mayors, and businesspeople. "What were you doing in that crowd?" asked Seeney, a bit hurt.

"I'm *not* in that crowd. Jack and Todd are both aware that you and I are friends. I sat several barstools away, but one of the guys opened a laptop on the bar. I saw the screen with the ServiceRate logo when I went past on the way to the restroom. Todd was showing the bartender."

"OK. I'm not sure what I need to do, but the first thing is to take the review down. Can you tell what day the post went up?"

"In the corner of the review is the date of the posting," said Tom. "I can't remember exactly, and I'm not looking at it now on a computer. I think it was only a few days ago."

"Yes," said Seeney. "I see it. Last Friday, so it's only been up for about four days. Thanks, Tom. I'll contact Mr. ServiceRate now."

Seeney was digitally re-routed several times before a live person at ServiceRate answered. "This is Tiffany, ServiceRate customer service representative. How may I help you?"

Seeney explained to the young woman that someone posted a review on the ServiceRate website that needed deleting. When Tiffany began listing the online process for removing a post, Seeney interrupted. "Tiffany! I read the process for disputing a review, and I don't have time to follow those steps. I want the review taken down immediately. Yesterday, if possible."

Tiffany advised Seeney to hold the line while she pulled the review up on her computer. In a few moments, Tiffany came back on the phone. "Ms. Tyson, I read the post in question, and I'm confused. The review, written by an official in your community, rates your business five stars. That isn't the kind of review most business owners typically want taken down. Unless something in this review is patently false, we can't arbitrarily sanction it."

Seeney did her best to remain calm with the pleasant young woman who was only trying to do her job. "Tiffany, you are a woman, so I think you'll understand my concern if you listen to me carefully. The man who wrote this review has never used my professional bookkeeping services—ever. I can prove that, so anything he says about my business is made up. On the other hand, everyone in my community knows I dated this crass man ten years ago. So, they are laughing at Foster's between-the-lines inuendos relevant to my possible sexual services to him a long time ago. I would hope ServiceRate wouldn't condone this sort of abuse of their very professional review site."

"Oh my God, Ms. Tyson! I'm horrified, and as I reread the review after your explanation, I find it disgusting. I'm sorry. Your complaint must still go through a review process here to verify what you told me, but I'll remove this post pending the results of that. In fact," Tiffany paused briefly, "as of this moment, the review is no longer visible to anyone."

"Thank you. So, what happens next?"

"We'll notify the ServiceRate subscriber who posted the review of the dispute, and our company will allow him to respond. If he doesn't reply within seventy-two hours, we'll remove the review permanently. If he responds with information that might validate his review, our legal department will conduct additional research. Fraudulent reviewers seldom want to push their cases to this extent."

"OK," said Seeney. "Thank you, Tiffany."

"You are welcome, Ms. Tyson. I'm so sorry for this." When Seeney hung up the phone, she dialed the number for Buster Aldrich.

Several days later, Seeney sat in Aldrich's office as he reviewed the papers Seeney brought him. When he finished, he removed his glasses, setting them on the desk. "I make a living off chauvinist bullies like Foster and Stiles, and I enjoy that part of my work. But, in this case, Seeney, I don't see enough evidence to pursue a legal remedy."

"That's what I thought you might say, Buster. I'm just so mad that I'm having a hard time letting this go."

"You shouldn't ignore it, Seeney," said Aldrich. "At a minimum, you should confront Foster. Maybe Stiles, too. Jack Stiles is still liable under a binding legal agreement with you and making you angry should concern him."

Seeney sat for a moment, thinking. "I'm not too bothered by Jack. I doubt the review was his idea—Todd probably included him in the joke afterward. I want Foster to understand I'm not some weak woman who's going to put up with his BS, though. Would you be able to attend a meeting between Foster and me sometime soon? I'd gladly pay you the four hundred dollars for an hour of your time."

"Sure, Seeney. If you buy me lunch in Tartan Springs, I'll even waive the fee."

Two days later, after lunch at Dillon's Deli on Main Street, Seeney and Aldrich strolled to the nearby municipal building. Seeney had called Todd earlier to request a short meeting for the two to "clear the air." Foster egotistically acknowledged that was in her best interest, and Seeney knew she had successfully set her trap.

On the way down the hallway to the mayor's office, Seeney stopped at Tim Howell's door. Tim was Tartan Springs' police chief and the father of one of Seeney's best high school friends. Howell seemed confused by Seeney's invitation to join her, but he walked with her and her attorney to Foster's office.

When Howell, Aldrich, and Seeney stepped into the mayor's office, Foster looked surprised. "Seeney, I thought you asked for a private meeting."

"What gave you that impression?" said Seeney innocently. "Todd, this is my attorney, Buster Aldrich, and you know the police chief."

The mayor stared at Aldrich with dark eyes, then questioned Howell in an irritated tone, "What are you doing here, Tim?"

"I just got invited, mayor. Would you prefer I leave?"

"What is this about, Seeney?" the mayor asked, ignoring the police chief's question.

"Let me answer for her, Mayor," said Aldrich. "On September sixteenth, you harassed my client and her friend at a high school reunion. You were drunk, and I believe someone called the police chief that evening to prevent trouble."

"But...," Foster tried to interrupt, but Aldrich didn't allow.

"Since then, you have continued to contact my client at her home by phone, and several days ago, you published a fraudulent review on a public website about her business. You are getting dangerously close to criminal harassment, and I'm putting you on notice to stop."

Finally able to speak, Foster said, "How can you call a five-star review *harassment*? I tried to help her out— and look how she repays me."

Aldrich listened impassively. "You, sir, have never used her professional services, so your review was, indeed, fraudulent. We're aware of your purpose for your insinuation-filled post, and ServiceRate removed it. If you continue to harass my client, I will pursue her case most vigorously, so I advise you to stop. Do you understand me?"

Foster didn't answer, and Aldrich said, "I asked you a question, Mayor."

The mayor mumbled that he understood and angrily declared the meeting over. As the group filed out, Foster told Howell to remain behind. "Did you know what would happen in this meeting, Tim?"

"Not a clue," said the police chief. "Seeney asked me to attend on her way to your office."

Frustrated, Foster said, "Well, remember who you work for, Chief. I'm not about to be bullied around by a tramp and her two-bit lawyer."

The police chief moved closer to Foster's face. "Mayor, you don't need to remind me who I work for. I'm an elected official, just like you, and I work for the people of this town—nobody else. It isn't my place to advise you, but if it were, I would tell you not to fuck with Buster Aldrich. He isn't a two-bit lawyer. Also, I have known Siena Tyson for most of her life, and she isn't a tramp."

The two men stared at each other for a few moments before Foster broke. "Get out of here, Howell!"

Outside the municipal building, Seeney thanked Aldrich. "I think that went well, Buster. I appreciate your help."

"My pleasure, Seeney. Including the police chief was a clever touch."

"A late-inning inspiration. Tim Howell's daughter is one of my best friends from high school. I spent a lot of sleepovers at his house, and I know him well."

"I doubt Foster will bother you anymore," said Aldrich, "but I'll follow-up this meeting with a strong letter to him. The correspondence will mean nothing, legally, but will be a useful piece of evidence if Foster ever tries to escalate anything."

"Thank you, Buster. What do I owe you?"

"Lunch again sometime," smiled Aldrich. Then, he added, "Or, better yet, keep your friend, Pastor Burns, out of the next poker game on Friday night."

"Is he that good?

"The guy is uncanny!"

"I'll see what I can do," Seeney said, smiling.

The Road ~~Not~~ Taken
"I'll see what I can do," Seeney said, smiling.

10 Holidays

Ty arrived at Seeney's house on Wednesday evening before Thanksgiving, and the couple went to Coroli's for a pizza and beer. After catching up on each other's lives for the two weeks since the USMC birthday bash, they returned to the house and went to bed early. The following morning, Ty checked the on-screen television guide for the day's sports schedule, and Seeney put supplies together for the afternoon's feast. By ten o'clock, she realized she needed to go back to the Whole Foods Market for some other things.

"I'll go with you," said Ty. "What do you need? You realize you aren't entertaining the pickiest eaters here today, right?"

"I know, but I have ideas for what I want to do, and I need a couple more items. You don't have to go, and I'm not going to be gone long."

"I haven't been out to the mall since I graduated. Let me call Tom. I don't think he planned to come this early, but I'll warn him we may be out of the house for a little while, just in case." When Ty reached Tom, the pastor had not left Compton yet. After Ty told him what Seeney and he were doing, Tom suggested they meet at the mall.

"A brand-new shooting range located at the end of the mall opened a few weeks ago," said Tom, "and I haven't had the chance to try it out. However, the range is open today. Do you do any shooting?"

"Not since basic training. I'm a pilot, not an infantryman, but I did well in basic. I earned a Sharpshooter badge for marksmanship. When did you start shooting?"

"Oh, I dabble. I shoot targets once in a while, but the closest professional range, until now, was in Morgantown."

"OK, I'll meet you in the Whole Foods parking lot. I assume I can come back to the house with you after we shoot? That way, Seeney wouldn't need to wait for us to finish."

"Yeah, that will work. I'll be there in about thirty minutes." Seeney and Ty held up their departure so they wouldn't beat Tom to the mall by too long. When they arrived, Tom's car was waiting for them, and Ty jumped into the pastor's Subaru.

The Bulls Eye Range was a state-of-the-art facility with about twelve long shooting alleys. The interior was well insulated to keep the gunfire noise inside, and a variety of revolver and rifle weapons were available for target shooting. The business required all new customers to complete a short safety lecture; after that, a trained employee personally escorted each customer to the shooting ranges.

About twenty minutes after they arrived, Ty and Tom stood in adjoining shooting alleys with Savage 110, bolt-action rifles positioned fifty yards from paper targets. Both men wore clear goggles and ear protection, and each had purchased thirty rounds of ammunition. They planned to use twenty shots for practice on the stationary targets. Then, they would receive scores from their employee escorts on ten rounds to a fresh, new, paper target.

Ty monitored his friend in the adjacent target lane, surprised at how comfortable Tom was with the weapon. Before the scoring round of ten shots began, Tom yelled over to Ty, "This one is for who gets the wishbone today."

Giving his friend a thumbs up, Ty carefully cradled the rifle stock against his cheek. Then, concentrating on the target, he pulled the trigger slowly, focusing deliberately on each shot. He could hear that Tom, in the next lane, finished his rounds much quicker than he had. When the target sheets mechanically rolled forward, Ty's employee instructor congratulated him.

"You did well, sir. Four bull's-eyes and nothing out of the first ring. That will earn you a high score."

Ty glanced over to Tom's lane, where the employee instructor conferred with his friend over the paper target. After a short conversation, Tom came over to Ty's side of the firing lane and offered Ty his hand. "You beat me. You nailed it with ninety-two percent. I only got seventy-two percent. Good job, Ty. Let's try revolvers."

"OK. Thanks. Here's my target sheet." Ty handed Tom his pockmarked, used paper target. "Let me see yours."

"Oh, I didn't keep it. I think they threw it away."

"No, we didn't," said the employee assigned to Tom, overhearing the conversation between Ty and Tom. "We still have it. We've never seen anything quite like it." The young man gave the sheet to Ty. The bullet holes on Tom's target centered around a spot perhaps one inch to the right of the bull's-eye and one inch below it. None of Tom's bullets entered the center ring, but if the innermost circle had been located a little to the right and down, all ten penetrations would have been within it.

Ty gazed at Tom in mild amusement. "Tight cluster there, Tom. Maybe the sights on your rifle were off a bit?"

"Yeah, could be. Anyway, you get the wishbone. I like this range. Thanks for joining me."

"I'm having fun. Good suggestion."

As Ty and Tom picked up the nine-millimeter Smith & Wesson M&P-9 revolvers supplied, employees rolled the range's targets closer, to twenty-five yards. During the twenty-round practice volleys, Ty assumed a classic two-handed stance, facing toward the target. However, he saw that Tom used a sideways position, holding the revolver with one hand.

After the practice rounds, Tom again finished the scored rounds well before Ty. This time, Ty's score was only eighty-eight percent; Tom's remained at seventy-two percent, identical to the score he recorded with the rifle. Tom reached over the rail to shake Ty's hand, saying, "OK, buddy, you win. Might not have been a fair fight with a minister against a Marine, but thanks for the chance to compete."

Ty shook Tom's extended hand but motioned for the employee to bring over the used targets. Ty's showed three bull's-eyes and seven shots reasonably well-placed around various parts of the center. Tom's target showed no bullets in the bullseye, but all ten within a one-inch area just high and to the left of the bullseye.

"Sights again?" asked Ty.

"Maybe."

Seeney surprised the men by showing up in the gallery to watch them. When they walked over to meet her, Ty said, "I thought you were going back to the house after you shopped. I didn't expect you to come over here."

"After I finished shopping, I thought I should check to ensure none of my hunters got killed. I don't see any game here for all the shooting going on."

"Only if you eat shot-up paper," said Tom, laughing.

"Well," said Seeney, "I have better food in the car, but I'm afraid the car presents a bit of a problem."

"Uh oh. What happened?" asked Ty.

"As I left the car, I realized I wouldn't need my purse, so I threw it back on the front seat when I got out. Unfortunately, I had already put my keys in the purse. I remembered that when the locks engaged after the door shut."

Ty chuckled. "So, the keys are inside the car?"

"Yes. Not a big deal. I have another set at home. So, I'll ride back to the house with you guys, and we can come back here to retrieve the car later."

"Hold on, hold on," said Tom. "Aren't the groceries also in the car?"

"Yes, but nothing in danger of getting stale in an hour. Dinner may be a little delayed, but you'll just have to deal with that."

Tom pulled something out of his pocket. "Before we abandon the car, let me see if I can jimmy the lock. I have some experience with this."

"Do you always carry a spare paperclip in your pocket?" said Ty, as he observed Tom twisting the small piece of metal.

"You might be surprised at how adaptable this simple invention is."

When they came to Seeney's car, Tom inserted the bent paperclip into the keyhole of the front door and leaned his ear close to the door's handle. Within fifteen seconds, all heard the distinctive click of the door's lock. Tom opened the door with a flourish and accepted the two-person applause graciously. Seeney and Ty got into her car, and Tom followed them home in his.

"Our friend keeps surprising us with new skills," said Seeney. "I wonder when he learned how to pick locks with a paperclip."

"You don't even know, Seeney! I just witnessed some of the most amazing marksmanship I have ever seen in my life."

"But Tom told me you outscored him in both the rifle and the pistol. Is that not true?"

"I did, but scores don't always tell the whole story. None of his shots either time went through the bull's-eye, but both times, he seemed to invent a personal target a little left or a little right of the real one. Then, he put every shot through the center of his individual bull's-eye. No variance between shots—no scatter—each shot almost the same. Pastor Tom Burns does a little more than preach, I think."

"What are you thinking? Should we be concerned?"

"No, not at all. I think Tom is a good person, and I'm certain he's a true friend to both of us." Ty stopped for a moment and added, "In fact, I'm delighted we're his friends—and not his enemies."

"That onion seems to have a lot of layers, for sure."

"Yes," said Ty, still deep in thought. "Remember in high school how he maintained a straight-D average, then scored an almost perfect SAT score?"

"How could I forget? That shocked everybody in the community. Didn't it even make the newspaper?"

"Yeah, it did, and the publicity irritated Tom. He didn't want that kind of recognition. When Tom and I met a couple of weeks ago in DC for a beer, we had an interesting conversation about uniforms. Tom said something like—' Uniforms can sometimes symbolize who we are—and other times present a mask for who we are.' "

"So, maybe for much of his life, Tom managed to create a mask for himself which isn't him?"

"I think so. Tom made people think he was dumb and that he didn't care about stuff—when he did."

"So, is he a pastor or not?"

"Yes. Tom's an ordained minister, but I don't think all he does with the Lutheran Children's Ministry involves the church."

"You're kidding! You think he's a spy or something?"

"Not sure, but he doesn't like to talk about it. I tried when we met for the beer in DC, and he changed the subject. So, let's not bring any of this up with him today, OK?"

"No problem. I'm just glad for the company at my table for Thanksgiving."

While Seeney busied herself in the kitchen, Tom and Ty sat in front of the TV watching the football game. The men had already finished one of the two growlers of beer Tom brought and were making a considerable dent in the second one. The cumulative effect of the activity was to raise the volume level of their conversations—and their laughter—to beyond that of the television's, which made Seeney smile. When she announced they could help her bring the food to the table, Ty and Tom responded enthusiastically.

"My Lord!" said Tom. "Who's going to eat all this, Seeney? Do you have more company coming? It looks amazing."

"I'm impressed," added Ty. "Even as well as you prepared hot dogs and beans on the trail, I had no idea you were capable of something like this."

Seeney laughed, and to deflect the attention, asked, "Who's winning the game?"

Ty's expression told Seeney he hoped Tom would answer her question. Tom's face indicated he had no clue which team was winning or possibly even who was playing. At last, Ty said, "I think Minnesota is."

"Strange, because the Vikings don't play until Sunday. Green Bay and Detroit are playing today."

"Busted!" laughed Tom. "The TV was a clever ploy to conceal our top-secret conversations. You caught us."

"Well, it didn't work. So, your spy techniques might need some adjustments, but now it's time to eat."

As they sat, Seeney said, "Pastor Tom, you're the most qualified among us to ask the blessing."

"Gladly." As the three bowed their heads, Tom remained silent for several seconds, then prayed. "Dear Lord, whoever you are—and wherever you may be—thank you for putting us on a path to this place, this table, and this feast before us. Thank you also for the glow of friendship among the souls gathered here, for it is at times like this we sense your presence most. We commit to you our promise to better understand your divine plan and your important mission for us as we go forward. Amen."

"Thank you, Tom," said Seeney. "Beautiful."

"It was," agreed Ty. "Thank you."

"My honor."

The three friends launched into the meal with pleasure and passion, making its creator proud of her accomplishment. After dinner, the two men helped Seeney clear the table, and Seeney announced she had one more course. "I purchased an apple pie at Whole Foods this morning."

Tom had a different idea. "Will the pie keep in the refrigerator? I brought a dessert that's in a cooler in my car."

"Tom!" said Seeney. "I told you not to bring anything."

"I remember, but as you may have discovered, I'm not always the best at following orders."

"Really?" said Ty and Seeney simultaneously in mock surprise. Tom rolled his eyes and retreated to his car. Moments later, he returned with what appeared to be a triple-layered cheesecake. One layer was pumpkin, one caramel, and the other looked like vanilla ice cream.

"Wow, Tom!" said Seeney. "Where did you find something this fancy around here?"

"I didn't *find* it, Seeney. I *made* it."

Seeney glanced at Ty. "Oh geez, *and* he can cook."

"What do you mean?" Tom didn't understand the nuance-filled glance exchanged between Ty and Seeney. "When you're single, a certain basic level of culinary skill is sort of necessary for survival."

"Right," said Ty, winking at Seeney. "It looks delicious. Let's see if the taste measures up to its appearance." It did, and the three friends remained at the table another fifteen minutes after each had finished the intricate dessert.

Finally, after checking his watch, Tom announced, "Folks, this whole day has been a joy. Thank you for including me, but now I need to get back to Compton." The three friends embraced, and Tom departed.

Seeney and Ty sat in her den on the large sofa after their guest left, but she didn't turn on the TV. Instead, the couple gazed at the flames from the gas log fire. Seeney's head rested comfortably on Ty's chest, and his feet were on a stool next to the coffee table. The peaceful atmosphere was relaxing after such a busy day, and the pair appeared lost in the pleasant reverie of personal thoughts. Ty was the first to break the silence. "The meal was beyond amazing, Seeney. Where did you learn how to cook like that?"

"Mostly from the internet and YouTube," she said. "I enjoy cooking for an enthusiastic audience like the one today."

"As Tom said earlier, the day was a complete pleasure for everyone. Thank you so much."

"I enjoyed it, too, Ty. Tom added a nice dimension to it. What a unique character our old high school friend has turned out to be!"

"That is an understatement. Just when you think you know him, he reveals a new layer. I think he's a good friend to have, though," said Ty. Then changing the subject, "Would you mind talking a little about the Christmas holidays?"

"No, Ty. I remember that you committed to visiting your parents even before we reconnected at the reunion. So, I understand and will work around your plans."

"Well, I would prefer that you work into my plans. I want you to come with me to Florida when I visit my folks."

Seeney sighed. "Oh, Ty, thank you, but I'm not sure I'm ready for that. What would your parents think?"

"They'll probably wonder why it took me ten years to find you again. But remember, Seeney, my parents know you. You aren't a stranger."

Seeney tightened her grip on Ty. "OK. I understand, but do they have room for both of us? You told me they lived in a condo."

Ty removed his arm from around Seeney's shoulder and stared at her with a grin. "Yes. Plenty of room. Their place has a guest bedroom."

"But, Ty, this isn't funny. How are they going to feel about us sleeping together in their home? Won't that make them feel uncomfortable?"

"Seeney, we're twenty-nine-year-old adults. My parents were born in the fifties, but they aren't naive. They won't think anything about us being in the same bedroom and might be more concerned if we weren't."

"OK, OK," said Seeney. "I guess we aren't the teenagers we were the last time I saw them. I just want them to like me."

"You be yourself, and they won't only like you. They'll love you!" As the couple compared holiday calendars, Ty said, "Because I'm the most junior officer in my squadron, I automatically draw Officer of the Day duties on both Christmas Day and New Year's Eve. That means I stay on base those days and sleep in a duty room at the Bachelor Officers Quarters. I won't be able to go to Florida until December 26. I had planned to spend three days down there to be back in plenty of time for OOD duties on the 31st. We can fly direct from either Dulles or BWI, but Dulles would be a little closer for you. What do you think?"

Now Seeney sat up to better think and engage in the planning. "My business is slow between Christmas and New Year's, so can I suggest an alternative to your plan?"

"Of course."

"Why don't I come to your condo on Christmas Eve? We can dine together that evening, and I'll spend Christmas day in your condo while you have the duty. Then, we can go to the airport on the 26th. When we return from Florida, I'll stay at your place until January 1."

"I love your plan. The military has no restrictions about you spending nights with me at the BOQ during my duty. It might be a little tight, though, because the bunk in the room is only a single bed."

"I won't take up much room."

"True," said Ty. "Also, since I won't be able to drink while on duty on New Year's Eve, we won't attend any wild parties."

"I'm relieved. That means no brutal hangovers. Is there a TV in the bunk room?"

"Yes. Why?"

"I'm looking forward to watching the ball drop from a cozy bunk."

"Perfect. I'll tell my parents you're coming. They'll be excited." The couple completed the plans and returned to their comfortable position on the sofa. As they watched the flames, Ty whispered to Seeney, "I still feel stuffed. I could use some exercise."

"Me, too. Let's get in bed."

"That's what I was hoping you'd say."

Christmas

The direct flight from Baltimore-Washington International Airport to Tampa, Florida, took a little over two hours and was uneventful. If Seeney was nervous, it didn't show, but Ty knew Seeney hid anxiety well. The couple had spent a delightful two days around Andrews Air Force Base, despite Ty's requirements as the duty officer for his squadron on Christmas day. As Ty suggested, Seeney stayed the last night with him in the duty bunk room, and, as Ty warned, the sleeping accommodations were tight. However, the close quarters bothered nobody.

Walking through the Tampa terminal, they looked for Ty's parents and found them in the baggage area. The older man and woman were easily identifiable by their matching Santa Hawaiian shirts and sandals with jingle bells. Seeney saw them first and laughed out loud. Ty rolled his eyes ever so slightly, drawing a harsh reaction from Seeney.

"Ty Harrell! Don't you dare act like you're too cool for this. Your parents are excited to see you, and, for them, *this* is Christmas day. Yesterday, many people in this airport met family in holiday attire like they are now."

"I'm sorry," said Ty, acknowledging the scolding. "You're right. Thanks."

As the two couples got closer, Ty embraced his parents. "You two look awesome! Thanks for bringing the Christmas spirit to the airport for us."

Orville shifted his balance from one leg to the other and avoided eye contact with his son and Mavy. "Sorry, Ty. The costumes were your mother's idea."

Before Ty could respond, Seeney swept in—delivering a full-on hug to both Mavis and Orville. "I think this is terrific! Thank you. You may not remember me from ten years ago—I'm Siena Tyson."

Orville smiled after the hug from Seeney. "Are you kidding me? Of course, we remember you! You were the prettiest girl at Tartan Springs High School, and now, you're the prettiest one in this airport. You haven't changed a bit."

"Mr. Harrell! Thank you. You're the same as I remember as well—except for maybe your eyesight, but I think I *like* that change. I hope you brought some costumes for us."

"You had to ask..." said Orville, looking toward his wife.

"Yes, we did," said Mavis, reaching into her oversized bag. "We brought these hats and some sunglasses for you." She handed two Santa hats to Ty and Seeney and then two pairs of sunglasses. One set of glasses had Rudolph appearing on the extended frame; the other one included a plastic image of Elvis Presley with a Santa hat on his head, holding a guitar extended from the edge.

Not hesitating, Seeney handed Ty one of the red Santa hats and the Elvis glasses. She placed the other Santa hat on her head and the Rudolph glasses over her eyes. Then, looking toward Mavis, she asked, "How do I look?"

"Adorable," said Mavis, smiling. "Absolutely adorable."

Ty surveyed the interaction between his parents and Seeney with some amusement and pride. She was doing this for him, he knew, and he loved her for it. To avoid further admonishment from Seeney, he put the Santa hat and Elvis glasses on. "I think we're ready to roll," he said, and the group left the airport amid appreciative stares and sporadic bursts of applause from bystanders.

Mavis had pre-prepared lasagna for dinner that evening, which allowed her to join in the family conversations without being occupied in the kitchen. Any awkwardness Seeney might have felt by being a new participant in this family's gatherings dissipated within minutes of sitting around the large coffee table in the den of the Harrell's condo.

Both Orville and Mavis expressed sincere interest in Seeney's business, and they kept her talking about her own life far longer than Seeney would have intended. Nevertheless, she understood what the sweet couple was doing, and she appreciated it. Additionally, the more she talked, the less nervous Seeney became. Finally, when Seeney seemed thoroughly acclimated to the Harrell family environment, the conversation turned to the group's collective memories of their years spent in Tartan Springs.

As stories extended into dinner, Seeney was astounded by the number of events in her youth she shared with the Harrells. She was also surprised by how many times their respective lives had intersected—and even collided. Similar occurrences in the same town witnessed from different perspectives added entertaining depth to the storytelling decades later.

Sometimes, the triangulation provided compelling moments of new understanding of the past; other times, it provided an increased level of comedy. By the time dinner was over and everyone departed for their respective bedrooms, Seeney seemed as comfortable with Mavis and Orville Harrell as Ty was. "Your parents are wonderful. Thanks for making me come down here."

"Yes, they are, and I know how lucky I am. You, though, were the hit of the day. What you did right out of the blocks at the airport was masterful. You should be a politician."

"Thank you. They gave me an opening early, and I didn't want to waste it. Thanks for playing along."

"Not sure you gave me an option. Where would I be sleeping tonight if I hadn't gone along?"

"Not with me," she replied, smiling." Ty didn't believe she was joking.

Official Christmas day this year in the Harrell's Florida household was December 27. Mavis planned a turkey dinner for late in the afternoon and Christmas presents after that. The two couples went to a mid-morning brunch at a favorite bayside restaurant in St. Petersburg, and the men planned to watch a college bowl game in the afternoon.

Orville's alma mater, Iowa Central, played Tennessee Southern in the Carhart Bowl in Charlotte, North Carolina. Neither team had played well enough during the season to receive an invitation to one of the more elite New Year's Day bowls. Still, the Carhart Bowl was one of the best of the second-tier bowls. Both Iowa Central and Tennessee Southern had young teams with solid coaches, and both programs projected to compete well in the coming seasons. Las Vegas odds favored Iowa Central in the game by a slim margin, and both Ty and Orville were looking forward to the game.

Seeney joined the men in front of the big screen television for the first half and had one of the Coors Light beers Orville provided. She knew that brand wouldn't have been Ty's choice, but she was glad Ty had expressed enthusiasm to his father when Orville showed him the case he had thoughtfully iced down for the game.

The first half of the game substantiated the various analysts' anticipation for it, as both teams moved the ball well and appeared to be evenly matched. With the score tied at halftime, fourteen to fourteen, Seeney joined Mavis in the kitchen.

"Can I help you with anything, Mavis?"

"I'm in pretty good shape, Siena, but if you're proficient with a knife, you can chop those three onions on the cutting board."

"I can handle that, and—so that you know, Ty calls me Seeney."

Mavis turned to face Seeney. "Well, his dad calls me Mavy."

"Great! Where would I find a knife, Mavy?"

"Right in this drawer, Seeney."

Seeney noted a half-empty glass of white wine near the sink as the two women busied themselves around the counter. Then, pointing to the glass, Seeney asked, "Is there any more of that kind of creativity fuel around?"

"Only about a half-gallon in the refrigerator. Help yourself. I'm afraid I don't buy pricey wine," she apologized.

"Cavit isn't bad Pinot Grigio, Mavy. I buy it at home when I can find it at Costco."

Seeney enjoyed talking with Mavis so much she didn't return to the den. However, frequent shouts—and occasional groans—from that direction suggested the game remained both close and exciting.

The addition of wine didn't improve cooking efficiency in the kitchen, but it tweaked the level of frankness and humor in conversations. Mavis told Seeney the story of how she and Orville met, how blessed they felt at Ty's birth, and how much fun they had as a family in Tartan Springs. Seeney filled Mavis in on some of the blanks in her own life, including the unfortunate circumstances of her divorce from Jack Stiles.

"Oh, Seeney, honey. I'm sorry you had to go through that. Men can be the most wonderful and useful of beasts if they do their thinking with the right head. But, too often, they do some of their more important critical thinking with the wrong one."

Seeney stopped what she was doing, a little shocked at Mavis's rather definitive explanation of a common fallacy of men. Then she burst out laughing. "Mavy, you're right. I never really thought about it that way, but you nailed it. So, tell me, how do you ensure your man continues to use the right head for thinking?"

Mavis laid her stirring spoon on the counter and stared into Seeney's eyes. "The best way to do that is to try to be in the vicinity whenever that other head starts thinking."

Seeney almost choked with laughter but reached over to hug the older woman. "Mavy, you are wise! You should write a book. Is that your secret to a thirty-plus-year marriage?"

"One of 'em, and it's an important one. I think the other thing that has made a difference for us is... we've always been friends. We *like* each other. We both have our human flaws, and each accepts those as a part of the whole package. The compromises become easier as we age and the longer we live together."

Seeney listened and then glanced at her glass of wine. She was no longer laughing but wondered if the effects of alcohol had perhaps magnified the moment in some way. She felt an overwhelming sense that her path had mystically led her to this specific time and place to listen to this sage of a woman—so that she, herself, would understand one of life's essential secrets about relationships.

"Thank you for sharing with me, Mavy. Your description of what creates a successful marriage bond is the best I have ever heard, and I'm going to remember it."

"I'm not so sure it's all that wise," scoffed Mavis. "Just how life has worked for us." Then, changing the subject, she said, "Orville and I both enjoy seeing our son as happy as he is, and I think you're a big reason for that."

"Believe me, that part is entirely my pleasure. Ty is a singularly special man, and my current goal is to keep him happy for a long time. You and Orville are an inspiration!"

A loud eruption of shouting interrupted the tender moment between Mavis and Seeney, and the ladies went to the den to determine the cause. Both Orville and Ty were hopping around the couch like drunken juveniles, pumping their fists and giving each other high fives. "What on earth is going on in here?" asked Mavis.

When Ty landed from his most recent jump, he said, "Only the most incredible finish to a college football game I've ever seen, Mom!"

Orville interrupted. "It was amazing, Mavy! Iowa Central was down by seven points with only about a minute to play..."

"...And," Ty broke in, "the Iowa quarterback drove down the field for a touchdown as time expired."

"But," said Orville, "Iowa Central was still allowed time to kick their extra point for the tie."

"Except," broke in Ty again, "the holder took the ball and skirted around the tackling melee to score a two-point conversion for the win!"

"Nobody touched him," added Orville. "It was unbelievable!"

Mavis smiled at her husband, then her son—and rolled her eyes toward Seeney, shaking her head. "Boys."

The Christmas dinner, prepared by Mavis with some help from Seeney, looked magnificent on the table. When all had been seated, Seeney surprised the group by offering to give the blessing. After a short pause, she said,

"Dear Lord, whoever you are—and wherever you might be—thank you for putting us on a path to this place, this table, and this feast before us. Thank you also for the glow of companionship among the souls gathered here, for it is at times like this we sense your presence most. We commit to you our promise to better understand your divine plan and your important mission for us as we go forward. Amen."

Ty, of course, heard this prayer several weeks earlier, and he smiled knowingly at Seeney. The first to speak was Orville. "That was a wonderful prayer, Siena. Thank you."

"Yes, it was," said Mavis. "Orville, she prefers to be called Seeney."

"Good!" Orville looked meaningfully at Seeney. "Thank you for that as well."

The bountiful and delicious meal matched the quality of the stimulating dinner conversation. When Orville recollected back to Ty's senior year in high school, he addressed his son while his eyes rested on Seeney. "You should have listened to me back then, son."

"I know, Dad. I know."

"What are you talking about, Orville?" asked Seeney.

"Ty was mooning around the house toward the end of his senior year, and I asked him who he was taking to the prom. Ty told me he didn't plan to attend, and I wondered why he wouldn't take the girl he talked about most of the semester—the one he worked with on the yearbook staff."

"And he told us," piped in Mavis, "that girl would never want to go out with him. He said she was just a good friend."

Keeping her eyes on Ty, Seeney asked, "He talked about me back then?"

"Oh, yeah. Not long conversations—just snippets. Like, something you said—what you wore to school—little things like that," said Mavy.

"We knew the poor boy had the worst possible crush," said Orville, "but we couldn't make him do anything about it."

"OK, OK," said Ty. "Looks like I'm the only one in the room who didn't know the score a decade ago. I screwed up! I'm glad I got a second shot this September."

Before Seeney could agree, Orville said, "We are, too, son. We are, too." Orville's statement touched Seeney, and, as she sat next to Ty at the table with this delightful family, she knew she belonged there.

On their last day in Florida, Ty went golfing with his dad, and Seeney went shopping with Mavis. That Ty had minimal golf skills suited his dad just fine. When they arrived home from the course, Orville proudly proclaimed he'd beaten his son by three strokes. "Wonderful, Orville," said Mavis, "What did you shoot?"

"A seventy-two."

"My goodness! The competition with Ty must've inspired you. You're seldom in double digits, are you?"

"Mom," said Ty. "We only played nine holes." When the laughter died, the group discussed plans for delivering the younger couple back to the airport the following day.

In bed later, Seeney lay awake next to Ty and nudged him. "Sorry, Ty, but I'm not ready to sleep yet. Will you talk with me for a while?"

Ty rolled over. "Sure. Something wrong?"

"No. My mind is just spinning from all that happened on the trip."

"The weekend has been fantastic. Thanks again for coming."

"No. Thank you for convincing me. Your parents are giving me a Ph.D. lesson in life. They're remarkable people, Ty."

"They are, and I love them."

"There's that word again—love. Of course, I love them, too. But a different kind of love. What a slippery word."

"You worry too much about that word," said Ty. "As humans, we're not finished inventing all the right words for the different kinds of love that exist. I think the *feeling* is more important than the word."

Seeney thought for a few moments. "You're right. Being a bookkeeper, I guess I like things when they're black and white. Of course, life doesn't work that way sometimes, but your parents' relationship is an inspiration to me. As I hear their stories and witness their interaction, I feel like I'm watching a movie about one of history's great romances—that hardly anyone knows about it."

"You might be right. We read about Romeo and Juliet, Cleopatra and Alexander, and Napoleon and Josephine. Yet, nobody will ever read about Orville and Mavis."

"But that doesn't make the romance any less important."

"Isn't that the same with many things in life? I'm in a business that creates heroes, but most real heroes are unknown to the public. A relatively small number get discovered or are officially recognized. However, that doesn't make the efforts of the unknown heroes less important or less meaningful."

"Right," mused Seeney, still thinking. "Having now witnessed your parents' romance, though, I'm grateful to whatever luck, fate, or road gave me the opportunity. It helps me to understand what it takes to create that sort of experience for myself."

"With me, I'm hoping?"

Seeney cuddled closer to Ty, placing her arm across his chest. "That's still something we need to talk about sometime. Not now, though. I love where we are and the path we're on, but I'm not the uninformed young girl I was ten years ago—or even the one I was a year ago. I'm now brave enough to open my eyes to all the things I don't know. A relationship like your parents is my new goal, and I'm going to make darn sure I get it right this time."

"So," said Ty, "you think I still have some work to do?"

"No, Ty. I do."

The following day the two couples exchanged parting embraces before Ty and Seeney left for their gate at the airport. All agreed the trip was an incredible success on many levels. Seeney expressed her hope to Mavis and Orville that the visit would become an annual tradition—a sentiment that touched the older couple deeply. None could have known, however, what was in store for the family in the coming year.

11 Spring

"I've known him my entire life," said Pastor Tom. "He isn't any different today than the next-door neighbor boy who played in my treehouse in the backyard. He proved to be a loyal friend and someone you could always trust then. He's the same guy now. I'm proud to call him my friend and believe anybody else who can say that is a fortunate person." Seeney and Tom were having lunch at the beginning of March, and Seeney wanted Tom's counsel on some personal issues relating to her relationship with Ty.

"I feel lucky about that, too," said Seeney. "I'm confused, though. In high school, I liked the fact Todd Foster was old enough to drive a car and take me places other boys in my grade couldn't, and I figured I must be in love. That was silly, of course, but then, when Jack Stiles provided a whole new kind of sexual enjoyment I had never experienced before, I thought that must be love. I'm an idiot, Tom! How do I know what I'm feeling now isn't just another level of something I haven't gotten to the end of yet?"

Tom laughed. "I can't answer that since I'm still a few levels below where you *have* already achieved. It could be love is a little like religion—an elusive concept we each discover individually. But, at a minimum, you're now experienced in some things you know the term *doesn't* mean."

"For sure," said Seeney, thinking. "I didn't want to go to Ty's parents' home at Christmas because I was afraid they wouldn't like me. I didn't want to take any chances on something hurting or changing the relationship Ty and I had. But then, during the trip, I witnessed the most amazing and loving bond between Ty's parents. They set a benchmark for marriage so high it makes me wonder if I'm capable of ever doing that. Ty deserves a relationship like his parents, and my track record hasn't been so good."

"You deserve a marriage like that, too. Unfortunately, life makes no guarantees, and we need to work with the data available to us. Ty appears to think you're up to the challenge."

"He does, doesn't he?" Seeney smiled to herself. "You're so right about him! Even in my foolish, uninformed, teen days, I noticed something different about Ty I liked. He wasn't the big man on campus at our school, he didn't drive the coolest car, and all the girls weren't talking about him. But, when I worked on the yearbook with him, I liked him. He was a nice-looking boy and in shape because of wrestling, but the part of the package I enjoyed most was talking to him. I wanted him to ask me to the prom, but he never did."

"He's told me he thought you were out of his league."

"Yes, he shared that with me, too. Then, in Florida over Christmas, his parents embarrassed Ty by telling me about the crush they said he had on me in high school. Isn't it strange, Tom? Here were two people who wanted each other a decade ago, and neither had the guts to do anything about it."

"I'm glad you both got another chance last September."

"When I saw Ty come through the door of the gym at the reunion, Tom, my heart jumped and fell at the same time. I felt like a giddy little teen again and thought my reaction to seeing him was just plain dumb. The whole scene seemed a little surreal."

"So, who made the first move?"

"Me, of course," said Seeney. "I figured I had nothing to lose, so I took a pretty direct approach."

"Good for you!"

"Yes, but later, when we danced, the band played a song about paths in life which spooked me. I felt like the song was a cryptic message meant just for me."

"*The Road Not Taken*? Stevie Liston, the lead singer, wrote that and recorded it. The song is doing well on the Indie circuit. You didn't like it?"

"No, I didn't. The verses seemed to be telling me I missed the opportunity to get on the path with Ty a long time ago, and now he represented the road *not taken* for me."

"But maybe the song didn't mean to refer to past roads as much as warn about future ones."

"I didn't interpret it that way, but maybe you're right. So now, here I am at another crossroads."

"From my vantage point," said Tom, "one road looks decent ahead, and the other one looks completely unknown. Why would you pick a road which appears empty?"

"Right! You're right, Tom. Thanks for helping me straighten this out in my head. I'm not sure why I was second-guessing myself. I need to marry this guy!"

"Wow! I'm glad to help you make up your mind, but do you think your decision might be presumptive?"

"What do you mean?"

"Well, doesn't he need to ask you first?"

"No," said Seeney. "Why should I wait for that? I'm going to ask him. I waited for him to ask me to the prom a decade ago, and he never did. I'm not going to let him make another mistake like that one."

"Silly me. What was I thinking? I'll warn him the next time I see him."

Seeney's cold stare made Tom shiver. "Just joking, Seeney. Just joking."

Frostdale

Two weeks later, when Ty called Seeney to confirm his plans to travel to Tartan Springs, Seeney said, "Change in plans, Ty. We're getting a late-season snowstorm this week, which will dump a foot of snow on us—more at the elevations. The interstates will be fine, so when you arrive on Friday, pick me up and let's keep going down to the Frostdale Ski Resort. Frostdale is only two hours from here, and we could be there by nine o'clock."

"Sounds great. I love to ski, but I don't own equipment anymore. I suppose I can rent some at Frostdale."

"I don't have any either, but no big deal. We'll rent it when we get there. Frostdale doesn't offer the most demanding skiing, but I'm only an average skier anyway."

"I skied at Frostdale when I went to WVU, and it's not too bad. The little resort is beautiful, and, with fresh powder, the skiing will be a treat."

"I'll make the plans. We'll pack everything into your Jeep when you get to my house since you have a four-wheel-drive."

"See you in a few days."

On Saturday, after a full day of skiing, Seeney and Ty had an early dinner at the resort's lodge. The couple had window seats with a spectacular view of the lower levels of the resort. The snow was still coming down in a light flurry against a mountain backdrop illuminated by a full yellow moon.

When Seeney and Ty came back to their detached cabin, Ty started a fire, and Seeney poured two glasses of a California Meritage she brought with her for the trip. They sat sipping the wine and watching the flickering logs in the fireplace for a long time without speaking. Then, at last, Ty said, "I want to talk to you about something and have been waiting for the right time. The atmosphere here feels right."

"Certainly, Ty, but I had something I wanted to ask you as well. You go first, though."

Ty was hesitant. "No, you go ahead. Mine may take a little longer."

"Okay," she said, setting her wine glass on the table and turning toward Ty. "My life has never been more enjoyable since the reunion in September, Ty. You're the reason why. We've only dated for about six months, but I love you. I want to know if you'd consider marrying me?"

Ty stared at Seeney, at once dumbfounded and amazed. Then, retrieving a small box from his pocket, he said, "Would you also like to give me this ring?"

"Oh, Ty, is this for me? Were you going to ask me to marry you?"

"That was the idea, but you beat me to the punch line."

"I'm sorry. Why don't you go ahead and ask me now?"

Looking a bit sheepish, Ty said, "Seeney, would you marry me?"

"Mmm, let me think for a moment," and she opened the box. The diamond, not oversized but beautiful, was perfect for Seeney. "Oh, yes! Yes, Ty, I will. Thank you! The diamond is gorgeous! Did you pick this out by yourself?"

"I had some help," admitted Ty. "Tom Burns came up to DC about a month ago, and we selected the diamond together."

"Interesting," said Seeney, smiling. "Very interesting. He seems to be everywhere, doesn't he?"

The question confused Ty, who was unaware of the conversation between Seeney and Tom two weeks prior. "I guess so. He's been a friend for most of my life, but especially since I reconnected with you."

"Yes. Tom has been particularly close to me since my divorce as well, and I'm glad. He's like a unique thread woven into the fabric of our lives together. Is there a plan for what comes next? When would you like to get married?"

"Tomorrow, if possible," said Ty, "but maybe that isn't realistic."

"I like the answer, Captain, but you're right. We have some things to think about and a few other people to consider, like your parents. Are they aware of this?"

"They knew I was going to ask this weekend. So, they made me promise to call them as soon as I had your answer."

"Where's your phone?"

"Right here," he said, reaching into his pocket. "You want me to call them now?"

"No. *I'll* call them now. Punch in the number and give me the phone."

Ty did, and handed the phone to Seeney. In a few seconds, she said, "Mavy, this is Seeney..." then retreated with the phone to the kitchen for privacy.

The conversation lasted several minutes, and Seeney was in tears for part of it. Finally, she came back to the den with Ty's cell phone still held to her ear. "I will," she said. "Yes, you, too—Of course, we will—Thank you. I love you both so much!—Absolutely, Mavy, I'll tell him." She disconnected from the call and handed Ty's phone back to him.

"They didn't want to talk to me?" asked Ty, pretending to be hurt.

"No, they got all the information they needed from me. Both told me to tell you they were proud of you for finally asking me to marry you."

"Did you tell them you asked first?"

"Of course, I did. They said that didn't surprise them, and they were proud of me, too."

"You're something else, Seeney."

"Yes, Ty, I am. I'm many things, but I'm not dumb. A long time ago, I waited around for you to ask me to the prom, and we both know how that turned out. I try not to duplicate past mistakes."

"Since you're usually ahead of me in planning this romance, did you and my parents discuss timing?"

"We did, and I told them to stay tuned," said Seeney. "We've established our intent, so I'm not in a hurry to rush the details. You'll find out about your upcoming orders by the summer. I want to finish my courses at the junior college, and I have a business in Tartan Springs to think about. "

"Okay, I understand, but my preference would be to see you more than every other weekend."

"I'm glad, but we aren't a couple of hormonal teenagers. We're adults with careers and responsibilities. Our life hasn't been unbearable since September, and I think we can deal with the inconveniences for a few months more if necessary."

"Alright, but one more thing to add to your list to think about," said Ty, "is once we're married, you qualify for full military benefits. If something were to happen to me, our government would still take care of you for life."

"Thanks, but that isn't the reason I'm marrying you. I'm fine on my own, and I want to see where you will be stationed next before making too many plans. It could make a difference in what I do with my business."

"Well, my detailer is probably starting to look at me right about now, so I could learn something as early as June or July."

"Then, let's wait until then before making any other decisions. I have some other news you'll appreciate this evening."

"What's that?"

"I'm back on birth control, so you can use the rest of what's in the package in your suitcase for water balloons if you want."

"Wonderful! Why didn't you mention that last evening?"

"I planned to, but you came dressed for bed, so to speak, and I didn't want to embarrass you."

"Are we done talking yet?"

12 Deployed

Spring passed quickly, and the couple had fun starting to plan a wedding for a date yet to be determined. Neither wanted a big wedding nor needed one to accommodate large numbers of family. Seeney had a sister and Ty, his parents, as close family. In addition, Ty and Seeney shared some high school friends, and Ty had military buddies who might be interested in attending the event. Both agreed Pastor Tom would conduct the ceremony, and they'd host a small reception someplace in Colgan County.

Ty made a surprise visit to Tartan Springs in the middle of a week in June. When he knocked on her door, Seeney suspected why. "You got your orders, didn't you?"

"Yes, I did. Do you want the good news or the bad news?"

"I don't want any bad news. Come on in. Do I need a drink?"

"No, Seeney. We're going to be fine. We just have some serious planning to do now." When they were comfortable in Seeney's den, Ty relayed what he knew about his pending orders. The good news was Ty was deep selected for early promotion to the rank of major and designated for a position in command. He would be the executive officer of HML-222, based in New River, North Carolina.

The need to fill the command vacancy in the squadron and the necessity for Ty to become familiar with the newest version of the UH-1Y helicopter, the Venom, required an earlier rotation from his current unit than expected.

HMX-1 would issue TDY orders to HML-222 for aircraft familiarization and Advanced Gunnery School in New River in September. After this, his tour with the new squadron would officially start in October. The bad news for Seeney was the unit would deploy to Bektistan in November as part of a joint force strategy with the Army to eliminate insurgent strongholds in the mountains of Bektistan. "That's not what I was hoping you would say," said Seeney.

"I know, and I'm sorry. The deployment is an unaccompanied tour which means families won't go with Marines. These tours usually don't last more than a year, and after that, the last two years of it will be in New River."

Seeney was holding back tears, and she hugged Ty to hide her face. "I guess since you're going to gunnery school, it means you'll be flying a helicopter which shoots guns?"

"Yes, I will be. Light attack squadrons are combat units. I won't be flying logistics like the last time I was in that part of the world."

Taking a deep breath, Seeney said, "OK, I guess we delay wedding plans for eighteen months or so. I don't like it, but as Tom says, we sometimes don't have a choice on where the path takes us."

"I thought we'd expedite the wedding plans, not delay them, Seeney. I want you to go with me to New River."

"That doesn't make much sense, Ty. You're going to be gone for a year right after you report to New River. What would I do down there without you? I couldn't run my business from there. So, if you aren't going to be in New River, I might as well keep my business up here and try to finish school while you're gone."

"But," said Ty, "you need to consider the military benefits. I don't particularly like that I'm going to be in a hostile part of the world or that I may participate in dangerous activities, but I want you taken care of if something does happen to me."

"And I'm telling you, Ty Harrell, I don't care about the benefits! I also don't want to be hanging around New River, North Carolina, waiting for you to come home in a box draped with an American flag. I love you alive, Ty, not dead. I don't want you to go, but there's nothing I can do about that. I'm not going anywhere, and I'll wait here to be your wife. I'm not going to wait in New River to be your widow!"

Ty, disappointed and a little surprised, thought for a moment. "I hear you, and I understand, but I'm not coming home in a box. I'll be home to marry you, as I promised. That means more to me than anything in the world—other than some other promises I made when I became a Marine."

"We comprehend each other then," said Seeney. "I don't like your job in the military, and I don't personally relate to why our country is involved in things happening in Bektistan, but I know about you and your integrity. I don't love you only for the man you look like. I also love you for the man you are beneath the skin. It is that man who made promises he won't break, friends he won't forsake, and commitments he'll honor at all costs. I'm not crazy about the career you chose or the job you do—but I'm holding you to the promise you made to me. So, get this tour done safely and get back here."

"I will, Seeney. Thank you." The couple talked no more of Ty's assignment nor of the wedding ceremony. Instead, they planned their events for the rest of the summer.

During their remaining visits, Ty spent time trying to make Seeney comfortable with the upcoming combat tour to Bektistan. On a return visit to Woodstock, Ty explained to Seeney, "More Marines lost their lives in training exercises over the past five years than in combat. Some of our deployments are to dangerous places, but we're well-trained and well-armed. We also aren't fighting traditional battles in Iraq and Bektistan."

"Thank you for the information, but would you call flying a helicopter in a combat squadron a safe occupation?"

"Well, no, but..."

"Would you call Bektistan a safe country to visit?"

"No, Seeney. Of course not. But..."

"Will armed soldiers who don't agree with the United States' point of view be aiming guns at you?"

"Maybe, but..."

"Save it, Ty! I support your choice for a career, and I appreciate your honor to serve. I'm not required to like it, though. I also reserve the right to remain worried. So, let's change the subject." That seemed final.

"It's supposed to rain tomorrow, so let's visit the local vineyards," Ty suggested.

"OK. We can ask Natalie this evening at dinner which ones she'd recommend."

The couple had driven to Woodstock separately from their respective homes on a Friday as they had on their first visit the previous October to this cute town in Shenandoah County, Virginia. They met at the Hampton Inn, located across the street from the Comfort Inn, where they stayed the last time. They had dinner reservations at the Woodstock Café for eight o'clock.

Natalie met them at the hostess stand when they arrived and led them to a table. "It's great to see you again," she said. "Is that a diamond ring on your finger, Seeney?"

"Yes. Ty and I were engaged in March."

"Congratulations!" said Natalie. "When's the wedding?"

"We're not sure yet," said Ty. "I have an overseas deployment this year, and Seeney wants to wait until I'm back. I'll be gone for about a year."

"Bummer! Listen, I hope you don't mind, but Renée is coming by before you leave tonight. She doesn't work too many evening shifts, but when I told her you had reservations, she asked if it would be OK."

"Of course," said Seeney. "We'd love to see her."

"She'll be here in a little while. I'll send Janine over for your order."

Renée stopped by the table as the couple finished dinner. "Natalie told me about the ring," she gushed, grabbing Seeney's left hand. "Beautiful! Congratulations. Way to go, Ty!"

"Thank you, Renée," said Ty. "Seeney gives you a degree of credit for this."

Renée laughed. "I doubt if I had anything to do with it, but I did say a prayer or two."

"Well, thanks," said Seeney. "How are you?"

"Terrific! Natty and Joe are doing outstanding with the business, so the job is fantastic. My boys are healthy and running me ragged with their activities."

"Sounds good, Renee. Listen," said Ty, "we were going to ask Natalie about wineries we should visit tomorrow, but you could probably make a recommendation on that."

"Sure, I could. I don't drink anymore, but I'm familiar with all the local wineries. How are you planning to go?"

"What do you mean?" asked Seeney. "Can't we just drive?"

"Sure, but there are three or four, and you might not want to be driving yourself after visiting two."

"Oh," said Ty. "I didn't think about that. Is there a shuttle people usually take?"

"Yes, one is available," said Renée, "but you need to schedule it in advance. I can drive you. My two boys are in camp this week."

"Oh, no," said Seeney. "We couldn't ask you to do that. Maybe we'll take in two wineries tomorrow and save the other two for another trip."

"I don't mind. I know everyone at the vineyards, and I'll enjoy seeing them. Let's start at ten o'clock in the morning. Where are you staying?"

Ty looked at Seeney, then at Renée. "If you're sure, Renée, we would love your company. I'll pay you for your time. We're at the Hampton."

"No, you won't be paying," said Renée, "but thanks. I'll be in the lobby a little before ten."

On Saturday, Renée drove Ty's Cherokee to Cave Ridge Vineyard, Kindred Pointe Vineyard, Shenandoah Vineyard, and finally, Muse Vineyard. Ty and Seeney thought the wines to be excellent and enjoyed meeting the friendly owners of each of the businesses. Seeney also found herself sharing more with Renée than she planned as the day progressed.

Ty became engaged in a conversation with the owners of the Muse Vineyard near the end of the day, and Renée cornered Seeney. "So, explain to me again why you want to wait until after Ty's deployment to get married?"

"You wear me out, Renee! Now you're taking advantage of me because I'm half in the bag, and you're cold sober."

Renée laughed. "Sorry, Seeney. Not my intention, but if it works..."

"I don't have a sensible explanation. I didn't need more time to plan a big wedding, and my reason isn't something most people would understand."

"OK, but I'm not most people. Try me."

Seeney, glancing in Ty's direction to ensure he was still talking to the vineyard's owner, said, "Ty's going off to war as the executive officer of a combat helicopter squadron. So, he'll be carrying a lot of responsibility, and, since I can't be there, being married or not doesn't matter a bit for the next year. And..." Seeney paused.

"And what?"

"And, if having a wife to worry about caused Ty one second of extra concern over there, I can wait. We don't need the certificate yet If it means an iota of additional burden. The other thing is, I'd rather not be married at all than end up a widow. Ty would be gone either way, so I'm not sure why I feel like that, but I do."

Renée listened quietly, then said, "I understand. I disagree with your decision, but I understand. I think Ty loves you the same, whether you're married or not. He most likely would prefer being married so that you would have military benefits if something happened to him."

"Yes, you're correct, but I don't even want the benefits if he's not going to be around. For me, the benefits would be a constant reminder of what I was missing because of the military. It would make me a bitter woman for the rest of my life."

"Got it," said Renée. "Looks like I need to ramp up the praying this year. We haven't known each other long, but would you keep me posted on Ty's deployment. I have sort of an emotional investment in you two now."

Seeney gazed at this woman she barely knew with a tear balanced on the edge of each eye. "Certainly, I will. Thank you. I may need someone like you to talk to."

When Ty got back to the table, he could tell by the expressions he had missed a deep conversation. "What now, Renée? The last time we were in Woodstock, you warned me I shouldn't 'blow it.' I've done my best not to, so what's up now?"

"So far, I think you're doing well, Major. Congratulations! Now, just get this stupid deployment over with."

"I'm planning on that," said Ty, looking at Seeney. "I have plenty of incentive."

"Your wife invited me to the wedding."

"Wonderful! You can drive us from the church to the reception."

The weekend was a success, and Woodstock had risen to the top of both Seeney's and Ty's list of favorite places. They canceled a trip to Virginia Beach planned later in the summer when Ty's gunnery training began a month earlier than scheduled. Seeney visited New River twice while Ty attended the school and while he transitioned into the H-1Y helicopter. The six-hour drive from Tartan Springs made more frequent visits difficult. The intensity of Ty's expedited training schedule at New River made trips to West Virginia impossible for him.

In November, when the equipment for Ty's squadron was loaded onboard the gigantic C5-A Galaxy aircraft at the New River Marine base, Seeney was there to see her fiancé off. She watched as husbands and fathers kissed their families goodbye and wondered how those left behind could endure the separation.

She was empty inside but didn't cry as Ty gave her a last hug before boarding the giant airplane. The aircraft taxied from the tarmac, and Seeney stayed in her place on the off-chance Ty could still see her from a window. Then, when Seeney was confident he couldn't anymore, she left.

After crying for many of the six hours back to Tartan Springs, she had no tears left by the time her car pulled up in front of her house. Seeney entered her home and went to the refrigerator, placing an "X" on the calendar. She silently hoped three hundred sixty-four "X's" later, Ty would be back home.

Seeney had refused to consider a wedding before Ty's deployment and, while that decision changed her life path's direction by only a few degrees, even this tiny adjustment would create unexpected consequences.

13 Fox Uni

Major Harrell's life on deployment didn't start overly exciting. For most of November, the men of the squadron kept busy reconstructing the Forward Operating Base. Marines had abandoned the remote outpost in the Kashir Province of Bektistan years earlier when it proved difficult to logistically service. A former administration also found the site challenging to defend. Officially named Damir Station, a group of past soldier inhabitants nicknamed it "Fox Uni." The moniker stuck. In the military phonetic alphabet, the letter, F, is called foxtrot, and the letter, U, is called uniform. To most military personnel, anything labeled Foxtrot Uniform is "fucked up."

The derogatory phrase was accurate for the base's condition when HML-222 arrived, but the motivated Marines made it functional within thirty days. Nobody believed the small base would remain operational long; it was merely well-located, not too distant from a more prominent Army Infantry location tasked with eliminating pockets of insurgent activity from the nearby mountains.

The rugged Kindu Hush range provided safe refuge for Tiloristan fighters. Senior military leaders hoped recent advances in heat-sensitive satellite imagery might present better evidence for locations of hidden terrorist units. Accordingly, HML-222's mission entailed supporting Army-led ground efforts to pursue identified targets.

A Forward Operating Base offers few of the comforts of home to military personnel inhabiting them. Fox Uni featured perimeter walls and security from previous employment and a flat, surfaced area for aircraft operations. The base's first military occupants placed first aid stations, a communications center, a small gym, and an enclosed mess hall inside several of the block buildings.

A gigantic, pre-existing, half-moon-shaped steel structure covered in deteriorating canvas served as a hangar bay for aircraft and combat offices for the squadron. Several generators provided power for essential equipment and some lighting. Plumbing was nonexistent, but freshwater came from a large, centrally located well. A tanker truck transferred water from the well to various parts of the base; the truck then pumped the water into elevated containers placed at critical areas.

Tent showers were available, and Marines washed clothing at a location near the well. The arid climate provided natural drying on clotheslines. All attached personnel stayed in tents erected over wooden platforms left by the previous occupants.

In the first two months of operations at Fox Uni, neither the Army units nor the USMC UH-1Ys was successful. Thermal *hotspots* reported by satellites turned out to be clusters of wild goats or sheep more often than armed soldiers. The mountains were also home to nomad tribes of sheepherders who created the same thermal image as Tiloristan fighters. By December, the squadron logged over three hundred hours of flight time but had not fired a shot in anger from their UH-1Ys.

Ty established a communications schedule with both his parents and Seeney during these initial months of deployment, which seemed to work for everyone. He sent his parents an email update each week and sent Seeney an email at the end of every day.

He wrote short messages to Seeney most of the time, but occasionally Ty used emails to give her longer descriptions of his deployment life. The couple usually talked by FaceTime once per week, and Seeney surprised Ty in December when she told him her plans to visit Ty's parents in Florida for two days over the Christmas holiday.

Within a day of receiving that information from his fiancée, Ty also heard the news from his parents. Mavis and Orville, delighted with

Seeney's plan, had already planned the costumes Mavy would take to the airport.

After the holidays, Seeney sent pictures to Ty of his parents and her wearing the silly Christmas attire. The photos brought a smile to Ty's face and a pleasant memory to his heart. Seeney also kept Ty posted on life in Tartan Springs, including the latest issues in her business.

With tax time approaching, all her clients required extra time. In addition, she had become quite close to one of the owners of her newest customer, Eastern Hydroponics. Terri Miller, the local manager/partner of the West Virginia location, was increasingly using Seeney's services for more than simple bookkeeping. Seeney was now performing functions for the aggressive start-up company generally reserved for CPAs. Ms. Miller gladly paid for the additional work, but the account occupied a significant part of Seeney's week.

The latest issue for Eastern resulted from the company's failure to obtain W-9 information from outside contractors for services performed during the year. Only three or four vendors had not completed the forms, but Terri asked Seeney to track down the necessary information before Eastern filed a tax return in April.

In January, the Army infantry units began having more success, which created a busier support schedule for the UH-1Ys of HML-222. The increase in activity also brought new elements of danger for the squadron's sorties. Two aircraft always accompanied missions, and several Venoms had returned to base with dented armor resulting from enemy ground fire. To date, HLM-222 aircraft had not encountered surface-to-air missiles, but enemy forces did send rocket-propelled grenades in their direction. When possible, pilots maintained altitudes above one thousand feet to stay beyond the effective range of a field-launched RPG.

When January ended, Ty sent Seeney a rather triumphant message: "Three months down, and only nine to go."

Seeney responded with her own message, "Only three months down, with nine months still to go. So, keep your head down!"

Seeney shared this short exchange of emails with her friend, Tom Burns, who admonished Seeney. "It appears Ty's cup is half full, and yours is half-empty, Seeney."

"No, Tom," she replied. "Mine isn't half-empty. It's totally empty and will only get full again when Ty gets back."

14 Water Problems

When Seeney returned from the holidays, she attacked the backlog of messages relating to her bookkeeping business. By late in the afternoon, she had responded to all clients, completed assignments for some, and set schedules for others. The last one on her list for the day was Eastern Hydroponics, her favorite customer.

The only thing needing resolution for this company was a missing W-9 from one obstinate vendor who had not answered repeated requests for the information. When hiring the services of unincorporated outside contractors, businesses are required to obtain certain critical tax information from the contractor using the W-9 form. Then, when a contractor completes services, the hiring business provides the contactor a summary of payments made through an IRS 1099 form.

Companies that utilize third-party contractors don't have to withhold income taxes or social security taxes from the payments made, so the filed 1099 forms ensure the IRS is aware of these payments. However, unincorporated businesses are responsible for paying their own taxes on earned income.

Eastern had been a little sloppy in the administrative part of their start-up in Colgan County the past year, failing to request W-9s from vendors who provided contractual services during the company's opening year. Seeney obtained the necessary documents from three companies, but the fourth, a water testing service, didn't respond to telephone, email, or registered mail requests.

State Testing Lab, which performed three thousand dollars' worth of water sampling tests for Eastern Hydroponics during the year, remained a holdout. Ensuring compliance with W-9 reporting requirements was beyond the service Seeney typically provided clients, but Eastern Hydroponics was a new company with a bright future. Seeney wanted to keep this account happy, and she decided to visit STL in person to complete this last hurdle before tax time.

Several weeks later, Seeney punched the address for State Testing Lab into the GPS app on her phone and began the drive. The GPS verified the business to be near the McCaskey Coal operations on Mullen Mountain, and the trip would take about twenty-five minutes from her location.

On such a beautiful and unseasonably warm day for February, Seeney enjoyed driving on State Route Four, one of the area's most scenic roads around Tartan Springs. Built to service the substantial activity of the McCaskey Coal operations during the peak years of the company's mining history, the road was wide and now only lightly traveled.

As it left town, the highway passed through rolling agricultural land before starting the long grade to the top of Mullen Mountain. The Siler River paralleled the road a little out of sight behind a line of trees, and Seeney could see traces of snow patches in several open areas near the mountain's summit.

Seeney's was the only vehicle on the highway this morning until she started the uphill grade; then, she came upon a Rural Valley Electric tanker heading up the mountain. A two-lane road for most of its distance between Tartan Springs and Mullen Mountain, Route Four featured several areas that widened to three lanes to allow cars to pass slower truck traffic.

Waiting for one of these opportunities, Seeney realized the vehicle ahead of her wasn't empty. It was full. The tanker slowed considerably on the steep uphill grade and downshifted to a lower gear several times as it struggled toward the top of the mountain. She had seen the truck pass through town on countless occasions over the past decade on its way to the McCaskey Coal operations, but it never occurred to her the vehicle was making a delivery and not coming for one.

Now, as she waited patiently to pass, Seeney wondered what liquid McCaskey Coal needed in tanker-load quantities. McCaskey Coal delivered coal by the truckload regularly to the various regional Rural Valley Electric power plants. What would return from the utility company in a tanker truck to the McCaskey mines? The answer didn't matter to her because she had no understanding of coal-mining operations nor any interest in learning.

A passing lane opened halfway up the mountain, and she darted around the truck. According to the GPS, State Testing Lab was a mile ahead, off a minor road intersecting with State Route Four. Mullen Mountain Drive was barely marked and not paved. She turned right as directed by the GPS and began looking for a mailbox or sign indicating one hundred Mullen Mountain Drive.

She found it where the unpaved road ended. The letters on the mailbox were no longer legible, but the numeral, one hundred, was spray-painted on the post holding the box. A rusty chain-link fence surrounded a dilapidated property that featured several junked trucks, a discolored double-wide trailer, and a large vinyl doghouse. A hand-painted sign on the doghouse read: Beware of the dog. He is aware of you!

An aged camouflage-painted Jeep Wrangler with oversized tires sat next to the doghouse. Behind the trailer were a dozen small, wooden A-frame enclosures. Roosters with short chains attached to a leg strutted in front of several of these.

From inside her car, Seeney looked for other dwellings in the vicinity and again checked her GPS. The message on her screen proclaimed, "You have arrived," and included a smiley face. She thought nothing about this place seemed smiley, and she surveyed the property for a sign identifying State Testing Lab.

When she turned off her ignition and opened the car door, she understood the sign's meaning over the doghouse. A huge black and gray pit bull bounded from behind the building, barking, snarling, and snapping his teeth. The dog's lethal intent was evident, and Seeney jumped back into her car. The vicious dog's progress abruptly stopped two feet before the fence when the animal arrived suddenly at the end of the chain attached to his neck.

Seeney surmised she needed to see no more and started the car when a man approached from the trailer. He gave a short command to the dog, causing the animal to retreat and stop barking.

Seeney got out of her vehicle again but kept the car door open. The scraggly-looking man reached the fence and asked, "What do you want?"

Still shaken from the dog's greeting, Seeney said, "Yes—well, actually, I'm looking for State Testing Lab, and my GPS brought me to this location. Are you aware of a business with that name around here?"

"Who's askin'?" questioned the stranger.

"Well, my name is Siena Tyson, and I'm a bookkeeper. One of my clients uses State Testing Labs for water testing, and I need to deliver some paperwork. I tried to call the company, and I also emailed, but so far have not been able to get a response."

"I got your messages, lady." The man sneered enough for Seeney to notice crooked and yellow teeth. "I'm not interested in filling out your paperwork."

"Okay, so, this is the correct location for State Testing Lab?"

"You have a problem with that?"

"No, sir. Then, you must be Justin Domship."

"What if I am?"

"I'm sorry, sir. I'm not trying to be difficult. It's just the IRS requires companies using outside contractors to file 1099s for the payments made. The contractors are supposed to complete a W-9 with certain tax information. I need to resolve the issue for Eastern Hydroponics about the work you performed last year for them."

"Well," said the man, "you're wasting your time. I'm not lifting a finger for the IRS or any other part of our government. Do you see how I live out here? Does it look like my government does anything for me?"

"I'm sorry, sir, but that doesn't change the law. I won't bother you anymore, but you should understand the IRS will be informed of the payments to STL by Eastern Hydroponics. You are liable for the taxes due on the income. Whether you pay them or not is up to you but failing to complete the W-9 won't stop the IRS from knowing about the income."

"You should probably get back in your car before I let Grizzly off his chain," warned the man.

Seeney sat back down in the driver's seat and shut the door. Then, with shaking hands, she started the car and glared at Justin Domship through the windshield as she left his property. The encounter scared her in the beginning, but now it made her mad.

She would provide Eastern Hydroponics her report and prepare the paperwork for the IRS explaining this vendor's refusal to complete the W-9, but she also planned to visit the town office. She wanted to find out who in that office would refer the criminal she just met to Eastern Hydroponics. She couldn't understand why the town would choose to use the services of someone like Domship.

As she considered this, she stopped the car, turned around, and parked in front of Domship's property, this time across the road from it. Not turning the ignition off, she opened the door and stood by the car. In a split second, the demon-dog named Grizzly heard the car door open, and the savage beast again charged the fence. Seeney waited a few seconds, and when Domship stepped out of his trailer, she snapped several pictures. She then waved pleasantly to Domship and got back in her car.

It took twenty minutes for Seeney to drive from Domship's property back to the town office in Tartan Springs. On her way, she called Elsie Morning, the town's financial manager. Seeney knew Elsie from the Chamber of Commerce networking meetings.

When Seeney entered the office, Elsie greeted her warmly, "Hi, Seeney, you said you needed some help with something."

"Yes, Elsie. I do. Thank you for meeting with me. I provide bookkeeping for Eastern Hydroponics, and one of the company's vendors refused to complete a W-9. The vendor is someone the town also uses, and you provided Terri Miller at Eastern Hydroponics with the referral for the vendor. Have you had any difficulty getting a tax identification number from State Testing Lab?"

"Oh dear, let me close the door." When Elsie sat back down, she said, "Terri Miller, from Eastern, asked me if I had a contact for someone to do water testing. That was almost a year ago at one of the first networking events Eastern Hydroponics attended. I told her I could give her a telephone number for a company the town uses, and I provided the information for STL. I wouldn't call it a reference because that vendor is also a problem for me. Domship was just the only contact I had."

"I understand. What are your problems with STL?"

"The same one as you mentioned. The owner won't fill out a W-9. I suggested to Mayor Foster we find a different vendor, but the mayor scoffed it off. He characterizes Domship as an anti-government hillbilly and tells me to ignore the paperwork in his case."

"That doesn't seem right, does it?"

"No. It isn't right. Technically, we're supposed to require outside vendors to complete the W-9 paperwork before they ever provide services for us. We're also required to examine their insurance coverage. The town would be in trouble if the wrong people found out we didn't do either with STL. I'm concerned but not sure what to do. Are you aware Justin Domship is related to the McCaskeys? Domship is the owner of STL."

"No," said Seeney. "Which McCaskey?"

"He's the son of Luther McCaskey's sister, Stella. Luther has managed the town's water plant for almost forty years and is Milton McCaskey's brother."

"Is that why Foster won't do anything? Milton's son, Four, financed Foster's campaign for mayor, didn't he?"

"I can't answer that, Seeney, but the whole thing makes me uncomfortable. I hope you won't tell anyone about this conversation. I need this job."

"I won't, but you should protect yourself, too. At a minimum, document somewhere that Foster told you not to pursue the W-9 paperwork. I'm not sure where your fiduciary responsibilities and your chain of command responsibilities coincide or overlap. Still, I'm fairly sure you aren't allowed to do something illegal just because your boss told you to."

"Thanks, Seeney. I agree," said Elsie.

Seeney left the town offices and saw Mayor Foster coming in as she was going out. "The invitation for dinner with me is still open, Ms. Tyson."

"Not interested, Foster." Seeney kept walking.

Foster stopped at the receptionist's desk and asked who Seeney visited. The young employee answered honestly, and Foster headed to his financial manager's office. Thirty minutes later, when Foster left Elsie's office, he told the receptionist he would be gone the rest of the day.

On his way up Mullen Mountain, Foster reviewed his meeting with Elsie Morning and the ensuing telephone conversation with Four McCaskey. Justin Domship had always been a royal pain, but Foster never expected him to do something so stupid as to expose his own family to trouble. Four McCaskey was angry and wanted explanations, but Foster had none. So, when he arrived at the headquarters for McCaskey Coal, Foster went straight to Four's office.

"Domship will be here in a few minutes, Foster," said a red-faced Four. "I'm not happy!"

"Well, don't shoot the messenger. All I did was tell you Siena Tyson was snooping around the town offices about Domship's W-9. I didn't do anything wrong. I continue to allow STL to perform the water quality tests—and pay Domship for the work despite his refusal to fill out the required paperwork, just as you asked when I got elected."

"What about this Eastern Hydroponics company?" asked Four. "When did you learn about them using STL?"

"About five minutes before I called you today."

"Okay, okay, sorry. That idiot, Domship! I should've known better."

The illustrious Justin Domship then arrived and sat down next to Foster. "Jesus, Domship!" exclaimed Foster. "Don't you ever bathe? You stink!"

"Cousin Four didn't give me time to clean up for this meeting, asshole," replied Domship. "He said I had to be here right away."

"Both of you shut up!" ordered Four. "We have a problem, and I need to find out how big it is now. Justin, when did you decide you could take on additional business using the company I set up for you?"

"What's it to you, Four?" asked Domship. "My name is the one on the state certification, not yours. You haven't given me a raise in eight years, so I thought I might give myself one with another account."

"You idiot!" yelled Four. "I pay you six thousand dollars per year in cash to perform four water quality checks per month for the mines. The town pays you the same amount for eight reports a month for them. The testing takes you maybe twenty total hours per month. It's a gift, Justin, plain and simple. We agreed you'd never do other water testing for anyone else. Our purpose was to keep you and your business a secret—not to advertise it."

"Yeah, well, thanks for the charity, but a man can't live on twelve grand a year, even if it's tax-free. I need to make more money."

"Your roosters aren't winning anymore?" asked Foster.

"None of your business, Foster!"

"Justin," said Four, "We aren't here to discuss your employment options. I can give you a job in the mine you can start tomorrow at twenty dollars per hour. You want money, but you never want to work. We may need to shut the water testing down and give you a vacation someplace. The wrong people connecting you to our operation could cause problems."

"Oh, Four! If you're worried about that bitch who visited me this morning, you can stop. You shoulda' seen her eyes the first time Grizzly charged the fence. I can make sure she doesn't say anything."

Four stared at his dim-witted cousin. "I can't believe I'm sitting here listening to this—or that you're in any way related to me. I don't want you talking to that woman, and you better not try to scare her. If you do anything to harm her, I'll personally make sure you spend the rest of your life in prison. Do you understand me?"

Domship acted surprised at Four's outburst and mumbled, "Yeah, right. I understand."

"For now, let's see if either Ms. Tyson or Eastern Hydroponics does any additional follow-up. We may need to change our way of getting samples from the town water supply. Our only purpose was to monitor the effects of the slurry pond seepage. It may be time to bite the bullet and stop the leak.

In Tartan Springs later in the evening

"Tom, can I run something by you which is bothering me?" said Seeney to her pastor friend.

"Sure," said Tom. "What's up?"

"One of my clients, Eastern Hydroponics, has a problem vendor I visited today. I'm trying to get some tax information from State Testing Lab, but in the process, I'm learning other things which are concerning."

"Does this require spiritual counseling?" joked Tom.

"No, only a friendly opinion. I know what I need to do to satisfy the IRS for my client, but the vendor causing the problem bothers me. On the other hand, I also think the vendor is just the tip of the iceberg for something that could impact our community. I don't want to get involved with any of this, but I have mixed emotions."

"Okay. If the bigger issue isn't your problem, why wouldn't you do the work for your client and forget about the rest? What issues could be so important for the community that you could impact?"

"I hoped you might feel that way. Other than satisfying my client, none of this is my business. I needed to hear that, though. I think Foster and the McCaskey's are hiding something relative to our water supply in Tartan Springs. Somehow, I happened in the middle of it, but I'm going to leave it where it is. Policing the town's water isn't my responsibility."

"Oh," said Tom. He said no more.

"You still there, Tom?"

"Yes, sorry. How did you say your client became involved?"

"I didn't," said Seeney. "Why?"

"I thought I heard you mention something about the water supply in Tartan Springs?"

"Yes. I did, but I didn't mention what my client had to do with that. Eastern Hydroponics received water quality reports from the same small company Tartan Springs uses for tests. Unfortunately, the vendor, Justin Domship, who owns State Testing Lab, refused to provide a W-9 to Eastern Hydroponics. So, Terri Miller at Eastern tasked me with running down the missing IRS forms."

"I see," said Tom. "And how does this relate to Tartan Springs' water supply?"

"Hold on there, Tom. You already told me you didn't think any of this was my problem. Why the sudden change?"

Tom coughed a little. "Right, except if you stumbled on something relating to the water your community consumes, isn't that a big deal? So, what makes you suspicious?"

"The whole thing does, Tom! Domship is a lowlife. I visited his address this morning to pick up the W-9 form in person, and he scared me. I couldn't believe our town would use such a scumbag, so I stopped at the municipal offices and checked with Elsie Morning, the town's financial manager. I didn't have to do this. I was just curious—and I wish now I hadn't been."

"Why?"

"Because Elsie appeared frightened when I mentioned Domship's name and closed the door to her office. She's had problems getting tax information from State Testing Lab, but the mayor told her not to worry about it. Elsie also told me Domship's relationship to the McCaskey's; he's Stella Domship's son. Stella was Milton and Luther McCaskey's youngest sister, who died a few years ago. Luther has managed the town's water plant for almost forty years."

"So, what makes you think any of this has to do with the town's water supply?"

"The whole thing is too fishy," said Seeney. "Why would the town contract with a no-load like Domship in the first place? Why would Foster tell his financial manager not to worry about collecting the required IRS forms? The town supposedly contracted Domship to run water quality tests, and the reports from these go to his uncle. Doesn't all that add up to something strange in your mind?"

"Yes. It does. I'm sorry about what I told you earlier. I'm not sure you can ignore this sort of problem. Tartan Springs is still your community, and I don't believe you can turn your back on something that might be dangerous to people in the town."

"Thanks for nothing," said Seeney. "I should have hung up ten minutes ago when I was ahead. My last several months have been traumatic with Ty leaving and all. After we marry, I'm not even sure Ty and I will stay in this area. Should I get involved in some dramatic episode that may or may not impact Tartan Springs now?"

"In the end, you'll make your own decision, and I'll support whatever that decision is. I know you well enough to realize you won't ignore this, though. I have a young friend who might have some unique insight. Could she call you?"

"I guess. Who is it?"

"Gina McCaskey. She attends my church, and she's the daughter of Four and Lisbeth."

"Lord, Tom! If any of this scenario with the town involves the McCaskey's, why should I talk to Gina?"

"Because she's a good person, and I trust her."

Tom said nothing else, and Seeney suspected the pastor knew more than he was telling her. She also knew she couldn't refuse her friend, but she now regretted calling him. She seemed to be plunging deeper into a hole rather than climbing out of one. "Okay," she relented, "but no promises about how I decide."

"Understood."

15 Trouble Brews

Todd Foster rechecked Seeney's Facebook page but didn't see new activity. Seeney's fiancé, Foster knew, was deployed, and the mayor expected she might post pictures of Harrell on her page. She hadn't, however, and it seemed Seeney preferred keeping her private life private. Foster had followed attorney Aldrich's advice and not bothered Seeney further since her confrontation with him, but his anger with her remained. He would one day even the score, but he realized he needed to be careful.

Foster tried to enlist Jack Stiles in his campaign against Seeney, but Stiles expressed no interest. The ex-husband exhibited fear in even talking about any such plan. The mayor presumed whatever Stiles had done to Seeney to cause her to divorce him gave her significant legal leverage over him. Stiles was not by nature a generous man, nor did he seem to be a forgiving one. Yet, schemes to retaliate for Seeney's lucrative settlement didn't appear to enthuse him. Still, Foster thought his newest idea for revenge might entice Stiles.

"Hey, Jack," said the mayor over the phone. "This is Todd."

"Hi, Todd. What's up?"

"Not much. Just a thought to run by you."

"Todd, if this is about Seeney, forget it. I told you I'm not interested in anything to do with her. She's a dangerous woman as far as I'm concerned, and I'm glad to be done with her."

"I know, I know," said Foster. "I learned that myself, believe me. Still, she's no smarter than either you or me, and she needs to learn a lesson."

"Well, you teach her all the lessons you want," said Stiles. "Just leave me out!"

"If you insist, but what I had in mind wouldn't hurt her either physically or financially. She also couldn't prove anything against us."

Stiles didn't answer right away, then said, "I'm listening... but that's all I'm doing."

"All I'm asking. Let's grab a beer at the Renegade tomorrow after work."

The following afternoon, Stiles and Foster huddled at a corner table in the Renegade with two pints of beer in front of them. Foster explained how he had managed to monitor Seeney's Facebook page for much of the past year and how she had registered for the SBAI organization in the Chamber of Commerce.

"She used the login: styson@satsun.com, with the password ST26537?," said Foster, "and I'm betting it's the same password she uses for her Satsun account."

"Probably so, unless she changed it in the last year. She tries to use the same login and password for everything."

"Then she most likely uses the same password for her cell phone?"

"Seeney doesn't have a password for her phone, to my knowledge," said Stiles. "She might now, but I doubt it. Why?"

"Just thinking. I haven't tried to access her Satsun account using the password she used to sign up for the SBAI account yet. If Seeney uses a different one, my plan won't work as well. Once I try to access her account, if her old password works, she'll receive an immediate warning on both her phone and her computer. Notifications are sent to customers when unfamiliar devices open their email accounts."

"So, what do you want to do?" asked Stiles. "You're not going to find any of her financial accounts, or much else important, through her

Satsun email account."

"Right. The whole thing will be fairly harmless, but we can make her life miserable for a couple of days as she fixes her computer and her cell phone accounts. After that, maybe she'll learn not to screw with us."

"OK, I guess I understand the computer part. What do you want from me?"

"If you can get her cell phone, we can execute a dual technology strike. First, we can use her cell to access her computer, and since her Satsun account will recognize the cell phone device, she won't receive a security alert. Then, after we send a few fake texts and email messages which will embarrass her, we'll change the password settings for both her phone and her Satsun email account."

Stiles thought about that for a moment. "She'll eventually straighten those out, though, so what would we accomplish? Also, how do you think I'm supposed to get her phone? Seeney and I don't see each other anymore and have no reason to now."

"Certainly, she'll be able to reestablish the accounts, but you know how long it takes to do anything with tech companies when things get screwed up. That might take days, and while she's doing that, we can mess with her and her business quite a bit." Foster continued, "I figured you could think of some reason to make her come to the agency. Perhaps a better warranty on the car you gave her—or possibly a deal to trade up for a newer model?"

"Well," said Stiles, thinking. "That might work. She could trade up now to a later model car, with a full five-year warranty, for almost no additional cash. Chevrolet has some deals going on. The warranty on the car she owns expires in two months, and Chevy will extend that for next to nothing. I could send her a notice, I guess. The problem is, even if I could get her phone, it wouldn't take long for her to figure out who messed with it. She'd remember where she was when the phone went missing—and I'm the only one with the old password information."

"So what? She's the one who is sloppy with passwords, and Seeney wouldn't be able to track our activity with her phone. She *might* determine who's responsible—hell, I hope she does! But neither she nor her asshole attorney will be able to do a thing about it."

"Let me think about it," Stiles said. "I've learned the hard way to be careful with her. Seeney has cost me a lot of money."

The mail notification about her car warranty surprised Seeney. The communication didn't appear to be a mass-mailed advertisement but rather a personal letter from the dealership. The last time she spoke to Jack Stiles was when he left the house over a year ago, and Seeney didn't believe he would try to do her any favors. So, she presumed Chevrolet automatically initiated such letters to car owners with impending warranty expirations.

The offer was compelling for a single woman with no aptitude for car repair. Two more years of coverage for an additional one hundred dollars per year seemed like a deal she should consider. She called the dealership and inquired what the process was for taking advantage of it. The receptionist informed Seeney she only had to visit the dealership and update some paperwork. Disconnecting from the call, Seeney hoped she might accomplish the extension without seeing Jack Stiles.

No such luck, she learned a day later. After filling out the preliminary forms, the receptionist asked Seeney to follow her to Mr. Stiles' office to approve the request. Seeney rolled her eyes but went with the young woman.

"Hello, Seeney," greeted Stiles. "This will only take a minute, but you should look at the 2017 models while you're here. You might be able to trade up to a newer car with no money down."

"I don't need a new car. I'll just extend the warranty on the one I own, thanks."

"OK," he said, hardly looking up. "Let me add some information to the application. You can put your coat on the chair if you want."

"Is this going to take that long?"

"No, just a little paperwork." Reluctantly, Seeney removed her coat and laid it on the adjoining chair over her purse. After writing on the papers in front of him, Jack asked for Seeney's car registration.

"It's in the car," said Seeney, a little annoyed. "Nobody told me to bring anything with me."

"Sorry, but I don't have the information from the original warranty, so I need the VIN for your car."

"Alright," said Seeney, picking up her purse. "I'll be right back."

Stiles hoped Seeney might leave her purse in his office, but he realized most women kept their car keys in their bag. He had a different idea for separating Seeney from her purse a little later, anyway. Seeney returned to Jack's office with the registration, and Jack typed some more on the form in front of him. As he did this, he said, "I told Joe Kearns to duck in and show you the new Malibus on the showroom floor. You said you aren't interested, but at least take a look. I'll finish with this by the time you're back."

On cue, a young-looking salesman peeked through the door, and Jack introduced Seeney to him. She rolled her eyes again but went with the salesman to the showroom floor. Stiles came from behind his desk and looked inside her purse as soon as Seeney disappeared through his door.

Her cell phone was on top of her wallet, and Stiles carefully removed it. He placed it under a corner of the desk where the device wouldn't be visible to Seeney. If, for some reason, she needed to make a call or check her phone before she left Stiles' office, it would appear the phone had fallen out of her purse to the floor.

Seeney came back into the office in less than ten minutes. "The new Malibus look nice, but I'm happy with my current vehicle for now. I don't want to take on additional debt, no matter how small."

"OK," said Stiles. "Thanks for looking. I'm done here. If you sign by the X, I'll send this in tomorrow. You'll receive an invoice by email within a couple of weeks."

"OK," said Seeney after signing the document. "Thanks. I'll see you around."

"I doubt it, but that suits both of us, I think."

Seeney put her jacket on, picked up her purse, and left Stiles' office. Preoccupied thinking about the strange visit to the dealership, Seeney didn't notice her cell phone missing when she retrieved keys from her purse.

When she arrived back home, Seeney hung her jacket in the hall closet, and set the purse on the kitchen counter. She picked a half-emptied bottle of white wine from her refrigerator, filled a glass, and opened her handbag to retrieve her phone. It wasn't there.

She felt around the other parts of the bag and looked in the side compartments, still not finding it. She thought for a second, then checked the pockets of the coat she had hung in the closet. Not seeing the phone, she tried to remember the last time she used the cell.

She had stopped at the post office before going to the dealership and made a call from the parking lot. Seeney remembered placing the phone back in her purse, though, which meant it must have fallen from her bag in the car or at the dealership. After checking her vehicle, she called Jack Stiles Chevrolet. The business was closed, as she expected it would be.

West Virginia: Tuesday, 5:00 PM
Bektistan: Wednesday, 2:00 AM

"I have it," said Stiles. "Where do you want to meet?"

"Come on over to the municipal building," said Foster. "We need to work fast."

Stiles was leaving the dealership when he heard the business phone ring and a call go to voicemail. He entered a code on his desk phone to listen to the message from the after-hours caller. The call was Seeney, inquiring about her cell phone, and she indicated she would call the following day when the business opened. She left her home number on the voicemail in the event someone heard the message that evening. Stiles smiled as he locked the doors to his business.

When Stiles arrived at the municipal building, Foster came to the front door and unlocked it. Stiles handed Foster Seeney's cell phone. "Now what?"

"Now we teach that bitch a lesson. Come on in."

Seeney's phone required no password to open it, as Stiles had predicted. So, Jack went to the settings window and changed the password to her Virtel account. To do this, Stiles needed to confirm it was Seeney requesting the change by entering some personal information—the maiden name of Seeney's mother and Seeney's favorite mascot. Jack and Seeney created their iPhone Virtel accounts at the same time, so he knew her answers to these questions.

Then, under Foster's supervision, Stiles accessed Seeney's Satsun email account from her phone. Entering the password she always used, he completed access to her settings, again changing her password. Foster understood this would generate a message to Seeney's other devices, warning of the change. So, when the notification showed up on Seeney's cell phone, Stiles deleted it. Foster then accessed Seeney's Satsun email account from the stolen phone, using the new password created, and removed the notification just received relating to the change in personal settings.

Foster looked at Stiles. "OK. I'm no tech geek, but I figure we have about twelve hours until Satsun can straighten Seeney's cell phone stuff out—maybe a little more. We may have about the same amount of time to access her computer email account without her knowing. She'll discover she can't open emails tonight or in the morning and will probably react quickly. Depending on how aggressive she is, Seeney might be back up and running with emails by tomorrow afternoon."

"OK. So, what are we going to do? And remember," Stiles warned, "I don't want her to be able to track this back to me."

"Oh," said Foster, "she'll undoubtedly guess who's responsible. No way she can prove anything, though. I have more to lose in this than you. It looks to me like you already gave her the ranch, so what more do you have to lose?"

Stiles stared at Foster for a long moment. "I had my reasons—which are none of your business! Now, tell me what you plan to do."

"Fine. Sometime after ten tonight, we'll send a couple of email notices to three or four of her clients to inform them she's dropping their business from her services. The announcement will anger the clients, but with a few calls, Seeney will be able to explain the mistake to them. The whole process will create a hassle for her, though. Second, we'll send her high and mighty flyboy in Bektistan a *Dear John* letter."

"What's that going to accomplish?" asked Stiles. "She'll be able to tell him she didn't send the message as soon as she gets a new phone. Any damage will be temporary."

"Of course, it will only be temporary. But the emotion created for a few days by the message will be monumental. We're making a statement to this bitch!"

"OK," said Stiles. "I guess, but it looks like a lot of work for not much revenge. As long as you're sure nobody can do anything to us for this."

"The only digital trail will lead to her personal cell phone," said Foster. "I told you before, she may figure out who's responsible, but she can't do a damn thing about it. She needs to learn not to fuck with us!"

By ten o'clock that evening, Foster and Stiles crafted several messages to various clients of ST Bookkeeping and a disturbing note to Major Ty Harrell, USMC.

16 Chopper Down

West Virginia: Tuesday, 10:00 PM
Bektistan: Wednesday, 7:00 AM

Ten o'clock at night in West Virginia is seven o'clock the following morning in Bektistan. Of course, the day starts earlier in this part of the world. Major Harrell had finished a short workout in the makeshift gym inside the canvass-clad, half-moon shell located at Fox Uni when he saw the text on his cell phone. It was seven-thirty in the morning, and he had flown a maintenance hop late the previous evening. That meant he wasn't due back at his unit's headquarters hanger for another four hours.

As he settled on a stool in the spartan surroundings of his hastily erected combat hut, he pulled up the message on his cell phone. A planet infrastructure of satellites providing service to backward nations as indiscriminately as more advanced ones facilitated communications with friends and family back home. Emails and texts between Seeney and Ty were not always daily, but they were frequent. For that reason, the text he read from Seeney this morning was both shocking and curious.

Ty - I'll send you a longer email today, but I must break off our engagement. I'm sorry and hope you can find it in your heart to forgive me - Siena

Since Ty had received a lengthy email from Seeney the previous day containing no hint of anything wrong, the short message stunned him. He was also hurt—but now, mostly confused. He reread the text and noted the time it had arrived on his phone: six forty-five AM. That meant Seeney would have sent the text just before ten o'clock PM, her time in West Virginia. Seeney seldom texted or emailed him after eight o'clock PM, her time, so the time for this communication was out of the ordinary.

He looked at his watch and decided not to wait for an email. Even if Ty woke her up, Seeney's text was too critical to ignore. He punched his "favorite's" icon on his phone and waited for Seeney to pick up. She didn't, and her recorded voice eventually instructed him to leave a message. He did.

After putting his cell phone away, he booted his laptop computer to life and checked for new emails. He had one from his parents and one from Seeney. Clicking on the email from Seeney, he noted the time stamp on the notification; six fifty-five AM, just ten minutes after the text. The message in the email was a more extended version of the one in the text, with the added information that Seeney had found someone new.

The news struck him like a bullet to the heart—but something still didn't seem right. He wondered how this could have come up so quickly with no warning signs. And why would Seeney sign both messages, *Siena*? He was beginning to be suspicious, but he sent a quick email reply to Seeney requesting she call him as soon as possible. Ty was reasonably sure Seeney wouldn't read the email for another six to eight hours when she awoke in West Virginia.

Ty was as perplexed as he was troubled by the two messages. He couldn't bring himself to believe Seeney would make such a dramatic decision this fast. And if she did, Ty didn't think this was how she would deliver the news. He needed to talk to her but knew this wouldn't be possible until later in the day.

He considered the text and the email as he changed into a flight suit. Not expected at the unit's combat headquarters until noon, he was the squadron's executive officer and had plenty of paperwork to catch up on. Moreover, recent Army-initiated ground operations had kept air support missions plentiful and the flight schedule busy. As a result, many of the unit's pilots, including himself, were getting behind on their collateral administrative functions. The commanding officer, Lieutenant Colonel James Hayden, was in his cubicle next to the hangar bay when Ty arrived. "Hey, Jim. Anything new this morning?"

"No. Things are quiet so far. We've got crews number seven and eight on alert status. Numbers one, two, and three are on duty rest from last evening. Your crew is also supposed to be on duty rest, Ty. Didn't you fly a test hop last night?"

"Yeah, but it was no big deal. I got enough sleep, and I'm not on the flight schedule today."

"Okay, if you say so," said the commanding officer. "Even though Captain Callahan's team is on alert, I let him take 433 up solo to calibrate the new nav system we just received. He's flying local, so if anything comes up, he could be back here in less than fifteen minutes."

"Roger. Who else is around?"

"Cooley, Dunn, and Short are at chow. Kilby is station Officer of the Day, and both Johnson and Lincoln are at the communications tent. Teams number five and six are flying perimeter surveillance over in Tigram this morning, and unit ten is ferrying 484 up to Kadun. They'll bring back the new ship this afternoon."

"Got it," said Ty. "That leaves us a little thin today, doesn't it?"

"A little, but you and I are still in reserve. Downs could also fly if he had to. His hand is better."

"Right," said Ty. "I'm going to try to catch up on the action reports this morning and, if I have time, I'll give you the fitness evaluations for the lieutenants later today. I'm aware those are overdue, but I have them almost completed."

"No problem. When you're operating on the front line, paperwork isn't the priority."

"Understood."

Thirty minutes later, the red phone on the duty officer's desk in the ready room rang. Captain O'Neill answered, listened, then hung up. He picked up the microphone attached to the hanger's public address system and announced: "Alert, Alert! Scramble units seven and eight. Make units twelve and thirteen ready in reserve: repeat, scramble units seven and eight. Launch immediately! Launch immediately!"

"Dammit! Dammit! Dammit!" yelled Hayden coming from his cubicle. Ty met him as he entered the ready room.

"What's up, Skipper?" asked Ty.

"I fucked up, Ty! That's what's up. We've got a fire team pinned down in Charlie Zone and need to launch our ready ships. But, stupid me has one of the alert pilots flying a navigation calibration."

"No problem. We've got this. I'm ready and will jump in for Callahan."

The commanding officer stopped for a second. "Okay. Go ahead, Ty. Callahan won't be back for at least ten minutes, and I think the 104 needs us right now! We pre-filed the manifest, but it lists Callahan as the pilot in command."

"A smart guy once told me when you're on the front line, paperwork isn't the priority. Someone can fix the manifest."

"In this case," said a still fuming Hayden, "*smart guy* seems a bit exaggerated—but go ahead, and let's launch."

Lieutenant Selby looked surprised when his executive officer slid into the pilot seat next to him. "Change in plan, George. You have the coordinates?"

"Yep. We're ready to fly. Master Sergeant Gunn is our crew chief."

"Great! I feel safer already. Going up!" The fully armed H-1Y, Venom, jumped into the air and fell in line behind the other helicopter. The ride was a short one to the opening of a rugged mountain pass north of the squadron's operating base. Lieutenant Selby was in radio contact with the Army fire-team leader on the ground, who reported their position and situation.

While entering an area of mountains believed to be unoccupied by the enemy, the relatively small seven-man Ranger fire team encountered heavy gunfire from two sides of the mountain pass. Miraculously, nobody was hit, and the squad retreated to a large outcropping of rocks several hundred yards in front of the pass.

The Army ranger reported his group had good firing positions and enough ammunition, but they were outnumbered. Enemy soldiers now also surrounded them on three sides. An armored division was en route to assist them, but the team leader didn't think his group could hold out long enough for the reinforcements to arrive.

Captain O'Brien, copiloting the Venom ahead of Ty's, was the designated mission commander, and he responded to the Army ranger over the radio. "Roger, Dog One. This is Fox One, and I copy. We'll come in low and abreast from the South with the Gatling's engaged. That should drive the bogies back toward the mountain. Are they armed with anything bigger than RPGs?"

"Negative, sir," said the ranger, "not that we've seen, but heavier equipment might be hidden back in the mountain."

"Copy, Dog One," said O'Brien. "For now, we'll concentrate on covering a retreat for your group, and we'll try to steer clear of the mountain. I have a visual on your position and will commence firing. Tell your men to keep their heads down."

"Roger that."

Ty steered his Venom to the right of the rocks, and Lieutenant Lewis, piloting the aircraft O'Brien was in, went to the left. A wall of lead laid down by the two helicopters found many targets and scattered more. Enemy combatants were retreating to their mountain stronghold after the choppers' first pass, and Master Sergeant Gunn reported from his station in the back, "Looks like around thirty or forty running. Can't tell how many might be down."

"Roger," said Ty. "Fox one, this is Fox two. I don't see grenade launchers, so suggest we hover over the rocks and fire."

"Two, this is one. Agree," said O'Brien. "Mission is to keep the back door open for rangers. Their armored division can bring bigger guns and more troops to take on what's in those mountains." Moving targets are always more difficult to hit than stationary ones, so hovering their aircraft was a calculated risk for Ty and O'Brien. The maneuver, however, allowed the two Venoms to guard the ranger unit's retreat more easily.

"RPG starboard!" crackled the radio, and Ty saw the telltale trail of smoke from the grenade coming in his direction. He juked his craft to the left, then spotted a second trail of smoke in front of them.

"Hang on!" Ty warned his crew. Ty's initial evasive maneuver caused the first grenade to miss, but the move put his Venom squarely in the path of the second one. The small bomb touched just above the cockpit and exploded near the engine compartment. The helicopter rocked from the impact, and all inside heard the ugly sound of shredding metal.

"We're going down," said Ty. "Buckle up. I'm going to try to set down on the riverbank as far from the mountain as possible. The landing might be rough."

The sinking helicopter was now auto-rotating toward the bank of a small river, perhaps three hundred yards from the rocks where the Rangers were evacuating. As the Venom moved slowly forward, descending, Ty ordered Selby to launch the two missiles attached to the bottom of their aircraft into the river to prevent them from exploding during the impending crash.

Just before hitting the ground, Ty managed to turn the Venom to face the mountain. Unfortunately, the maneuver caused the helicopter's tail to touch the ground first, creating a violent jolt as the forward part of the machine came down. Ty felt a sickening crunch in his back and noticed a piece of metal from the seat assembly protruding from his left leg.

"Roll call," said Selby into the mic after the crash.

"Gunn here. Woke me up, but I'm here."

"Harrell here. My back is hurt, and I've got some metal in my leg. Not sure I can move, and I need to stop the bleeding from my thigh."

"Okay," said Selby. "I'm good, so I'll tend to the major. Sergeant, you set up a defensive perimeter. We have an M-29 with a scope, right?"

"Roger," said Gunn. "We've also got twenty clips of thirty rounds for the M-29 and one pissed-off Master Sergeant. So, these guys are outnumbered."

Ty winced with pain but had to smile at Gunn's remark. "Before we lose coms, let Fox one know our status."

"Roger," said Selby.

When Selby reported to the mission commander, O'Brien replied, "Roger, Fox two. Copy. We have a blinking fuel light with possible damaged tank but will relay your information to base. We'll get someone back here to pick you up. The ranger unit is out of the rocks and safely across the river. Their leader said they used up most of their ammunition during the battle, so I'm not sure they can assist. Can you hold out for an hour or so?"

"Fox one, Fox two. Affirmative, if we can get Major Harrell's wound under control."

"Okay. Good luck, Fox two. Out."

With some help from Master Sergeant Gunn, Selby removed the jagged metal piece from Ty's leg. Blood ran freely from the wound, and

Selby stuffed it with gauze. Then he bandaged the leg as tightly as he could with tape. When the lieutenant finished his medic work, Ty asked for the binoculars. "I won't be able to do much besides lookout, but I'll keep an eye on the mountains for activity. The bad guys saw us go down, and they know someone will be back for us, so they won't take long to try to reach us first."

"Why wouldn't they just launch an RPG or two our way, then?" asked Selby.

"They might," said Ty, "but I doubt it. We're worth nothing to them dead. If they can, they'll want to take us alive. Also, they don't know for sure if any of us even survived the crash. What's the range of an RPG, Sergeant?"

"Maybe five hundred yards, with a lucky shot," said the Master Sergeant. "And, for what it's worth, being taken alive isn't an option!"

"Okay, then, here's what I suggest," said Ty, "but I defer to your judgment, Master Sergeant. I'll monitor with the binoculars and relay the info to you two. We should have at least two hours of battery time for our helmet communications."

"That's about right," said Gunn.

"The guys on the mountain need an RPG launcher on this side of the rocks to be effective, and, with the binoculars, I should be able to see anyone carrying one of those. If they send troops our way, I propose we allow them to advance close to our position before we react. You two hide behind those rocks in front of the helicopter, and I'll tell you when enemy soldiers are within thirty yards, which is the effective range for the Glocks."

Master Sergeant Gunn and Lieutenant Selby agreed with the plan, and they crawled out to a position in front of the downed helicopter. Sergeant Gunn carried the M-29 with the scope. Lieutenant Selby had both his and Ty's service Glock handguns. They expected the enemy to fire test shots toward the crash before advancing too close, but the team resolved not to reveal themselves if this happened.

The armor around the cockpit would protect Ty from any standard rounds from a rifle or pistol. On Ty's verbal signal, both Sergeant Gunn and Lieutenant Selby would fire on the marauders. With the more accurate gun, Sergeant Gunn would focus on anyone with a radio antenna; Lieutenant Selby, with both Glocks on automatic, would empty all his rounds in the vicinity of anyone standing.

All in Ty's small team hoped this first, brief, surprise attack would create a delay from the almost inevitable assault from the enemy's more significant force. The gunfire from Ty's group at the short distance would also not disclose the Master Sergeant's possession of a high-powered marksman's rifle equipped with a scope.

The M-29 had an effective range of a half-mile, and Sergeant Gunn had assured Ty he was an excellent marksman. With three hundred rounds of ammunition for the rifle, Gunn felt confident they could hold off a small force for an hour, especially since the enemy wouldn't be able to move to a position behind them because of the river.

The landscape in front of the downed aircraft was still, and Ty thanked his luck for being able to crash-land with the cockpit facing the mountain. That decision certainly improved his team's chances of survival. As he continued to monitor the area between his position and the massive elevation before him, Ty caught a whiff of something sweet in the air. Poppies, maybe? In this temporary calm, the beauty of the rugged mountain range also mesmerized him.

The pastoral thoughts were interrupted when Ty noted movement at the base of the mountain. Ty calculated the enemy's position to be about six football fields, or a little over a quarter mile away, and it appeared that a small scout team was coming to survey the wreckage.

When the group of four men reached the rocks where the Ranger unit had been, all fired their automatic weapons toward the downed Venom. Several shots pinged off the aircraft's metal, but none landed near where Selby and Gunn lay. Ty watched through the binoculars from just above the level of the Venom's front bubble window as the enemy soldiers approached. They were now carrying their weapons casually, apparently convinced nobody survived the crash.

The scout team advanced to within thirty yards of Selby's and Gunn's position, and Ty said into his helmet mic, "Okay, guys. Four men. Directly in front of you with weapons relaxed. The one in the middle right, Sergeant, has an antenna extending from his back. On my mark—one, two, three!"

The volley from Selby and Gunn was wholly unexpected by the approaching troops, and Lieutenant Selby took credit for three of the four men down in front of them. Gunn reluctantly agreed with Selby's claim but noted the waste of ammunition on the lieutenant's part. Gunn had fired one shot, eliminating the target with an antenna, while Selby had emptied full magazines of two pistols - thirty-four bullets in all.

Ty brought them both back to reality with his command. "Good job, team! Retreat to the helicopter!" His two crewmen hurried to the downed craft while Ty kept his eyes on the battlefield through the binoculars.

Smoke still drifted above the spot Gunn and Selby had been, and the strong smell of cordite enveloped the area. No other movement was evident. Tall grass hid the bodies of the soldiers dispatched by his crew, and Ty was troubled by conflicting emotions.

To protect his men, Ty assisted in ending the lives of four others. He wondered if Moses's stone tablets were too small to include the entire sentence for the seventh commandment. Could the complete version have been, *Thou shalt not kill unless thou are about to be killed*? He decided Religion and War were two subjects that shared no common or overlapping territory, and perhaps the two terms should not even occupy the same page of a book. Not only were Ty's thoughts becoming confused, but his sight was getting blurry.

When the Master Sergeant and Lieutenant arrived, Ty handed Selby the binoculars. "I'm a little dizzy, George, so you're now the spotter. Pistols won't be effective during this next phase, anyway."

"Major! You gotta hang on. Our guys are going to be here soon."

"I know. I'm not going anywhere. I just know my capabilities now. You need to be the eyes and the Master Sergeant the talent. We've got a few hours of daylight, and the folks on that mountain won't want to waste it."

Gunn set his rifle on a ledge of the side window of the helicopter and adjusted the scope. Then, ignoring rank, he suggested Lieutenant Selby check for enemy activity through the binoculars. The junior officer did and directed Gunn's attention to the left side of the mountain. "Some movement around the base on the port side. I see three guys, and one has a launcher."

Gunn, peering through the powerful scope attached to the M-29, confirmed, "Roger. Visual. Let's see what they're going to do with the launcher before I do anything. No sense in letting them know we've got a long-distance rifle until we need to."

"Roger," said Selby. The M-29 model Infantry Automatic Rifle, built by Hecker and Koch, had replaced the venerable M-249 in 2010 and was a reliable all-around automatic weapon. It was capable of the high rate of fire of a machine gun but featured the lightweight portability of a rifle. The weapon also had a lethal range of nearly two miles and a practical target range of over six hundred yards. Each Venom crew attached to HML-222 carried one M-29 with twenty magazines in the aircraft. "Looks like they're going to set the launcher up right there at the base of the mountain."

"Yeah," said Gunn, "which is fucking dumb! The launcher can send a grenade as far as we are, but not with much accuracy. They must've decided when their buddies didn't come back, we weren't worth the trouble to take alive."

"Too bad," said a nervous Lieutenant Selby. "Are we going to let them use us for target practice?"

"Nope. Even at that range, they might get lucky." Then, aiming his rifle carefully while peering into the scope, Gunn pulled the trigger manually three times in quick succession.

"Two down, and one running back to the woods," announced Selby. "Nice shooting!"

"Nice shooting would have been three down, Lieutenant," said Gunn, still looking through the scope intently. "But their boss must've told somebody to retrieve the launcher. Here comes one sneaking out of the woods on his belly."

"Copy," said Selby, confirming through the binoculars what Gunn saw through the scope.

Gunn fired the rifle, and Selby watched the grenade launcher topple over six hundred yards away. "Okay, Master Sergeant, now you're just showing off," he said. Then, the man who had been coming toward the RPG launcher stood and raised his middle finger toward the downed helicopter. Gunn fired the M-29, and the man pulled his hand down, darting back to the woods. "Missed," noted Selby.

"Nope. Didn't miss. I shot the bastard's middle finger off!"

Lieutenant Selby laughed and glanced over to the salty Master Sergeant. Gunn wasn't laughing, and it was evident he had not been joking. "Well, I guess it isn't a secret we have a long-range rifle equipped with a scope and somebody who knows how to use it."

"Nope. Hand me two magazines for the rifle and load full clips in the pistols. Now, we need to convince them we have more than a rifle. On my count, aim at the base of the mountain and unload the pistols on fully automatic. I'll do the same with the M-29. You won't hit anything with the Glocks, and I probably won't either, but we'll make a lot of noise. That might make them stall."

Thirty seconds later, on Sergeant Gunn's count, the two Marines unleashed a volley of bullets toward the mountain. Gunn reloaded the rifle with a new magazine, and Selby put fresh clips in the two Glocks. "Now what?" asked Selby.

"Watch and wait," said Gunn. "In a perfect world, we'll hear the sound of friendly helicopters before we see those guys decide to mount a full-on assault. Our main problem is that the enemy outnumbers us, which is their advantage whenever they choose to use it" Then Gunn shouted to Ty, "How are you doing, Major?"

"I'm a little dizzy, but still here," said Ty.

"Hang on, sir, and do your best to stay awake," said the Master Sergeant. "Fight the urge to shut your eyes. How's the pain?"

"I'm sort of numb," said Ty, "so the pain isn't too noticeable."

"Okay," said Gunn. "It won't be long now." As he finished speaking, the three Marines heard a volley of machine-gun fire coming from the mountain, and Gunn warned, "Cover-up!"

The bullets raining down on the shell of the helicopter sounded like hail on a metal roof, but nothing penetrated. Gunn peeked over the side. "Okay, here they come. They're firing from the woods to keep our heads down while the assault team comes this way. I see at least one grenade launcher." Gunn, concentrating and peering through the scope, pulled the trigger slowly four times. "The RPG launcher is disabled, but about fifteen men are coming this way." The sergeant continued to shoot his rifle methodically.

Fox Uni

After securing the Army Ranger unit's retreat, Captain O'Brien disengaged and radioed the situation back to his base. His chopper was low on fuel due to a leak in one of the tanks, possibly caused by enemy ground fire. Nevertheless, he supported Ty's belief that the major's crew could hold out for an hour until a rescue bird could return. "Fox Uni, this is Fox one. Fox two has a solid defensive position in front of riverbank, six hundred yards from last known enemy location. Crew chief is experienced marksman with M-29 and three hundred rounds ammo."

"Roger, Fox 1, copy. Units twelve and thirteen are fueled and ready to launch. One will require equipment adjustments to accommodate three passengers. ETA overhead - forty-five minutes."

"Copy Fox Uni," said O'Brien. "Because I know the lay of the land, the exact location of enemy, and disposition of downed bird, suggest hold rescue crew fifteen minutes. With me in one of the rescue birds, mission safer for all."

"Copy, sir. Stand by." After a delay of thirty seconds, the radio sounded in O'Brien's helmet again. "Fox one, this is Fox Uni. Base confirms your plan. Expedite return and units here will hold."

"Roger, Fox Uni. Out."

Lieutenant Colonel Hayden agreed with Captain O'Brien's suggestion and instructed the ground crew to fuel the Venom that Captain Callahan just landed from the navigation calibration hop and equip it to act as the medevac vehicle.

As an afterthought, he told the ground crew to replace the Hydra missiles usually attached beneath the aircraft with fuel pods. "I'll fly the medevac bird solo with a corpsman," said Hayden to his operations officer.

Within forty-five minutes of Captain O'Brien's first report, three helicopters lifted off for the rescue mission. Captain O'Brien piloted one Venom; Captain Callahan was pilot in command of the second helicopter, and Lieutenant Colonel Hayden brought up the rear with the third chopper. The three Venom's arrived near the river, and when all onboard observed the group of enemy combatants approaching Ty's downed aircraft, they knew they had gotten there in the nick of time. Captain O'Brien directed the attack while Lieutenant Colonel Hayden maneuvered his helicopter into a position to land close to Ty's aircraft's wreckage.

When the three marines on the ground recognized the distinctive roar of several M134 miniguns from behind them, Lieutenant Selby smiled and gave the sergeant a thumbs up. Both glanced toward Major Harrell with concern.

The survivors of the hail of 7.62 MM caliber bullets delivered at a rate of three thousand rounds per minute raced back to the cover of the mountain. Three HML-222 Venom helicopters flying abreast of each other passed over the Marines' heads with the Gatling-style mini guns still firing. The noise from the rescue team was the last sound Ty heard before closing his eyes.

Two of the Venoms continued forward while the third hovered over the wreck. While the two lead aircraft continued to engage and provide cover, the third chopper dropped to a landing near the disabled helicopter. A medic with a portable stretcher raced toward the wreck, and Lieutenant Selby briefed him on the situation. "The Sergeant and I are fine, but we need Major Harrell evacuated right away. He's unconscious, lost a lot of blood from a leg wound, and his back might be broken."

The medic acknowledged and signaled for Selby and Gunn to help him place Ty on the stretcher. After the three Marines hauled the major into the helicopter, the corpsman slapped a needle into Ty's arm, hanging a bag from a cargo rail above the stretcher. Next, he motioned Lieutenant Selby to the copilot seat and the sergeant to his crew chief's location. Then over his mic, he said, "When your copilot straps in, we are ready for liftoff, sir!"

Selby climbed into the right seat of the cockpit and realized his commanding officer was the pilot. When Selby plugged in his headset, Hayden told him, "I flew up solo with the medic. Five people are all we can hold with a stretcher. Let's get outa' here!"

The rescue bird lifted off, and the other two Venom's disengaged the enemy to join the skipper's aircraft in a trail position. Only an hour and fifteen minutes had elapsed since Ty's helicopter had gone down.

A few minutes into the flight, with Ty's team on board, the medic called the commanding officer over the intercom. "Skipper, we have a problem back here. Major Harrell is unconscious and has lost a lot of blood. He also has a broken back. The back isn't what is going to kill him, though. Is it possible for us to divert to the hospital in Kadun?"

"Affirmative," said Hayden. "I put on extra fuel pods in case we might have to do that." Lieutenant Selby radioed the other two helicopters and told them what they were doing. The lieutenant also radioed ahead to Kadun, letting the military hospital know they were coming.

"Copy and good luck!" said O'Brien. The medevac chopper then turned north for Kadun.

17 Disconnected

West Virginia: Tuesday, 5:00 PM
Kadun: Wednesday, 4:00 AM

Seeney dialed the dealership, and the call went to an after-hours voicemail system. She left a message with no expectation of receiving a return call that evening. Jack's business was the only place her phone could be, but if found there, Seeney doubted her ex-husband would go out of his way to return it. So, she resolved to go by the business the following morning.

She used the landline to dial her cell phone number, on the off chance someone who had found her phone might answer, but the call went to the cell's voicemail system. She sipped her wine, idly wondering how the phone might have fallen from her purse at the agency in the few minutes she had been with the car salesman.

Seeney was only beginning to speculate on whether Stiles might have taken the phone. She thought about this as she booted up the computer on her desk. When Seeney got to the screen to check emails, a notification informed her the password entered for the account was incorrect. Thinking she had typed a wrong letter by accident, Seeney reentered the password. Her computer again denied access.

Strange, she thought, and she almost clicked on the *forgot password* button but stopped. Seeney knew this would necessitate creating a new password, and she didn't want to do that yet. Having no absolute necessity to check emails this evening, she decided to wait until the following morning to address her Satsun email account and her lost cell phone.

Seeney had difficulty sleeping because something about the phone and her Satsun account problems gnawed at her. At a little after six o'clock, she got out of bed, made coffee, and went back to her computer.

She received the same response as the evening before when she tried to access her email account, and after a couple of tries, she clicked on the *forgot password* button. A new screen requested verification of Seeney's Satsun security information. She entered the pertinent data, but when she answered the first security question, her mother's maiden name, the screen indicated her answer was incorrect.

Seeney reentered the name, Bell, being careful to capitalize the "B." Once again, the answer was wrong. Finally, she opted to select a different security question: her favorite team's mascot. When Seeney typed in "Mustangs," the mascot for Tartan Springs High School, the screen again indicated an incorrect answer. Until she could verify her identification, the page told her she wouldn't receive a new password.

Crazy! She was beginning to fear someone had hacked her account. She wrote down the number for technical support and called it from her landline. After several rings, she received an automated response giving her options. She picked the one for a "live person" to assist.

After a short delay, she listened to another digital message apprising callers that Satsun technical service was available seven days per week from eight in the morning to six in the evening, Pacific Coast Time. That meant she would have to wait almost three hours to speak to someone about her problem. The car dealership didn't open for another hour, so Seeney decided to shower and dress. The day hadn't started well, but she committed to resolving her cell phone and Satsun issues that morning. So, at nine o'clock, Seeney dialed Jack Stiles Chevrolet.

The receptionist told Stiles his ex-wife was on the phone, and he picked up the receiver. "This is Jack Stiles," he said, answering as if he didn't know who was calling.

"Yes, Jack. This is Seeney. Did you happen to find my cell phone in your office after I left? It wasn't in my purse when I got home."

"Phone? No. Where might you have left it?"

"I wouldn't have *left it* anywhere, but I thought it might have fallen from my purse while I was in your office yesterday."

"Hold on." Jack held the receiver away from his ear for a few moments, pretending to look around his desk. "I checked around the chairs and under the desk but found no phone. So, where else did you use it?"

"No place before I came there. It was in my purse when I left the house."

"And you looked in your car?"

"Of course, I checked the car," said Seeney in an annoyed tone. "Do you think I look for reasons to call you?"

"Listen, Seeney," spat back Jack. "Don't give me attitude! I'm not the one who lost the phone. You did. I'm just trying to help."

"Fine. Thanks." She hung up.

Fear now grew inside her. Perhaps the whole car warranty initiative was a ploy orchestrated by Jack to steal her phone. That didn't make sense to her, though, because she couldn't imagine what Jack could accomplish by having her cell phone.

She dialed the number for her carrier, Virtel. After explaining to the customer service representative that she had lost her phone, the Virtel employee told Seeney, other than the necessity of purchasing a new phone, Seeney need not worry. The Virtel "Cloud" held all the contacts, pictures, apps, and personal information in her lost device. Seeney could reload all this back into a new phone at the local Virtel sales center in Compton. Seeney thanked the representative and planned on driving to Compton later in the morning.

At the stroke of eleven o'clock or eight in the morning on the west coast, Seeney called the customer service center for Satsun. What should have been an easy process to reset Seeney's Satsun account with a new password was not easy since Seeney now knew none of the answers to any of her security questions. Further complicating the issue, Seeney had no cell phone to receive a unique authorization code from Satsun to confirm her identity as the valid owner of the Virtel email account.

"I lost my cell phone yesterday at about the same time I found I no longer had access to my Satsun account," said an exasperated Seeney.

"Couldn't you just send the authorization code to my computer?"

The representative, Julia, waited a few seconds to reply, perhaps trying to think of a delicate way to answer without implying Seeney was stupid. "Ma'am, I know you're upset, but sending the code to your computer will not help you. Your Satsun account isn't available for you to access."

"Oh, God! Of course. I'm just not thinking. What should I do?"

"Ma'am, don't be concerned. We'll figure this out," said Julia. "From what you told me, it seems possible the loss of your phone and the changes in your Satsun account may be related. I'm looking at your record now, and someone made the password and security question changes last evening. When did you say you lost your phone?"

"Oh, no," said Seeney, now piecing the puzzle together herself. "It was yesterday in the late afternoon."

"Was your phone protected with the same password you use for your Satsun account?"

Seeney hesitated because the answer to that question embarrassed her. "No, Julia. I didn't require a password for my phone."

"Oh, dear. That's too bad because that means anybody could access the information in your cell."

"I realize, but I figured nobody but me would ever have my cell phone. I was wrong. What can I do now?"

"Well, our company will treat this as a malicious hacking situation. We'll lock out your account so no additional changes can occur. We'll also prevent further messages from the account. People who try to email you will receive a notice that your account is out of service for a short time."

"But," said Seeney, "I need the Satsun account for my business."

"We should be able to have it back up fairly quickly after our fraud department does some research. Someone from that office will contact you in the next two hours. Do you believe you'll purchase a new cell phone soon?"

"Yes. I'll be leaving in a few minutes for the closest Virtel office. If I miss the call from your fraud department while I'm gone, is there a number to get back to Satsun directly?"

Julia gave Seeney a number, and Seeney prepared to leave for the Virtel store in Compton. But, before she left, she made another call to the Jack Stiles Chevrolet dealership. "Jack Stiles speaking."

"This is your ex-wife again. I'm on my way to Virtel to purchase another cell phone, and I'm sure I know what happened to the one I called about this morning. If, or when, I confirm what I think I'm going to discover about my missing phone, I'm going to take out a full-page ad in the Colgan Register to inform everyone in this county why I divorced you!"

"What? What are you talking about?" sputtered Jack. "I don't have a clue what happened to your damn phone, and if you even think about breaching our legal agreement, I'll sue you for your last penny!"

"That's fine, Jack. You do that. Because if I find out you're the one who stole my cell phone and screwed with my internet account, you violated the legal agreement. If that's the case, I'll make sure nobody in this town would want a car from you—if you were giving them away—for fear they might catch a disease!" Then Seeney hung up.

Stiles held the receiver of the phone in his hand for several seconds. Then he replaced it, picked it up again, and dialed the number for the mayor of Tartan Springs.

Kadun

West Virginia: Wednesday, 10:00 AM
Kadun: Wednesday, 7:00 PM

Medics rushed to assist when Lieutenant Colonel Hayden landed on the helicopter pad at the Saould Dhan Military Hospital in Kadun. With Sergeant Gunn's and the Marine corpsman's help, they transported the stretcher holding Major Harrell inside. The medical attendants took Harrell to a cubicle in the emergency room, and his fellow Marines waited outside.

The hospital was a modern-looking facility with four hundred beds, and many employed there had received their medical training in the United States. The services provided by the hospital were extensive and, in at least one area, controversial. The facility provided critical care to Becktistan National military soldiers and their allies, including United States service members, but the hospital also dedicated two floors for the urgent care of Tilorstan fighters.

As Lieutenant Colonel Hayden looked around, he knew it possible injured members of the group responsible for his executive officer's injuries might be receiving treatment in the same facility. Within thirty minutes, a young doctor who spoke excellent English visited Hayden and his men in the waiting area.

"Good afternoon, sir. I am Doctor Faould, and I went to your University of Virginia. Your friend is still unconscious, but for the moment, his condition is stable."

"Thank you, Doctor," said Hayden. "Can you tell us the extent of his injuries and a prognosis?"

"Yes, sir," replied the polite physician. "I can tell you his injuries, but I cannot yet speculate on a prognosis. The Major sustained a compression fracture to his spine. We stabilized his more life-threatening conditions, but we have not conducted an MRI. He lost a substantial amount of blood, which is what caused the unconsciousness. We're replacing that now. His heart rate was low when he arrived but is improving. The increasing pulse rate is a positive sign, but it's too early to tell if he'll be okay. He lost nearly forty percent of his total blood supply, and this is a level that is often fatal. We're doing what we can, but now his body must assist. We'll know more in a few hours."

"Okay," said Hayden. "Thank you. I'm the commanding officer for the squadron to which Major Harrell is attached. He is, in fact, my executive officer, and he's also my friend. So, I provided my contact information to staff at the front desk and will count on you to keep us apprised of Major Harrell's condition. My aircraft has enough fuel to fly back to my base, so unless there is a reason for me to stay, I'll take my group and leave."

"Thank you, sir. You can do nothing more here. May I ask if one of these gentlemen with you dressed your friend's leg wound in the field?"

Lieutenant Selby said, "That was me, Doctor. Did I make a mistake?"

"No, Lieutenant. You did an excellent job using the limited supplies at your disposal, but the wound severed the femoral artery. Without immediate attention, this type of injury can be fatal due to rapid blood loss. The gauze you placed against the open wound, wrapped tightly with tape, is what kept him alive long enough to get here."

"Thank you, Doctor. I'm glad I paid attention during the first aid course in basic training. I still don't think I want your job, though".

"Well," said the doctor, smiling, "I don't want yours either."

The Marines filed out of the waiting area and boarded their helicopter. Major Ty Harrell continued to lie still in the emergency room, unconscious.

Tartan Springs

West Virginia: Wednesday, 11:30 AM
Kadun: Wednesday, 8:30 PM

"Okay, Foster!" yelled Stiles through the phone. "It isn't even noon, and Seeney has figured out what happened to her cell phone! I just spoke with her, and she's threatening all kinds of stuff. Trouble from Seeney is exactly what I didn't want to happen."

"Calm down, Stiles! Calm down!" said Foster. "I told you it wouldn't take her long to figure out what happened, but so what? You should be glad she thinks you're involved in this somehow. What the hell can she do to you now? She can't sue you because she can't prove a thing, and she's already taken most of your money. So, what's your problem?"

Stiles had no intention of divulging to Foster what else Seeney knew about him. "As I told you before, Seeney Tyson is a dangerous bitch. I can't imagine what she might be able to do, but she scares the shit out of me. For one thing, my fingerprints are all over that phone."

"In about twenty minutes, the phone will be at the bottom of the Siler River. Nobody is going to ever find it, much less any fingerprints on it. I deleted the messages she received from two of her clients since we got the phone. I also trashed the email from Harrell to Seeney requesting her to contact him. I can't do much more with the account, so I'm going to ditch the phone. No matter what she might suspect, she can't prove anything. Just don't go weak and start talking."

"Okay. You might be right. I guess she can't prove what we did. You make sure you keep your mouth shut, too. You had your fun. Now leave it there."

"I'm not an idiot, Jack. It may not be much, but maybe Siena Tyson learned a little lesson. See you around."

Jack hoped this escapade was over because the petty revenge on Seeney didn't justify the stress. However, his bigger problem was to believe Foster when the mayor assured him he wasn't an idiot. The mayor *was* actually an idiot.

Compton

West Virginia: Wednesday, 12:15 PM
Kadun: Wednesday, 9:15 PM

Seeney arrived at the Virtel retail store in Compton just after noon, and as she expected, the place was busy. She waited patiently for one of the service counters to become free and introduced herself to the attractive young lady behind the first one that did.

After explaining her problem to the customer representative, Sylvia, Seeney took her driver's license from her wallet. She also placed her last two Virtel bills on the counter. Sylvia looked at Seeney's driver's license and copied the two invoices' account numbers. Next, the representative entered information on her computer and asked Seeney when she discovered her phone was missing.

"Yesterday at about four-thirty," said Seeney, "and I'm almost certain I can name who took it if that helps any."

"No, ma'am," said Sylvia. "We have no legal standing there. You may wish to pursue that on your own, but our only concern is to protect your account with us and, to the extent we can, protect the information stored in your device's memory. In addition, our company utilizes an application that can determine the location of a lost phone if the phone is still on. Would you like me to see if I can find where your old device is?"

"Wonderful! I had no idea that was possible."

After entering some information on the computer in front of her, Sylvia said, "Your phone is still active and located in Tartan Springs."

"No surprise. Let me guess. Is the address three hundred Spartan Way? That's the location for Stiles Chevrolet."

"No, ma'am. It is at one hundred Main Street. Are you familiar with this address?"

"Yes," said Seeney. "I am. Our Municipal Building in Tartan Springs is there."

"Well, your phone is too. Do you have a contact to call who might retrieve the phone? Getting your old cell back would preclude the necessity of purchasing a new one."

"I know many people there, but the person who most likely has my phone won't want to return it. So, I'm not sure what I should do now."

"Well," said Sylvia, "if you don't believe someone will return your phone, we can freeze your account. This will allow nobody to access the account and prevent further communications from it. We can also set you up with a new account and a new phone."

"Okay. Can we do both? Will you be able to transfer the contents and information from my old phone to a new one?"

"Yes. You have quite a bit of information to transfer, so that will take a little while, but we can do that."

"Will I need a new number?"

"No. Your previous number will transfer to the account we create today."

"Can you tell me the changes to my settings since four-thirty in the afternoon yesterday?"

"Yes, ma'am." She typed additional information into her computer, and after a short pause, said, "It appears that around eight o'clock last evening, some of your settings changed. Only someone who knows your password and the answers to at least two of your five security questions would be allowed to make these changes. When this information is changed, a text message and an email are automatically sent to your account, notifying you of the changes. Do you remember receiving this email?"

"No, because the person who stole my phone also changed the password to my Satsun account. Satsun locked my email account last night as a result."

"Oh, my. This sounds like someone you must have trusted at some time."

"Yes. An ex-husband. I didn't change the passwords on my accounts after the divorce."

"I'm sorry, but you aren't the first to make this mistake. Hang on—let me see what I can do. Do you want to pick out a new phone while I'm checking? I can give you a customer number that will allow you to get back to me with little or no wait once you're ready."

"That would be great," said Seeney. "Thank you."

After Seeney found a model she liked, she went back to the line in front of Sylvia's counter. Sylvia motioned her forward, and Seeney told her the model of the phone she picked out.

"Okay," said Sylvia. "This is an excellent selection, and, with your account discount, the phone will cost you four hundred sixty-five dollars. Do you want us to add that to your next invoice, or would you prefer to pay for the new device now?"

"I'll pay now." Seeney retrieved a credit card from her wallet. "I want new selections for passwords and security questions. Can you take care of that?"

"Yes, ma'am. We can do those things right here. Let me get a new phone from the back, and we can start. I'll run your credit card to complete the transaction. You'll also receive an automatic three-year warranty as a part of the transaction."

"Thank you."

Sylvia completed the transaction and recorded Seeney's new settings. She then told Seeney it would take at least forty-five minutes to transfer her last cell phone contents to the new one. "Would you like to wait?"

"No. Can I come back in an hour or so?"

"No problem. Your new phone should be ready by then."

Seeney thanked Sylvia, then asked if she could access a phone to make a personal call. The representative offered Seeney her own cell phone, and Seeney dialed the number for Tom Burns. Her friend answered on the second ring. "Hey, Seeney. What a nice surprise on a Wednesday afternoon. Where are you?"

"Well, Tom, I'm right down the street at the Virtel store. I'm sorry I didn't warn you I was coming, but can I buy you lunch?"

"I'm at lunch now with some old folks at the Greenway Assisted Living Center on Route Twelve. I can meet you when I finish here. What's going on?"

"Oh, nothing," she said, then thought better of the answer. "Sorry, Tom. Something is going on, and I think I need you. Where can we meet?"

Tom agreed to meet Seeney at his church office at two o'clock after picking up her new phone. She went to a TGIFriday's restaurant next door to the Virtel store for lunch by herself. After eating, she returned to the Virtel store, and Sylvia waved her over to her counter.

"I uploaded your apps, your photos, and your saved messages to the new phone," said Sylvia. "You'll be able to link your contacts to your Virtel account when you have your Satsun email account back online. You only need to create a password for your phone now. This iPhone supports fingerprint recognition, which is what I suggest you use to open it. You won't need other passwords if you choose this method."

"Sounds good. Thank you, Sylvia. Am I able to see messages sent from my old phone when it was out of my control?"

"Yes, ma'am. You can unless you or someone else purposely deleted them."

"Mmm, that might be an issue, then. Let's check." Seeney executed the procedure for password protecting her new phone with her forefinger print with Sylvia's assistance, then opened her screens. She went to her messages, but the folder was empty. "Is there like a trash bin for deleted text messages?"

"No. We have no feature like that in Virtel accounts. Once someone deletes a message, we don't keep it anywhere else in the system."

"Okay. Thank you, Sylvia. You were most helpful. I'll send a note to Virtel about what an outstanding representative you are."

"Thank you, ma'am. I appreciate that!"

When she reached her car, Seeney called the direct line for Satsun support. Her representative from earlier, Julia, answered. "Hi, Julia. This is Siena Tyson. Your fraud department might have already called me, but I haven't been home. However, I do own a cell phone now that you could send an authorization code to."

"Hi, Ms. Tyson," said Julia. "According to the notes for your case file, Jay Jennings from our Fraud Division left you a message on your home phone about thirty minutes ago. I can transfer this call to him or send a new authorization code to your phone. Using the code might be the quickest way to fix your account."

"Okay, let's do that. I'll wait." Within fifteen seconds, Seeney's new phone lit up with a notification from Satsun. "It worked! Yea. The code is 726543."

"Got it," said Julia. "You'll be able to access your email account as soon as you create a new password. If you aren't at your computer, you can do this through the Internet Explorer option on your phone."

"Thank you. Can I also do this from a different computer?"

"Yes. Our Fraud Department may still want to talk to you, but you can reach them after you recover your email account."

"I certainly will, Julia. Thank you so much."

It was almost two o'clock, so Seeney decided to make the changes to her Satsun account at Pastor Tom's office rather than through her phone. Burns was waiting for her when she arrived at the Lutheran Church. Seeney relayed the traumatic events of the last day, and Tom listened without comment. When she finished, Tom asked, "Do you think you need to speak to Buster again?"

"Yes, I do, but first, I need to see my email account and check what those bastards Stiles and Foster might have done."

Tom invited Seeney to bring her chair to his side of the desk, and he booted his computer to life. After accessing the Satsun website and entering the authorization code provided, Seeney completed changing her password. This time, she used: sH91616!.

"Seeney," said Tom, "considering what you've just been through, would you like to reenter a password while I'm not watching?"

"Next to Ty, you're my closest friend. I'd trust you with my life, and besides, I doubt that password is one you're going to be able to remember, anyway."

"You're correct on part of that. You *can* trust me with your life, but I'm sure I'll be able to remember that password."

"Really? Why?"

"Because," said Tom, "you used the initials you'll have one day, with the more important one in your opinion, H, capitalized—and the anniversary of the date you reconnected with Ty. The exclamation point at the end is for emphasis."

Seeney stared at Tom in amazement. "You, Mr. Burns, are downright scary. Do you think those initials are a little presumptuous?"

"No, Seeney. You're engaged, so I think the initials are inevitable. Considering the issues with this phone and the computer mess over the last day, the letters could also stand for Shit Happens, though."

Seeney laughed for the first time in almost twenty-four hours. "Let's check out the damage."

Everything seemed to be working in her account, and, at first glance, nothing appeared out of the ordinary. Seeney noticed several solicitations scattered among her email messages, along with some other generic notes from clients. "See anything unusual?" asked Burns.

"Not really. The only thing a little strange is a message that isn't here."

"What one is that?"

"Ty almost always sends me a short email every day. I send him one as well, usually at the end of the day. I couldn't last night because of being locked out."

"Maybe he's on a mission or something," said Burns.

"Possibly, but he didn't mention anything coming up two days ago when we talked. So, here's the last email from him," Seeney said, pointing to one of the messages. "This came early yesterday, and Ty says nothing about any looming operations that would take him away from his base overnight."

"Can I check something?" asked Tom.

"Sure." Seeney moved her chair over to allow Burns better access to the computer.

"Look at this," said Tom. "This is the recycle bin, and it keeps deleted messages for up to thirty days. I see two recent messages *to* you in the folder—and several *from* you sent in the past twelve hours."

Seeney saw the incoming message from Ty and clicked on it. Ty had only requested she call him as soon as possible, which surprised her. When she clicked on the sent message, purportedly delivered by her to Ty, she realized why Ty's note had been so short—and urgent. She gasped, "Oh, my God, Tom! Look!"

Tom read the *Dear John* letter. "Those sons of bitches!"

"I need to call Ty right away."

"What time is it over there?"

"About two o'clock this morning, but it doesn't matter." Seeney punched in the number but had no way of knowing that Ty's cell phone was on the desk in his combat office—or that he was at this moment lying in a hospital bed in Kadun, unconscious.

Ty, of course, didn't answer, so Seeney left a lengthy message on his voicemail. She also sent him a text and an email explaining what had happened. She ended each communication, "Ty, I love you more than anything in this world. Please call me as soon as you can!"

As Seeney finished these messages, Tom surveyed the other recent messages in the recycle bin. "Looks like you, or someone, sent three different emails to three of your business accounts telling them you were dumping them. One of the incoming messages to your account was from one of those businesses."

Seeney looked at the emails Tom found. "Jack Stiles would have no idea who my clients are, except for the Ford dealership. So, Foster had to have helped with this part of the scam. He's involved with the Chamber of Commerce activities, and I'm a member of one of the Chamber's sub-organizations. That's how Foster found out about the BusinessRate reviews. One of my clients posted a review she had written for me to my Facebook account, and Foster saw it."

"I figured you would have blocked Foster from your Facebook account by now."

"I did, Tom, long ago. The Small Business Alliance Initiative has a Facebook page, though, and I allowed that organization as a *friend* in my personal Facebook account. The mayor is also a member of the SBAI."

"I see. That makes sense. So, he can probably figure out some of your business clients through Facebook posts?"

"Yes."

"Clever," said Tom. "Not clever enough to keep you from figuring out who was behind the scam, but maybe enough to avoid prosecution for criminal activity. Since Foster and Stiles used your phone to send those messages, I'm not sure you'll be able to prove the fraud—unless they admit to it."

"Those bastards! They most likely *want* me to know who did this. Foster does, for sure. Do you really believe there is no legal case?"

"I'm not an attorney, Seeney. Ask Buster that. First, though, you should reach out to the clients who think you dropped them."

"Right." She made the calls from Burns' desk, and all three customers were understanding. They each questioned who Seeney suspected of the fraud, but she declined to speculate. She finished these conversations and called Buster Aldrich. When the receptionist said the attorney couldn't take Seeney's call right away, Seeney instructed the woman to ask him to return the call to Tom Burn's office.

As she waited with Burns, she apologized for occupying so much of the pastor's day. "This isn't a problem," said Tom. "Helping people is one of the things I'm supposed to be doing in this occupation."

Aldrich returned the call a few minutes later, and Seeney spoke with him for almost a half-hour. She reviewed the conversation with Tom after she hung up. "Aldrich agrees with you. Stiles and Foster most likely committed fraud, as well as a theft of my phone, but no hard evidence exists. Buster said if I did anything in reaction, such as publicly sharing the reasons for my divorce, Stiles could sue me for damages, based on the agreement we both signed last year. Doesn't seem right, does it?"

"It isn't right," said Tom, thinking. "Other options, besides legal ones, may become available, though."

"What do you mean? You aren't suggesting illegal options, are you?"

Tom laughed. "Of course not, Seeney. Ethical alternatives may exist, which could even be better than legal ones. Todd Foster isn't going to be able to avoid bragging to someone. His ego is just too big. When the right people find out what he's done, it could be damaging for Foster—and even worse for Stiles."

Seeney didn't pursue her friend's mysterious logic, but she knew him well enough to be certain Burns had a plan evolving. For now, she had more important things to do than try to catch a couple of petty criminals. Her current priority was to communicate with Ty Harrell.

Back home and now equipped with a cell phone and an active email account, Seeney checked for new messages on both. Seeing none, she called Ty's parents in Florida. The call went to voicemail, and Seeney left a message for either Mavy or Orville to call her back.

It was five o'clock in West Virginia, which meant it was around two in the morning in Bektistan. Ty had sent no other messages to her since the previous evening—which she didn't see until a few hours ago. He usually emailed at the end of his duty day in Bektistan, which was about nine in the morning in West Virginia. However, Seeney saw no messages from him today. He also had not responded to the email Seeney sent him after Satsun reactivated her account that afternoon.

Perhaps he had a mission that took him from his base overnight, but there had been none of those types of operations to date on the deployment. Considering the *Dear John* letter Ty received, supposedly from her, Seeney was concerned. She tried to keep herself from panicking.

From her computer, she found the number for Marine Headquarters, Quantico. The military provides an excellent service for keeping relatives apprised of deployed soldiers and a live person connected promptly. Seeney told the young lady Ty's full name and rank, and the soldier, Corporal Jensen, asked Seeney to hold the line for a moment.

"Okay, ma'am," said Jensen. "Major Harrell's information is here. He's attached to HML-222 as the squadron's executive officer and has listed next of kin as Mavis and Orville Harrell, who reside in Florida. Are you Mrs. Harrell?"

"No, ma'am. I'm Siena Tyson, Major Harrell's fiancé."

"Oh, I see. My problem, Ms. Tyson, is I'm not allowed to provide any information relative to Major Harrell except to his listed next of kin."

"But I'm going to be his wife!"

"I understand, ma'am, and if you *were* his wife, I would be able to give you the same information as Major Harrell's parents. But I can't give that to non-family members. Is it possible for you to reach Major Harrell's parents?"

"Yes, ma'am," said Seeney. "I can, and I have left a message for them. I appreciate your help, and I'm sorry you aren't able to assist me." Seeney hung up and started to regret the decision she made not to marry before Ty's deployment. She tried the Harrells' phone again in Florida and left another message.

After completing these calls, she looked at her watch. It was almost five o'clock, and she wondered if she could still catch Mayor Foster at the Municipal Building. After dialing the number, the mayor came on the line, surprising her.

"Good afternoon, Ms. Tyson. Been a while since we talked. What's the occasion?"

"Don't be cute. You know why I'm calling. You and Stiles are in a lot of trouble," she said.

"What are you talking about?"

"Are you aware Virtel has an application that can track where a lost cell phone in their system is?"

"No," said the mayor. "What does that have to do with me?"

"You and Jack Stiles somehow stole my phone and used it to hack into my Satsun email account. You sent several of my clients' fraudulent messages, among other things."

"You're crazy, Seeney! And if you try to slander either Jack or me with this bullshit, I'll sue you right out of this community. I can promise you no phone of yours is on this property, and I don't care what Virtel told you."

"I'm certain it is no longer at your office, Todd. You probably disposed of it in the landfill by now. But, while I may not be able to do anything legally, I'm not going to forget this. You're a sorry excuse for a human and in similar company with Jack Stiles. Good luck—because you're going to need it!" Then, she hung up.

Before he left his office, Foster called Stiles. "Hey, Jack, your ex-wife called me."

"She's figured it out, hasn't she?" asked Stiles.

"Of course! I told you it wouldn't take her that long—and I also told you there would be nothing Seeney could do about it. She can't prove anything, but she *did* tell me something I didn't know."

"What's that?"

"Virtel can track the location of a lost phone."

"Shit! That means they could track her Seeney's cell phone from my desk to your office."

"Right—and so what? A custodian could also pick the phone off the floor in your place and drop it in a trash can over here. Nobody could prove any different. The phone is at the bottom of the river now, where nobody will ever find it. Seeney admitted to me, herself, she has no legal recourse. So, just keep your mouth shut. I warned her I would sue her if she tried to slander either of us. I doubt she's going to fool with us anymore."

The two men hung up with viewpoints at different extremes. Jack Stiles had the good sense to be worried; Todd Foster had the poor judgment to feel victorious.

Bektistan

West Virginia: Wednesday, 10:00 PM
Kadun: Thursday, 7:00 AM

Lieutenant Colonel Hayden sat down behind his desk in the morning after successfully delivering his executive officer to the hospital in Kadun, and his administration officer, Captain Eric Kilby, knocked on his door. "What's up, Eric?"

"Just a little paperwork snafu," said the captain. "Lieutenant Selby filed the Combat Action Report from yesterday, and Captain Lincoln finished the Aircraft Casualty Report on aircraft #455 this morning. We just received a message from headquarters that the two reports don't correspond. Colonel Simpkins advised us to delay notifications to next of kin until we resolve the inconsistency."

"So, what's the issue? We need to make Major Harrell's parents aware of Ty's condition."

"Yes, sir. I understand. The problem is the manifest for yesterday's flight involving #455, the chopper we lost, still listed Captain Callahan as the pilot in command. Our Personnel Casualty Report filed with the Combat Action Report lists Major Harrell as the pilot in command and as the casualty."

"Shit! I forgot about that! We never changed the manifest after Major Harrell jumped into 455 for Callahan. I'll call Simpkins."

Hayden called his superior at Marine Headquarters and explained what happened; his boss instructed Hayden how to correct the paperwork. It didn't present a significant or even an unusual problem, but everything needed to be accurate before notifying the next of kin. Colonel Simpkins reiterated to Hayden that relaying erroneous information could exacerbate the stress for the loved ones of service members stationed overseas in combat situations.

Hayden hung up the phone and called Captain Kilby. After explaining to Kilby the procedure to correct the paperwork error, the commanding officer instructed his administrative officer to make no notifications until proper clearances from headquarters. "I doubt that Major Harrell's parents would call us here, but if they do, refer them to the Casualty Section of Marine Headquarters, Quantico. That will be their best way to track their son's medical condition and recovery."

"Roger," replied Kilby.

Kadun

While Lieutenant Colonel Hayden was resolving the paperwork issue, Major Harrell's body was doing its best to recover from the problems created for it by the previous day's combat activities. Doctor Faould checked on Ty regularly, and the Marine regained consciousness sporadically during the evening. Ty's heart rate improved, and Faould hoped Harrell could be moved from the emergency room sometime soon. The doctor wanted to assess the extent of the injuries to Ty's back through an MRI, but not before the injured Marine was fully conscious.

By mid-morning, Ty's eyes fluttered open more frequently, and a nurse called Doctor Faould to visit Ty's bed. "Can you hear me, sir?" asked the gentle doctor to his patient.

Ty opened his eyes partway. "Yes. I can. Where am I?"

"You are in the Daould Khan Military Hospital in Kadun. Your friends brought you here last evening. You lost a lot of blood from a leg wound, and your back is injured. Do you feel pain?"

"Yes, Doctor, I do," said Ty, "but not in the leg."

"That is good, sir. I would be more concerned if your body were numb. I believe crushed vertebrae may be close to or touching the nerves in your spinal cord. This contact would cause pain. We stitched and bandaged your injured thigh."

"I'm also tired and a little dizzy, Doctor. Are my friends still here?"

"No, sir. They returned to your base, but I promised I would update them on your condition."

"Thank you, Doctor. They were courageous yesterday."

"If I can keep you from sleeping for a while, I would like to perform an MRI to diagnose the injuries to your back. I would prefer not to administer additional medication for your pain until after that procedure. How significant is the pain?"

"About a seven on a scale of ten," said Ty, "but I can stand it if I need to. How long will the MRI take?"

"Maybe fifteen minutes," said Doctor Faould.

Later, when a nurse rolled the gurney holding Major Harrell back from the MRI tunnel, Doctor Faould thanked him for being patient about the pain. "I'll give you a shot which should reduce your discomfort, sir. The medicine will also make you sleepy. I'll learn more about your back later today."

Ty next awoke several hours later, no longer in the emergency room. Instead, a plastic curtain surrounded his bed, and he could see an array of monitoring devices attached to various tubes sticking from his body. He felt groggy but cognizant and glanced around for close-by medical personnel.

A nurse attended one of the bags suspended over his bed, and he asked, "Can you tell me where I am?" The nurse politely curtsied and held up a finger, speaking in a language he couldn't understand. Then, she disappeared, returning in a few minutes with a young doctor by her side.

"Good afternoon, sir," said the doctor.

"Good afternoon, Doctor. I seem to remember you, but my mind is a bit foggy. We have met before, right?"

"Yes, sir. This morning. You were awake briefly, and we spoke. After completing an MRI examination, I administered medicine for your pain," said the doctor. "This medicine would make you groggy and confused."

"Then, you may have told me where I am, but I don't remember. I'm sorry."

"That is quite alright, sir, and perfectly understandable in your condition. I am Doctor Benzi Faould, and you are in the Daould Khan Military Hospital in Kadun. Your friends brought you here almost twenty-four hours ago, unconscious and near death from a loss of blood due to a wound to your leg. You also suffered compressed and broken vertebrae. We must operate on those soon to prevent further damage to your spinal cord."

"Thank you, Doctor. I don't remember much since hearing helicopter units from my squadron coming to rescue me yesterday."

"Yes, sir. Your situation was critical when you arrived, but the immediate danger from blood loss has almost passed. Your heart rate is close to normal, and your body is now regenerating blood on its own."

"I understand," said Ty. "Will I be disabled from my back injury? Will I recover?"

"We should operate soon to preclude the broken vertebrae from impacting your spinal cord. Successful removal of the fragments and repair of the compression fractures should ensure that you have no significant long-term effects from the injury. You will, however, require a rather lengthy rehabilitation."

"Thank you, Doctor. I assume the friends who brought me here are back at the base?"

"Yes, sir, but I'm in touch with them," said the doctor.

"What about my parents and my fiancé? Are they aware of my location?"

"I cannot say because only your military can release such information. However, I'll ask your commanding officer when I next talk to him."

"Thank you. When do you think you'll operate?"

"With your military's permission, this evening, sir."

"Is there a reason someone would withhold permission?"

"In a case such as this one, I expect your superiors to grant permission. Sometimes, your military prefers that the larger hospital in Randstuhl, Germany, manage unusual injuries to their personnel. However, the trip to Germany would be a long and uncomfortable flight for you, sir, so I think you would be better off if we operated here."

"Okay, thank you, doctor. I appreciate the information. Your English is excellent. Are you from here?"

"Yes, sir, but I graduated from your University of Virginia. Go Wahoos!" the doctor said, smiling.

Ty fell back into a deep sleep after Doctor Faould left, and the physician called Lieutenant Colonel Hayden to update the commanding officer on Major Harrell's condition. When Faould asked about the notification to Major Harrell's parents and fiancé, Hayden told him about the administrative issue delaying those. He hoped Major Harrell would be well enough soon to be able to talk to his family himself. The commanding officer confirmed he would contact the necessary department in his chain of command for the operation's authorization.

West Virginia

West Virginia: Wednesday, 10:00 PM
Kadun: Thursday, 7:00 AM

It was ten in the evening when Mavis Harrell called Seeney back. She apologized, but the Harrells dined out with friends and had just gotten back to their condo. When Seeney related to Mavy what had happened and her concern for Ty, Mavis said, "Don't worry, Seeney. I'm sure he's okay, but I'll call the number you provided for Quantico tonight. I doubt they'll answer, but if I find out anything, I'll call you back."

Fifteen minutes later, Seeney's cell phone rang. It was Mavis. "Listen, Dear, that number you gave me is great. They take calls 24 hours per day, seven days a week. That part is good. What they told me isn't so good."

"Oh, no! Oh, no!" cried Seeney.

"Hold on, Seeney," said Mavis. "I didn't mean to alarm you. The phone call was just a little strange. The lady who answered confirmed all Ty's personal information then insisted on calling me back on my cell. She did this to make sure it was actually me who was calling about Ty's medical status. When she called back, satisfied I was Ty's mother, she told me Ty's condition was classified. She said this appeared to be a temporary situation and that I should call back tomorrow."

"What does that mean, Mavy?"

"I don't know, but we'll find out tomorrow. I'll call you when I have more information."

"Thanks, Mavy."

Laying down on her bed at the end of the most emotional day in her young life, Seeney cried. She felt alone, lost, sad, and guilty, without the power to fix any of those things. Her poor selection in past partners had now perhaps jeopardized her hopes for attaining a future one she coveted. By naïvely allowing the theft of a cell phone foolishly unprotected with a password, she facilitated a scam that could devastate two lives.

Her irrational refusal to marry Ty before the overseas deployment now complicated her ability to learn either his location or condition. Wallowing in her self-recriminations and pity, Seeney wondered how one person could make so many wrong turns. At the depth of her despair, she felt hopeless and defeated.

Then, her new cell phone rang. Hoping the call was from Ty's parents with more news about Ty, she grabbed the device, pulled it from the charger connection, and knocked over a bedside lamp. The screen showed the caller was Pastor Tom Burns.

"Hey, Tom."

"Hi, Seeney. Sorry to call so late, but I wondered if you heard anything more about Ty?"

"No," said Seeney. Then, she began crying softly into the phone.

"Seeney, what's going on? Are you alright?" Seeney recovered and provided her friend a summary of her thoughts of the past hour. She ended the melancholy narrative with another audible sob.

"Are you done now?" asked Tom.

"What do you mean?"

"I mean, I hope all this whiny, self-centered, pessimistic despair is now out of your system? I'm sympathetic, but this isn't like you, and I don't think you have time for it now."

Somewhat stunned by her friend's criticism, Seeney said sarcastically, "Gee, Tom. Thanks for your gentle compassion. I'm not sure I needed so much sympathy tonight."

"Quit the BS, Seeney! You're one of the strongest women I know, and you never give in or give up. A long time ago, back when I was on the missionary trip to South America, Pastor Sinn told me something I never forgot. He said, 'When you find yourself in a hole, the first thing you should do is quit digging.' It sounds to me like you're at the bottom of your hole. You should start looking up to see how to get out of it now versus looking down to see how much deeper you can make it." Seeney didn't answer for a long time, and Tom asked, "Are you still there, Seeney?"

"Yes. I am—and thank you. You're right. I spent the last hour feeling sorry for myself. That isn't going to help the situation, so do you have any suggestions?"

"Yes," said Tom. "You aren't going to sleep in your present state of mind, anyway, so don't try. Instead, get out of bed, find some paper, and draw some pictures. Make a list of all the elements of your current problems. Then, draw Xs through those things you can't do anything about. Draw lines connecting the things you can impact and wake up tomorrow with a plan to start to correct the path."

"Thank you for calling, Tom. I needed this conversation and may need more help tomorrow. I'll try to get an update from Ty's parents, and if I do, I'll let you know. I'll also get out of bed and start drawing."

"Okay," said Tom. "You've got this!"

"Yes, I do!"

Seeney then reconnected her phone to the charger, got out of bed, and looked at herself in the full-length mirror by the dresser. To the image, she said, "Get your shit together, Woman! You made some mistakes you can't correct, which caused some things you need to fix. They aren't going to fix themselves." Then, she went to the refrigerator and poured a glass of wine. She carried the glass to her home office area, pulled a legal pad from her desk, and started drawing pictures as Tom suggested.

Within an hour, the paper was full of boxes, names, arrows, and connecting lines. Many of the items on the paper had bold Xs marked through them. These included the names, Stiles and Foster. She could do nothing about them now, so she wouldn't waste time on them.

A long path of blocks connected by lines started with a box containing the name *Me* and ended with a box containing the name *Ty.* The line connecting these two boxes had an X through it; another line connecting *Me* with the *United States Marine Corps* also had an X drawn through it.

Finally, a third line from the *Me* box connected to the one labeled *Orville/Mavy*. A solid line then joined that box to the *United States Marine Corps* block, followed by another solid line connecting the *United States Marine Corps* block to the *Ty* block.

Next, a solid line connected the *Me* block to one named *Business*. A similar line connected a block labeled *Tartan Springs* to the *Me* block. The *Tartan Springs* block joined the block tagged *Bektistan* with a solid line. Finally, Seeney wrote three lines at the bottom of the page:

1. *Communicate with Ty.*
2. *Put the business on hold.*
3. *Get to Ty!*

When she finished, she felt confident about the abbreviated plan. Her priority was to establish communications with her fiancé. The diagram confirmed the only way to do this now was through Ty's parents. She reread the last email Ty sent her several times, noting the time he sent it.

Seeney - Pls call me as soon as possible! - Ty

Sent at a bit after eight in the morning in Bektistan, the message occurred within thirty minutes of the time the fake note from Seeney's account to him was posted. Ty's short message didn't express emotion, just an urgency for Seeney to call him. Ty would have known Seeney wouldn't likely see his message until six or seven hours later when she awoke in West Virginia. He, therefore, wouldn't anticipate a reply from her by phone, text, or email until later in the afternoon of his day in Bektistan.

Seeney now knew, though, through her conversation with Mavy, something happened to Ty yesterday. He probably didn't get back to his phone or computer. She pondered this and decided Ty had not accepted the fraudulent communication from Seeney's account at face value. His response to her, she thought, would have been longer. He only wanted an explanation because he was confused.

The explanation was impossible for Seeney to send because of the problems with her account. Still, even if she had, Ty might not have had an opportunity to read it because of whatever happened later in his day. Ty had incorrect information that Seeney needed to straighten out as soon as she could. She felt certain Ty would understand what happened and be relieved by her explanation. Now, she just had to figure out how to get that information to him.

The line from Seeney's box to her business reminded Seeney to responsibly inform her customers of the current trauma in her life. Seeney had already missed a deadline for a sales tax filing from one customer. The following day, she would call that client to explain the mistake and offer to pay the late fee from her own account.

The pesky W-9 issue relating to Eastern Hydroponics still needed resolution, but Seeney decided that could wait a week.

Seeney would attempt to forecast immediate needs for the rest of her customers and complete as much work in advance as possible. However, she would also warn them that her availability would be limited over the next few days.

And last, Seeney would research the ways of cutting the geographical distance between herself and Ty. She had no idea whether it was even possible for her to travel to where Ty was, but she would find out. Based on the minimal information Mavy shared, Seeney couldn't guess what the mystery surrounding Ty's condition involved. Perhaps she didn’t need to get to Ty’s location, but additional delays wouldn't accrue because of the need to plan if she found out she did.

Satisfied, she had done what she could for the evening, she finished her glass of wine and went to bed. Glancing in the mirror again before lying down, she said, "That's more like it!"

Kadun

West Virginia: Thursday, 10:30 AM
Kadun: Thursday, 7:30 PM

Ty's operation started at eight in the evening, and by eight-thirty, Doctor Faould instructed his nurse assistant to close the wound. The doctor stitched the two incisions he had made in Ty's back and helped the nurse roll the gurney back to Ty's room. The doctor was sitting beside the bed when the injured Marine awoke from anesthesia. "Good evening, sir."

"Hello, Doctor," said Ty sleepily. "How did the operation go?"

"Not well, I'm afraid. I started the procedure but couldn't complete it. Several bone fragments from the injury are lodged near the spinal cord. One fragment punctured the Dura Matur, which forms the outer layer of protection for the spinal cord. We must remove this fragment without allowing further movement of it, and no surgical instruments utilized in the operation can touch the spinal cord."

"So, what does that mean?"

"Sir, the bottom line is that this is the most delicate of all possible operations, and a specialist should execute it. I'm an excellent surgeon, but I suggest finding a doctor with more experience than me in this type of procedure. The negative consequences of even the smallest miscalculation or mistake would impact you for the rest of your life. Therefore, I closed the incisions and related this information to your military."

"I'm sorry to hear all that, Doctor, but I appreciate your concern and professionalism," said Ty. "Am I in further danger now by waiting?"

"Very little, as long as we keep you immobilized," said the doctor. "You won't be comfortable, but we'll try to source medical alternatives for you quickly. Your commanding officer informed me earlier this afternoon he had received the clearances to contact your parents. He told me he did not yet have authority to notify others, but he seemed certain your parents would call your fiancé."

Thank you, Doctor Faould."

Fox Uni

West Virginia: Thursday, 10:30 PM
Kadun: Friday, 7:30 AM

Lieutenant Colonel Hayden listened to Doctor Faould's

explanation, thanked him, then got on the phone with Marine Corps headquarters. Within an hour, Colonel Fitzpatrick from the Casualty Assistance office in Quantico called Hayden back.

Fitzpatrick informed Hayden one of the best neurosurgeons in the world, Doctor Walt Shapiro, practiced at the Randstuhl Regional Medical Hospital in Randstuhl, Germany. This was one of the largest overseas military hospitals in the United States Department of Defense network. Colonel Fitzpatrick said that orders were being "chopped" as they spoke to transport Harrell from Kadun to Randstuhl the following day. Hayden relayed this information to Doctor Faould in Kadun, and Faould said he would make certain Major Harrell was ready for the flight.

Tartan Springs

West Virginia: Thursday, 1:30 PM
Kadun: Thursday, 10:30 PM

At one-thirty in the afternoon on Thursday, Seeney's cell phone rang. "Seeney, it's Mavy. The Casualty Assistance office at Marine Headquarters finally called me back. Ty is in a hospital in Kadun. He suffered a leg wound and a back injury during a mission, and he will undergo an operation sometime today. The corporal told me she would call me with updates. Ty's command delayed the information because of some confusion about his identity."

"Oh, thank you, Mavy! What a relief. Will you be able to talk to Ty soon?"

"I'm not sure, Seeney. Everything is a bit sketchy, but I'll call you with any news as soon as I get it."

"I know you will, Mavy. Thank you. Ty wanted us to marry before he left, and I didn't want to do that. What an idiot I was! If we had gotten married, I'd be able to get this information myself. I'm so sorry."

"Seeney," said Mavy. "You *are* next of kin! It doesn't matter what your last name is. We'd be sharing things just like we are now whether you were married or not."

"I guess you're right, Mavy. Thank you. Hug Orville for me. I love you both."

The news, while not complete or what she wanted to hear, relieved Seeney. Ty was alive. Before turning off her computer, she pulled up a map of Bektistan and located Kadun. She then typed in the URL for Orbitz and checked airline schedules in that part of the world. Not surprisingly, the alternatives were minimal, and the travel site listed a full page of warnings, restrictions, and requirements.

West Virginia: Friday, 8:30 AM
Kadun: Friday, 5:30 PM

Mavis called Seeney early on Friday with other news. "The Casualty Assistance office gave me an update on Ty. Our military is moving him sometime tomorrow to one of our Department of Defense hospitals in Germany. The doctors in Kadun were uncomfortable with the complexity of the operation required for Ty's back." After Mavis provided Seeney these details, Seeney thanked her and hung up. Then, she opened her computer, and an hour later called her friend, Tom Burns.

18 The Operation

West Virginia: Friday, 9:30 AM
Kadun: Friday, 6:30 PM

"Tom," said Seeney, "Ty is being flown from Kadun to someplace in Germany, the Randstuhl Regional Medical Hospital. His back is broken, and he needs a neurosurgeon to operate on it."

"That sounds serious.

"He had a wound to his thigh and lost a lot of blood, but he's recovering from that. He's stable, but a doctor in Kadun started to operate on his back and decided it was too delicate to continue. So, our military is picking him up tomorrow and flying him to the hospital in Germany."

"Randstuhl is our largest military hospital overseas. It has an excellent reputation, and I think I'm acquainted with some people who work there."

"Why does that not surprise me? Are you ever going to tell me what you really do, Burns?"

"I *have* told you, Seeney! My association with the Children's Ministry merely exposes me to a variety of professionals in a lot of different countries."

"Right, right," said Seeney, not sounding convinced. "Listen, this may sound stupid, but I want to fly to Randstuhl. I need to see Ty!"

"Whoa! Flying there is a bigger deal than you might think. Randstuhl isn't the easiest place to get to from here, and I'm not sure you'd be allowed into the hospital once you got there. Won't you be able to talk to Ty soon on a telephone?"

"I don't know. He hasn't been able to speak to anyone yet, except his doctors in Kadun. His own parents haven't talked to him."

"Because of military clearances or his medical condition?"

"I can't answer that, Tom! That's the thing. All this is a mystery that even his parents don't understand, and nobody will tell us anything. I think I need to be in Germany when he gets there and see for myself."

"OK. Settle down. I get it, but you need to realize this may not work. We might be unable to obtain clearances to go inside the hospital, so we could travel to Germany and still not be able to see Ty."

"Tom, I'm not asking you to go with me—I'm just asking you to help me figure out how I can get there."

"And I'm giving you that. You can't make this particular trip by yourself—and you don't have my connections. So, when do we leave?"

"I was thinking of a flight from Dulles with two stops leaving after midnight tonight. It will take over twenty-four hours to travel there."

"I need to make some calls," said Tom, " but I can do that. Let's take my car to Dulles. I'll pick you up around eight this evening. My suggestion is—pack a carry-on and a backpack. With two stops, the chances of finding checked luggage at the end are marginal. Do you need a credit card number to book the flight?"

"No. I'm cashing a CD for this trip to cover the credit card bills."

"OK, I'll pay you back."

"Not likely."

"Seeney! I'm aware of the cost of these types of flights. You can't do that."

"This isn't a vacation, Tom. You're doing it for me."

"*And* Ty. He's *my* friend, too."

"Are you planning to marry him?"

"No, but still..." started Tom.

"I'll tell you what. Let's throw in that you'll do our wedding ceremony for free. OK?"

"I was going to do that anyway."

"Oh, gosh! You're too slick for me. You win. See you around eight." Then Seeney hung up.

West Virginia: Friday, 8:00 PM
Kadun: Saturday, 5:00 AM

Tom picked her up that evening, and Seeney threw a small carry-on bag and a stuffed backpack into his backseat. "I hid about a thousand dollars in cash all over my body, Tom. Will that be enough?"

"With the thousand dollars in my wallet, it should be."

"Good. I paid a little extra for an open return which gives us some flexibility on coming back."

They arrived at Dulles in plenty of time to park in the cheapest satellite parking lot available and take the shuttle to international departures. After passing through security, Tom asked, "Have you traveled internationally before?"

"No, but I applied for a passport four years ago, hoping Jack would take me someplace. He never did. Now Ty is."

"Well, this won't be a treat, I'm afraid. We're in economy class, so I hope you can sleep sitting up. Our flight doesn't leave for a few hours, so let's enjoy a decent meal here. We may not eat again for quite a while."

"OK. I brought some extras of these if you need one," she said, holding up a container of pills. "Doctor Chavez gave them to me last year to combat my stress relating to the divorce with Jack, but I never needed one. So, I called her before you picked me up, and she told me a single pill would allow me to sleep like a baby to Europe."

"I generally don't indulge in self-medication, but after dinner, I might consider the offer."

Seeney and Tom had a big meal at a high airport price before boarding their flight for the first leg of their trip. Though they occupied middle seats, at one-thirty in the morning, they both fell asleep before takeoff.

Announcements and other passengers in their aisle needing to use the bathroom interrupted their naps sporadically, but by the time they arrived in France to switch planes, the couple was well-rested—if a little stiff. The following two flights were short, and both Seeney and Tom remained awake until they landed in Ziestrucken, Germany.

West Virginia: Friday, 7:30 AM
Kadun: Friday, 4:30 PM

Lieutenant Colonel Hayden called Doctor Faould to inform him about the flight coming from Germany the following day, and Faould reported that Major Harrell would be ready. Faould asked the commanding officer to ensure the C-130 aircraft would be equipped with a hospital gurney to transfer the Major. Hayden assured Doctor Faould those arrangements had been made and thanked the doctor for his care of Ty.

Before leaving the hospital that evening, Doctor Faould checked on Ty. The injured Marine lay still on his back while a nurse fed him soft food from a bowl. "Good evening, Major Harrell. I'm glad you are receiving sustenance from something other than a tube. How are you feeling?"

"Not as confused as the past several days. There is little pain if I lie still."

"Excellent. We tried to keep your dosage of pain medication as low as possible because of the drug's side effects. Tell us, however, if your discomfort becomes greater. I will need to administer a rather strong dose tomorrow before being transported to the airplane taking you to Randstuhl. Even small aircraft movements will cause you pain."

"Thank you, Doctor, and thank you for making these arrangements."

"You are welcome, Major." The doctor peered at one of the monitors beside Ty's bed before he left. Then, he placed his hand on Ty's forehead. "You have a slight fever, and we don't like these after surgeries. They can be indications of infection resulting from surgical procedures." Faould then spoke in another language to the nurse feeding Ty. "I instructed Badrai to monitor your temperature closely this evening."

After eating, Ty went back to sleep. At two in the morning, an alarm from one of the monitors near his bed awakened him. A nurse entered and silenced it, but seeing Ty awake, motioned for him to wait while she left for a moment. She returned with another doctor.

The Becktistani didn't speak English as well as Doctor Faould, but Ty could understand him. "Temperature too high," said the doctor. "Must fix!" The doctor removed a vial of medicine from one of the drawers in the cart near Ty's bed. Then, snapping the top from the bottle, he attached it to a tube on Ty's left arm. The doctor gave Badrai additional instructions and departed.

At seven o'clock, Doctor Faould was again beside Ty's bed, gazing at several monitors in the room. Then, realizing Ty was awake, he said, "I am sorry for your discomfort, Major Harrell. Your fever got worse last evening, and the medicine administered didn't bring it down as it should. Therefore, I must give you more medicine to control the fever as well as antibiotics to destroy the infection I fear is causing it."

"Will this impact my ability to fly today?"

"We will see. Several more hours remain to monitor the fever before deciding. If it subsides by your scheduled departure time, you should be safe to fly."

That didn't happen, though. Ty's temperature rose some, despite the medicine, and the patient was uncomfortable. Doctor Faould made a call to Ty's commanding officer with the bad news. "I'm sorry to tell you this, sir, but I fear if the Major's fever would increase during the flight, he might convulse. He could damage his spinal cord permanently if this happened. Therefore, I believe the risk is too great for Major Harrell to travel."

"I understand, Doctor Faould. Thank you," said Lieutenant Colonel Hayden. "The flight is scheduled to land there soon and doesn't need to depart until tomorrow morning. If the fever came down significantly this evening, would your opinion change?"

"Yes, sir. If Major Harrell's temperature returned to almost normal, I wouldn't be concerned for him to fly. We began administering antibiotics for the potential infection we believe responsible for the fever, and sometimes this medicine works quickly."

"OK," said the commanding officer. "At this point, I won't make further notifications. Call me tomorrow morning, and we'll make a final decision."

By Sunday morning, Ty's fever was down, but not enough for Doctor Faould to rule Ty safe for the long flight to Germany. "Thank you, Doctor," said Hayden. "I understand, and I will inform headquarters. We'll try to re-book the flight for later in the week when Major Harrell recovers from the infection."

The Casualty Assistance Office reached Mavis and Orville Harrell with this news, but not in time for them to stop Seeney from traveling to Germany. Seeney's flight from Dulles departed before the Harrells learned the change in plans for their son.

West Virginia: Sunday, 5:30 AM
Germany: Sunday, 11:30 AM
Kadun: Sunday, 2:30 PM

After arriving, Tom surprised Seeney by having transportation arranged from the airport to the hospital. "When did you do that?" asked Seeney.

"On the last flight. The internet connection was reliable, and since we're only going to the hospital, we won't rent a car. The ride by Lyft, which is a service like Uber, is short."

"Apparently, you know your way around. Isn't this the same airport the C-130 from Kadun will land to bring Ty?"

"Yes, as a matter of fact, it is. How did you find that out?"

"I'm just a naïve girl from West Virginia who's never been out of the country, Tom—but I'm not stupid. I did a little research before we started the trip."

"Sorry," said Tom. "Naturally, you would. The plane bringing Ty from Kadun will taxi right over there to the military side of the airport. Military schedules aren't published, but the C-130 should be here in the next hour."

"Yes. Ty's mother told me it would be around eleven o'clock this morning, Randstuhl time. So, I picked the flights I did partly for that reason, but how did you know the time? I told you the day, but we never discussed times."

"Right, Seeney. I'm not trying to spook you, but I advised you I had friends here. Ty is coming here because one of the best neurosurgeons in the world practices at this hospital. His name is Walt Shapiro, and he's a board member of the Lutheran Christian Children's ministry."

"Of course, he would be," replied a sarcastic Seeney.

"Seeney, that happens to be true! I can't claim that Doctor Shapiro is a friend, but he's an acquaintance, and we're familiar with each other's work. I texted him somewhere over the Atlantic, and he told me he was coming to meet Ty's plane today. Doctor Shapiro will operate on Ty tomorrow."

"I'm not sure if this is a good dream or a bad dream," said Seeney, "but it *does* spook me. Honestly, Tom! What are the chances that the one doctor capable of operating on Ty would be a friend of yours in Germany? Doesn't that strike you as odd?"

"We aren't gambling, so the odds aren't important. Whatever they are, you need to deal with it! You may not have any faith—and I'm OK with that—but others do. Be thankful that folks are praying for you and Ty and consider the remote possibility of the power of prayer. Perhaps the people who pray are smarter than you, after all!" Pastor Tom, clearly irritated with Seeney, finished his short tirade with an apology. "Sorry. I didn't mean to raise my voice. We've had a long day."

Seeney grabbed his hand before Tom could turn away. "No, Tom. I'm the one who should be sorry. I appreciate you and all the others who help with their hopes and prayers, and I apologize for being so selfish and thoughtless. I probably don't deserve these blessings, but I promise you I'll do better. Can you forgive me for my presumptions and my skepticism?"

"Forget it, Seeney. The world is full of things none of us can understand. For now, whether we're blessed or just lucky, we need to keep moving forward. Let's go check that military terminal."

When they reached the terminal located on the other side of the airport, Seeney saw various types and sizes of military aircraft on the tarmac. Some displayed German emblems on the tail sections; other aircraft had French flags, Spanish flags, and United States flags. They entered the terminal building, and Seeney felt relieved to see no military-oriented security.

The waiting area was mostly empty, but Tom recognized someone as soon as he arrived. "Doctor Shapiro is over there." Ty nodded his head toward a distinguished-looking older gentleman seated near a window. As Tom and Seeney headed in the man's direction, Shapiro noticed them and stood.

"Pastor Burns!" said Shapiro. "You pop up in the most unusual places. Your text message surprised me."

"I bet," said Tom. "My visit isn't official. I'm accompanying my friend here, Siena Tyson. Coincidentally, her fiancé, Major Harrell, is the injured soldier coming from Kadun for your professional attention."

"The world does sometimes seem exceedingly small, doesn't it?" said the doctor, shaking Seeney's hand. "You might be aware of this, but perhaps not. I only received the news myself moments ago. Unfortunately, Major Harrell didn't make this flight because he wasn't well enough to travel. Nevertheless, the aircraft should land in about fifteen minutes, so I thought I might get some additional information about what happened from medical personnel on the plane."

Seeney looked distraught. "No, doctor. This is news to us, but we've been out of touch with the world for most of the last twenty-four hours while we traveled." She turned to Tom with eyes full of tears. "What do we do now, Tom?"

Tom looked at Doctor Shapiro. "You say you just found out?"

"Yes. I received a text from my office. Someone contacted us after the flight took off from Kadun with the information. It must have been a last-minute decision."

"Seeney," said Tom, "let's wait here with Doctor Shapiro. Someone on the airplane might be able to tell us more. We're here for the evening anyway, and when we get to the hotel, you can call Ty's parents. They may have more information."

Twenty minutes later, a C-130 Hercules aircraft taxied to an area in front of the terminal building. The four engines stopped, ground crew chocked the wheels, and fifteen people disembarked. The massive cargo door at the rear of the aircraft lowered, and several more people departed by this exit, including two strapped to rolling hospital gurneys. Seeney observed Doctor Shapiro talking to one of the medical attendants and, after a short conversation, the doctor returned to where Seeney and Tom waited.

"Major Harrell was to be on this flight, but the co-pilot scratched his name from the manifest before the airplane taxied," Shapiro said. "The doctor who accompanied one of the fellows who came off the plane on a stretcher said he heard Major Harrell had developed a high fever and couldn't travel. That was all he could tell me."

"Thanks, Doctor," said Tom. "We'll try to reach Major Harrell's parents in Florida at our hotel. They may have received more news while we were in route."

"OK." Doctor Shapiro handed Tom a card. "Here is my contact

information. The hospital security is tight, but I can get you inside if you need me. Good luck."

Tom and Seeney thanked the doctor and turned to leave when Seeney suddenly stopped and touched Tom's arm. "It's happening again."

"What's happening?"

"The thing we discussed earlier. Religion, luck, fate—whatever. I've met that man." Seeney pointed to one of the crew members departing the plane.

"Which one? The pilot?"

"Maybe he's the pilot," said Seeney. "He's the one in front, holding the canvas bag in his left hand." Seeney went to the door and waited for the Marine officer to enter.

"Major Jackson?" she said to the tall airman as he entered the terminal.

"Yes, ma'am." The pilot plainly didn't recognize Seeney immediately.

"My name is Siena Tyson, and I met you..."

Before Seeney could finish, the pilot said, "... at the officers club at Andrews Air Force Base for the Marine Corps Birthday party. That was the year before last. You were with Ty Harrell!"

"Exactly! You and your wife came with us to National Harbor that night after dinner."

"Of course! And neither my wife nor I remember much about the evening after that. What on earth are you doing in Ziestrucken? Ty is with HML-222, isn't he? Did you two marry?"

"We're engaged, Steve. We couldn't get married before his squadron deployed. I'm here because he was wounded in Bektistan and was supposed to be transported from Kadun today on your airplane. He didn't make the flight, though."

"Oh, my God! I'm sorry. I didn't look at the manifest myself, but we had to adjust it for one less passenger before taxiing in Kadun. That must've been Ty. I had no idea!"

"One of your passengers told us he became too sick to make the flight."

"I'm so sorry, Seeney. The Marines operate a two-plane detachment here, and we make the run to Kadun regularly. He might be able to make the flight next week."

"I'll find out more when I can talk to his parents later tonight from the hotel," said Seeney.

Jackson wrote some information on a small pad he pulled from one of the many pockets of his flight suit and handed it to Seeney. "This is the number you can usually reach me. My wife and I live in temporary quarters not far from here. Our detachment at Ziestrucken Airport is small, only about twenty people total, with six pilots, and I'm the Officer in Charge. Our office space is over in that maintenance hangar. Call me when you have more information about Ty."

"I will. Thank you."

"Where are you staying?"

"My friend and I reserved rooms at the Westin, but we haven't checked in yet. The hotel is supposed to be near the hospital."

"It is. If you can wait here for about fifteen minutes, I'll give you a ride there."

"OK. Thank you."

Tom watched the interchange from a short distance away, and when Seeney returned, he said, "Who has the connections now? How do you know him?"

"Eerie, isn't it? None of this seems real. That was Steve Jackson, and I met him and his wife, Charlotte—he calls her Charlie—at the Marine Corps Birthday Ball. He was in HMX-1 with Ty and was one of Ty's closest friends in that squadron. He's now in charge of a two-plane detachment stationed here. I think his main unit operates out of California."

"Did he know anything about Ty?"

"He knew Ty was in HML-222, but he had no idea Ty was scheduled to be on this flight. He wants me to call him if we find out anything from Ty's parents. He's also giving us a ride to the hotel."

Major Jackson and his copilot dropped Tom and Seeney in front of the Westin. After checking in, Seeney and Tom met in Seeney's room. She booted up her tablet and saw the email from Mavy.

Sometime after Seeney and Tom had departed for Germany, Mavy and Orville received the notification of the change in plans for Ty. Their son had developed an infection at the hospital in Kadun, causing a high fever. His doctor in Kadun had judged Ty too sick to travel, and the Marine Casualty Office would review other options for their officer.

"The good news," said Tom, "is Ty is still alive."

"The bad news ... he needs the back operation but is still in Kadun."

"Right. I promised to give Doctor Shapiro an update. I'll call him. You call Major Jackson."

Tom was working from a small table in Seeney's room, and he waited patiently after his call to Shapiro for Seeney to complete her conversation with Jackson. She disconnected, and he asked, "Are you tired yet?"

"After only twenty-six hours of continuous traveling, catching naps in the sitting position? Is that a rhetorical question?"

"Sorry, no. I'm tired, too, and we both need some rest, but let me tell you what I learned from Doctor Shapiro. A doctor in Kadun started the back operation on Ty but stopped when he realized the potential for severe complications. So, he called our military and suggested that Ty fly to Randstuhl, but Ty became too sick to travel."

"That coincides with what others told us."

"Yes, it does. It sounds like Ty needs this operation, and our government is trying to do everything it can to make it happen. So, I'm thinking, if the United States can't bring Ty to Doctor Shapiro, why not take Shapiro to Ty?"

Seeney gazed at Tom for a moment. "If you're going to now tell me you can call Marine Headquarters to order that, I'm going to—I don't know—I think I'm just going to go ahead and wake up from the dream."

"No, I can't do that," said Tom. "But, between us, we might be able to make it an easier decision for headquarters."

"I'm listening."

"Doctor Shapiro is an important physician at the Randstuhl hospital, but he's working as a contractor for the Defense Department. His schedule tomorrow is busy but includes no critical surgeries. He told me this. You are friends with the Officer in Charge of the Marine detachment of C-130s located here, who also happens to be a friend of Ty's." Burns became more excited the more he talked. "I'm certain Major Jackson gets his flight scheduling from central operations, but he most likely has some input to it. He has to balance the schedule against crew availability, aircraft maintenance, and a host of other variables."

"So?" asked Seeney.

"So, why don't you call Jackson back and ask him straight out. If we find a way for Doctor Shapiro to be cleared to travel tomorrow, what are the chances Jackson could arrange another emergency flight to

Kadun? His command may already have completed a flight schedule which precludes that possibility, but if not—what harm is there to ask?"

"But what if he can make the trip, but then Shapiro can't get clearance to go?" asked Seeney.

"Major Jackson just cancels the flight."

"Do you think Shapiro's chain of command would allow him to be away from here for a whole day?"

"Not sure, but there's only one way to find out."

Two hours later, Seeney and Tom compared notes. Major Jackson's second C-130 was currently down for maintenance, so no flight operations had been scheduled for it. However, Jackson thought the plane could be operational by tomorrow afternoon. He said he would volunteer to take the flight to Kadun with another pilot if that happened. This flight would require a clearance from his commanding officer in California, but Jackson felt confident he would receive this.

Tom told Seeney that Shapiro was willing to travel to Kadun for the operation on Ty, but the Department of Defense would need to clear that. Shapiro suggested to Tom that the wheels of bureaucracy sometimes moved slowly but less so when it came to the care of critically wounded soldiers. "This may not work," said Tom. "There are hundreds of details to resolve and quite a few challenges, so don't get your hopes up."

"I'm not, but I'm glad we're trying. I was ready to go to bed a couple of hours ago, thinking we had done everything we could, but you didn't give up. Thank you."

"I'm more experienced with this than you. Governments are no different from corporations or people. Often, they want to do the right thing and say *yes*. We just need to make it easy for them. I don't think there's anything more we can do tonight, though."

"Good," said Seeney, "because I don't have much more energy. Do you want one of my magic pills?"

"No. Won't need it. I'm hoping I'll be able to remove my clothes before I fall asleep. Call me when you're up tomorrow."

Germany: Monday, 7:00 AM
Kadun: Monday, 9:00 AM

By seven in the morning, Randstuhl time, both Seeney and Tom were awake and communicating. Each had gotten almost seven hours of restful, uninterrupted sleep, and they were functional, if not wholly rejuvenated. They had breakfast together in the hotel's restaurant and afterward began working their cell phones in Seeney's room.

By nine o'clock, Seeney provided the first positive news. Major Jackson told her his second aircraft was now deemed safe for flight and in an operational status. Including himself, the major had a crew of four ready to make the trip to Kadun in the afternoon if he received clearance from his commanding officer in California.

Soon after, Doctor Shapiro called Tom to report Major Harrell's status in Kadun. The attending physician there, Doctor Faould, told Shapiro that the antibiotics were working, and that Ty's temperature was dropping back toward normal. However, Faould remained concerned about the possibility of loose vertebrae fragments touching the spinal cord potentially causing permanent damage. Shapiro had relayed this information to his superiors, hoping it would expedite a clearance for him to travel to Kadun. He had not yet heard back from the Department of Defense.

At eleven-thirty, Shapiro called Tom to report he had received approval to fly to Kadun if military transportation was available. Lieutenant Colonel Hayden from Ty's squadron had appealed to Marine Headquarters in Quantico, which sent a request to DOD officials in Washington, DC. Pastor Tom gave Doctor Shapiro the number for Major Jackson's direct line to coordinate a departure time.

In minutes, Seeney received a call from Major Jackson. "We're scheduled for a one-thirty departure this afternoon, and Doctor Shapiro is on the manifest."

"Oh, Steve, thank you! Thank you so much! You don't know what this means to me. Good luck, and please keep me posted about Ty. I'm so worried."

"Well, uh, OK," said the major, "but I thought you and Pastor Burns would want to come with us."

"We can do that? I had no idea. Of course, we do!"

"I'm not sure of the legalities, but in this case, I'm not taking a chance by asking. We don't have time. So, I'm making a command decision that Major Harrell's primary clerical advisor and the pastor's assistant seem like reasonable exceptions to normal protocol. See you here as soon as you can get to the terminal."

Within ninety minutes, Tom and Seeney were sitting next to the eminent Doctor Shapiro in the austere environment of the C-130's passenger cabin. No cocktails, in-flight meals, or other amenities were available, and the ambient noise inside the venerable old warbird made conversation impossible. The seats reclined almost to horizontal, though, and with earplugs, the muffled rumble of the four massive turbine engines made sleep easy.

Kadun

Germany: Monday, 6:00 PM
Kadun: Monday, 8:00 PM

The big transport aircraft landed, and an armored ambulance met it at the terminal. Seeney asked the C-130's crew chief, "Will my friend and I have problems with clearance to enter the hospital?"

"No," said the Sergeant. "The laws are a little loose here. It's a dangerous place, especially for Americans, so stay inside the vehicle away from windows. Then, when you're safely at the hospital, don't leave it for any reason."

"Thank you, Sergeant. We won't. Where do you and the crew stay when you're here?"

"The boss tries not to schedule flights where we remain overnight here. This one is an unusual exception. We'd rather bust our duty flight time a little and fly to Kadun and back on the same day when we can. When we do stay, we camp out on the plane. These old birds are secure, well-armored, and equipped with duty racks. We also carry an arsenal of weapons, so folks don't mess with us much."

"Great! We'll look forward to seeing you again tomorrow early."

"Best of luck with the operation, ma'am."

Their vehicle delivered the small group to the hospital, and all went inside. Doctor Faould met Doctor Shapiro at the door and extended his hand. "Thank you, Doctor, for making this long trip. Your patient is waiting, and three of my staff besides myself are available to assist. We'll be ready whenever you are."

"Thank you, Doctor Faould," said Shapiro. "I would like to review the MRI images before starting and perhaps talk to you about what you encountered when you began the operation before. Did you sedate the patient yet?"

"No, Doctor. We weren't sure how soon you would want to start the operation after you arrived."

"As soon as possible," said Shapiro, "so have your people begin the anesthesia now. Our discussions should take no more than fifteen minutes. How is Major Harrell's fever?"

"It dropped last night, sir, but he was much too sick to travel for the past two days. We administered more medicine than I would have preferred in his condition to fend off the infection."

"I understand," said Doctor Shapiro. "It's a delicate balance. What is his overall condition?"

"He is weak, Doctor Shapiro, but I believe he can withstand the operation. His options are limited. One of the fragments in his back is dangerously close to the conus medullaris."

"Thank you, Doctor. Then, let us not delay."

Tom and Seeney heard most of the exchange between the two doctors, and Tom reached over to hold Seeney's hand. "We've made it this far, Seeney. These guys sound like they know what they're doing. Let's find a quiet place to wait."

The couple sat in the hallway outside the operating room until a nurse motioned to follow her. She led them to a waiting area with some chairs and a small sofa. The nurse showed Seeney and Tom where water was available in a bathroom adjoining the waiting room.

Within two hours, Doctor Faould came to the area, still wearing his medical gown. "Doctor Shapiro completed the surgery, removing several small fragments near the spinal cord and repairing one vertebra. With some luck, Major Harrell will require no additional surgery. He's resting now but may awaken from anesthesia within the hour. You can wait in his room if you'd like. I must warn you when he awakens, he may not recognize you or be able to speak. Due to medicine for his infection, the narcotic for pain, and anesthesia for the operation, his mind could be cloudy and confused. Keeping him engaged by talking to him for a short time would benefit him. Your friend has been through a trying ordeal."

"Thank you, Doctor," said Seeney. "We'll wait in his room. We understand your warnings and won't expect too much."

The storm inside Ty's head raged, fueled by narcotics, antibiotics, and the effects of anesthesia. An overwhelming desire to sleep waged war with an equally compelling command to wake up. Ty's dreams were sporadic and unconnected, punctuated by gunfire, a referee's whistle, music, and voices.

People moved in and out of his subconsciousness so quickly he couldn't recognize them, and a silent voice insistently repeated, "Wake up! Open your eyes! Don't sleep! No! No! No!" Ty briefly saw Gabe Sullivan and a man in a striped shirt prepared to slap the mat while he, on his back, struggled.

He heard Sergeant Gunn scream, "Hold on! Hold on!" But Ty felt he needed to sleep, had to sleep... just for a few minutes... please... just for a few minutes.

Then, a man with a collar...was it Tom? ... screamed, "No! It's time to wake up! You have to wake up!" The turmoil was relentless and exhausting until Ty finally found himself in a field, looking up into a clear blue sky. A summer breeze cooled him as he relaxed on a soft bed of green grass. The feeling was euphoric, and Ty nearly succumbed to the calmness and blessed tranquility.

But—he picked up a mild scent. It was the lilac petals scattered in the grass on which he lay... and once again, the voice inside him commanded, "Open your eyes! You must open your eyes! Do it! Do it! Do it now!"

Ty didn't want to open his eyes; he felt he didn't have the strength; it was too hard... but finally, using all his power, he forced his eyes to open... a little, almost... "Again!" said the voice. "Again! Don't stop! Again!" And, once more, Ty tried to execute this one specific command. He opened his eyes—and the scent of lilacs became stronger. It was no dream. The violets were standing next to him—In the form of a female person—who held his hand.

"Seeney?" he said—or thought he said, the name whispered so softly he couldn't hear it himself. But the person next to him answered.

"Yes, Ty! It's me. I'm here. Oh, my God! I have been so worried. Thank you, thank you, thank you for opening your eyes!"

Ty's mind was now slowly coming to life, and he had much he wanted to say, but he couldn't make his lips move. He became desperate to speak but could only form a small smile and squeeze Seeney's hand ever so lightly. Doctor Faould stepped from somewhere in the room and took the hand Seeney was holding.

"Major Harrell, you endured quite an ordeal," said the doctor, "but I think you're going to be OK. Your body has willed you to live. I want you to try to remain awake for a short time. Your ability to think and speak will improve dramatically as the effects of the pain narcotic and the anesthetic subside. You have caring friends here who accomplished extraordinary feats to be with you. I'll leave you with them for a little while."

Ty again tried to speak and thought he said, "Thank you," but he couldn't be sure. Seeney and Tom stepped back to the side of the bed. Ty's eyes widened when he saw Tom, and he remembered the recent dream—or was it a dream? "Did you..." started Ty, "Were you..." but he couldn't finish his question. The confusion and inability to form words frustrated him, but his friend answered.

"Yes, buddy, I did, and I was," said Tom, smiling. "I'm glad you remembered."

Ty smiled, and Seeney looked at Tom in wonder. "Tom! What on earth are you talking about?"

"Nothing, Seeney. I'm just answering idle questions to keep Ty talking. That's all."

Seeney looked skeptical but refocused on Ty. "We know it's hard for you to talk, Ty, so don't try for a while. Would you like to hear how we got here?"

Ty smiled slightly and relaxed. He squeezed Seeney's hand and, in his mind, thought he winked in Tom's direction. Seeney then spent the next fifteen minutes describing the exciting journey she and Tom made from West Virginia to Kadun. Finally, she ended the description of the travelogue, glancing at Tom. "The truth is, Ty, I'm not sure how we got here. Tom's connections in this world—and other worlds—might have had something to do with it. Maybe Renée's prayers in Woodstock, or a dance shared at the Marine Corps birthday party. Maybe you willed us here, Ty, or possibly this was just a trip meant to be—on that crazy road through life we keep discussing. I don't know, but I *do* know getting here was important, and I'm glad we did."

Ty listened as Seeney spoke, and the longer her descriptions went, the more active his mind became. The fog in his brain was lifting, and by the time Seeney finished, Ty was able to comprehend every word. His words remained soft when he spoke, but they were now clear. "I promised you I wouldn't come home in a box, Seeney. I'm not."

Seeney wanted to hug Ty, but the number of tubes protruding from different parts of his body precluded that. "I remember, Major, and you always keep your promises." Doctor Faould reentered the room, signaling the welcome-back-to-the-world reception for Ty was now over. His friends told Ty they would visit again before they departed back to Germany.

Ty's medical condition wouldn't allow a four-hour flight today, but Doctor Faould predicted he might be ready for such a trip in a week. "And what happens to him after that?" asked Tom.

"Medically?" questioned the doctor.

"Yes," said Tom. "How long will he be in Randstuhl, and what kind of recovery can he expect?"

"I can't accurately estimate that yet. Much of his recovery will depend on his own body. Major Harrell is in no danger from the back operation now, and I believe we eliminated the infection that caused the past fever. However, his rehabilitation from the injury will be lengthy. Most of that will occur in your country."

"Thank you, Doctor," said Seeney.

"Yes," said Tom. "Thank you. Do you have a few more minutes that you might talk to me, Doctor?"

"Certainly, Pastor."

Tom looked at Seeney. "This won't take long. Wait for me where we were this morning."

When the two men stood alone outside of Ty's room, Tom said, "Doctor Faould, I'm impressed with your service and professionalism. Thank you."

"You are most welcome, my friend, but it was your Doctor Shapiro who performed the delicate back operation, not me."

"I'm aware, Doctor. It was you, however, who decided Doctor Shapiro should operate."

"Yes, sir. Doctor Shapiro was better qualified for this type of surgery."

"Perhaps," said Burns, "but you had little to lose by performing it yourself. I admire your unselfishness and your sense of duty in the case of my friend."

"Thank you, Pastor, but I didn't do this because he was your friend or because he was from your country. Are you familiar with the Hippocratic Oath?"

"Yes, I am. It is a remarkable promise that knows no geographical boundaries and has withstood the test of time for all in your profession."

"Correct. Not all in our profession always honor the sacred oath, but the Hippocratic Oath provides consistent guidance for true healers. As doctors, we don't look at nationality, skin color, or political allegiance. Our mission is to heal the sick and wounded wherever they may be, and whoever they may be, in the best way possible. Furthermore, we are charged as physicians to share our talents for the common benefit of all. I think this philosophy helped your friend."

"Without doubt," said Tom. "Do you believe he also benefited from something else?"

"Do you mean something spiritual?"

"Perhaps."

"That, sir, is more in your area than mine," said the doctor.

"Maybe, but I'd be interested in your perspective. It seems to me you deal in a professional universe with similarities to mine. We understand much about the human body, but that is still only a small fraction of what we must yet learn. I think religion, or spirituality, or faith, or whatever you want to call it—is the same."

"But, Pastor," said Doctor Faould, "your Christian Bible is immense and full of guidance. Are you not comfortable with the answers provided there?"

Pastor Burns smiled. "Are you certain, Doctor, of all the answers contained in the Koran?"

"Let us sit in my office," suggested Faould.

Tom found Seeney in the waiting area and warned her he might be delayed a while longer with Doctor Faould.

"Is this about Ty?"

"No, Seeney. Something even more important. The human race." Tom smiled, so Seeney relaxed and told him to take as long as he needed.

Tom sat across from Doctor Faould in the physician's small office. The young doctor confirmed, "I believe your friend, Major Harrell, received assistance in recent days by someone—or something— more powerful than just his friends who rescued him or the doctors who attended to him. It might have been your Lord Jesus, my God Allah—or Zeus or Apollo, or one or more of the many spiritual figures worshiped by the indigenous people of your country. Or maybe it was none of those. With respect, Pastor, I don't believe anyone truly knows those answers."

"It may surprise you, Doctor, but I agree with you. I adopted a faith within a religion I think is more right than wrong, but I openly profess to my peers and my parishioners my doubts and my ignorance. I encourage all to continue to seek the answers. Collectively, this effort may eventually bring us all closer to the Great Truth. Our respective faiths diverge in some areas, but they intersect in many more, and I believe if we focus on those areas of similarity rather than the areas of disagreement, our chances are better for true understanding."

The doctor thought for a long time before answering. "I have met few clerics, before you, with such an open mind."

"I believe you may have, Doctor, but you just didn't know it. Many spiritual scholars have questions, but we feel uncomfortable allowing our followers to perceive this. When the congregation looks to us for answers, we feel a responsibility to provide those."

"Ha! Our professions are alike in many ways, then, as you stated earlier. Thank you. Like you, I believe a common thread of truth runs through most religions, but sometimes I think we look for guidance in the wrong places. We tend to raise our eyes to the heavens—beyond the universe when we pray. Perhaps we should focus inward. Do you think it might be possible each of us contains the true spirit of life within ourselves? That the answers to those things we don't understand are in our hearts, and souls, and consciences?"

"Yes, Doctor. I do. We are boxed, as humans, into concepts we can hear, see, touch, taste, or smell. I think it possible other senses exist, which we have not yet developed. Things like dreams, and love, and honor, can't be quantified using just five senses, yet we know they exist."

"I enjoyed this conversation, Pastor," said the doctor. "You understand our universe better than most. The good things people do are perhaps random manifestations of divine guidance. Virtue exists in all cultures and all parts of the world, and perhaps our civilization would benefit by discovering its roots. In the meantime, we can only go forward in our ignorance with an inner faith driving us to try to do the right things."

"I agree. Thank you for speaking with me."

Doctor Faould showed Tom and Seeney to a vacant room in the hospital with two beds. Doctor Shapiro was lying, fully clothed, on one bed in the room, sleeping. Looking at the remaining bed, only a single-sized unit, Seeney and Tom decided the bed could still accommodate both if neither moved much. Then, exhausted from days of near-constant travel, they napped soundly on their backs for several hours.

When they awoke, Doctor Shapiro was no longer in the adjoining bed. Seeney peeked into the hallway and saw him talking to Doctor Faould. The two doctors completed their conversation, and Shapiro walked back toward Seeney.

"Major Harrell had a restful evening, and Doctor Faould is encouraged," said Shapiro. "The fever is gone. Faould says the major asked for you this morning, Seeney. There is little time to talk to him because we must leave here in about an hour. Major Jackson would like to depart by eight o'clock this morning."

"Thank you, Doctor Shapiro, and thank you for making this trip."

"You're welcome, ma'am."

A nurse guided Seeney and Tom back to Ty's recovery room, and Tom stayed back as Seeney approached the bed. "Seeney!" Ty appeared much more lucid than a few hours earlier. "I was afraid I might have been dreaming that I saw you before."

"No. It wasn't a dream. Tom and I visited you last night after the operation. You couldn't talk much, so I babbled at you for about a half-hour."

"I remember the conversation now. Doctor Faould says you must leave soon. Is Tom still here?"

"I'm here," said Tom, walking from the back of the room.

"Hey, Tom. Thank you for taking care of Seeney. How on earth did you two manage to get here?"

"A long story for a different time," said Tom. "It wasn't easy. Let's just say that once this woman gets an idea in her head, she's hard to stop."

Ty laughed and said, "I know, Tom." Then, addressing Seeney, "Are you aware that someone sent me a message using your cell phone and your computer, Seeney?"

"Ty! Half the reason we're here is because of that. I didn't find out until you were here in this hospital, and I couldn't reach you. I worried that you might believe the message actually came from me."

"No. I would have never believed that. I know you too well, Seeney. I tried to call you before I went on the mission that morning to warn you someone may have hacked your computer, but I couldn't reach you."

"I'm so relieved, Ty! Thank you for trusting me. You were right about wanting to get married before you left. I was wrong. Since I'm not officially related to you, the military won't update your condition. So, I had to resort to imposing on your parents."

"I never thought about that, but it makes sense. It doesn't matter. You're here now, and the doctor says I'm going to survive this. We're going to be alright."

"Yes, we are," said Seeney, "but Tom and I need to go back to Germany now. Your old friend, Steve Jackson, is our pilot, and he helped us to get here. He oversees a two-plane attachment at Ziestrucken and bent some rules to allow us on his plane. I'm also certain we aren't supposed to be in Kadun. You'll be in Germany, though, soon, and then back in the states. I love you so much—oh—by the way, Tom says he'll marry us for free since I paid for his ticket here."

"Way to negotiate! Thank you for—well, just thank you. I love you, both."

The three friends gave light hugs and left Ty's room. Doctor Shapiro was waiting for them, and they followed him to the armored vehicle outside. Within fifteen minutes, they were back at the C-130. Two of the four giant propellers were spinning when they arrived, and by the time the three passengers strapped into their seats, the airplane taxied.

When Ty awoke the next time, Doctor Faould was at his bedside. "Good morning, sir. How do you feel?"

"Better, Doctor. I feel only slight pain in my back, and my head is clearer today."

"Excellent, sir. We administered no pain medication since the operation last night, so this is a positive sign. Your fever also subsided, and you're only a degree above normal. Therefore, I believe we neutralized the infection."

"So, what comes next?"

"Your C-130 will return late in the week, and if we're pleased with your progress, you should be able to make the flight to Germany. You'll most likely stay there for a while before flying back to your country."

"And the operation went well?"

"Yes, sir," said Faould. "It went very well. Your Doctor Shapiro is a fine surgeon, and I felt honored to assist him. I also enjoyed meeting your friends, Mr. Burns and Ms. Tyson. They are exceptional people."

Ty smiled. "Yes, they are, Doctor. One is my fiancé, and the other has been my friend since I was four years old."

"You are a fortunate man, sir, for such friends. Pastor Burns invited me to speak to his congregation in West Virginia by satellite in several weeks."

"That sounds interesting, Doctor. Are you giving a sermon?"

"No, sir. I believe I'm sharing my perspective on how different cultures and religions share many common elements. Your pastor friend possesses an unusually open mind in this area."

"He's blessed with a brilliant mind, and you two would be outstanding partners."

In Tartan Springs later in that week

"How's Ty doing?" asked Tom.

"Great, I think," said Seeney. "He flew to Germany on Tuesday, and I talked to him a little when he got to Randstuhl. His fever is gone, and doctors believe the back operation was successful. He'll probably be in Germany for a couple of weeks but could be in the states by April."

"I'm glad we went out there. What an adventure, but I think it was important for Ty."

"Adventure? An understatement, for sure. You're right, though. I think our visit had a positive impact on Ty. Something changed when he realized we were next to his bed after the operation."

"We'll never know what might have happened if we hadn't made the trip. What did occur, though, was amazing. So, how's everything down there after the cell phone debacle?"

"Fine, I guess. I still can't believe Jack or Todd would do something like they did, but I'm past them now. Ty will be home soon, which is all that matters.

A week later, Ty left Kadun for Randstuhl, Germany. Doctor Shapiro met him at the hospital when Ty arrived, satisfied with the recovery since the operation. Shapiro told Ty he believed the stopover in Randstuhl would be relatively brief, as direct military flights from Germany to Dover Air Force Base were frequent. From there, the drive to the Bethesda Naval Hospital was a short one.

Major Harrell arrived in Bethesda on April 10th as Doctor Shapiro had predicted he would, not quite a month since the last time he piloted a helicopter. For Ty, the period seemed much longer, but he felt relieved to be back in the United States.

19 Recovery

After Ty arrived at the Naval Hospital in Bethesda, Seeney drove from Tartan Springs almost every weekend to see him. She found a small boutique bed-and-breakfast near the hospital, which she made her headquarters for these visits. Physicians confined Ty to his hospital room when he first arrived, directing him to perform light exercises from an apparatus attached to the bed. Doctor Sheila Roberson told Seeney Ty progressed well but that she wanted to take it slowly. The doctor projected Ty might start physical therapy out of bed within two weeks.

Once Ty began short workout sessions outside of his hospital room, his recovery picked up speed. Doctor Roberson reported to Seeney that Ty improved weekly at a nearly miraculous rate, and she thought he might be released from the hospital in less than a month. However, she warned Seeney that after Ty's release, he still faced a long period of consistent physical therapy.

On one weekend, Ty told Seeney his therapist had suggested he could now leave the medical facility for short periods of light activities. "Like walks?" asked Seeney.

"Yes. I think Doctor Roberson meant that. She believes getting away from this room on occasion would be healthy for me as long as I don't try to overdo anything."

"Wonderful! Where would you like to go?"

"Well," said Ty, looking for the right words. "I've got some equipment which hasn't been checked out here at the hospital. So, I would sort of like to see if it all still works."

Catching his drift, Seeney said, "I understand. Will you need technical assistance with this? I may know someone familiar with the equipment."

"Yes. Who do you have in mind?"

Well, that would be me. I'm a little out of practice, but I think I remember how everything works."

"That's what I hoped you'd say. The equipment already seems to be responding to verbal stimuli. A good sign, right?"

Seeney glanced toward Ty's belt. "Yes. That is an excellent sign, but I think we need to get it to a garage right away and on a rack where I can have a closer look."

"Great! I'll drive."

"Nah, I will," said Seeney, winking at Ty. Rain fell lightly as the couple reached the door of the bed-and-breakfast. Well past lunchtime, neither Ty nor Seeney were hungry.

Seeney and Ty lay next to each other not long after, listening to the rain splatter against the window. Ty inquired, "Everything worked okay, right?"

"Yes. The things appear to be fully functional, but that was only a single test drive, and I'll need to do some additional analysis. So, let's allow the engine to cool down a bit and take another spin later."

"Where do we find such responsible mechanics?"

"You can't, so don't start looking." And she cuddled against his chest. In this microcosm of the world, on a rainy day in the nation's capital, in a small room with a population of two, all seemed right, at last.

Seeney returned to Tartan Springs energized. Ty strengthened each week, and the horrors of February were becoming ever more distant in her memory. She had met with Terri Miller at Eastern Hydroponic and explained what Eastern needed to do relative to the missing W-9 from

State Testing Lab. Terri understood and apologized for the trouble the issue caused Seeney. She also informed Seeney her company had sourced another firm to perform future water tests.

Seeney heard nothing more from Tom Burns, and Gina McCaskey had not called her. She hoped this meant other events might have overtaken the necessity of her involvement relative to the Tartan Spring water supply. She wanted nothing more to do with Justin Domship, Todd Foster, or any of the McCaskey clan.

She pulled into her driveway and walked back to retrieve the empty garbage cans left in front of her house. The two containers stayed in a three-sided enclosure in the rear of her home, which hid them from the side street and neighbors. She turned to walk back to the front driveway and noticed a cigarette butt just off the sidewalk near the back door. Picking it up, she dropped the litter in one of the empty cans. Then, as an afterthought, she tested the back door to ensure it remained locked. It was.

When she parked her car inside the garage, Seeney left the garage door open and walked around to the front door. On her way, she checked the ground for other cigarette butts. She found none and unlocked the front door.

After closing the garage door from the inside, she decided to check some other things outside. She strolled around the house's perimeter, starting from the front door looking for other cigarette butts, checking particularly carefully underneath windows. She found no more and went back inside. The single butt at the back door bothered her because no reason existed for anyone to be there. Her mail and package deliveries came to the front door, and neither meters nor utility connections were near her back door.

She had successfully spooked herself, so she went ahead and checked the security of all her windows. Jack never believed the couple needed a home security system in a town as safe as Tartan Springs. Instead, motion-activated lighting at the front and back porch sufficed for him. Seeney didn't think about it much after Jack vacated either, until now. Since she might not even live at this house after the wedding, installing a security system didn't seem cost-effective. At a minimum, she committed to adding some additional motion-activated lighting around the perimeter of her property.

20 Gina McCaskey

After another visit to Bethesda, Seeney had four messages on her home voicemail that concerned her. One was from Terri Miller at Eastern Hydroponics; one was from Georgina McCaskey; two were from nobody. They were hang-ups. Since the encounter with Justin Domship, and the unexplained cigarette butt by her back door, Seeney found herself skittish of anything unusual. Hang-ups weren't unordinary, but to her now, they were unnerving.

Also, before seeing the vehicle at Domship's property, Seeney was sure she had never seen his dilapidated, camouflage-painted Wrangler before. Now, it seemed to be every place. She knew this was probably her overworked imagination, but it was always in the back of her mind.

The April 15th tax filing date had passed, so Seeney hoped Terri Miller's call had nothing to do with improperly filed paperwork. It didn't. Eastern received its first water quality check from the new testing lab, and Terri wanted to show Seeney the results.

"Nothing overly unusual," said Terri on the phone call, "but I want you to look at something. The water quality report is a two-page document, and STL only ever provided us with one page. We didn't know this, of course. We never checked at the top of the page STL sent us, which indicated page one of two. Based on what is on the full report we just received, we're adding something to our filtration process."

Seeney, uninterested in water quality science, politely committed to meeting with Terri later in the week. "That is fascinating, Terri. Thank you for calling. I'll look forward to seeing your information."

When Seeney reluctantly returned the call to Georgina McCaskey, Georgina answered. "Hello, Siena. Thank you for calling me back."

Seeney said, "Our mutual friend must have provided you my business number and not my cell. I would have called you back sooner if I'd received your message on my cell."

"Yes, ma'am. Pastor Burns gave me this number a few weeks ago. As he suggested, I wanted to call you earlier, but I couldn't muster the courage until now. Would you meet me in person?"

"Sure, Georgina. Where would you like to meet, and when?"

"Would tomorrow evening be too early? I know where you live, and I could come there."

"Sure. Would seven o'clock be OK?"

"Yes, ma'am. See you then."

Seeney recognized Georgina McCaskey when she came through the front door but couldn't recall from where. Perhaps from seeing the young woman around town. Tartan Springs was, after all, still a relatively small community.

"Hi, Ms. Tyson," said Georgina. "Thank you for meeting with me. I'm sorry for making this so mysterious."

"It's OK, Georgina. I guess our mutual friend believes this conference is important."

"Pastor Burns is an incredible person, isn't he?" Before Seeney responded, Georgina added, "I go by Gina."

"And I go by Seeney to my friends, and a friend of Pastor Burns qualifies. Come on in."

Gina glanced through the window near the door and then to her watch before following Seeney to the den. Seeney noticed and asked, "Are you expecting someone else to join us?"

Gina appeared surprised by the question and replied, "No, ma'am. Not at all. I need this meeting to be as private as possible. Why do you ask?"

"Well, you looked out the window and then at your wristwatch. Are you concerned someone followed you?"

"I'm sorry. I'm scared, paranoid, and probably shouldn't be here. I could be getting myself into a lot of trouble, but I don't want to cause you difficulties because of the meeting. It isn't dark yet, and I'm afraid someone passing your house might recognize my car in front."

"I can't even imagine why you're here, Gina, but let's move your car to my garage. The left side is empty."

Gina parked her car safely in Seeney's two-car garage, and the ladies resumed their places in the den. "Do you remember the cheerleading camp you helped coach in the summer of 2004?" asked Gina.

"Yes! That's it! I've been racking my brain for where I know you—and it's that camp! You were thirteen or fourteen years old. Two of the other high school cheerleaders and I conducted the camp for the County Recreation Department."

"Yes, I was thirteen and going into the seventh grade. We had about a dozen girls and one boy in the group. You were the most amazing coach, and you taught me how to do a back handspring."

"Thank you for bringing that memory back to me. You were the youngest girl in the class and so cute. I do remember showing you how to do the handspring, but I also recall something else now. After the class was over, I saw you just about every summer day practicing that handspring in front of your uncle's bottled water company."

"Yep. That was me. It must've worked because I got to cheer for four years in high school and then three out of four years in college."

"You look like you could still do the acrobatics," said Seeney. "Where did you go to school?"

"West Virginia."

"Division I athlete. Congratulations! When did you graduate?"

"2013, with a degree in mining engineering. I stayed another year to complete a master's in environmental engineering."

"Why does the degree in mining not surprise me, but the master's in environmental engineering does?" said Seeney.

The question seemed to rattle Gina, and Seeney apologized. "I'm sorry, Gina. I sounded rude and judgmental, which isn't what I intended at all."

"That's OK. Yours was an honest and logical observation, given my family's business for the past seven generations. Also, your question is relevant to my reason for being here. Before we go into that, though, can I ask you about your friend, Pastor Burns?"

"Of course. We graduated from high school together but didn't become close friends until last year. Do you attend his church in Compton?"

"Yes," answered Gina. "I started going on summer breaks from WVU right after his ordination. He was young and different from any ministers I ever met before, and I enjoyed it when he gave the sermons. I could relate to them. I was comfortable talking to him about things, and before my senior year at college, we had a conversation that changed my life."

"OK, Gina. Stop right there. My interest is piqued, and unless you're in a hurry, I'm going to pour myself a glass of wine. I'm sure the reason you're here is serious, but I promise I can function with wine. I already like you, and we don't need to rush this. Would you like a glass? Your choices are white ... or other white."

Gina smiled, a little surprised, and said, "Thank you, Seeney. I would love a glass—and would prefer white."

When they resumed their conversation, Gina asked, "Do you know about Pastor Burns' sister, Adele?"

"Not much. Adele died when I was in like seventh or eighth grade. A suicide, right?"

"Yes. Adele was five or six years older than Pastor Burns and was involved in beauty pageants from when she was a baby until she died. Right after Adele graduated from high school, she was a quarterfinalist in the Miss West Virginia competition. She died a couple of years later, after failing to make the final eight of the same competition. Most in the community believed her poor showing was the reason for the suicide. She didn't leave any notes."

"An awful story," said Seeney. "I was unaware of the background."

"Adele's death was tragic, but Pastor Tom gives his sister credit for the inspiration changing his life. Years before she took her own life, Adele told Tom he should never try to live up to the expectations of others—but only to those he set for himself. Adele apparently felt trapped into a life she didn't create or plan and was miserable. She warned her brother not to make the same mistake."

"That explains so much about this man who I adore but don't always understand. I'm a bit surprised Tom never shared this with me—because Tom and I are close. He knows things about me nobody else in the world does. Tom's a private person, so why did he share this with you?"

"Because it was a unique gift to me from him which related to my situation. Pastor Tom was certain I could benefit from the same advice his sister had once given him. In one of our many conversations during an adult Bible study he sponsored, I confided to him about my destiny. I'm the only direct heir to seven generations of McCaskey's in this county. I was supposed to be the fifth George McCaskey to run the family coal business, but I turned out to be a girl. So, there will be no George Milton McCaskey V, just Georgina Millicent McCaskey. Despite any regrets my father felt in not producing someone to carry the name, he tried to raise someone who could carry the business. I went to West Virginia University to be a mining engineer for that reason. Then I had the conversation with Pastor Burns."

"He convinced you to live your own life, not one somebody else planned for you?"

"He didn't convince me of anything," said Gina. "He only passed on good counsel his sister once gave to him. He shared his belief that people are free to create their own paths, not be bound by those set by others. I thought about that, and I agreed with him, so I stayed another year at WVU to earn a master's in environmental engineering."

"Whew! You make me glad to be unburdened by family legacies and responsibilities. I understand how you must feel."

"Some difficult moments for sure, but Pastor Burns helped me through these. I'm confident about what I can do with education, energy, and access to resources unavailable to many others. I need to do my best to use these assets in the most productive ways strategically possible."

"Where do I come in?"

"Want another glass of wine? You're going to need it," Gina warned.

"I better open a bottle."

Back in the den, Gina said, "I apologize in advance for what I'm about to tell you. I thought about this and believe I'm doing the right thing. You may disagree, though, and I'll respect whatever your decisions are after this evening."

"That is quite an opening, Gina. Go on."

"Several weeks ago, maybe months," started Gina, "you attempted to obtain tax information for State Testing Labs."

Seeney interrupted Gina. "Gina, you may need to go no further. One of my bookkeeping clients required a W-9 form for service STL performed. The owner of STL refused to provide the information, and I notified my client of what her company should file in such cases with the IRS. I did the necessary due diligence to obtain the information, and my work and professional obligations are complete. I'm aware now that STL does work for McCaskey Coal, but that isn't my business or concern."

Gina listened patiently, and when Seeney finished, said, "I understand, and again, I'm sorry. In the process of doing your job, you also discovered STL does work for the town and that Mayor Foster informed his town's finance director to avoid sending a 1099 for STL's work."

"True, but I'm not planning to cause trouble for either the town or Mr. Domship. As I said, I finished my personal responsibilities to my client."

"Yes, and I wish I had a way to avoid involving you. I don't. I'm not here this evening because of what you *plan* to do, but because of what you *can* do. Through our mutual friend, I'm also aware of your character. Pastor Burns says most people believe two choices exist for them in life—to do the right thing or do the wrong thing. Others suggest a third option, which is to do nothing. Burns argues doing nothing is no different from doing the wrong thing, and I agree with him. He confided to me where he thinks you would stand." She paused. "You might want some more wine now."

Seeney took a large sip from her glass and relaxed back into the chair, realizing she was past the point of no return in the current conversation. Gina continued, "The client requesting the tax information is Eastern Hydroponics, and all you learned in your research for them is accurate. Justin Domship, the only employee of State Testing Labs, does testing work for McCaskey Coal and Tartan Springs. Justin is my aunt Stella's son, and not much good for anything, as you found out."

"You heard about my encounter with him?"

"Yes, and I'm sorry about that. Justin is a degenerate. Anyway, my grandfather provided the funds for Justin to take the course required by the state for certification as a water sample chemist. Justin's only clients were supposed to be McCaskey Coal and the town of Tartan Springs. My family paid him off the books for this work, and Mayor Foster agreed not to require a W-9 from Justin. The income was a form of charity on the part of my grandfather to care for my no-load cousin. But unfortunately, Justin got greedy a year ago and started taking on other work, which is what led you to identify him."

"That, and he scared the bejeezus out of me when I visited his trailer to try to pick up the W-9 in person," said Seeney.

"Right, and with a little more research, you would discover that the most senior employee on the town's payroll is Luther McCaskey, my grandfather's youngest brother. Luther has run the water plant for almost forty years."

"What does he have to do with this?"

"I'm getting to that, Seeney. Sorry. You've seen the tanker truck from Rural Valley Electric that passes through town about once per month, right?"

"Of course. My parents died in an accident involving one of those trucks in 2008."

"I'm aware. If you called the Department of Transportation, which manages the state's weigh stations, you'd learn the tanker enters our area fully loaded and leaves empty. Rural Valley Electric might not be willing to tell you the contents of tanker loads from their plant sites, but you could easily check the state's Department of Transportation for permits issued to parties transporting toxic materials. With this information, you might become worried, and you might find that Tartan Springs Water, our bottled water company, stopped using water from the natural spring in 2008. Since then, the bottled product is the same municipal water that comes from the fixtures in your house."

"So, if the water company no longer uses the spring water, are you telling me McCaskey Coal polluted our water supply for at least nine years without letting anyone know? Why would you want your family discovered, and why do you want me involved?"

"I'm trying to protect my family, which is why I want you involved. I feel terrible about engaging you in this, but I'm desperate. So, allow me to finish, and you may understand my dilemma."

Seeney was now inwardly fuming that her friend, Tom Burns, arranged for this meeting. "OK, Gina. Go ahead."

"The coal industry has been declining for decades, and when my grandfather inherited the company in 1965, McCaskey Coal was a shell of its former self. Then, he did something in 1975, which pretty much ensured the company would never again be economically competitive in the West Virginia mining business. Are you familiar with the term MTM?"

"No," admitted Seeney.

"It stands for Mountain Top Mining. Put simply, the MTM process blasts the top of a mountain away with explosives, exposing the veins of coal. Whoever invented the system should be hung, and whatever politicians allowed it to continue should be placed in our national Hall of Shame forever. But, at the small price of ruining the beauty of our gorgeous mountains, MTM expedites the mining of coal. The process is less labor-intensive and requires no expensive tunneling. Despite the pressure to keep McCaskey Coal profitable, my grandfather couldn't bring himself to resort to this process for mining coal. He left the decision to my father ten years later, neither encouraging him nor discouraging him. No matter what you or others in the community may believe, my father is a good person, not driven by greed. He, like my grandfather, refused to embrace the concept of Mountain Top Mining."

"But McCaskey Coal is still operating, so your dad must be doing something right," said Seeney.

"Our company's coal production declined to just a trickle through the eighties and nineties, with revenues in many years not covering the cost to produce it. In 2007, a representative of Rural Valley Electric approached my father with a proposal to utilize our company's existing infrastructure and provide needed revenue for the business. RVE needed places to store toxic waste resulting from operations at their four area power plants, and McCaskey Coal had multiple empty slurry ponds available. So, in 2008, RVE began bringing a tanker truck per month to our location. One of these trucks holds about eight thousand gallons of sludge per trip, so in nine years, our largest pit is only about two-thirds full, and we own two other empty pits RVE can use. McCaskey Coal earns almost three hundred thousand dollars per year from the storage."

"Not a bad business since the slurry ponds are already there."

"The problem is our slurry pond leaks. McCaskey Coal employs someone to check the water in the Siler River just below our mining operations monthly. We've been doing this since 1965. Now you also know McCaskey Coal's relationship to the person in charge of water for the town. These measures aren't to help McCaskey Coal hide the existence of contaminants resulting from our operations. We take these precautions to make sure our business never harms the citizens of the community. For generations, we have ensured that McCaskey Coal becomes aware of problems right away—not after the fact. Our tests indicated trace levels of sulfur and hexavalent chromium in the aquifer after the first year of the storage program, and my father presumed the cause was a leak in the retention pond. Sulfur isn't a problem, since it isn't toxic. The hexavalent chromium, called CR-6, alarmed him. CR-6 is the chemical at the center of the crisis made nationally famous by the movie *Erin Brockovich*."

"Oh, no!" interrupted Seeney. "We've been drinking water that can cause cancer?"

"Not really," replied Gina. "Even after the interest created by the movie, the EPA specified no standard for levels of CR-6 in public water supplies. The only standards apply to total amounts of chromium present. Amounts of one-tenth of a milligram per liter or one hundred parts per billion are considered unsafe. Our tests never registered more than fifty parts per billion in thirty-plus years, and even these small amounts are removed from the town's water supply before anyone drinks from it. When Uncle Luther discovered traces of CR-6 in the municipal water, he instituted a different filtration process, called reverse osmosis, to remove the chemical. Tartan Springs Water also quit using water from the natural spring for bottled water."

"Gina," said Seeney. "I'm not sure what to say or what you expect me to do. Even if your family did try to protect citizens, I don't think your company should knowingly cause dangerous pollution of the municipal water supply, no matter how insignificant that might be. Why hasn't your father just fixed the leak in the retention pond?"

"That isn't so easy, and the remediation would cost money the company no longer has."

"So, let me get this straight," said Seeney. "You're the anonymous whistleblower providing essential facts to a case impacting the collective health of our community, but which might also destroy your family?"

"No. I'm an environmentally motivated activist providing a way for *you* to fill in some missing information relative to a situation potentially affecting our citizens. What you do with the information is entirely up to you, and I believe you'll do the right thing. I can't in good conscience destroy my family. My goal is to help them, not hurt them. We've done much over the past seven generations to benefit this town, and we can do more. McCaskey Coal just needs to pause and reset now."

"So, why don't you suggest that to your father?"

"Because, as much as my father and grandfather love me, I'm still a kid to them. They remember me practicing handsprings in front of the bottled water business, not graduating with a degree in engineering. So, they do their best to shield me from the unpleasantness of our current business, and they're sad because they think they somehow failed me."

"In a perfect world, what would I do?"

"You would request a meeting with my father. He's concerned by your research into SLT. You could do a bit more research, perhaps using the hints I provided, and maybe convince my father the time has come to address our problems intelligently. You inadvertently stumbled on information that others could have found, but to date, haven't. Your logical questions could provide the critical catalyst necessary to effect an overdue solution."

"Don't you think Mr. McCaskey would receive such a meeting as a threat?"

"I guess that depends on you, Seeney, but I don't think your message would have to come across like that. Are you familiar with the Elizabeth Whorton Scholarship?"

"No. Should I be?"

"Not necessarily, but since your fiancé was once a recipient, I thought you might have heard of it. George McCaskey III created it to honor his wife, my great-grandmother. Originally endowed with one million dollars, the scholarship can only fund college for Tartan Springs high school students. Back when McCaskey Coal made a lot of money, the McCaskeys reinvested heavily into their community. You're familiar with the McCaskey library and the McCaskey Town Park, but the family did much more. If you approach my dad and grandfather to alert them —warn them —that a solution to a significant problem is overdue, I don't believe you would appear threatening."

"I see, and I'm betting you're working on a plan for after that. By the way, how did you know about my fiancé and his scholarship?"

Gina smiled. "Tonight's meeting may have appeared spontaneous,

Seeney, but I planned it. I wouldn't waste your time by not being prepared. But, as you suspect, I do have a plan."

"Do I need more wine for this?"

"No. The worst is over, and I appreciate your patience. I believe your meeting with my father will generate a family discussion, and my father will invite me. By the time this happens, my additional research may surprise the family. I have ideas that will help to address the current issues as well as protect the McCaskey legacy."

"Like what?"

"Well, I'm not ready to share everything yet, but I'm friends with smart people who are in the business of re-purposing old mines. I went to school with one of them. I'm also aware that millions of dollars in federal and state grant money exist for bona fide projects designed to clean up the mess left behind by our former dependence on coal. And lastly, I'm certain RVE's resources for other viable locations to bring toxic waste are limited."

"Why am I surprised you're so prepared?"

"Because you're only prior experience with me was as a thirteen-year-old cheerleader wannabe."

"Maybe so. That certainly changed. Can I think about all this for a few days? As you guessed when we first began talking, I don't want to be in the middle of something this dramatic and this important now. My fiancé just returned to the states after narrowly avoiding death as a Marine Corps pilot. We have a wedding to plan—and I want to think about a happy life together, perhaps away from this community. So, getting involved with a local problem isn't at the top of my list of priorities."

"I understand," said Gina, "and I'll accept any decision you make without attempting to further involve you. I'm grateful for your time this evening."

Gina left after eleven o'clock, too late for Seeney to call either Ty or Tom. The wine made Seeney sleepy, but the evening's conversation kept her awake until the early hours of the morning.

21 Meeting of Minds

Seeney called Tom Burns as soon the following day as she thought he might be at the church. "Pastor Burns speaking."

"Hello, Pastor Burns. This is your former friend, Siena Tyson."

"Seeney! You called on the work phone and not the cell. What do you mean, former friend?"

"I called on the work phone because this involves work, and I said *former* friend because no real friend would ever try to involve me in the community scandal of the century. I'm joking about the former part, of course—but you're still in trouble."

"I'm guessing you talked to Gina McCaskey?"

"Right. How much of what she told me last night do you know?"

"I'm not sure all she told you, so I won't speculate—but I'm aware of quite a bit."

"And, you couldn't have warned me?" asked Seeney.

"Not with a clear conscience, Seeney. Especially since I'm the one who suggested for Gina to speak with you."

"Well, she did. We talked for nearly three hours last night, and I'm not sure what to do."

"If you're asking me, I can't answer for you. You'll have to decide for yourself what the right thing is and then do it."

"Sure, Tom. Real simple," Seeney said sarcastically. "The right thing for me? The right thing for Ty? The right thing for Tartan Springs? The right thing for Gina? Or are you talking about the right thing for God? Which right thing am I supposed to do?"

"Whatever the right thing is, is the right thing for all those."

Seeney thought about what Burns said for a second. "You sound philosophic, Tom, but I don't think it's so easy. The legally correct option would be to turn all this evidence over to the police and let the courts decide. McCaskey Coal has knowingly allowed our water supply to be contaminated, maybe dangerously, and that is wrong! However, if I turned what I know over to the legal system, the results could be disastrous for McCaskey Coal, devastating for Gina and her family, and would involve me in a long and contentious trial that wouldn't be good for me in any way."

"Let me ask you something, perhaps unrelated," said Tom. "When we boarded the military aircraft, illegally entering Becktistan, did we break military laws or maybe some international visa laws?"

"Probably a bunch of them."

"But was the result of that trip positive for Ty?"

"Yes."

"How about you—was the trip good for you?" asked Tom.

"Without a doubt!"

"Did we hurt anyone by breaking these laws?"

"No."

"So, you agree the right thing morally and ethically isn't always the lawful thing?"

"I guess," said Seeney. "Doing nothing wouldn't make me feel any better."

"I didn't think so. That isn't an option for Gina, either. She's sure this situation needs resolution."

"She's a strong lady, Tom. If she hadn't been the one to dump all this guilt on me, I'd like her a lot."

"I think you like her anyway," said Tom. "You may not like how she's attempting to involve you, but I think you respect what she's trying to accomplish."

"How close a friend is she to you, Tom? Your admiration for her is plain."

"I met her shortly after being ordained, and, yes, I'm proud of her. She's a remarkable and bright young lady who will succeed in life wherever she goes."

"High praise coming from you," said Seeney.

"Deserved, too. Perhaps my highest reference for her, however, is that she reminds me of you."

"Wow! Just keep piling on the guilt."

"Didn't mean to," said Tom. "I trust you'll make the right decision—the same as I trust her to. If I'm not missing anything, she's only asked that you engage her father in a meeting. Correct?"

"Yes. She's given me some hints about where I can find additional information that would be relevant to the meeting."

"I might be able to help you with that," offered Tom.

"Meaning, you already conducted that research?"

"Possibly. We have discussed in the past that my network and connections now are unusual." When Seeney didn't reply right away, Tom asked, "Are you still there?"

"Yes. We're on a church line, and none of the responses I had in mind seemed appropriate. How were you so sure you could convince me to go along with Gina's plan?"

"Because it was the right thing to do. You are only obliged to take a meeting, Seeney. Gina will do the heavy work after. She just wants you to create an opening for her. If her plan works, she may create a chance to address the McCaskey company's issues, preserve the McCaskey family's reputation, and help build a better company that would benefit our area and maybe the world. On the other hand, if she isn't successful, she at least tried, and she'll join another engineering business someplace to become fabulously wealthy."

"Alright. Let's meet so you can share with me what you know. Then, I'll call Gina to tell her I'll schedule the conference with her father. I'm going to ask Ty for his opinion, too—unless you beat me to that. Did you?"

"No. Until this evening, Gina's conversations with me were professionally privileged. Just between her and me."

The following morning, Seeney made a short list of things she wanted to research before scheduling the talk with Four and Milton McCaskey. Based on what Gina told her, Seeney already knew the answers additional research would yield, but she wanted to create her own plausible trail for it.

In addition, doing the extra investigative work would protect Gina's confidentiality, as well as insulate her from potential legal liabilities if the situation took an ugly turn. Finally, working backward from a known answer was infinitely more manageable than trying to discover the unknown solution hidden amidst volumes of relevant and non-relevant data.

Now aware of the contents of the Rural Valley Electric tanker that arrived regularly at the McCaskey Coal-mining facilities, Seeney, to protect Gina, needed to think of a way she might have discovered this on her own. So, opening the bottom drawer to the filing cabinet next to her desk, she retrieved a thickly bound file. The label on the folder read, "Accident - 2008". Seeney remembered the day she secured the file with a cloth ribbon and placed it in the cabinet.

She and Millie deposited the insurance company's settlement check relative to the interstate accident that killed their parents. While neither sister had thoughts of pursuing a claim against Rural Valley Electric for negligence involving the crash, the family of the driver of the tanker truck had. That family's insurance company requested Seeney's parents' insurance company to join the suit to make the case stronger. Seeney and Millie approved the request, and RVE quickly settled the claim out of court for about ten percent of the amount stipulated in the lawsuit. The settlement check came with a thick dossier outlining the company's case against RVE, which neither Seeney nor Millie ever read.

Seeney opened the bound folder and turned to the description of the accident. In addition to a narrative detailing the incident, the sworn testimony of various people corroborated different aspects of the insurance company's legal case. Police officers responding to the accident described the scene, and the coroner's report revealed in more detail than Seeney wanted the precise causes of her parents' death. A state chemist testified none of the contents of the tanker truck escaped to the highway because of the crash.

Flipping a few pages, Seeney read the deposition provided by an executive of Rural Valley Electric. This document also explained the tanker driver's assignment in meticulous detail, including the carrier's contents and destination. Bingo!

In all the years of seeing the RVE truck travel through Tartan Springs, Seeney had never thought about what it carried ... or didn't carry. Most likely, nobody had. It was just a big commercial vehicle servicing a local mining operation, and its occurrence was no more unusual than all the other vehicles traveling between the mining operation and the interstate.

Without knowing it until now, Seeney had the answer for the tanker's contents in a file cabinet. Four and Milton McCaskey would certainly not be surprised that, considering Seeney's unique connection to a runaway RVE tanker truck years earlier, she might be familiar with what they stored at their mining operations.

With this fact in her pocket, Seeney hoped she wouldn't need it. This information was, in effect, her *stick*; she hoped she might accomplish her mission using a *carrot* instead.

Seeney's next call was to Terri Miller at Eastern Hydroponics. After confirming with Terri when she would stop by to pick up copies of water quality reports completed by STL, Seeney called Elsie Morning at the Tartan Springs municipal building.

"Finance, this is Elsie Morning."

"Hi, Elsie. This is Seeney."

"Oh, hello, Seeney," said a lukewarm Elsie. "I really can't talk to you more about the things we discussed earlier. I got in a lot of trouble for meeting with you the last time."

"I'm sorry, Elsie, but you didn't do anything wrong. Some others are doing something very wrong, however, and I need your help. I promise I'll protect you, but you would be better off staying on the right side of this."

"Seeney," whispered Elsie, "I have three children, and Clem's company laid him off. I need this job in the worst way, and I can't afford to move. After we spoke the last time, Mayor Foster threatened me. I'm sure he'll fire me if he finds out I talked to you again."

"I understand, and I don't want that to happen. Nobody knows better than I what a bully Foster is, but he can't fire you for providing public information to a citizen. I promise you, if he does, his legal problems will become even bigger. You'll be able to provide what I need without Todd ever finding out, I think."

"I'm so scared, Seeney, but what is it you’re looking for?"

"Just copies of the last two water quality reports submitted by the water plant. These tests must be retained and are a matter of public record, so I doubt you would even have to ask anyone for them. You can probably access these documents yourself."

"Yes. That one is easy because a copy of the form accompanies the requisition request from the water plant for a check to reimburse State Testing Lab. I can provide two of those to you but would prefer if you didn't come here to pick them up."

"Of course not. Why don't we both get gas this afternoon after work at the Fill-N-Go? I have some pictures to show you from the last Chamber networking lunch."

"Okay. That will work. I usually leave here at four-thirty, so I'll be at the Fill-N-Go at around four-forty. I'll bring the paperwork for your business license renewal as well."

"Thanks. See you a little later."

That evening, after receiving the two reports from Elsie and the four incomplete reports from Terri Miller, Seeney spread the papers on her dining room table. As Terri mentioned to Seeney earlier, the reports from STL for Eastern Hydroponics were single pages, cut off at the bottom. The reports from the town were also individual pages, but both the front and back contained data.

The town's documents included two reports for each of the two dates of samples taken for a total of four forms. For both dates, one form had data for samples taken at the inlet valves of the water plant, and the other one recorded the results for water sampled at the exit valve. The records for the inlet valve samples indicated traces of chromium in the water. However, tests from the exit valve showed no chromium present in the water.

On all four of the STL forms for Eastern Hydroponics, the line for chromium was missing. Also, no information appeared on the back of the paper. As a result, Seeney felt confident the new tests for Eastern Hydroponics conducted by a different contractor would look like the town's tests, complete with two pages, not one, and showing trace amounts of chromium.

Seeney believed she had the information she needed for the meeting with Four and Milton McCaskey. Her supposed motivation for the conference was to request additional data relating to water samples the

McCaskeys might have at the mining operations to validate discoveries from the Eastern Hydroponic tests.

Her "good Samaritan" pretense to Four and Milton would also alert them to the existence of a potentially dangerous element in the water if they didn't already know about that. Positive that Four and Milton were aware contaminants originating at the mine escaped to the aquifer, Seeney still hoped this approach would be less threatening to them. She would default to the information derived from her parents' accident only if her softer strategy didn't work.

Satisfied with her plan, Seeney called Ty and briefed him. "Should you review with Gina or Tom before you call Four to schedule the meeting?" asked Ty.

"I don't think so. Both Tom and Gina have more information than I do now, but I don't want anymore. I'd like to protect Tom and Gina by not allowing Four and Milton to suspect their role. I believe Four will understand that the data I found is readily available to anyone and that proactive solutions are overdue. Gina will take the ball from there."

"Good luck, Seeney. Update me on how the meeting goes."

"Of course, I will."

The following morning, Four's secretary transferred Seeney's call to her boss. Surprised to hear from Seeney, Four didn't act overly enthusiastic, but agreed to a conference later in the afternoon. Seeney hung up the phone, took a deep breath, looked in the mirror, and said to herself, "Once again into the fire, girl!"

George McCaskey IV extended his hand to shake Seeney's, and he introduced Seeney to his father, George Milton McCaskey III. The older man rose from the table politely to greet Seeney, telling her to call him Milton. "And most folks call me Four," said George IV.

"Thank you," said Seeney. "My friends call me Seeney."

"Well, Seeney, what can we do for you? We don't get too many visitors up here on the mountain anymore." Seeney was sitting in a small conference room located inside McCaskey Coal corporate headquarters on Mullen Mountain. The building was over one hundred years old and seemed mostly empty. Mullen Mountain was one of three ranges where McCaskey Coal owned mineral rights and was twenty miles west of Tartan Springs.

"I'll only take a few minutes of your time. As I told you on the telephone, I'm trying to close the loop on a pesky little W-9 matter for one of my bookkeeping clients, Eastern Hydroponics."

"Yes. I thought we provided what you needed, even though we didn't have much to contribute."

"Yes, sir. You did. You told me Justin Domship performed water quality tests for your company, but you paid him in cash and not through payroll. You indicated this was a form of charity, and you didn't include expenses for this work in your financial filings."

"Yes, Seeney. Unfortunately, that is correct. It may not be the proper thing to do, but as we told you, Justin is a relative. He's a little off and doesn't believe in government, so I doubt he files taxes."

"Right," said Seeney. "I met Mr. Domship and agree he's somewhat strange, but I couldn't care less how he handles his personal life. Eastern Hydroponics filed the necessary paperwork with the IRS explaining the missing 1099s information, and that company won't be using Domship in the future. That isn't why I'm here, though." At that, Seeney pulled several official-looking forms from her briefcase. "Are you familiar with these documents, Four?"

Glancing at the water analysis sheets quickly, Four said, "Yes. We receive the same form for water quality checks here at the operations." He looked toward his father casually with a hint of panic in his eyes.

"Correct. These four forms on the left are the last reports completed for Eastern Hydroponics by State Testing Lab, your relative, Justin Domship. The ones on the right are from around the same date. STL took these tests for Tartan Springs. You can see that the forms on the left are all cut off at the bottom, missing about three lines of information."

Four looked at the two sets of documents for quite a while without saying anything. Finally, he said, "I see what you're talking about. Justin tends to be sloppy, but I'm not sure what your interest in us is. We don't oversee STL's work."

"No, sir. I understand, and I tried to obtain the completed copies of this report from Mr. Domship for my client with no success. The missing information concerned Eastern Hydroponics, so I went to the town offices to find a copy of the same form with no missing lines. Sally Ingram, the plant supervisor at Eastern, told me that someone from the town's administration referred STL to their company. So, I assumed

Domship provided the town with the same form. As it turns out, your nephew does two monthly tests for Tartan Springs, one at the intake valve from the river to the town's water plant and one from the exit valve before the water goes to the water tower. Those are the four reports on the right."

"Okay," said Four becoming irritated. "Why am I looking at these, and what am I supposed to see?"

"I'm sorry, Four. I just wanted to bring something to your attention. I discovered it totally by accident. You may be aware of this, but if not, you may want to be. One of the missing lines from the Eastern Hydroponics forms is the one that records levels of chromium in a water sample. Eastern Hydroponics wants to know if this element is present in their water because, at higher levels, it can be dangerous for human consumption."

Four snuck a glance at his father as Seeney continued to speak.

"In the town's four completed forms, all the lines for tests are included on the sheet, as you can see. Chromium is present at the intake valve but not when it exits the water plant. The town takes appropriate measures to filter the element from the drinking supply. Eastern Hydroponics has now contracted someone besides STL to perform water quality tests, and if they find chromium, the company will institute appropriate filtering. Since you also take many samples, I wondered if you could check your records as well?"

Four's head shifted from his father to Seeney. Not sure what to say, he stalled. He had no way of knowing whether Seeney might have additional, perhaps even more damning, information, so he believed it essential to keep her friendly. Finally, to create time to consider things, he said, "Goodness, Seeney! The analysis of a water sample is rather technical for a bookkeeper. You provide quite a service."

"Not really, Four," said Seeney, glad he had given her the opening she needed. "The issue with the W-9 just made me notice the missing lines on the form, which led me to the easiest place I might find a complete form. The folks at Eastern Hydroponics can handle the rest, but then I saw chromium listed on the town's water report. *Erin Brockovich* was one of my favorite movies, and I remembered hexavalent chromium was the culprit chemical in the show. The element is unusual, and if it might be coming from something you do here, I figured you'd want to be informed. I'm sorry I bothered you with this."

"Not at all, not at all," said Four. "We take pollution seriously, despite what people may say. I'll check our reports this week. Would you like me to call you back with what I find?"

"No. You might give Sally Ingram at Eastern Hydroponics a call sometime to compare notes. She's the plant supervisor. If she has traces of chromium show up in her next water tests, but you don't, then she might be able to narrow down where else it might be getting into the aquifer. She's a scientist, like you, and will be interested in these sorts of things."

Seeney left the meeting room, and Four looked at his father. "Now what, Dad?"

Milton shook his head. "I'm not sure, Four, but I think we all suspected this might happen eventually."

"I guess, but over a stupid W-9 form? What was that idiot thinking? He knows he wasn't supposed to go after outside business."

"We're the dumb ones, son. We trusted somebody with no brains and no morals with something important. Do you think this Seeney gal is what she purports to be, or is she trying to become the next Erin Brockovich?"

"No telling, Dad," said Four. "She's a mystery to me. I found it a bit scary a bookkeeper would do so much follow-up on the technical side of water."

"Yeah. Me too, son. But you know what? If it weren't her, it would be someone else at some point. She just expedited our deadline to take care of this—if we can. So, call Gina, and let's meet this evening."

"Okay, Dad. I'm sorry."

"For what, son?"

"For allowing us to get into this storage thing with Rural Valley Electric in the first place."

"Four, you did what you thought you had to do to save the remnants of this old company from final collapse. We both had opportunities to cave to the pressure of mountain top mining—but we didn't. The storage of RVE waste was a bridge to get us to another day."

"You're right. Thanks," said Four. "Our work is cut out for us now, though."

Milton smiled. "It is, Four, and the prospects exhilarate me. At eighty-two years old, I'm tired of the company left to me and looking forward to hearing what that granddaughter of mine thinks."

Seeney arrived home and called Gina. "Okay, lady, I did it. I didn't like it and felt a little bad about the acting, but I'm sure your father and grandfather are concerned."

"They are," said Gina. "My dad just asked me to join a family conference this evening. Thank you for doing this."

"You're welcome, Gina, and good luck. For your information, the only thing I used was the Eastern Hydroponics water reports compared to the same documents for the town. They think I'm an *Erin Brockovich* junkie—and they probably hate me."

"I doubt that, and after this evening, it won't matter. I think I'll be able to convince them about what we need to do."

Later in the evening at the McCaskey home

After the meeting concluded and Gina and Lisbeth left the room, Milton stayed behind with his son. "She's quite a daughter, Four."

"And quite a granddaughter, Dad."

"That too," said the old man, "and I'm extremely proud, but you and Lisbeth are responsible for Gina. So, I'm proud of you two as well."

Four appeared touched. "Thanks, Dad. I wish I could have done more with the company. In some ways, I failed you and Granddad."

"Nonsense, son! If anyone failed the former generations of McCaskey, it was me, not you. I had to live with the failure for most of my life, but tonight I feel better than in decades."

"Why, Dad?"

"My granddaughter, for one thing," said Milton. "She makes me want to get up tomorrow morning and start helping her with the plan. She's smart, passionate, committed, and I think she's right. Her ideas could work. The other thing, son, is this—sometimes doing nothing is better than doing the wrong thing. You and I both made a decision that didn't benefit our company financially, but I think we made the correct choice."

"Are you talking about the MTM?"

"Yes," said Milton. "Mountain Top Mining could have kept the coal company more profitable for a few more decades, but we'd have ruined the geography in which we live. I don't think the McCaskeys before us would have approved."

"You're right. Your father, my grandfather, once told me, 'You must always be proud of the place you're from and live your life so your place is proud of you.' If we had blown away the tops of the surrounding mountains, I don't think our place would be too proud of us."

"I heard your grandfather repeat that quote many times. I think Abe Lincoln said it, and I like it. By not allowing the destruction of the beauty of the place we live, I believe we've sustained the family's legacy beyond the odds against us for the past fifty years."

"The best part of our legacy might be Gina," said Four, smiling at his father.

"I'm okay with that. In fact, I'm darn proud of it. When Jules died, I had no strong desire to keep going myself. Feeling guilt for leaving you a business in poor shape but incapable of finding a way to make it better, I patiently waited for my time to end. Tonight, I don't want it to end. I have contacts; I know people; I can bring relevant experience to Gina's plan. Her energy inspires me, and her pride in our family humbles me. I think I can help her and want to spend my remaining time doing that."

"I'm glad, Dad. I think the four of us, including Lisbeth, can be an excellent team. Until tonight, Gina was my baby, who I sheltered from the business. I should have resourced her intellect and energy sooner. What would you think of naming her Vice President of Development tomorrow?"

"I think that would be a day late. Gina has work to do, and the title will help her open doors. Can you ask her to join us again now?"

The following morning, Gina phoned Seeney. "Your meeting worked better and quicker than I ever imagined possible. Can we meet again?"

"Sure," said Seeney. "Where and when?"

"How about this evening at your place? I'll park inside your garage again if that's okay?"

"Okay, see you around eight o'clock. I'll leave the garage door open."

Gina settled into a chair across from Seeney. Visibly energized, she opened her briefcase and accepted the glass of wine Seeney offered.

Before sipping, she clinked Seeney's glass. "Thank you, Seeney—so much."

"Gina, I didn't do anything but participate in a short meeting. Tell me what happened. Why are you so excited?"

"Well, for several reasons," said Gina. "First, my new title at McCaskey Coal is Vice President of Development."

"Wow! Congratulations! Sounds like your presentation went well."

"Yes. I spoke to my dad, mother, and grandfather, and I think I surprised them with my knowledge of the company and our industry. I gave them a vision of what we might do with our current resources and proposed a plan for resolving some critical issues. They thought I was a little wide-eyed and naïve at the beginning of the conversation, but after hearing my research, they engaged."

"So, what's next?"

"What's next started today. I called the Vice President of Operations for Rural Valley Electric and will meet with him tomorrow in Sikeston. His name is Ted Brokeman, and my sense is, he didn't want to talk to me. But then, I told him some things which got his attention."

"Like what?"

"Like the fact I was aware the next closest option for RVE's toxic waste disposal was about two hundred miles away and that the site charges almost double what McCaskey Coal does. I also informed Mr. Brokeman about the chromium hexavalent showing up in their waste and the reason for that. The chemical is present in the solvent utilized by RVE to wash down their stacks every month. RVE owns four power plants, and the company systematically cleans smokestacks at each plant to preclude dangerous buildups. Then, they carefully capture the residue from these cleanings and ship the collection to McCaskey Coal."

"How did you get this information?" asked Seeney.

"Not that difficult. RVE is a public company with reasonably accessible records. I also called one of their four power plants and pretended to be a salesperson for a competing cleaning solvent. The maintenance supervisor told me the product they were using satisfied them and provided me the product's name. From there, I went online to find out what was in the solvent."

"So, what do you hope to accomplish at the meeting with RVE?"

"Two things," said Gina. "I believe I can make a case for the company to switch cleaning solvents. Even though RVE is doing nothing wrong by using a cleaning product containing CR-6, the fact waste containing the chemical may be getting into a community's aquifer would be bad publicity. Second, I think RVE might consider financing the work required to line McCaskey Coal's slurry ponds to prevent further leaks."

"I didn't think about that. Helping your company fix the leak could be cheaper for RVE than switching to an alternate facility."

"For a corporation like RVE, such a project wouldn't be overwhelming. Upgrading our slurry ponds could preclude the necessity for RVE to transport waste two hundred miles further away at twice the price. RVE would want some long-term contract for continued storage at McCaskey Coal, which I'm not excited about. I could live with five years, though."

"So, the chemical causing concern would no longer be in the waste delivered, and even if it were, the McCaskey Coal slurry ponds wouldn't allow further seepage?"

"Right," answered Gina.

"Brilliant! Why hasn't your father pursued this before?"

"Because he didn't think he had any leverage with RVE, and he didn't know how the CR-6 was getting into the waste coming from them. Dad also had no idea how scarce approved toxic waste dump sites in our general region are. Ten years ago, neither the federal government nor the state had such strict requirements for storage, and McCaskey Coal's limited financial resources precluded capital improvements to the ponds' infrastructure. Consistently monitoring the area's water supply to ensure it remained safe was the less expensive alternative. As we've discussed before, the level of chromium in our water system here, even before filtration and treatment, is well below dangerous levels. After filtering, the CR-6 is nonexistent in the water we drink in the community."

"Except in private wells, where no treatment is applied?"

"Yes," said Gina.

"What do you think the timeline for remediation might be?"

"Pretty quick if I can scare Mr. Brokeman enough. RVE could switch out the cleaning solvent on a day's notice. Plenty of effective cleaners exist that don't contain CR-6. Lining the slurry ponds is less intensive than it sounds. Large cattle operations in the Midwest developed cost-effective and efficient ways of sealing the gigantic tanks containing runoff of manure products from feeding lots. The same materials would work for our ponds. RVE needs to apply lining to one of our unused pits, then pump the sludge from the pond currently being utilized into the upgraded one. The whole process could be done in thirty days once men and material were on site."

"How much would it cost?

"In the half-million-dollar range. Hauling the waste an additional two hundred miles and paying twice the rate charged by McCaskey Coal for storage would increase RVE's costs by close to three hundred thousand dollars annually." "

"So, they'd recoup their investment in two years?"

"Or a little less. They'll most likely want a ten-year contract in return for the investment, and I'll try to negotiate for five."

"That would be a win for McCaskey—and the community. Did you discuss some of your other ideas with your father and grandfather?"

"Yes, but not in detail. My family is enthusiastic about rebranding the company as McCaskey Energy versus McCaskey Coal. They're also interested in meeting my friend who is re-purposing a coal mine in Pennsylvania. I want him to meet your contact at Eastern Hydroponics, too. Scientists in New Zealand are using an old mine to grow unusual plants for the pharmaceutical industry. We might be able to duplicate that here, and I'm certain grant money exists for these sorts of projects."

"You had some day," said Seeney. "You should be proud."

"I'm feeling better, Seeney, but your assistance was critical. I put your values on the line to trust me with this, and I won't let you down. It would have been much easier for you to turn what you knew over to the authorities and let them do what they had to do."

"As I listen to you, I'm convinced the publicity might have destroyed McCaskey Coal, shamed your family, and left you no platform for your vision. Good luck with your meeting tomorrow. Do you think your youth, or your gender, will work against you with some crusty old male corporate VP?"

"It might—in the beginning, but I think I'll prevail. There's a quote I keep on my wall from Mahatma Gandhi that says, 'First, they ignore you; then they laugh at you; then they fight you; then you win.' Well, I'm going to win."

"I would bet on it," said Seeney.

22 Business To Finish

Pastor Burns went to the Renegade four nights in a row before he caught his fish. He sat at the bar, sipping a single beer on all four evenings, watching sports on the bar's TV, and chatting with the bartender. He never had more than a beer, and, on two of the evenings, he had a sandwich, but Burns was always gone by eight-thirty. Then, on the fourth night, a Thursday, he saw the mayor of Tartan Springs arrive.

Burns monitored Foster through the reflective glass behind the bar as the mayor drank two beers with his rowdy friends. When the third beer came to the table, Foster excused himself and headed toward the restrooms. Burns said hello to him as Foster passed the bar, but Foster barely acknowledged him. The two were not friends but Burns believed tonight was his chance to snare Foster, so he ordered another beer.

As he nursed the second beer, he watched the mayor and his group consume at least two more rounds. Foster left his table again, but he stopped at the bar this time. He was standing close to Tom's seat, appearing to be interested in the football game on TV. He said relatively casually to Tom, "You seen your friend, Siena Tyson, lately?"

"Done," thought Burns. "Game on!" Then, looking down at his beer reflectively, Burns said, "Yeah. Coupla' days ago. She's not doing so well."

"Really? What's going on?"

"That asshole, Stiles, stole her cell phone and used it to send out a bunch of messages. One was to her fiancé overseas. She's pretty upset, but her attorney says she can't do anything about it."

"Huh," grunted Foster. "You know what? She had it coming to her. She took Stiles for quite a bundle."

"I guess, but I never figured Jack Stiles to be so smart. To get her phone, understand how to hack into her computer and send those messages... that took some planning!"

Foster laughed and sat down on the empty stool next to Tom's. "Would you be surprised, Burns, if I told you Stiles didn't plan any of that?"

"What do you mean?" Burns asked innocently.

"What I mean is—Siena Tyson is an uppity little bitch! I'm aware you are big-time friends with her, but she can't always get away with the kind of shit she's been pulling. Maybe with Stiles—but not with me! The only thing Stiles did last month was steal her phone."

"Whoa!" said Burns in faked amazement.

"That was my idea. When Jack brought the phone to me, I'm the one who sent the messages. I'm the one who sourced her business accounts through the chamber website. You're right about two things, though. Number one, Siena can't do a single thing about it. Number two, Jack Stiles couldn't pull off something like that! So, who's the smart one now?"

"Hmm," said Tom. "Not you. Stiles is just a sleazeball. You're an idiot and a sleazeball!"

Foster stood from the bar and appeared to be ready to punch Burns. Tom stopped him by saying, "Do you want to strike a minister in a public place when you can't pass a sobriety test, Foster? I don't think so. I'm a man of God, though, and I want to try to help you. Take this card because I think you're going to need it." Burns handed Foster a small business card and left the bar.

After Burns departed, Foster glanced at the card. On the front was a Bible verse: "Do unto others as you would have done unto you." The back listed a website address for a company called DisappearRU.S.com.

Foster started to throw the card away, but he put it in his pocket as an afterthought.

When Tom Burns got back to his apartment behind the Lutheran Church, he pulled the TCTEC pen from the front pocket of his shirt. He had ordered the gadget from Amazon the week before and tested it at home. A writer friend of Tom's told the pastor about using the device for capturing random notes related to his writing while he drove. Tom had wondered if the same technology would work for recording "notes" in a barroom conversation.

The pen operated simply enough, but tonight was the real test. He retrieved the tiny memory stick lodged in the pen's barrel and plugged the adapter cord provided into one end. Next, he inserted the USB connection into his computer and searched for a file. He clicked on the flash drive, and a sound file started to play on his desktop.

Burns listened to the first words recorded on the device: "You seen your friend, Siena Tyson, lately?" Then, he sped to the end of the recording and heard, "So, who's the smart one now?" The audio sounded crystal clear. Burns saved it to his desktop and sent a copy to a blank USB drive. He thought about saving another copy for Seeney but decided not to. Her plate was already full.

Tartan Springs Town Council Meeting, May

Tartan Springs' town council meetings occurred monthly on the third Tuesday, at five o'clock. Today's meeting would be well-attended, perhaps because of a Facebook post circulated through the community in the past week. The post encouraged citizens to attend to hear exciting news about council leadership. Mayor Foster saw the message but had no clue what it referred to. When he asked town council members if they knew, none did. The reason mattered little to him because he liked to perform before a crowd.

Seeney and Tom arrived together, and as they sat down near the back of the chamber, Tom whispered, "Do you know what this is about?"

"No," she said. "I haven't heard a thing since you told me to circulate the Facebook posts."

"Did you post those from your account? I forgot to check."

"No. I sent it from the SBAI account."

"Good. I guess we'll see soon enough."

Outside the building, a stream of vehicles began parking anywhere available. Then, leaving the cars came groups of United States Marines in service dress uniforms. The men and women, officers and enlisted, younger, and older, found seats where they could among the vacancies scattered throughout the room.

The unusual presence of so many uniforms caused whispers from the dais where council members sat, but none of the town officials could explain the Marines' attendance. Mayor Foster hammered the gavel at five o'clock and called the meeting to order. At the end of his opening comments, he welcomed the many attendees in military uniforms.

When all business topics scheduled for the meeting concluded, the mayor asked, "Is there other business to be considered from the community? If not, we customarily reserve this time for citizens with topics to bring before the council."

Nobody immediately stepped to the small podium in front of the seated council members, and then a tall, thin Marine came from the back of the room. When he arrived at the podium, he adjusted the gooseneck so he could comfortably speak without stooping. "Good afternoon, council members and citizens of Tartan Springs. My name is Colonel Holden Storm, and I am the Chief of Staff for Marine Corps Systems Command based in Washington, DC. You may have noticed that I brought some of my friends with me today. To you, these men and women may appear similar because they all wear the same uniform, that of a United States Marine."

Several in the gallery applauded.

Storm continued, "But they're different in many ways. Among those in Marine uniforms here are young and old, enlisted and officers, men, and women. They come from different places all over our country. But every Marine in the room today does share one thing not all might notice. It's a small colored ribbon on their chests. That is a purple heart, and those who wear the badge suffered wounds in combat."

Storm paused and quietly surveyed the room. "You may also observe that several of my friends are missing body parts—an arm here—a leg there. These wounds are evident, but I assure you, each one of the soldiers in this room has other wounds you cannot see—and will never see. One of your former citizens and a brother of ours shares this medal with us. Major Tyrell Harrell lies in a hospital in Bethesda, Maryland, recovering from injuries he received in Bektistan. He didn't send us here today, and he isn't aware we're here. We, his brethren in the Corps, traveled to Tartan Springs on our own time. Our mission is to share a problem we have."

Mayor Foster hammered the gavel. "Sir, with due respect, this time is allocated for citizens of the community to bring business before the council. All here are proud of Major Harrell, but if your business does not relate to the functions of this town, I must interrupt your address."

Several in the audience voiced disagreement, and the Vice Chairman of the Council, Jean Simpson, said, "Mayor, I think we can allow the Colonel to finish."

"Thank you, ma'am," said Colonel Storm. "I will delay you no further with additional introductions. Today, mayor, we're here to resolve an issue that is out of our realm of jurisdiction. We're hopeful the patriots of your town will handle the matter. I have a USB drive in my hand," said Storm as he pulled the small flash drive from his pocket, "which I'll leave to the care of your police chief. This device contains a recorded conversation in which you admit, Mr. Mayor, to sending a false message to Major Harrell, using his fiancée's stolen cell phone. In the recording, you name your partner in this fraud as Jack Stiles, who I believe is a local businessman in the community. The message to Major Harrell, from someone pretending to be his fiancé, Siena Tyson, indicates she was ending her marriage engagement to Major Harrell. Unfortunately, our comrade, Ty Harrell, didn't find out this *Dear John* communication was a shameful fraud until after his recovery from the serious injuries he incurred during combat. In our military system, Mayor Foster, methods exist for handling this sort of treasonous activity. Our military family cannot, however, presume control of a civilian matter. Therefore, we leave this injustice to your community to address. Thank you."

Someone in the back of the chamber shouted, "Ten-hut!" and the Marines in the room snapped to attention. When someone called the order, "Fall back to your vehicles!" Marines marched to the rear of the room and out the doors. A hush remained in the place for a few moments until someone stood and applauded. Then all in the room did the same.

Finally, Foster began slamming the gavel to the dais, proclaiming,

"Meeting adjourned! Meeting adjourned!" The hall emptied, and the police chief and assistant mayor asked Mayor Foster to join the rest of the council members in council chambers. When Foster arrived in the room, Police Chief Howell touched a button on the computer at the table, and Foster listened to his own voice say, "Would you be surprised, Burns, if I told you Stiles didn't plan any of that?"

Foster said, "Where did Storm get this? Turn that thing off!"

Howell said, "Not sure, but the conversation sounds like one you might have had with Pastor Burns up in Compton. I don't think anyone questions whether that's your voice on the recording."

"Fine!" said Foster. "Try to take that to court. I didn't authorize any recordings of my conversations. So, the tape is illegal."

All in the room remained quiet until Jean Simpson said, "Todd, this doesn't need to stand up in court. Nobody here mentioned anything about court. We all know who perpetrated this horrendous deed, and we don't want you representing our town anymore. You're a disgrace to the community. You may resign this evening, or we'll start the proceedings for a recall tomorrow."

"Really? Really? Okay. I resign. I don't need this bullshit!" Foster then stomped out of the room.

Seeney was still discussing the exciting events of the council meeting with Tom Burns in the parking lot. Tom said, "I guess you can tell Ty this weekend about how his friends all rode into town. It was like an old-time cowboy movie. Colonel Storm would be an excellent choice for the big-screen version."

"Yes," said Seeney, eyeing her friend suspiciously. "When you told me to pass the news about the meeting, did you know all this was going to happen?"

"Colonel Storm told me a group of Marines would be visiting us, but he didn't send me a script."

"How did he get the flash drive? Did you record Todd?"

"You need to ask the Colonel. He appeared to be a resourceful guy and may have just had good connections."

"Mmm," said Seeney. "Good connections, huh? The resolution appears to have been an ethically correct one to a problem that might have been difficult to handle legally."

"Yes, it does, doesn't it," agreed Tom. "I told you something like that could happen."

"Right. You make uncanny predictions sometimes." Tom could only smile.

The first call Todd took the following morning was from Jack Stiles. "What the fuck did you just do?" yelled Jack through the phone.

"Oh, shut up, Jack. Who's giving you your information?"

"Jim Headley on Town Council. He's a customer of mine—or, I should say, a former customer now. He told me what happened at the council meeting yesterday and about the recording someone played in chambers."

"Nobody can do anything with that," said Foster. "Somebody recorded the conversation illegally."

"You dumb shit! You had to go brag about what you did, didn't you? It doesn't matter that the recording may never be used in court because everyone in town knows whose voice was on it—and you implicated me as well."

"Relax, Stiles. I'm the one who got hurt, not you. I lost my job as mayor."

"Right. You lost a thirty-five-thousand-dollar per year job, and I may have lost a multi-million-dollar per year business! How does that compare?"

"What the hell are you talking about?"

"Half of my employees didn't show up this morning for work. That hasn't been much of a problem for the business because we've had no customers all day. My voicemail this morning was full of nasty messages, and I had to shut down my email. When someone catches you pulling a stunt like ours against a combat veteran, especially when the veteran is a local hero, you don't need a court to do anything. The public will take care of it. My parents won't even speak to me!"

"The whole thing will blow over in a week," said Foster, "and nobody will remember it."

"We'll see, but I doubt that. Who recorded the conversation anyway?"

"The only one who could have done it is Tom Burns. He tricked me into talking about what we did when I was at the Renegade one night. The marine who gave Tim Howell the tape didn't say where it came from, but I bet it was Burns."

"Well, thanks for ruining my life, asshole!" said Stiles before hanging up.

Foster checked his cell phone and counted twenty-seven voicemail messages. He'd listened to three earlier and didn't need to hear more, so he clicked the *delete all* button. Then he dialed the number for the Compton Lutheran Church.

"Compton Lutheran, Pastor Burns speaking. How may I help you?"

"You can't, jerk! You already did enough!"

"I'm sorry," said Burns. "To whom am I speaking?"

"This is Todd Foster, and you're in a world of hurt, Burns. You think you're so smart with your illegal little recording. You cost me my job, and now you're going to have to look over your shoulder every time you go someplace. This time, you screwed around with the wrong guy, Mister!"

"Ahh, yes, Foster. You aren't getting any smarter, I see. You just called the church's public hotline, and every call coming in here gets recorded automatically. So, thank you for so clearly enunciating your name when you delivered your threat. That will make filing for a restraining order easier. I might ask the sheriff's department to add a few other names to the list for protection as well."

Foster held the cellphone to his ear on the other end, not knowing what to say. He finally punched the *end call* button on the phone as hard as he possibly could. The violent slam only registered as a gentle click on Tom's end.

Life for Foster spiraled progressively worse in Tartan Springs. When he shopped for groceries at the Food Bear, every checkout line he entered closed just as he reached the register. Gas pumps inexplicably turned off when he tried to fill his car. Employees of area restaurants told Todd they had no open tables when he asked for service, and the apartment manager for Foster's complex said he wouldn't renew Foster's lease at the end of the current one.

Even his favorite bar, The Renegade, never had the beer Foster ordered anymore. On one occasion, he became outraged by management's refusal to serve him at the restaurant, and he called the County Sheriff's office from his place at a table.

"Sheriff's Department, Sergeant Dove speaking."

"Yes, Sergeant Dove, I'd like to report an incident of extreme discrimination. I'm sitting at The Renegade Bar and Grille, and, for no reason, management is refusing to serve me."

"I'm sorry, sir. Could you state your name, please?"

"Yes, this is Todd Foster."

"Thank you. Could you hold for just a second?"

"Yes."

After a short pause, "This is Chief Donelson, Mr. Foster, and I understand a public restaurant is refusing you service. Am I correct?"

"Yes. That is correct."

"Okay. We know the location of The Renegade. I'll send a unit out there to look into this."

"Thank you," said Foster. "How long will that take?"

"Well, we're stacked up at the moment, but we might be able to send someone in a couple of hours."

"A couple of hours?" exclaimed Foster. "I'm not going to sit here two more hours to wait to eat."

"That's up to you, sir, but if you aren't there when officers arrive, we won't be able to complete an investigation or file a complaint."

Foster hung up and stormed out of the bar. Then, after two weeks of driving to Sikeston, thirty miles away, in disguise, to purchase groceries, he checked in his top desk drawer for the business card Tom Burns gave him several weeks earlier at The Renegade. Foster typed the website URL listed on the reverse side of the card into his computer. Three days later, Foster left Tartan Springs with everything he owned packed in his car, never to return.

Jack Stiles fared no better with the outraged community. In a town divided often by opposing opinions on politics, religion, economics, and sports, citizens of Tartan Springs united in their condemnation of the recent horrific actions of Jack Stiles and Todd Foster.

Jack's parents understood the implications for the Chevrolet dealership and sold the business at a cut-rate price to Tartan Springs Ford. Jack Senior made a few calls to old friends in his network and was able to find his son a sales job in a small car business in Montana. Jack's parents helped him move but suggested Jack limit his visits back to West Virginia.

Sitting with his father in the small new apartment, Jack lamented about his bad luck. "How is that, Jack?" asked his father.

"Well, three years ago, I had a nice house, a big car, a beautiful wife, and a successful business. Now I've got a crappy sales job in a two-bit town, and I live in a small, rented apartment."

"So, how do you think that happened?"

"Seeney and Foster did it. They ruined me."

"What did Seeney do?"

"She went to that lawyer and took half of everything I owned."

"Hmmm, and what did Foster do?"

"He mouthed off to the minister."

"I see," said Jack Senior. "And what about you? What did you do?"

"What do you mean, Dad?"

"Did you do anything to Seeney to make her go to the attorney? Did Foster say anything to the minister which wasn't true?"

"Whose side are you on?"

"I'm on your side, son. Always will be but being on your side now requires making you understand that what happened to you is your fault—nobody else's. Until you take responsibility for your actions, your life won't improve much. You're thirty-five years old with many years ahead of you if you're lucky. Whether that life is fulfilling or miserable is up to you. You learned a harsh lesson, but it's better to learn now than when you're sixty or seventy. Your mom and I will help you whenever and wherever we can, but today would be an excellent time to grow up and start taking care of yourself."

23 Life Planning

The Naval Hospital released Ty in May but required him to maintain a daily schedule of prescribed physical therapy. Officially, his Marine Corps status was Temporary Limited Duty (TLD), pending recovery from his injuries. He was assigned to the Naval Shipyard in DC to participate in regular physical therapy and complete his rehabilitation. A Medical Evaluation Board (MEB) would eventually determine if and when Ty would return to duty. The board would also assess any limitations to the types of responsibilities Ty would be able to perform.

Ty suspected what the probable conclusions MEB would reach. His physicians had been honest with him throughout his recovery, warning him that returning to military flight status was a remote possibility. He had choices to make but at least six months to make them.

The rigorous standards for a military combat pilot differ significantly from those for a private civilian one, and Ty's injuries would likely not prevent him from flying outside of a military environment. After finishing the lengthy period of physical therapy, Ty would be eligible to continue his career as a United States Marine Corps officer in a variety of administrative positions. If Ty desired, he could, alternatively, choose an honorable discharge at the end of his rehabilitation.

Ty knew all these choices were no longer his, alone, to make. Seeney would own an equal, if not the deciding vote. In the meantime, he had temporary accommodations at the Bachelor Officers Quarters (BOQ) at the Naval Shipyard to continue physical therapy and all his weekends free to travel to Tartan Springs.

"Do you want to stay in the Marines, Ty?" asked Seeney during his first visit to Tartan Springs in almost a year. "You still look good in the uniform, and you already invested eight years of your life in the Marine Corps."

"I'm not sure. I enjoyed flying, and I won't be able to do that anymore. Twelve years of sitting behind a desk, possibly doing something I don't like, seems like a long time to me."

"Where would you be based?"

"It could be anywhere the Marines have an administrative location," said Ty, "and they could transfer us every three years. I guess the thing to think about is, I would only be forty-two when I retired, which is still relatively young."

"As you said, though, twelve years is a long time. What would you do with those years if you didn't stay in the Marines?"

"I thought about that some," Ty said, smiling at Seeney. "You might think my idea is silly, though."

"Only if it involves joining a circus or becoming a bull rider in a rodeo."

Ty pretended to think about those options seriously before answering. "Shoot! I hadn't thought of those two, but I'll put them on the list if you don't like my idea. What if I went to work for you? Your business is growing, and my education is diverse enough to take courses to qualify to take the CPA exam. In the meantime, you can teach me how to do the simpler bookkeeping tasks for QuickBooks. I might also stay in the Marine Corps Reserves. That would bring a little extra money in and leverage my active-duty time into a reserve retirement in twelve years."

"How do the Reserves work? Would you be deployed again?"

"Probably not, especially since I wouldn't be able to fly. The idea for the Reserves is to keep qualified military personnel who no longer want to make the military their primary career engaged. The government spends a lot of money training men and women, and rather than lose the benefit of all this training, Reserves provide a way to continue to access it. Reservists train one weekend a month at a military location and usually two weeks per year of active duty."

"Can they send you someplace dangerous for active duty?" asked Seeney.

"Reserves are part of the military, so they're subject to active-duty call-ups in emergencies, but this isn't a common occurrence. To answer your question, honestly, though, our government and the Marine Corps determine where reservists who are called up go. Individual reservists don't have a say in those choices."

"Don't like that part much," said Seeney. "What about when there isn't some national emergency? Are you paid for the time you spend in Reserves?"

"Yes. Reservists receive compensation for drills and their two weeks of active duty. At the end of twenty years of combined active and reserve service, Reservists earn a retirement. Unlike active-duty retirements, reservists don't earn military benefits until they turn sixty, but at that age, they receive a monthly pension and are eligible for complete medical coverage. If we continue to live in the general vicinity of DC, my weekend drills and active-duty requirements would most likely be geographically convenient."

"OK, an extra paycheck, and I still get to see you once per month in a uniform? That part doesn't sound bad. Am I missing anything else?

"Nothing much," said Ty, smiling. "I also have an idea where my Reserve unit would be and what I might be doing."

"Don't start turning into Tom Burns and becoming mysterious. What would that be, and how do you know?"

"Sorry. It isn't so mysterious," said Ty, "and just sort of lucky. I called Jim Hayden last week about being my best man, and he asked what my plans were. I told him what I was thinking, and he was bummed about my prognosis. He understood how I felt, though, and told me to call Colonel Simkins in DC. You might remember that Simkins is the one who cleared the way for the C-130 to bring Doctor Shapiro to Kadun. Anyway, Simkins says he has a spot for me at a USMC reserve unit which works out of the Pentagon. He told me all I had to do was let him know when I completed my active duty."

"Was it our friend, Pastor Burns, who told us that rules, regulations, and processes are only applicable when network breaks down?"

"Ha! Tom is obsessed with connections. Maybe he's right, though."

"Well," said Seeney. "Nothing you have told me is bad except for the possibility of being called back to active duty for something unsafe. I'll take your word that the possibilities for that are remote. Why would you assume I'd think your consideration relative to my little company to be silly? It's brilliant, but most men's ego wouldn't allow them to even think of working for their wives. The fact is, Ty, we're a team, and if we do this, you won't be working *for* me, but rather *with* me. Do you think we'd stay around Tartan Springs?"

"That's up to you, but it wouldn't be my first choice. For me, living anywhere with you is better than living anywhere else without you, but my impression is you might like to see someplace new. This whole drama involving the McCaskeys and the town water hasn't made life here easy for you."

"Very perceptive, sir. I *would* like to see something new, but what about my business?"

"Seeney, about one-third of the population of the United States is within three hundred miles of Tartan Springs. Your business depends on a computer and a telephone for the most part. If you visit here occasionally, I don't think many existing customers would leave you. Besides, wherever we live, with two of us working, Tartan Springs will soon represent a minority of our business. We don't need to live on the west coast. There are lots of places within a few hours of here that I think we would enjoy."

"This is exciting, Ty! I love it. Thank you. I'll finish at the junior college this month, and I'll hold off applying at Shepherd University until we decide where we're going to end up."

"Whoa, girl! We're not going to decide that quick. Half the fun of moving is looking for the right place. You have a home here, and I need to finish the TDY at the shipyard. The wedding is just around the corner, so we don't need to decide this today."

Seeney sighed, smiled, relaxed back into Ty's arms, and turned off the TV.

"Ready for bed?"

"No. Just didn't want you to be distracted."

Since neither Seeney nor Ty wanted or needed a large wedding, it was easy to plan. They picked early August for a date, the Compton Lutheran Church for the ceremony, and Pastor Tom Burns for the officiant. They reserved the Hampton Inn banquet room for a reception and a block of rooms for their out-of-town friends. Ty also negotiated a price for Benny V to bring his band up from Woodstock for the event.

Planning a honeymoon location proved more challenging since neither Ty nor Seeney was up for a long flight anywhere. Ty's back injury would make him uncomfortable in a cramped seat for more than a couple of hours, and Seeney's flying marathon in March tempered her desire to fly again soon. Long car drives would be no more comfortable for Ty than long plane rides, so when he saw the ad for a cruise from the nearby Port of Baltimore to Bermuda, leaving on August 9, Ty thought he found a good alternative.

"Perfect!" said Seeney when Ty called her from his BOQ room. "We can drive to Baltimore on the eighth and stay at the Inner Harbor for the night. It sounds like fun."

"OK. I'll book it now. When I spoke with the reservations department earlier, few cabins remained. So, I'm not sure what kind of room will still be available."

"As long as it has a bed and located inside, I don't care," said Seeney. "Have you ever been to Bermuda?"

"No. How about you?"

"Ty, I haven't been any place—except for Germany. Everyplace is new for me."

24 Uninvited Guest

Feeling exhilarated after the conversation with Ty, Seeney finished her wine, did some more wedding administration, and went to bed. With the recent traumas in her life seemingly behind her, sleep came easier these days. She drifted off, looking forward to the following day's planned trip with Marie Chavez to pick a wedding dress in Compton.

At one o'clock in the morning, Seeney didn't know what made her wake up. She lay quietly in bed, listening, but the house was quiet. Her bedroom was near the rear of the second floor, and Seeney could tell the motion-activated lights installed at the back door were still off. She left her bed and walked to the other end of the house, relieved the security lights at the front door were also still off.

She glanced through a window in the hall located on the side of the house closest to the street and detected a tiny light glow from some distance down the side road. It quickly went out. She continued to stare at the spot where the light had been but didn't see anything more. Just as she turned away, though, she caught sight of the light again in her peripheral vision. She snapped her head back to the spot and glimpsed a momentary red glow.

The night was dark, with no moon, and the light she witnessed came from at least twenty to thirty yards down the side street. She continued to stare at the spot, and another short glow rewarded her patience. The light then arced into the air, dropping to the ground several feet away.

A cigarette! Somebody was smoking a cigarette at one in the morning on her crossing street. Parked cars were present on the road, but she couldn't distinguish colors or types, just dark shapes. Then, almost on cue, the Colgan County Register delivery truck turned on the street. Ever so briefly, the headlights from the large vehicle illuminated the parked cars, including for a split-second, a camouflage-colored Jeep.

Her heart went to her throat, and she dashed to her bedroom. The motion lights had not activated, but she was certain Justin Domship lurked out there—somewhere. Keeping her head behind the curtain, she tried to look below to her back door, but it was too dark. She reached to the bedstand for her cell phone, and as she did, the rattle from the back doorknob downstairs alarmed her. Her security lights had still not activated, but someone was undeniably at the back entrance to her house. She dialed 911, fumbling with shaky hands.

"Emergency services, how may I help you?"

"This is Siena Tyson, and someone is trying to break into my home," Seeney whispered. "Please send the police right away!"

"I'm sorry, ma'am," said the responder. "I couldn't understand what you said. Are you reporting an emergency?"

The back door rattled violently and more audibly, and Seeney decided now was no time to whisper. Instead, talking plainly, but with a trembling voice, she said, "Someone is trying to break into my house, and I need help."

"Okay, ma'am. I heard you this time. Please give me your name and address."

"Siena Tyson at one twenty Whispering Way in Tartan Springs." Seeney kicked the door to her bedroom closed and locked it.

"Thank you, ma'am. We dispatched a police unit to that address a while ago. Did you call earlier?"

"No," cried Seeney. "I didn't. Who else called?"

"I don't have that information, ma'am."

Now, Seeney's mind raced, processing the worst possible scenarios. Was the town involved with this somehow? She thought about who else to call but knew nobody who would be able to respond in time. The sounds coming from her back door terrified her, and she realized she still held her phone. "Ms. Tyson, are you still there?"

"Yes, yes, sorry."

"Sergeant Mathers from the Tartan Springs Police Department

reports he's on-site. Do you see him?"

Seeney peered out the window and saw an officer with a large flashlight talking to someone hidden under the back porch roof. Another officer pointed a revolver toward Seeney's back door. "Yes, ma'am. Two officers are at my back door. Thank you! Thank you so much!"

Seeney clicked off her cell phone and raced downstairs, turning lights on as she went. When she arrived at the door, the two police officers had moved their suspect from under the porch roof. The intruder stood with his back to Seeney with a zip-tie now securing his hands.

Seeney opened the door and peeked her head through the opening. "Can I come out?"

"Yes, ma'am," answered the officer, Jimmy Mathers, who had been two years behind Seeney in high school. "Hey, Seeney. Do you know this no-load?"

Seeney didn't need the man to turn around. "I've met him."

"Yeah, sorry about that," said Mathers. "His name is Justin Domship, and he's not saying why he was trying to break into your house. He had this in his pocket, though." The other officer held up a small pistol. "We've already checked the serial number on the gun, and it isn't registered. Probably stolen. Anyway, we'll be taking Justin in, and he'll be booked for attempted breaking and entering and illegal possession of an unregistered firearm."

Mathers finished, and another man joined the small group, walking in from the darkness of the street. It was Four McCaskey.

"Well, hello, Justin," said Four. "Fancy meeting you here."

Domship, surprised by his cousin's presence, asked, "What the hell are you doing here, Four?"

"Oh, I'm the one who sent out the invitations," said Four. "Well, not to Ms. Tyson. I'm sorry for this, Siena."

"I'm confused, Four," said Seeney. "What's going on?"

"I'm embarrassed to say this good-for-nothing criminal is related to me. After our meeting several weeks ago, Siena, Justin said something that concerned me. Since then, I have been monitoring him." To Domship, Four said, "You don't follow directions very well, do you, Justin?"

"How'd you know I was coming here, Four?" asked Domship.

"I attached a simple little GPS device with a magnet under the front bumper of your Jeep. Amazing little toy I bought off Amazon. I guess parents use these to track where their teen children are going. At any rate, the gadget has an app that sends my cell phone a message anytime your vehicle moves more than one hundred yards."

"You asshole! That can't be legal!"

"Not sure about that, but it works well. When your Jeep headed here, I called 911." Four focused on the two police officers and said, "If anyone at the department wants the location for local cockfights, I might be able to provide information."

Sergeant Mathers said, "That would be the state police's jurisdiction, but I'm sure they might be interested. Justin, you ready for a little ride?"

Domship only grunted but gazed at Four. "You and I should talk before they take me downtown."

"You can have the conversation when you're in the car," said Mathers.

Four and Mathers escorted Domship to the squad car, and the other officer asked Seeney if she was okay. "I'm fine, now, but I was terrified. Thank you for getting here so fast."

"No problem, ma'am," said the young officer. "You were never in real danger because we were here before Domship even got to the door. We couldn't do anything until he physically tried to break in, though."

"I understand." Seeney then gazed at the motion detection lights, wondering out loud to the officer, "These lights didn't work well, did they? They're supposed to come on when something moves out here."

The officer pointed his flashlight to one of the lights and reached up to twist it. The light illuminated immediately. "Not screwed in completely." The officer started to reach for the opposite fixture, and Seeney stopped him.

"Leave that one alone for now," she said. "I'll bet your department will find Domship's fingerprints on it."

Seeney retreated inside her home, considering her recent carelessness. The day she found the cigarette butt at the back door and checked so carefully for other butts around the perimeter of the house, she never thought to check the lights. She resolved now to install a security system the following day.

Mathers secured Domship in the police cruiser's back seat and allowed Four to approach the vehicle's window to speak to him. Justin glared at his cousin. "You think you're so smart, Four, but I better be out of this by tomorrow, or you're going to be in a lot of trouble."

"How is that, Justin?"

"I'm aware of a lot of things, Four. If I'm going down, I'm taking you with me."

Four smiled grimly at Domship. "What you think you know, Justin might fill a paragraph. And while that might embarrass me, I'm guilty of nothing. I, on the other hand, have quite a bit of information about you." At this, Four pulled an envelope from his pocket. "Here's some reading material for this evening. You'll be processed downtown, and officers will check inside this envelope to ensure it contains nothing but paper, but they'll return it. What is written on the documents is nothing you'd want them to see. You'll be glad, I think, to give this back to me tomorrow when I visit."

"You're a jerk, Four."

"And you're a lowlife scumbag who I'm embarrassed is a relative. I'm certain your mother died asking forgiveness for bringing you into this world. You might spend a short time in jail or, depending on how many find out the envelope's contents, a long time. Whichever it is, when you get out, I'll do you one last favor. I'm going to give you enough money to relocate to another part of the country where I'll never need to hear from you again." Then Four turned and left.

25 McCaskey Energy

Ty, horrified to hear about Seeney's adventure of the previous evening, asked if he should come to Tartan Springs before the weekend. Seeney told him it wasn't necessary. With Domship behind bars and Todd Foster no longer in town, she didn't think anyone else left in the community wanted to harm her. Seeney mentioned to Ty how Four McCaskey had been looking out for her without her knowing it.

"Well," said Ty, "does Four know you looked out for him as well? You would never have had to deal with Domship if you hadn't met on Mullen Mountain with Four and his father."

"I doubt Gina ever said anything to her dad. My agreement with her was to provide the opening to address the water issue, and she'd take it from there."

"Does she know about last night?"

No. She'll find out soon enough, though. She'll call."

The couple finished their conversation, and Seeney cheerfully took the spiral notebook labeled *wedding* from her desk drawer. With just two months until the event, she still had planning to do. In the afternoon, she received a call on her landline, which still served as her business line. "STL Bookkeeping, may I help you?"

"Hi, Seeney, this is Four McCaskey. I wanted to call again to apologize for what happened last evening."

"Oh. Thank you, Four, but I should probably be calling to thank you for your role in helping me."

"Not at all. Domship was my problem from the beginning, and you should not have experienced such a terrorizing event. I'm embarrassed for my relative and express regret for my company. I visited the jail this morning, and I'm certain nobody will need to be concerned about Justin for quite a while."

"Well. Thank you for calling and for taking the extra precautions on my behalf last night."

"You're welcome, Seeney. I had one more thing I wanted to ask you. Would it be possible for my father and me to meet with you again? Our last conference generated discussions that led to exciting changes in our company, and we want to share some of those with you."

Caught off-guard, Seeney hesitated. "Sure, Four. When would you like to meet?"

"Anytime convenient for you, but if you could revisit the mountain, we can show you something I believe will please you. Almost any day this week would work for us."

The week was only two more days long, so Seeney understood when Four mentioned *anytime*, he meant *anytime soon.* To accommodate them, she said, "How about tomorrow at three o'clock?"

"Perfect. I'll tell my father."

When Seeney arrived at the McCaskey offices, a secretary led her straight back to Four's office. There with his son, Milton sat at a small conference table to the side of Four's desk. Milton rose and said, "Thank you, Seeney, for coming up the mountain today. Four told me about your difficult experience with Justin Domship, and I'm so sorry."

"Thank you, Mr. McCaskey, but everything worked out okay, thanks to your son. Hello, Four."

"Hi, Seeney," said Four. "I appreciate you accommodating us this week. I know you are busy."

"My pleasure. You mentioned you wanted to show me some plans?"

"Yes. After we met with you in May, we had a series of family discussions that impacted our company. Do you know my daughter, Gina?"

Seeney didn't want to lie. "Yes, Four, but only on a social basis. She and I have some mutual friends."

"Wonderful," said Four. "We're most proud of her, and during our family meetings, she made suggestions that frankly surprised us. Her education is in mining engineering, and her understanding of our business with its challenges is remarkable. As a result, my father and I gave her a position in the company as Vice President of Development."

"She sounds like an excellent choice. Gina impresses me as a bright person, but how does this relate to me?"

Milton said, "We want to show you something occurring on our property as we speak. It relates to the reason you requested a meeting with us in May."

"Yes," added Four. "We believe the chromium showing up in the Tartan Springs water supply originated from the waste product we store for Rural Valley Electric. Gina convinced us to resolve the issue by allowing RVE to assist in lining the holding pond retaining the waste. As a result, the utility company completed insulating one of our empty slurry pits last week, and we're pumping material from the old pond to the new one now."

"That was quick!" said Seeney.

"Yes," said Four. "We should have done this years ago. Gina has additional ideas for alternate uses for our mines. A college friend of hers in Pennsylvania is involved with the successful repurposing of an old mine up there. We're meeting with him soon."

"Four and I are excited about Gina's ideas," said Milton. "We're going to announce a change in our name from McCaskey Coal to McCaskey Energy next month."

"All this happened in six weeks?" said Seeney. "Incredible!"

"We think so too," replied Four. "I want you to meet Gina on a professional level at our next meeting."

"I'll look forward to it. Did you want to show me the slurry pits?"

Seeney called Gina from her car on the way back from Mullen Mountain. Gina didn't know about the meeting her father scheduled with Seeney but was glad he had taken the initiative. "Did you see the pumps transferring the waste from the old slurry pit to the new one?"

"Yes," said Seeney. "I'm surprised you could get the work done so quickly. Your father said the old pond should be empty in another four days."

"Yes. RVE had a strong incentive to work as fast and as quietly as possible. We settled on a seven-year contract for continued storage."

"Did RVE's willingness to do the repairs surprise your father?"

"It shocked both he and my grandfather. Neither had any idea of the advances made in lining materials and because the two ponds are so close to each other, virtually no excavation was required. My friend in Pennsylvania believes the effects of any past seepage will work through the aquifer system in less than a month. We plan to convert our water bottling plant back to spring water by late July."

"That would be worth a press conference, except nobody around here ever knew you switched from the spring water in the first place."

"Right," said Gina, "but we might still include the issue of water quality in the announcement we make about our name change. We think we'll be able to make our new name public within the next sixty days. My friend from Pennsylvania, who attended WVU with me, Neil Strom, is visiting next week. Would you be available to meet him?"

"Sure. Just tell me when."

"Okay, I'll get back to you. Neil is bringing his girlfriend, Lei Singh. She's also a scientist with a degree in chemical engineering from Lehigh University."

With no commitments at the Naval Shipyard until the following Monday, Ty drove to Tartan Springs on Wednesday evening. He looked forward to joining Seeney to visit Gina McCaskey and her friends on Mullen Mountain.

Gina attended WVU with Neil Strom, a year behind him in the university's mining engineering program. John Young, president of Young Mining, located in Rileyville, Pennsylvania, hired Neil right out of school. Young was the patriarch of a wealthy coal-mining family from the southwest area of the state, and he made national news in 1998 when he closed the family's last two mining businesses. An ardent environmentalist, Young refused to embrace the industry trend of Mountaintop Removal, also called Mountain Top Mining, for the efficient recovery of coal.

Instead, Young hired educated young scientists like Neil and Neil's girlfriend, Lei Singh, to research alternative uses for the family's old mines. Young, an expert on the nation's complicated network of state and federal grants, knew where grant money originated, what agencies controlled it, and the rules for accessing it.

Neil smiled and shook hands with Ty and Seeney, then introduced them to Lei. Gina said, "We've spent the last day showing Neil and Lei our resources here. I think my dad and my granddad's heads are still spinning."

"No," said Neil. "Your dad understood everything we talked about, Gina. Your grandfather was probably a little lost in the science, but I think he understands the vision and the potential."

"Maybe," said Gina. "You two didn't give them a rest, though."

"No time to rest," said Neil. "Opportunities, particularly in the financing, exist now that won't be around in five years."

Gina addressed Ty and Seeney. "Neil and Lei converted an old mine in Pennsylvania to a miniature hydroelectric plant capable of providing enough power for a small town. Solar panels generate the only energy required in the facility. Their company achieved eighty percent of the financing for infrastructure through federal and state grants, and income generated was tax-favored for the next decade."

"Wow," said Ty. "Why isn't everyone doing that?"

"Because," said Lei, "the technology is new, and most people give up before getting to the second or third level of the bureaucracy for obtaining state and federal grants. Also, nobody does more research in the field of repurposing old mines than John Young. He's an amazing entrepreneur as well as a world-class environmentalist."

"Neil and Lei say our mine is almost a duplicate of theirs in Pennsylvania," said Gina, "with the added advantage of being closer to water, the Siler River. They believe the same technology used in Pennsylvania would work here."

"Do you know how to get the grants?" Seeney asked Gina.

"We'll help," said Neil. "We developed a template for grant applications."

Ty looked from Gina to Neil and back to Gina. "That's a lot of work, Gina. Will Neil and Lei or Mr. Young be partners in your operations here?"

Gina glanced at Neil, who said, " It's okay. I trust these two if you do."

"Not for publication, but we spent the last several hours talking about how a partnership might work," said Gina. "Neil called his boss, and Mr. Young is coming here tomorrow to meet with dad, granddad, and me. Mr. Young thinks we should consider taking McCaskey Energy public before the end of the year. He can't devote time or extra resources to manage an expansion in West Virginia, but he's certain his systems, created with Neil and Lei, will work here. He doesn't mind sharing his proto-type and patented processes with a team he feels confident can execute the project if he can invest in the company early. If we're successful, his return will be the rising stock price. In Young's opinion, this is the easiest way to leverage his investment in research and development before competition floods the market."

"It may not seem like it during some political administrations," said Neil, "but our government generally understands the damage that reliance on fossil fuels has caused the planet. As a result, the national budget features chunks of money earmarked for cleaning things up. These funds won't be available forever, but entrepreneurs with proven track records can apply for them to use for sanctioned projects. The quicker we can expand, using federal and state grants, the further we'll be ahead when competition becomes more intense, and grant monies become scarcer."

Gina said, "Young Utilities is already a public company with ninety percent of the stock owned by the Young family. Mr. Young wants to show my father how he can create a similar company without giving it away to outsiders."

Ty watched Neil and Lei as Gina talked. "Do you two own Young Utilities stock?"

Lei smiled. "Of course! We each own five thousand shares, which Mr. Young gave to us. When the shares released for purchase at the Initial Public Offer they had a par value of ten dollars per share. Today the stock is valued at over ninety dollars per share."

"Wow," said Ty. "That kind of growth can keep you motivated."

"Yes, it can," said Neil. "Sometimes, to a fault. Lei and I want to get married, but we can't find the time for a wedding!"

"It doesn't matter," interjected Lei, grabbing Neil's elbow. "This whole adventure is fulfilling, and we're building a team that will soon be able to lighten our load."

"I know Gina from school," said Neil, "and her family already owns much of the grid for the needed system. So, this collaboration appears to be a win-win."

"How exactly does a miniature hydroelectric plant using an old mine work?" asked Ty.

"In layman's terms," said Neil, "water is pumped from the Siler River to the top of the mountain. The tunnels and outlets made by past mining operations are blocked, so the mountain eventually fills up with water. Then, engineers equip narrow passage raceways inside the mountain with turbines, just like a dam. When water is allowed through these channels, the turbines revolve, creating electricity. Excess power generated is stored in giant batteries. It doesn't take as much water as you might think running through the small raceways at the speed of gravity to turn these efficient turbines. The exit water is recirculated to the top of the mountain by pumps powered by solar panels."

"So, it takes no energy to create enough power to light a town?" asked Seeney.

"Not quite," said Lei. "The process requires a significant amount of energy, but most of it is provided by the sun every day for free. Our only cost is the initial investment in the equipment needed to capture that energy. The sun produces one point nine seven to the twenty-sixth power of terawatts per square foot of Earth in energy every day. But, as you know, we use extraordinarily little of this."

Ty whistled lowly. "Mind-blowing! I never thought something like this would happen in my lifetime."

"It is remarkable, Ty," said Lei, "but alternative energies are still in their infancy. What we can currently produce from a small plant like this one will only power a town, not a county or city. And the cost of the equipment to accomplish this isn't insignificant. Unless our government helped with the initial investment for projects like this one, they wouldn't make economic sense. The good news is, once we invest, minimal reinvestment is necessary. The equipment is durable and lasts a long time. Also, as we use the technology, we get better at it with continued evolving efficiency."

"Scientists have told us for centuries," Neil said, "that perpetual motion is impossible. In a micro sense, this is true, but our sun's energy will be perpetual for another five billion years. If the planet keeps spinning, wind and current will also be continuous. In conjunction with the moon's and the sun's gravitational pull on water, the wind will also ensure the wave action of our oceans. All these forces provide energy sources that are free and sustainable. We just need to learn how to harness the energy cost-effectively."

"I'm as excited for your new company as you are," said Ty to Gina. "I never felt more hope for our planet than I do now listening to these intelligent people. Thank you for including Seeney and me today, Gina."

"You're welcome, Ty. Seeney played an important role in getting us to our discussions today."

On a beautiful evening in late July, the front lawn of the Tartan Springs Water Company hosted most of the town's constituents. Four and Milton contracted a small carnival featuring rides, food stands, a petting zoo, and a bandstand to set up on the property. Workers built a stage on the porch of the business, and folding chairs lined the area below the podium. A fountain to the left of the stage shot water thirty feet into the air, which fell into a makeshift pool created around the base.

A giant projection screen stood to the right of the stage.

The high school orchestra performed on the bandstand, and at eight o'clock, when the band finished a song, Four McCaskey stepped to the podium. "Thank you, friends and neighbors, for joining us this evening. It's a beautiful night to be alive in West By God Virginia, isn't it?"

The audience applauded enthusiastically, and Four continued. "My father, Milton, my wife, Lisbeth, and I couldn't be prouder of this community in which we live and that seven generations of McCaskeys have been so intimately connected." The audience cheered again. "Thank you. Tonight, I introduce a new spokesperson for our family to share exciting news about our company. She is my daughter, Gina McCaskey, who is our company's new Vice President of Development."

The crowd applauded, and Gina stepped to the microphone.

"My God!" said Ty. "Look at her!"

"She's beautiful," agreed Seeney.

"This is going to be good," said Tom.

Female executives sometimes emulate their male counterparts in public appearances, opting for stodgy business suits, but not Gina. Her gray, straight skirt and blue sports coat were professional, but Gina did nothing to hide her youth or femininity. Her confident presence and demeanor defied anyone to find fault.

"Thank you, Dad," said Gina in a firm voice. "We've had a busy summer at McCaskey Coal, but before I tell you about that, indulge me with a short exercise. Officials from our state's water quality division are with us today, and while I speak, they will begin a test on the water spraying from the fountain to your left. These tests will take a little time, and I won't delay our ceremony, but you'll see their findings displayed on this screen as the chemists work. The fountain water comes directly from the natural springs for which our town derives its name."

Officials in white laboratory coats approached the basin below the spraying water as Gina spoke.

"Our county is among seven in the state ranking in the top third of all counties in the nation for fewest water-related health violations. Bragging a little about the six prior generations of McCaskeys before me, McCaskey Coal has always made this county's water quality a priority in managing its coal business. Our company takes extraordinary measures to preclude the possibility of the company's mining activities impacting your drinking water negatively. This summer, in cooperation with Rural Valley Electric, we made additional plant improvements to ensure this record would continue." The audience clapped, and Gina looked toward the large screen.

"You can see that some data is starting to appear on our display, and we'll review that soon. Our planet is almost four point five billion years old, with human life existing for around two hundred thousand years of it. To put that in perspective, if Earth were one day old, we humans arrived only in the last thirty-eight seconds. Yet, in the past hundred years humans have depleted more of the planet's resources than all life forms combined in the previous four point five billion. Scary thought, isn't it? Scientists say the sun will last another five billion years, so, technically, Earth should survive the same amount of time. But not if we continue to use its limited resources at the rate of the past century."

Gina paused while the audience considered her last statement, then continued. "Coal is still an important source of energy for much of our world, and we at McCaskey will mine a limited amount of it into the foreseeable future. However, our operations will only utilize traditional methods that impact our environment minimally. Therefore, we have not, and will not, ever employ Mountain Top Mining!"

Loud, spontaneous applause stopped Gina's speech, and she waited to go on. "Reinforcing this commitment, as of today, our company will be re-named McCaskey Energy." Four and Milton removed a canvas from a display behind the podium, which showed the company's new name and logo.

McCaskey Energy
Making Energy for a Better Planet

When the applause died, Gina said, "To meet our stated vision, we will utilize this country's most important national resource. Not coal, not oil. I've asked Mrs. Murdoch from our school system to display a sample of this resource today." At that, one of the community's more popular teachers, Elvira Murdock, led her kindergarten class of children to the stage. Twenty-three beautiful youths took seats amidst the ovation of an adoring audience.

"Aren't they something?" exclaimed Gina. She then held up a fist-sized brick of coal. "This piece of coal in my hand might be powerful enough to give a dog a headache if I threw it hard and my aim was accurate. But when a quantity of this is cleaned, crushed, processed, distilled, and refined, it can light cities, power factories, and create weapons dangerous enough to destroy our planet. However, more potential power exists in the brains of these children on stage, and all like them, than what I hold in my hand. Filtered in elementary school, processed in middle school, distilled in high school, and refined at schools like West Virginia, Penn State, and Virginia Tech, these minds can change our world. Raw intelligence is born into the wealthiest homes of our most affluent neighborhoods and to the poorest homes in our inner cities. Strong minds only need development to reach full potential. Two of my guests here today bring such highly evolved brains to this gathering. They are Neil Strom and Lei Singh, who created a process for converting an old mine into a miniature hydroelectric plant in Pennsylvania. We at McCaskey Energy plan to start construction for a similar plant. Using only solar power, the facility will produce electricity with no waste product." Applause again rippled through the audience, interrupting Gina. She directed the crowd's attention to the giant screen when the crowd noise died. "Our guest chemists completed the water analysis. Remember, the water tested from this spring comes from the same aquifer as the water you use in Tartan Springs to drink, bathe, and water crops. The red line on each column denotes the danger level for any mineral or chemical tested. Note that nothing in the sample registers more than trace elements of anything but H2O. The analysis confirms we enjoy some of the cleanest water in the world here in Tartan Springs."

The crowd responded with thunderous applause, and Gina asked her father to fill a glass from the water spraying from the fountain. When Four returned the full container to his daughter, Gina drank it and smiled. "The initials for our new company spell *ME*," she said. "Besides standing for McCaskey Energy, those initials remind our employees who is responsible for ensuring that we deliver energy good for our customers and healthy for our world. We hope these initials may also remind the other *MEs* on this stage, in this audience, and outside the pages of this book of who is responsible for taking care of Earth. Thank you for your attention today and for your support in this community."

The crowd rose in unison, and Gina placed a box in front of the podium. One of Mrs. Murdoch's students walked toward the microphone, and Gina lifted her to the box. The adorable girl was brown-skinned with kinky curls braided in ribbons. When she smiled, all in the audience noticed the missing front tooth.

Her name was Laticia Adams, and her two grandfathers, four uncles, and father were or had been Colgan County coal miners. As the band played the opening bars of *America The Beautiful*, little Laticia began singing. Tissues appeared throughout the audience, and, by the second verse, all in attendance sang with the young girl. Gina's apt finale succeeded in metaphorically connecting the county's historic coal legacy to the country's future.

Seeney, standing between Ty and Tom, said to Tom. "You were right, Tom. I'd follow her into battle or vote for her for president. She's astonishing!"

"She is, Seeney, but for every Gina McCaskey, there are a host of helpers in the background whose work is just as important if not as recognized. You had a hand in this performance today."

"Because of you," said Seeney.

"As someone once said, 'it takes a village.'"

"I think I know what to do with my military service severance check next month," said Ty. "When do you think McCaskey's IPO will happen?"

"Gina thinks before the end of the year," said Tom.

The three friends edged toward the podium where her fans in the community still surrounded Gina. Milton and Four watched Gina with evident pride, and when Four saw Seeney, he motioned her in his direction.

"Your daughter did an excellent job with the announcement," said Seeney. "I think this group would elect her as Governor today."

"She wouldn't be a bad choice," said Milton, "but she's going to have her hands full for the next few years here, I think."

"Right," said Four. "I doubt any time will remain for politics—or much else."

"We want to invest when McCaskey Energy goes public," said Ty. "Will you save some shares for us?"

Four said, "Yes. We're starting a list, but we might fully subscribe by the time we're ready to announce. Mr. Young from Young Utilities wants one hundred thousand shares, and so does Rural Valley Electric. Tartan Springs' finance manager wants to reinvest part of the municipal employee pension fund in the company as well. Gina's friends, Neil and Lei, also requested shares."

"How exciting, Four," said Seeney. "All the McCaskeys before you would be proud."

"Thank you, Seeney. You may not be aware, but you had a role in what transpired today."

Playing naïve, Seeney asked, "How's that, Four?"

"It was our meeting with you in May, which convinced us of issues in our operations needing expedient solutions. We called a family conference to discuss this, and Gina surprised us with much of the plan you heard today. We had no idea what a resource we had in Gina until then."

"Well, I'm honored to have helped." As Seeney spoke, Gina joined the group.

"Seeney," she said. "I was so pleased to get your invitation to the wedding. Thank you. I'm coming!"

Ty said, "We received your RSVP, and I have some Marine friends coming up from New River who will want to meet you."

"Good! Then I'll have somebody to dance with. Are you excited, Seeney? It's just over a week away."

"I am, Gina! Thank you. Ty and I took an interesting route here, but nothing worthwhile is ever easy, I guess."

"Nobody is looking forward to the event more than me," chimed in Tom. "My sermon is down to an hour and thirty minutes, and I'm not sure I can take much more out."

"Well, keep working on it, Pastor," said Seeney. "You only need to cut about another eighty minutes."

The friends laughed together as the last rays of the summer sun descended beyond the mountains to the west. The high school orchestra played an instrumental version of *Country Roads*, and the twinkling lights of the carnival combined with the sweet smell of popcorn and cotton candy to create a Norman Rockwell-like moment in small-town America.

Pastor Tom gazed toward the sky for a moment, then smiled and joined his friends on their way to the carnival's midway shooting gallery. He saw the young singer, Laticia Adams, with her parents and called to her, "Laticia, you did an awesome job with *America The Beautiful*. I'm a pretty decent shooter, so if you come with me, I think I'll win you a stuffed animal."

26 Big Event

Mavis and Orville took their places in the first row of pews in the church, and many high school friends of Seeney's and Ty's sat in the seats behind. A slimmed-down Bill Busby with his wife sat next to Jude Stevens. Susie Thompson sat next to Sally Howell and Sally's new boyfriend, Earl. Sally's father, the former police chief and now mayor, Tim Howell, was several rows behind his daughter with his wife. Buster Aldrich, his wife, and most of Seeney's bookkeeping clients, including Terri Miller from Eastern Hydroponics, occupied seats on the bride's side of the gathering. Slipping in just before the ceremony began, Gina McCaskey took a seat in one of the back rows.

A contingent of dapper men in suits sat together on the groom's side. Ladies accompanied many of these, but some were single. None wore uniforms, but nobody in the room doubted what they did for a living. Their haircuts, posture, and air of confidence gave them away. HML-222 returned from deployment in July, and several carloads of Ty's friends from his former squadron drove from New River for the wedding.

Seeney's sister, Millie, and Marie Chavez helped Seeney with her gown in the Vestry, and they now rummaged for other things to do.

Since Seeney insisted on no elaborate hairstyling or extreme makeup applications, the ladies resorted to nervous conversation.

Seeney asked Marie to check the hallway. She wanted to move to the small room adjacent to the narthex if it remained vacant. This space contained the sound and light controls for the building and a window from which Seeney could see the front area of the church. She could observe things through the window, but stained glass prevented others from seeing into the room.

With Seeney situated, Marie hugged her and left for her station near the pulpit. Millie accepted an escort to a front pew, leaving Seeney by herself. Twenty minutes remained before the ceremony's scheduled start, and Seeney enjoyed the quiet solitude of this private space to reflect on the journey which led her to this moment.

The weather in West Virginia is usually hot and humid in August, but today felt comfortable. A thunderstorm the evening before dissipated the humidity, and the outdoor temperature registered only eighty-eight. The music from the gigantic organ was magnificent and entertaining. Seeney and Ty had selected a mix of classic hymns and romantic love songs, which the talented organist incorporated into an enchanting medley. The popular melody playing now, *Heaven*, sounded like a sacred elegy.

Less than two years ago, Ty walked through the doors of the gymnasium to attend the couple's tenth-year high school reunion. She remembered the moment as both exciting and a little sad. Her heart had stirred, but Seeney realized the two had chosen different paths a decade earlier and lived dramatically contrasting lives since graduation. The event seemed to provide an occasion to refresh an old friendship, but little more.

As the evening unfolded in unexpected ways, though, Seeney did bold things to make the best of her second opportunity with Ty. The two years between the reunion and this day had provided memorable moments but just as many traumatic ones. The couple overcame a mountain of challenges thrown their direction... but had somehow arrived today near an altar together.

Along the way, Seeney learned about love. Confused for years by a term so many used casually for a wide range of emotions, Seeney now understood love wasn't a *word*. It was an essence, a notion, a process—and it defied simple expressions or rational explanation. It was a feeling, and Seeney knew she had it. She felt certain Ty did as well.

Seeney also rediscovered Faith. Assisted by her friend, Tom Burns,

Seeney accepted it was OK to have questions and still not wholly understand all aspects of spirituality. Seeney realized she had not traveled her arduous path or mastered its many hurdles by herself. She received help, as did Ty. Seeney attended church again, not to embrace a particular religious philosophy but to use the time to think deeply in a suitable place. She would never again question the faith of others but try to listen and learn.

As people filled the pews, Seeney considered the mysteries of the human connection. In the church sat old friends she had known most of her life, but over half of those present were new acquaintances from the past two years. Girlfriends from childhood she once regarded as soulmates didn't make the guest list, replaced by newcomers now vital to her present life. And yet, amid the capricious ebb and flow of personal relationships, Tom Burns and Tyrell Harrell were notable constants. Only minor supporting players in her earlier life, the two stepped into starring roles when she needed them the most. Did they always have that potential?

The first strains of *If I Loved You* began, which signaled Seeney to cue herself near the end of the aisle leading to the altar. When she arrived there, she saw Ty at his place near the pulpit. He smiled at her, and she winked from across the room.

When he heard the initial bars of the love song from the musical *Carousel*, Ty stepped to his place before the congregation with his friend and former commanding officer, Jim Hayden. Doctor Marie Chavez, stunning in a cream-colored formal dress, joined them from the other side of the altar. Moments later, Seeney appeared at the end of the aisle, and Ty couldn't suppress his smile.

Her pale white gown with a sheath design hugged her body until arriving at the hips; from there, it dropped straight to the floor. The neckline tantalized without showing cleavage, and the thin straps highlighted Seeney's bare shoulders. The fabric was simple and sheer enough below the waist to allow a faint silhouette of Seeney's legs when she moved.

With hair and makeup as close to natural as the formal occasion allowed, her radiant smile accentuated a face needing no additional help. Nobody in the chapel would mistake Seeney for a giddy, fragile, tentative child-bride. She was clearly a mature and confident woman, happy to be here.

When Seeney winked, Ty remembered their debate about this song for the processional. He loved the lyrics but believed they described the couple's feelings twelve years prior, not today's.

Longin' to tell you,
But afraid and shy,
I'd let my golden chances pass me by

"Exactly!" Seeney had countered. "Which is why I want to march down the aisle to that song at the wedding. It means something to me. We almost let a *golden chance pass us by* a long time ago, but life gave us another one. We didn't waste it, and here we are. Walking to you from the back of the church to *If I Loved You* will be my metaphorical victory lap over what could have been an unkind Fate. I think the song is perfect!"

Ty agreed, and now he found it difficult to listen to the melody without emotion. He also regretted Seeney didn't have a father to escort her in the traditional fashion for this part of the ceremony. Unbeknownst to him, however, she wouldn't be making this short trip alone.

Seeney's appearance and demeanor surprised nobody in attendance, least of all Ty, but what she did next did. Glancing to her right, she reached for the elbow of a man who suddenly emerged from that side of the entrance. Pastor Tom Burns smiled as Seeney took his arm, and the two proceeded forward slowly to the music toward the altar. When Tom nodded slightly to him, Ty fought to maintain composure.

Observing two of his favorite people in life walking to him, Ty wavered between laughing and crying but settled on a warm smile. The pastor and the bride reached Ty's position, and Tom presented Seeney's hand to Ty, taking the two steps to his place behind the pulpit. The music ended, and Pastor Burns invited the congregation to be seated.

"Welcome all to the Compton Lutheran Church. It is an honor to perform this ceremony for two people I have known since my youth. More than friends, they provide me in my profession with benchmarks for kindness, trust, love, and perseverance. They overcame the challenges of time, distance, and hardships to be here together before us today. To say their path to this altar was *meant to be* would not only be trite but inaccurate. Neither Ty nor Seeney serendipitously fell into a beautiful trail destined to bring them to this place at this time; they fought to build that road themselves. In doing it, they provide us with a valuable lesson. We are humans with the power to control some part of our destiny, and it *is* possible to achieve better results... but the effort required is seldom easy. This couple reached a summit today, and I believe Seeney has something to say to Ty, which she is willing to share."

"Thank you, Pastor, I do," said Seeney in a firm voice all in the church heard without the benefit of electronic amplification. "Ty Harrell, I *love* you and will until the end of my days. I also *like* you and want to spend the rest of my life with you. I like you rich or poor, sick or healthy, in uniform or not, and I promise this will not change from this day forward."

"Wonderful!" said Pastor Burns. "Ty, do you have something to say to Seeney?"

"Yes, Pastor Burns, thank you. Siena Tyson, I am honored to be your friend, lover, and partner, and I promise to maintain the high standards required to keep these three relationships valid as your husband. I will be happy with you in a tent or a castle, whether you're awake or asleep, while you're young and when you're old. I will cherish the ground we walk together for the rest of my life."

After the couple exchanged rings, Pastor Burns smiled and said, "Ty, you may now kiss the bride."

Ty turned to Seeney, whispering in her ear, "Let's not miss any more proms!" Their kiss was gentle and sweet with evident passion appropriately restrained for the public ceremony. Long enough to conclude the service successfully, but not the story, the embrace caused some to sigh, a few to cry, one to touch the cross on her necklace lightly, and all in attendance to feel good.

Pastor Burns smiled and proclaimed, "I now, gladly, pronounce you Man and Wife!" Then turning to the congregation, "I introduce you to Ty and Seeney Harrell."

The precious and lovely moment hung silently in the air for only a heartbeat because Ty's Marine friends could no longer contain their enthusiasm. Somebody yelled, "Oorah!" and at once, all in the church became Marines, standing to repeat the cry in unison. Seeney clutched Ty's elbow, and the couple walked together between the aisles, each feeling this was the best day of their respective lives. And it wasn't over yet.

Dillon's Deli catered a buffet dinner at the reception in the banquet hall of the Hampton Inn. One corner of the room featured a full bar, and Benny V and his band from Woodstock moved equipment to a stage at the opposite end to provide live entertainment.

Besides Ty's parents and Seeney's older sister, guests mainly comprised high school friends and some of Ty's USMC buddies. Renée Prichard, the spunky server from Woodstock, surprised the couple by driving up for the wedding. She had already informed guests about her partial responsibility for the event—because of the praying she had done.

Mavis and Orville sat at a table with Seeney's sister. Millie and Tom Wharton divorced several years before, and Millie appeared better for the change. Pastor Tom occupied a place at the same table with Doctor Chavez and the Aldriches, Buster and Shauna.

When Buster arrived earlier, the attorney had headed directly toward the bandstand area. Benny, finishing sound checks, stopped when Buster approached. The two men embraced, and then Shauna also hugged Benny. As the musician introduced the couple to the rest of the band, Ty and Seeney joined them.

"Sorry, Ty," said Benny. "We'll get started in a moment. These two are old friends of mine, and I couldn't believe it when I saw them here."

"No problem, Benny," said Seeney. "We're in no hurry. Where do you know Mr. Aldrich from?"

"Buster, Shauna, and I played in the same band together thirty years ago in DC. Shauna sang lead for us, and she met Buster when he joined our group. He was one of the meanest guitar players in the city."

"Well," said Seeney, "now he's one of the meanest lawyers in this area. How does that translate, Buster?"

"I'm not sure, Seeney," said Buster, laughing. "I worked my way through American University and George Washington Law with a guitar and caught Shauna as a bonus from the music business."

"Do you still play?"

"Not much. I own a six-string acoustical I mess with once in a while."

"What about you, Shauna," said Ty. "Do you sing?"

"Sure do. In the church choir."

"Well," said Benny, "we may need to invite you two for a guest appearance tonight."

"In that case, we better get a drink, Honey!" said Buster to his wife.

Before the music started, Ty brought his bride to the table of Marines who had driven from North Carolina. Jim Hayden and his wife, Sally, were there. Also, Skip Callahan and Scott O'Brien with their wives. Josh Lewis and George Selby, both single, rode up with Ginny and Joel Gunn. Ty had noticed his Master Sergeant friend at the church earlier and could hardly believe his eyes.

Ty had only seen Gunn in combat fatigues at Fox Uni, where the seasoned veteran presented the iconic and fearsome image of a walking war machine. Today, he looked like a Wall Street banker, with his starched white shirt, blue suit, and stylish striped tie. The black shoes, spit-shined to a sparkling finish, provided the only clue to his actual profession. His wife appeared to be as fit as the Master Sergeant.

Seeney wanted to stay at the table longer, to learn more about the people responsible for ensuring her husband lived long enough to make today's ceremony possible, but the band started to play. As the table quickly emptied, she remembered from the Marine Corps' Birthday Bash that Marines didn't only know how to shoot and fly. They liked to dance!

Benny played to his audience, and within only a few songs, guests packed the floor. Experienced entertainers can accurately read a crowd to engage all with music, and Benny's first set established the tone for the evening. "Can you believe this, Ty?" asked Seeney. "Isn't it amazing?"

"It is. Look over there." Ty pointed toward Orville and Mavis, who danced to an old Elvis Presley love song. It was a waltz, but the older couple periodically added twirls and pirouettes between steps, creating a shag-like choreography that attracted attention from those around.

"Wow. They're adorable. Did you know your parents could dance like that?"

"No. I've never seen them dance at all." Orville and Mavis returned to the table, and Ty asked his father, "Where did you learn how to do that, Dad?"

"Oh, somewhere along the way. When I was young, a guy had to be able to dance to score with chicks. It must've worked because I met your mom that way, and once I did, I never danced with anyone else."

Mavis glanced at Seeney knowingly and said to her husband, "Because, dear, I never again let other women near you when the music started!"

Seeney stifled a laugh as she covertly gave Mavis a nod. Later, as the men engaged in conversation at the other end of the table, Seeney told Mavis, "I won't ever forget what you taught me about keeping a good man honest. I still chuckle when I remember our talk in Florida about that!"

"I doubt you'll ever have to worry but take nothing for granted."

"I won't, Mavy! Thank you."

"I love you, Seeney. And I love you and Ty together even more than I loved my son by himself if that's possible."

"I understand, Mavy, and I love myself more with him. I think I'm a better person with Ty."

"Great partnerships are supposed to work that way."

Pastor Tom asked Millie to dance, but Seeney's shy sister declined. Renée heard the rejection from her place a table away. "I'll dance with you, Pastor," she said and grabbed his hand before he could reply.

The couple didn't sit for nearly twenty minutes, enjoying themselves, oblivious to their surroundings. Renée may have been devout, but her dancing was expressive, and many of her steps bordered on suggestive. Tom played the supporting role well, feigning shock at Renée's more provocative moves but keeping up with her step for step. Several stood to applaud the cleric when he performed a perfectly executed Michael Jackson-style moonwalk to leave the floor.

Seeney and Ty observed the display in awe, and when Tom returned to a seat at Renée's table, Seeney commented to Ty, "*And* he can dance."

After their lively dance set, Renée and Tom began an intense philosophical discussion at their table. Ty stopped there to listen, and Tom complained in pretended exasperation, "Where did you meet this woman, Ty? I never met someone so sure of herself about things she knows nothing about."

"Hold on there, Pastor!" said the feisty Renée. "I don't know what kind of school would give you a collar, but you have some messed-up theories." Ty quickly excused himself from the debate. The chemistry between Renée and his friend, Tom, was evident, but the relationship didn't appear to be one made in heaven.

Seeney's maid of honor, Doctor Chavez, an accomplished physician, and a fetching divorcee, also enjoyed dancing. An extrovert with no lack of self-confidence, Marie pulled Orville or Buster to the floor when either didn't dance with their wife. The table represented the most senior of the guests at the event, but the occupants didn't act so old.

After the band's first break, Seeney witnessed Buster, Shauna, and Marie confer with Benny V. Then, when the band resumed, Benny surprised everyone by introducing *guest* musicians to open the second set. Doctor Chavez, on lead vocal, with backup from Shauna Aldrich, sang a rousing version of the classic *La Bamba*, complete with a guitar solo in the middle by attorney Aldrich. Seeney just shook her head in awe. "Who knew?" she asked Ty.

Ty had his own *who knew* moment about fifteen minutes later. He heard the first strains of the ubiquitous Electric Slide coming from the band area and politely excused himself to use the men's room. He privately wondered why every wedding reception required this silly dance ritual, and he suspected Seeney would want him to join. His best chance to avoid that was to be absent as she attempted to find him.

The ruse worked, and when Ty returned to an empty table, it didn't surprise him. What he saw on the dance floor did. Master Sergeant Gunn led the Electric Slide-- with two of the younger Marines positioned in the line between himself and his wife. Lieutenants Selby and Lewis desperately tried to follow Gunn's drill-instructor-like commands for the steps to the dance, with only modest success. The Sergeant's personal choreography, on the other hand, blended the grace of Broadway with the precision of a march, creating an effect that was ... entertaining. His two students, or anybody else who observed, dared not smile at the performance because Gunn's commitment to perfecting this frivolous line dance seemed equal to his disciplined approach as a warrior on the battlefield.

The last time Ty had seen Joel Gunn, the man protected him, expertly and heroically, with an M-29 rifle. Now, Ty found Gunn's enthusiastic display on the dance floor as profound as it was surprising, and he wondered which was the more genuine persona: the one in Bektistan or this one. He decided both were, and he respected each.

Gina McCaskey gravitated to the Marines' table and held her own in the fierce party atmosphere there. Striking in a simple red dress, she had discarded her matching high-heeled shoes to accommodate her athletic dance style. George Selby and Josh Lewis were obviously delighted with Gina's attendance at the reception. Only slightly older than the young woman, the two junior lieutenants and Gina shared the same interests in music and compatible energy levels.

Ty and Seeney stopped at the table during the band's break, and Jim Hayden stood. "Ty, this may not be the right time, but I might not see you tomorrow before we depart. I brought something from New River for you."

"Jim, I told you the rules. We specified no gifts.

"This isn't a gift, Ty. It's something you earned." All at the table now focused on Hayden and listened. "I understand you'll soon be discharged from active service and will join the Marine Corps Reserve. What I have for you could be presented at a more formal ceremony but never among more appropriate comrades. Before I left to drive up here, I received three Bronze Stars for you, Master Sergeant Gunn, and Lieutenant Selby." Hayden opened the small box in his hand to show Ty and Seeney the medal. "You'll notice this isn't just any Bronze Star; this one has the letter V, for Valor, attached to the ribbon. Sergeant Gunn's and Lieutenant Selby's are the same. Not so many of these exist. Thank you for your service, Marine!"

Hayden finished speaking and handed a similar box to Master Sergeant Gunn and Lieutenant Selby. "George, Joel, I'll need to get these back for the official ceremony in New River, so don't lose them between here and North Carolina." Gunn and Selby accepted the medals solemnly, thanking their commanding officer.

Seeney, overcome with emotion, hugged her husband. Then, turning to Hayden said, "Thank you, Jim. Thank you so much—for everything." After embracing Hayden, Seeney did the same with Joel Gunn and George Selby.

Seeney and Ty left the table, and Gina, with tears in her eyes, whispered, "I don't understand much about what I just witnessed, but I found it touching and powerful. I hope someone will explain it to me."

Gunn said to Gina, "The three of us got into a bit of a pickle in Becktistan, and the military sometimes hands out medals to folks who manage to save their own butts in these sorts of situations." Then, pausing momentarily and pointing to Selby, Gunn continued, "The lieutenant there did most of the heavy work. He was firing a Glock in each hand and looked like Wyatt Earp at the OK Corral!" Gunn gave Selby a wink when he finished his story.

"Thanks, Master Sergeant," started Selby, "but your version is a little exaggerated ..."

Gunn cut Selby off before Selby could say more. "They don't give these medals out for exaggerations, son." Selby understood Gunn's message and said no more. Gina now eyed the young lieutenant with more than casual interest.

Later, in a private moment with Gunn, Selby said, "Thanks, Master Sergeant, for your remarks a few moments ago. You were the hero that day, though, not me. I'll never forget it."

"Wrong, lieutenant! All of us were heroes, including the guys back at the base who didn't participate in the encounter. Now, though—

tonight—you need that little piece of metal more than me. You'll find kids like shiny things—bright objects keep them amused. Of course, you hope as they age, they'll learn to like things that aren't as shiny, such as courage, loyalty, commitment, and love. But, sometimes, if you keep them distracted long enough with the things they can see, they may start to appreciate the more important things they can't." Gunn nodded toward his wife. "Ginny there is no kid, and she doesn't need to see more medals. She knows I can do a lot more than shoot." George Selby shook hands with his wise friend and returned to the table and the young lady who now infatuated him.

Surprised that Pastor Tom and Renée appeared to be departing before the party ended, Ty took Seeney to the exit to say goodbye to their two friends. Renée had gone ahead of Tom, and the pastor, seeing the newly married couple approaching, stopped. "Sorry, Ty and Seeney. The reception has been wonderful, but Renée and I need to leave. Our theological debate has reached a decibel level that could offend other guests. She suggested we find a more private place to continue our discussions."

"Mmm," said Seeney, smiling. "Do you think Renée can be saved?"

Tom smiled. "I can guess what you might think, but you should remember this quote: Judge not the path to righteousness, for it is not always clearly marked."

"Good one," said Ty. "Is that from Matthew, Mark, Luke, or John?"

"None of them," replied the pastor. "It's from the Book of Tom."

"You better hurry before she closes the church or loses the spirit," said Seeney.

"Yes," said Tom. "Wise counsel. We'll talk again soon."

The Marines, particularly the younger ones, didn't appear ready for the party to end as they headed toward the doors. Ty and Seeney overheard Gina providing directions to a club that stayed open late in Compton, and apparently, George Selby would travel there in Gina's car. While the men visited with Ty and Seeney before departing, Gina plopped down in a chair next to Orville and Mavis. She held her red high heels in one hand, and the ribbon once used to tie her hair back now appeared to be a neck ornament.

"Mr. and Mrs. Harrell, my name is Gina McCaskey. I'm sorry I didn't introduce myself earlier, but I'm sort of a new friend of Ty's and Seeney's."

"Goodness, Gina!" said Orville. "Look at you! I remember your dad bringing you into the post office on his shoulder. You were his pride and joy, and I bet you still are."

"Maybe," she laughed, "but lately, I have given them some stressful moments. I didn't want to leave without telling you how much I respect Ty and Seeney. They're two of my most trusted mentors."

"Thank you, Gina," said Mavis. "We're, of course, prejudiced, but I don't think you could pick better friends."

Gina's eyes fluttered briefly, and she paused for a moment, searching mentally for words. Finally, she said, "Seeney recently helped me negotiate a difficult path when she had more important things to do than worry about me. I'll never forget it and plan for Ty and Seeney to be a part of my life for a long time." Realizing she had shifted into an awkward philosophical mode, she tried to recover. "I'm sorry. Ty's friends haven't been a good influence on me. I'm babbling."

"Oh, don't be embarrassed," said Mavis. "Thank you for telling us about your feelings for our kids, but I can't agree that Ty's Marine friends are a bad influence. They seem like excellent company and well qualified to provide the very sort of evening a young person like yourself should enjoy. They're quite a handsome crew."

Gina smiled. "You might be right, Mrs. Harrell, but I think I'm going to feel pretty tired tomorrow morning. I might be smart to quit while I'm able."

"Gina," said Mavis, "tonight still has hours left in it for some fun. You can sleep anytime."

"Mmm, Mrs. Harrell. Good point."

Orville added, "When you get older, I doubt you'll spend much time looking back on all the nights you went to bed early, but you'll enjoy the memories from the ones you didn't."

Gina laughed. "I'm going to remember those words tomorrow when I don't feel so hot, Mr. Harrell. Thank you." Seeney came to the table, and Gina said, "We've never had a better party in this county, Seeney! Thank you for inviting me."

"I'm glad you came, Gina. It looks like you made some new friends," Seeney said, noting the young Marines heading back in Gina's direction.

"Yes. These guys are a riot, and guess what? They invited me to come to New River in November for the Marine Corps Birthday Bash. I think I might go. Have you ever been to one of those?"

"Oh yeah," said Seeney, smiling. "They're a blast, but don't plan on driving home the next day."

"I think I catch your drift," said Gina, winking at Mavis and Orville.

"Have a good time, Gina. We'll talk again when Ty and I are back in a couple of weeks."

Ty and Seeney checked out of the Hampton Inn the following morning, and Seeney wondered about Ty's haste to leave so early. Their cruise from Baltimore didn't depart until the next day, so they hadn't planned to check-in at the Inner Harbor hotel until that evening. "I have a little business along the way and something to show you," said Ty. On I-81, he continued to drive south when they reached the exit to go east on I-66.

"Did you just miss our turn?" questioned Seeney.

"No, I need to go down to Woodstock before heading to Baltimore." They traveled through the quaint town to a few miles south of it, and Ty turned on a narrow road heading toward the river. After twisting and turning down the single lane to a lower elevation, the Shenandoah River came into view on their right side.

The car arrived at a tiny neighborhood nestled against the mountain a short distance later that reminded Seeney of the entrance to the Frostdale Ski Resort. The community's paved road ended at the driveway of an older home sitting among a grove of oak trees, and Ty turned in. Seeney noticed children playing with a puppy behind a fence surrounding the spacious yard, and she asked, "Do you know these people?"

"Yes, I do. You might recognize them as well. Over there is Angela," he said, pointing to a tall woman, "and that one is Justine. They work at the Woodstock café, and we've met them several times. I assume the little ones are their children."

"What is your business with them?"

"Well, get out of the car, and you'll see."

As Ty opened the door, Justine approached. "Hi, Mr. Harrell. Everything is ready, and Angela's family will stay here as long as you need. We're going to get some lunch, but Angela will be back in about an hour."

"Thanks, Justine. You might remember my wife, Seeney, from our earlier visits."

"I sure do," said Justine. "Congratulations on the wedding!"

"Thank you," said Seeney, looking at Ty curiously.

After Justine and Angela returned to their cars with the kids, the puppy romped up to Ty's feet. Grabbing the dog's ears playfully, Ty said, "Hey, little buddy, how you doin'?"

"Ty," said Seeney. "Do you want to tell me what's going on?"

"Honestly, Seeney. I didn't think that would be necessary. I thought it would be obvious to you! Look around. There's the big house—still needs some work, by the way—but it's big. A picket fence surrounds the yard and look at the dog! He's little now, but he's going to be big. He's a Black Labrador mix that will end up being around a hundred and twenty pounds. Tartan—that's his name—came from the shelter located a mile from here." Ty grinned, waiting for Seeney to respond.

As her gaze wandered from the mountain to the house, fence, and finally the puppy, she turned back to Ty. "Ty, are you telling me you own this house?"

"No. *We* own this house—if you want to. I only made a small deposit to hold it for this weekend, depending on what you thought. Natty, from the café, has an uncle who is a realtor, and for the past month, he has researched properties we might like in the area. I wanted the house to be a surprise, but I wouldn't make a decision like this on my own. If you like the property and agree we should buy it, Angela's family will live in it and take care of Tartan for us until we can be here permanently. We do own Tartan now-- wherever we live."

The dam behind her eyes broke in a flood, and Ty grasped Seeney before she could collapse. She cried softly into his chest, and Ty asked, "Is this one of those times..."

He couldn't finish the question before she said between sniffles, "Yes, Ty! It is. Just be quiet and let me enjoy this for a minute." Ty complied, and when she lifted her head, she said, "I love this house. I also love this town, and I love you. Will the real estate company hold the property with your deposit until we get back? I don't want to risk losing it."

"Yes. I only need to tell Natty's uncle we want it for sure. I'm glad you like it." As Seeney continued to gaze at the surrounding geography, Ty said, "You can check inside if you'd like. We'll want to change a few things, but it's in good condition."

"Don't need to, Ty." Seeney then pulled her cell phone from her purse and tapped the app for her stored photos. "Does the interior look anything like this?"

"Where did you get these?" asked a stunned Ty as Seeney thumbed through several pictures of the house behind them.

"Renée gave them to me at the reception. When you and I talked about different places we might live a few months ago, I called Renée and told her to keep her eyes open for anything nice that might become available down this way. She found this house listed but warned me someone had a contingency contract on it when she showed me the pictures yesterday. I told her I'd get back in touch with her after the honeymoon."

"What a coincidence!"

Seeney thought for a moment. "I don't think so, Ty. Since you and I managed to get back on the same road together, wouldn't it be logical for us to see the same sights and come to similar conclusions?"

"Maybe, but ...,"

"No maybes about it! And what's *coincidental* about a big house with a picket fence and a dog? You *promised* me that on the night of our tenth high school reunion ... and somehow, I *knew* you weren't joking. I like a man of his word, and I like it even better in a husband." Then, as her eyes rested on the fenced area in front of the house, she asked, "You know the only thing missing in that yard, Ty?"

"No, what?"

"Some kids!"

"That's what I hoped you would say."

The End

Made in the USA
Middletown, DE
22 January 2023

22809216R00182